MARI'S WAY

Romance and Revolution

D1289680

Gilbert and Valerie Lewthwaite

Cover design by Lance Buckley

ISBN: 978-0-244-86426-2

PublishNation LLC
www.publishnation.net

Contents

Preface

In December, 1826, Maryland's *Easton Gazette* published a short story, entitled "Modern Chivalry," by Catharine M. Sedgwick, the Jane Austen of early American letters.

The heroine was a rebellious, well-bred English girl. Her defiant, trans-Atlantic pursuit of self-fulfilment against 18th century restraints took her from the privileged comforts of the old world to a life of adventure, hardship and romance in the new.

The story was fictionalized, but in the opening paragraph Sedgwick declared, "the leading incidents of the following tale are true."

In "Mari's Way – Romance and Revolution," we have followed Sedgwick's clues to identify as many of the actual characters, episodes and locations as possible, bringing to life a classic romantic adventure, based firmly on historic fact, with a few liberties taken on personalities and relationships.

PROLOGUE

November 6, 1765 - Ravenhill, the English country home of Sir Joseph Westin. Westin's old friend, David Garrick, the most famed actor of the day, was a guest and had promised to read one of Shakespeare's plays to the family.

Garrick, Lady Westin told her young daughters, was bent upon reviving Shakespeare and making him a popular playwright again. How stupefyingly ignorant of the English, she said, that they should allow the writing of such a master of the language to have fallen into desuetude.

As the family gathered in front of the fire-place in the library after dinner, Garrick took out his copy of "The Winter's Tale."

Mari and Sophie, Sir Joseph's daughters, were enchanted, particularly by the part of Perdita, the shepherdess who turned out to be a princess.

How romantic a tale it was.

Garrick's voice rose and dropped softly. No loud theatrics or flamboyant gestures. He spoke so quietly that Joseph Westin, who had supped a glass or two, all but fell asleep, but the children with their sharp young ears caught his every word.

Lady Westin, who knew the story well enough, sat back in her chair, hands crossed peacefully on lap, enjoying the effortless performance.

Listening so intently, there in the coziness of their home, Mari wondered how anyone could hear him in the vastness of an auditorium. That they could, her mother later told her, was part of Garrick's magic.

The actor's eyes, face and voice conveyed every emotion as he spoke: the malignant fury and later sincere remorse of King Leontes, who rejected his daughter as a bastard; the outrage, hurt and forgiveness of Hermione, his wronged wife; the essential goodness of the honorable Camillo; the impulsive rapture of Florizel for his sweetheart, the sweet, innocent Perdita.

Mari, the older girl, was enthralled as Garrick seemed to direct his words right at her, relishing the romance and drama.

She and Sophie talked about it for days afterwards, fantasizing they might each meet their own prince one day, and hear him say "But, come; our dance, I pray: your hand, my Perdita; so turtles pair that never mean to part."

Mari declared she would remember that evening always, little knowing how soon she herself would be called Perdita, but not by any prince, or how long she would have to wait for the dance she dreamed of, and that when she finally enjoyed it, it would be not simply a celebration of romance, but also of a revolution that was brewing far, far from Ravenhill.

BOOK ONE

ENGLISH BEGINNINGS

I

Spring, 1768 - Mari was the first to sense something was wrong. They were taking the short cut home to Ravenhill, across the south corner of Strawberry Farm's five-acre field, scuffing through sweet green grass and wildflowers.

Her brother, Tom, and his friend, George, were having a friendly argument, bragging of their knowledge of where the best trout rose in the estate's stretch of river.

The rolling pasture seemed empty, but Mari heard an animal noise, a brute's strangled cry of protest, and, looking back, there was Myrmiddon, Squire Roberts' prize bull, hauling his bulk over a rise in the ground. Thought and argument were wiped out as alarm blasted through them.

"Run like the Devil," yelled George, taking off as if his feet hardly needed purchase on the ground.

They all fled, but Mari outran the boys, thanking fortune she was wearing Tom's old britches. They pounded over the turf toward the gate, and Mari launched herself without thinking at the top stave. She had never done such a thing before, but she copied by instinct what she had seen the boys do.

She flew at the gate, grasping with both hands on the top, and vaulted over, letting go at the apex of the jump and landing on the packed earth of the lane.

Tom came over next in a graceful one-handed vault, laughing all over his face, then George in a clumsy, scrambling fall. Out of breath from laughter as much as the effort of running, both boys fell rolling on the bank, spluttering and choking with mirth, hardly able to speak.

Mari just stared at them and back across the field, where the formidable Myrmiddon had come to a standstill in the middle of the pasture, glaring at them with mean, bloodshot eyes. A mountain of an animal, he snorted and pawed the ground a few times as though in contempt, then lowered his head to graze.

Mari was breathing hard, unable to speak from fright, and she couldn't understand the boys' laughter.

"T'was a mock charge," coughed George, getting his breath back.

"My, you can run, Mari. I felt I was standing still, you put so much distance between us. Old Myrmiddon, he just wanted to put a scare into us."

Tom sat up, grinning.

"Little Sis, you cleared that gate like a tumbling artist at a traveling show. You beat George and me by a length, and we are pretty fair at taking the other fellows on at school."

"Tumbling artist," spluttered George, and the boys fell back on the grass again, rolling with laughter.

"Raggy-assed apprentice more like," cracked Tom, and they were helpless again.

Mari affected pique at their teasing, but stalked off up the track toward home, hiding a grin. She had prevailed upon Tom to include her on their jaunts, and, not for the first time, her brother had risked a beating for giving in and lending her a set of his old clothes.

"You can't have any of my good stuff," he warned.

"Just what I use for ratting in the barns with Scotty and George, and you'd better stuff your hair in one of my old caps. If Pa finds out you've been traipsing around with us like a gypsy, you'll be confined to barracks but I'll be for a flogging."

He and George, both, regarded outings with her following along as something of a lark. Her first time out with them, Tom had criticized the way she walked.

"Don't mince along avoiding puddles, stride full out, and don't squeal and go all girlie on us."

She was compliant, happy with his conditions, loving him for his easy-going ways. He teased her, but she sensed that he was quite proud of her spirit to join in and share some of the same freedoms as the young men.

The track crested a slope overlooking the Ravenhill estate and Mari paused to view the scene below. Bright morning   sunlight washed over everything.

The house stood beautiful and remote amid the fields, as though stranded with the green Essex countryside flowing around it. The only movement was at the far end of Ravenhill's drive, where the sun splashed a reflection off the glossy side of a carriage turning in from the road.

Behind Mari's shoulder a moan came from Tom, "Lord, now we are for it. It's Aunt Matty. Why isn't she at home tormenting Uncle Fred?"

The three of them took off again, cantering down the hill, making for a thicket of mixed honeysuckle and briar that camouflaged the outdoor privies.

"Change tumble-artist to quick-change artist," puffed Tom. "Get your skirts on quick while we stand cave."

Mari snatched a housedress, hidden earlier, from a tangle of flowers and pulled off her shirt in one of the huts. Yanking the dress over her head to hide the britches, she didn't bother with stays, too much of a hindrance. Then they fled the mingled odors of sweet honeysuckle and sour midden, and raced for the house.

Up the back stairs – fast as you like," urged Tom. "We'll head off the aunt at the pass!"

He and George waited for Mari to gain the upstairs hall to her bedroom, then ploughed to the front of the house gasping with laughter to intercept Aunt Mathilda Ashford. They failed.

Uncle Frederick was there, and delighted to see both young men, engaging them immediately. Aunt Mathilda was already half way up the front hall stairs on a foray, determined to nose around, making demands of household staff, brooking no evasive answers to her sharp questions. Reaching Mari's room, she marched in on a disheveled niece, who was stuffing a pair of britches into an old trunk.

"What on earth are you up to, child?"

Mari, flushed and guilty, mumbled something incoherent about a pantomime for Sophie.

Aunt Matty didn't believe a word of it, and took a seat, sitting upright and imperious to survey Mari as she finished dressing. The girl pulled on hose and a worn petticoat carelessly and tugged at stays that were laced lopsided. Her face and arms were tanned, and her hair a brighter gold than usual, from too much sun Mathilda thought. Tumbled about Mari's shoulders in wisps and straggly curls, her hair had obviously not been dressed in days. Fidgeting around trying to tidy herself, Mari saw her aunt's expression and waited for a litany of criticism. For once, none came.

Mathilda was feeling a stab of guilt, mentally chiding herself for her neglect of her nieces.

Their mother, Anne-Marie Westin, had died two years previously. She had been a beauty, elegant and gracious, with a rare sweetness of nature. She had been too good, in Mathilda's opinion, for Joseph Westin. Mathilda had an elder sister's exasperated affection for Joseph, but she knew his faults, and deplored his treatment of his wife in her last illness. His indifference to his daughters afterwards, she neither forgave nor excused.

Young Tom seemed to fare well enough with his father, but the girls seemed to be disregarded. Left for the most part in the care of housekeeper and governess, their days were casually ordered and lightly supervised, Sir Joseph being rarely there.

In Mathilda's opinion, his daughters and Ravenhill came a poor third after the demands of northern business interests and the London social scene.

Mathilda judged that Miss Pardoe, the governess, did well enough by seven-year-old Sophie. The little girl loved her, obeyed her, and certainly benefitted from her care and instruction.

Teen-aged Mari was another kettle of fish. Headstrong and impatient, she was way beyond any nursery discipline, and Mathilda suspected that the girl ran rings around Miss Pardoe. It was clear, too, that Mari spent too much time unsupervised, gallivanting around with her brother and his country friends.

She caught her niece's wary gaze in the mirror, and eyed her keenly. There was neglect here. The girl was wild-looking. Tall and thin, active and awkward, wearing ill-chosen clothes and odd accessories, she hardly looked the daughter of landed gentry.

She had her mother's beauty of face - the resemblance, in fact, was quite uncanny - but none of her quiet, gentle nature. In fact, Mari reminded Mathilda of herself at the same age. The girl had a mind of her own and wit to go with it. The aunt nodded to herself with satisfaction. Fair face, wit and character could trump lack of shapely figure and a complaisant nature.

Sophie, for her part, seemed to be out-growing her clothes, but at least looked tidy and well brushed, thanks to the governess.

Heaven knew, there was fortune enough for the daughters of Sir Joseph Westin to be dressed in the finest, and to mix in the best circles. Mathilda had at first rationalized her brother's attitude as due to grief, but that was no longer acceptable so long a while after his bereavement. His behavior now seemed more petulant resentment against his dead wife for abandoning her family duties than genuine grief for the loss of a good woman.

Mathilda remembered her late sister-in-law with great affection. Ravenhill had been a vibrant, hospitable place when Anne-Marie Westin had been alive. The Westins held large house parties attracting brilliant and amusing guests. That had all passed.

Sir Joseph Westin became remote and disinterested, particularly toward his daughters. He departed Ravenhill in favor of his house in London. He would occasionally return to rouse and criticize the household, but soon leave them again to their own devices. At his departure the house would settle back into the usual daily round as dust settles after a disturbing wind.

Mathilda stirred from her reverie, to ponder and plot how to handle her brother. The housekeeper, Mrs. Trant, had said that he was expected back at Ravenhill the next day. Mathilda determined to be ready for him and settle his hash.

Snapping her fan sharply against her knee, she startled Mari with, "We'll have him. We'll have him girl!"

Then added, "You know, it's high time I arranged an entertainment for us. A ball would do nicely."

She brushed her skirt and made for the door, feathers on her hat fluttering as if trying to escape. She paused to say, "Get one of the maids to tame that mane of yours, and come down to welcome your uncle. He'll be with us for dinner, but then I'm packing him off back to his business at home. He will prefer that to supporting me in a family fracas, anyway."

Formidable Mathilda was underway. She smiled and sailed from the room, leaving a confused niece behind her.

* * *

Sir Joseph arrived the next day looking irritable and distracted, perhaps at finding his sister waiting for him. Mathilda greeted him pleasantly though and bided her time, determined to prevail.

A good supper followed by several glasses of splendid port mellowed Sir Joseph Westin enough for him to succumb to Mathilda's argument on her nieces' behalf.

A little modest social life would benefit the girls, she offered casually.

"Yes, Matty, you have the right of it."

They would become dull and countryfied, too much confined at Ravenhill.

"Very likely, Matty, m'dear."

They would come to no harm in Chelmsford. They could hardly go astray.

"It's a comfortable old town, Matty. No place for anyone to stray there. Take 'em, and whilst you're about it, buy 'em some clothes. They both look a fright."

Perversely irritated at his manner, Mathilda gritted her teeth and was forced to accept an easy victory. She had wanted to harangue him vigorously. He deserved it. She was intensely dissatisfied with her brother, and always suspected his motives, but, for once, he had given in with quite good grace.

Complacent, Westin smiled again. He was off back to London in any case. The girls were free to go and dance to Mathilda's tune.

Ravenhill coasted along nicely as expected in the hands of his factor and would not require his own attention for some time. He settled back in his chair to pay further homage to the port, and consider his return to London.

It was strange and exciting for Mari and Sophie to leave Ravenhill so abruptly. Their father waved briefly stood gazing after them as the coach set off down the drive.

Aunt Matty did not wave back to him, but ordered the coachman to pick up the pace, "in case he changes his mind," she said, and smiled at no-one in particular.

* * *

The Ashfords' house was a small classical villa. It was not too grand, but had large reception rooms downstairs, opening onto a gallery, ideal for airing family portraits, dancing, and setting card tables.

Mari accepted with interest and good humor Mathilda's plans for her, though Uncle Frederick was not straight away convinced of the need for a ball.

"A rout no doubt, that's what it will be," he grumped.

"I'll be expected to prance about with the neighbors and watch old General Huffington down my best brandy."

Mathilda told him to cease muttering behind his newspaper and put a good face on it. She announced she had some new arrivals to season the usual crowd of their acquaintances - a very pleasant family, the Hunters, merchant people on a relaxing trip away from their busy London round.

"Stop shaking your jowls at me, Freddy," she said. "It's past time anyway that we livened ourselves up and put out for the young folk."

Frederick realized that she was on a mission for her nieces, and Mari was her main focus.

Sophie, being too young for the social scene, was left to the safe custody of her governess. Unaccustomed to so much attention, a bemused Mari was to be measured and fitted for new finery.

Mathilda's dressmaker was a plump woman in sober blue grosgrain, whose pink face beamed beneath a pumpkin shaped wig, an array of fat, stiff ringlets jiggling around her neck as she pulled out bolts of fabric and trailed them around the room.

Joseph Westin was to be spared no expense in the outfitting of his daughter. With Uncle Frederick as an ally though, Mari gave a firm refusal to suggestions of powdered patches and pomade.

"She's a perfect, fair complexion – as all young'uns should have," huffed Frederick.

"And hiding gold curls with false hair and paste would be travesty. Leave her be herself, Matty!"

Mathilda did not press it, knowing when her mild-mannered husband meant business. She allowed that Mari's curls, washed in lavender water and soft soap, would be hard to beat by any wig loaded with trinkets.

The dressmaker smiled happily and approved any of the choices the ladies might make, from silk damask for an evening to fine lawn for a summer picnic. Finally, however, Mathilda had delved into a store chest and produced a length of the palest yellow silk, patterned with hand-painted flowers.

"French – Lyon's best," she said proudly. "This will be for your first ball gown."

"Kent smugglers!" interposed Uncle Freddy as he eyed the spread of colored silk. "Matty will have us in the Tower one of these days."

"Oh, hush yourself," Mathilda shot back. "What about your French brandy."

Being turned out as a young lady was a mixed blessing. Mari loved the silk dress with the painted flowers, but had to stand imprisoned in a tightly-laced corset and whalebone hoops as it drifted over her head to settle in a whisper over its foundation. She liked what she saw in the looking glass, but chafed at the cage around her. Activity was limited to sitting or standing stiffly, and parading with dainty steps. No striding about, running or scrambling, dressed like this.

Tom was supposed to be joining them for the evening, and he would hardly recognize her. No wonder men offered their arms for support. Ladies were sensible to take them against the risk of falling over. Secretly she was nervous at the thought of appearing clumsy in public, and said as much to Aunt Matty one afternoon during a fitting.

"Well – yes – you have to learn a little deportment, and to move in a more measured way, as a lady."

Mathilda paused as if she hadn't considered it before, and flapped her hand dismissively.

"You're right, of course. We're on display. You for the fellow to size up, and the likes of me to keep them in line, and, of course to play one up on the other matrons. 'Tis an endless game, niece."

Mathilda enlarged the theme as she downed a glass of ginger cordial.

"Your dress is both armor and uniform – yes, we have it, just as the men have theirs, but never fear, you'll be in fine fettle when I've finished with you."

She poured herself more cordial as Mari pulled at the detested stays.

"I never wear these at home. I despise them," she muttered. "Uncle Freddy said once that women's undergarments were unnatural contraptions."

"Well, of course, he would say that. He's a man," came back Mathilda.

"Now walk about the room and show me your silhouette, and practice smaller steps. No wonder you frazzle poor Miss Pardoe. You glower at the idea of behaving like a proper lady, stamp on your stays, and run around like an urchin at home. Your father has much to answer for."

She went silent again and gazed fuzzily at the near empty cordial bottle.

"I'll be half cut if I down any more of this."

Looking at her, Mari felt a rush of affection and a stab of panic. When Tom went for the Navy soon, as she knew he would, Aunt Matty would be her only ally at home.

Tom aided and abetted her on their jaunts at Ravenhill, but, in the end, he probably expected her to toe the line as a dutiful daughter, marry a man of her father's choice, and take her place as a matron in society. "Gossiping in the parlor," as he put it. She flinched at the idea.

* * *

Dropping efforts to primp and pose, Mari sat down next to Mathilda.

"If you really do wish to set me up as a presentable catch, Aunt Matt, you'll have to ease the pace."

She chuckled and leaned over to give her aunt a hug, but winced as her dress hoops creaked and nipped.

"It's impossible to be easy wearing these things. How can I dance in them?"

But came the evening, dance she did. Under instructions from his wife, a resigned Frederick Ashford started off the frolics with his niece.

"Mind you, why my beloved Matty would have me show off like this, I can't imagine. I'd much sooner watch you young'uns from the safety of the card tables"

He flourished unnecessarily with his arms, and made an alarming turn.

"I can't dance any better than my favorite mare."

He batted his wig straight, and pointed a foot extravagantly. Mari had no argument with him, and was reduced to giggles.

While Frederick labored against the music and Mari cheerfully maneuvered around him, Mathilda's new friends, the Hunter family, arrived. They stood framed in the gallery doorway as Mathilda made introductions.

Dan Hunter's nephew, Bryce, stood a little apart, waiting to pay his respects to his hostess and surveying the guests. Down the line of dancers, the pastel silks of the women's dresses flared and billowed as they turned, trailing the quicker swirls of their partners coat tails.

At the far end of the set, a bright haired, slim girl caught his attention.

She and her clumsy partner were lost in merriment, skipping and hopping to keep up with the rhythm of the dance. She seemed to mischievously improvise a step or two, and was a focus of light and laughter under the candelabra, as her dress, the color of pale sunlight, floated a cloud of flowers around her.

Moments later, the music released them to bow and curtsey, and, beckoned by Mathilda, Frederick led his niece to greet the late arrivals.

Bryce fixed his gaze on Mari Westin as though she were the only one present. Looking up as she approached on her uncle's arm, Mari locked eyes with the young American and was stunned by her own reaction.

He wore a well-cut coat of fine wool that held close purchase on strong shoulders. The deep wine color of the coat was offset by just enough gold lace for a young man's vanity to carry, and a snowy cravat was slightly, not unbecomingly, askew.

Bold eyes, almost black, matched against tanned skin and bronze hair caught in a queue, gave him the air of an exotic animal, let loose in the Ashfords' home.

They smiled at each other as if in recognition, and only a tug on her arm from Uncle Frederick steered Mari to be introduced to the elder Hunters first.

There was a kind greeting, and shrewd, amused regard from Dan Hunter, and a quizzical look from his wife, Alicia. Mari exchanged automatic curtseys with the jolly, beaming sisters, Maybelle and Arabel, and carefully dipped another curtsey to their cousin, Bryce.

Standing near him, Mari was vibrantly aware of everything about him, cloaked in warmth as though in an enchanted circle. She felt a startling impulse to reach out and touch him, but stopped herself for propriety's sake.

The rest of the evening was a melange of pleasure, anticipation, and frustration as they partnered each other whenever possible between social duties to the other guests.

14

He flirted expertly with her, filling her head with tales of plantation life in Virginia, of sultry, blossom-scented evenings drinking fruit punch on verandahs, horse racing after church on Sundays, with even the local pastor joining in. He teased her with a wonderful fantasy of sailing to the Americas with him in a stout ship.

"I'll be sailing home soon. Just suppose if we could take passage together - what a fine trip we'd share. I would parade you around the deck on my arm, and we would dine with the captain. The sailors would dance for you and you would sing for them."

Mari was transfixed by his words, imagining following the pathway of a westering sun with him.

Later, Aunt Matty found them on the gallery terrace, where dripping laurel bushes and damp, gritty stones underfoot, went unnoticed, so absorbed they were in each other.

Smiling only a little, she firmly steered Mari inside for mulled wine before retiring. The party had mostly dispersed, and the Hunters were about to leave.

As the Ashfords stood waving them off, Bryce's smile blazed back at Mari over the heads of his prattling cousins. Mathilda led Frederick and Mari to the drawing room.

"My, but I thought young Parson Bell would never go home. He's so anxious to please and repetitive with his thanks and felicitations. I think that shy wife of his is with child already. Well, I am off to my bed and a warm posset. Tell me all your party gossip tomorrow, though Mari looks too dreamy eyed for much chatter."

This last said with a knowing glance at her niece, who had the grace to blush as she gave her aunt a hug.

"Away to your bed, child, and dream your dreams," said Mathilda.

Mari, flushed with her first infatuation, obeyed her, but lay awake going over every moment of the evening. Bryce Hunter's attention had overwhelmed and fascinated her. His words now crowded her head with visions of life beyond the confines of her own at Ravenhill.

With Aunt Matty in Chelmsford, she suddenly felt the possibility of life opening up. Before drifting off to sleep, a longing for change fed a whirl of dreams about Bryce Hunter.

The sudden shock of attraction was a wave lifting her up, giving new perspective. Her jaunts with Tom and George now seemed childish pranks. They had given her small tastes of freedom but left her confined still in their narrowly proscribed circle.

Then, just as she drifted into sleep, came an uneasy recollection: the evening's dancing…the formal movement of each partner as if posing for a picture…. the men looking as if they knew it for a game… the women more like pretty marionettes with someone else pulling the strings.

The thought troubled Mari.

II

Frederick Ashford gazed at his wife with amiable resignation, surrendering hopes of a quiet glass of wine and a perusal of *The London Gazette*.

"You can't kill the messenger, Matty."

Ravenhill groom Dobby Baines threw a thankful glance at him, and looked back stolidly at Mathilda.

"Why are you so exercised?" Frederick continued. "I thought that you wanted Joseph to have his girls with him more. I'm mystified as to your objections."

Baines had been sent with a message that Sir Joseph Westin's daughters were to return home immediately, and prepare for a visit to London.

Mathilda fretted at this abrupt change of plan for her nieces, making her umbrage clear to the groom. There was no response, and up against stolid male impassivity she dismissed him to the kitchen to coax a piece of pie from the cook, then paced, flicking a fan with irritation.

"He'll manage to loiter until he's back in time to miss his evening stable chores,' she muttered, and turned to set her husband straight.

Seeing Mari in the doorway, she curbed her temper and glared at Frederick instead, muttering about questionable company in the London house.

Frederick blandly ignored her and cheerfully called to Mari, "Come and have a sup of Madeira and a biscuit. You look such a stripling, as though you need feeding up. You'll see new sights and enjoy yourself in London, and Aunt Matty and I will certainly visit and make sure that you do."

* * *

The Ravenhill party was deposited outside the Westin townhouse in Conduit Street.

Instead of entering the house immediately as she normally would have done, Mari found herself warily holding back with Sophie to wait for Miss Pardoe, who was organizing the disposal of their boxes and baggage.

There was a bustle of activity as the coachman lowered his bulk from the driver's perch to help the groom and a footman, who ran down the steps from the front entrance.

The footman had been waved forward to the task by Mrs. Pynchon, the Westins' housekeeper in town, who came down to greet them, looking relieved to see Miss Pardoe with the girls. She seemed, somewhat ill at ease and distracted as she gazed at them. She bowed her head politely, but greeted them perfunctorily and turned to conduct them indoors.

Would they care to rest themselves in the room she had ready for them before dining? Or had they dined on the way?

They had expected to be greeted by their father, but Mrs. Pynchon explained that he was out, though expected back for supper. She stated this uncertainly at first, and then again repeated herself – "Yes, he will surely be back for supper."

She then added in a rush, that meanwhile Sir Joseph's companion and guest had expressed a desire that they should go up and see her as soon as they arrived.

"Though," she continued, glancing up the stairway and pausing as though listening for a sound upstairs, "the lady is still abed, I think – so we must wait, and in any event you must all be parched and jolted from your journey and in need of refreshment."

Sophie held tightly to Mari's hand and didn't let go even when they entered the bed chamber they were to share.

"Here. Here we are. You are both together, but it is a most comfortable and spacious room. You must remember it – quite the best after that of Sir Joseph, of course, and your mother's – um – ah – the mistress's."

The housekeeper paced the room. She lifted and replaced the lid of a pot-pourri, went silent, and paced the floor some more. She appeared distracted again. Miss Pardoe, after hesitating politely, took the initiative and dismissed the footman, who was patiently standing by the doorway waiting their pleasure after depositing the baggage and adjusting the curtains at the window. She turned again to the housekeeper.

"Mrs. Pynchon! Mrs. Pynchon!"

She spoke sharply to gain her attention.

"Mari and Sophie will need a maid to help them unpack and see to their comfort, and I don't see that having just arrived after a long journey they should have to satisfy the curiosity of a guest before attending their parent, who" – here she allowed some disapproval to sound in her quiet voice – "I note is not yet here anyway to greet them."

Her small, straight figure exuded propriety.

Mrs. Pynchon stared at her and started to comment, but changed her mind and sighed instead, and requested a few words privately with the governess.

Miss Pardoe, now perplexed and irritated but curious at the housekeeper's behavior followed her into the upstairs hallway, closing the chamber door behind her after urging her charges to refresh themselves and await her return.

Mrs. Pynchon, after looking about her on the landing, raised a finger to her lips to signal silence, and conducted Miss Pardoe back downstairs and along to the privacy of her own parlor at the rear of the house.

Mari and Sophie were left standing, holding hands like two waifs. Neither had spoken hardly a word, apart from a formal greeting to the housekeeper.

Mari was at a loss to think what was going on. It was as though they were expected but not welcome, and she sensed some confusion as to their disposition.

Little Sophie stayed close to Mari even when her elder sister tried to disengage her hand and move around the room. Sarah moved with her and held on to Mari's skirt.

"Who's Papa got as a guest? Will we be having a party, Mari? I don't really like parties much, having to curtsey to a lot of strange people."

Her sister gave her a quick hug.

"Let me take your cape off – are you hungry little sister? Come over here and sit on the bed."

Mari busied herself, helping Sophie to put on some house slippers.

19

"If Mrs. Pynchon doesn't send us up a tray soon, I'll go down myself and find Abby. She, at least, will be pleased to see us. Mrs. Pynchon seems at sixes and sevens."

She went over to the door and stepped into the hallway, looking and listening toward her mother's room. Sophie slid off the high four-poster bed, and went to her side, guessing what Mari intended to do.

"Can we go and look at Mama's room – will it be the same, Mari? Would it make Papa angry?" Mari smiled down at her.

"Papa is not here, and hasn't forbidden us. The rooms haven't been changed."

She looked again at Sophie's trusting, hopeful face.

"Let's take a peek, shall we Sophie, whilst no-one's about."

They passed to the end of the hallway and stopped in front of their mother's boudoir.

Mari found that she was holding her breath as she stretched out her hand to the gilded handle of the door of their mother's dressing room. She was about to press down the door handle when she and Sophie jumped back, as if scalded, at the sound of a raucous shriek from behind the door.

"Aagh! Oh! Oh! Have a care! 'Tis a tender part of me you are raking, you wall-eyed witch! Have a care! Get away!"

The lusty yells were punctuated by several thuds and cracks and the sound of something metal bouncing and clanging on the floorboards. There were some indistinct muttering sounds from inside the room.

The sisters stared at each other, eyes wide and startled like young fawns. Mari plucked up courage to knock on the door, wondering who had invaded her mother's sanctuary. There was a sudden silence.

"Get up you whey-faced wench before I drag you out! Come out from behind that settle and answer the door!"

The two sisters heard footsteps, and the door opened before them a little way to show a maid hastily straightening her cap with one hand while clutching some sort of pincers with the other. Mari could just see that her apron was drenched with something, and there was a sharp smell of wine, or vinegar, mixed with the sweeter scent of roses coming through the doorway.

"Who is it?" demanded a full, throaty woman's voice. "Open the damn door, Maisie."

The maid complied without saying a word to either of them, standing back so that her mistress could have a full view of the girls through the now wide-open door.

Tamsin Tallentire was leaning back upon a brocaded couch in deshabillé. A plump, white left arm was raised by her ear, as, with a frown, she tenderly, if inelegantly, probed among the copper colored fuzz of her underarm. A blue silk robe slid off her right shoulder and gaped open. Her upraised left arm, free of the robe, pulled the globe of a well-rounded breast almost clear of her embroidered shift, revealing a pearly pink nipple.

Not at all fazed by their presence, she gazed keenly at the slim figures, standing hesitantly outside the door, her arm still lifted for ministration.

She had fine hazel eyes, thick-lashed and slightly protuberant, and fine teeth in a wide generous mouth. Her hair was curly and a rich chestnut gold color, intriguingly cropped short like a boy's, the better, Mari supposed, to fit under a fine wig. The urchin hair-style belied the voluptuous curves of its owner.

"Well, what are you selling, ladies? No posies or potions today."

Mari, finding herself for once speechless, cleared her throat to try to say something.

The woman on the couch was an unexpectedly unnerving sight. The last time the daughters of Joseph Westin had been in this room was two years earlier, and it was also the last time they had seen their mother in it.

They had been admitted to her presence only when she had finished her toilette, and was ready to display her impeccably groomed and elegant self to her daughters. She would have a tray of chocolate set for them, and would let them help her choose some item of jewelry, or other.

The intruder finally lowered her arm and reached to take a fig from a bowl of fruit, casually adjusting her robe and scratching her breast as she did so.

"Well, cat got your tongue? Maisie, damn it, wipe up that witch's brew on the floor, and take your stuff away."

She turned her attention again to Mari and Sophie, still standing, transfixed, watching her, but before any more was said, Mrs. Pynchon and Miss Pardoe appeared behind them.

21

Miss Tallentire roared with laughter when apprised of the fact that the two young girls were Sir Joseph's daughters, not ribbon and posy peddlers.

She insisted that, of course, she had recognized who they were, and didn't Sophie, surely, take after her father, and Mari after her mother.

Miss Pardoe and Mrs. Pynchon stared at her, dismayed. It was entirely unacceptable to them that this woman, albeit ensconced as Joseph Westin's mistress, should have the effrontery and ill grace to comment on his daughters, especially referring to their late mother, the exquisite Lady Westin with whom the likes of Mistress Tallentire could never have had acquaintance.

Mari, herself, felt not so much affronted as confused and bemused. Folk always remarked on her likeness to her mother, that she took for granted.

What was stunning was the very presence of this newcomer exercising such familiarity in her father's house. They had had no warning. Presumably this explained Mrs. Pynchon's lack of composure at their arrival.

The woman called Tamsin, though, seemed not at all affected by the reticence of the other women, and rattled on amiably and gaily about what times they would have together in London.

She immediately announced that she would supervise Mari's wardrobe, introduce her to some young friends of hers, at which the housekeeper looked askance and the governess turned pale. They would visit Vauxhall and Ranelagh, and take trips on the river. They would attend the theater and show off their finery and cut such figures.

The full flow of her enthusiasm was interrupted only briefly by the return of her maid, Maisie, who entered again with a fresh bowl, containing, by the sharp smell of it as she passed, more of the wine and rose water concoction.

Maisie looked uncertainly from her mistress to the quartet of onlookers, gazing at the spectacle of this exotic female, who seemed totally unaware of the social niceties. Sophie, at least, had ceased to appear anxious and nervous, and was now simply fascinated.

"You're not going to drink sour wine are you, lady?" The little girl had found her voice at last.

Miss Tallentire, unabashedly lying back on the cushions and freeing her arm again from her robe chuckled.

"No poppet. Maisie has a receipt to wash my underarms. It don't do for a sporting lady to have parts smelling of old men's socks – so Maisie will swab me and help me get rid of some fuzz without pulling me to bits and pieces into the bargain – won't you, wench?"

At which last comment she glared at Maisie, who sniffed and wore a martyred expression as she wrung out a small kerchief in the bowl.

At this point, Miss Pardoe and Mrs. Pynchon both spoke at once, each insisting that she was busy and the girls needed some rest and refreshment, and they would no doubt see Tamsin with their father, at supper.

Whereupon, the fascinated sisters were ushered out, and Tamsin Tallentire shrugged with easy indifference.

As the door closed behind them, she held her hand in the air, studying with appreciation the heavy rings adorning her pale fingers, whilst the hapless Maisie bent to a decidedly thankless task, and the murmurings of two thoroughly routed retainers faded as they shepherded their charges away down the corridor and back to the safety of their own chambers.

* * *

Joseph Westin came back to his house in Conduit Street late that afternoon.

After summoning the Ravenhill party to the library, he harrumphed a greeting at them, omitting any affectionate gestures toward his daughters. He questioned Miss Pardoe cursorily as to their health and well-being, and accepted her earnest replies in an off-hand, apparently disinterested manner.

He had not invited them to sit in his presence, and they, all three, stood in line like housemaids hoping for employ, not speaking unless spoken to. Sophie had, once again, fastened like a limpet to Mari's hand and stood close as though hoping to conceal herself behind her sister's skirts.

Their father finally noticed his own lack of consideration and waved them to sit, whereupon all three managed to squash themselves onto the same small couch.

Westin went silent, and stood pondering to himself, as if at a loss as to how to communicate with his own family, and impatient and somewhat exasperated at the need to do so.

The room was quiet, except for the ticking of a fine ormolu clock on the fireplace mantel and a fire that crackled in the grate. It was elegantly furnished and would have been warm and welcoming were it not for the constrained atmosphere.

Westin walked to the tall windows and gazed out onto the street, hearing a cab rattling over the cobbles, and the sing-song voices of a couple of street vendors.

Mari was overtaken by a tide of resentment at the reception they had had from their father. She noticed that the attitude of some of the servants had the tenor of that of the staff at Ravenhill.

The old retainers were warmly, if discreetly, welcoming, but Mari had sensed a feeling of pity toward herself and Sophie that was unsettling.

She had noticed, also, one or two of the newer servants in the London house exchanging knowing smiles, and their glances at the two girls had become blank-faced expressions when caught by Mari's sharp scrutiny.

She felt angry for herself and even more so for Sophie, gentle little Sophie, who wouldn't say boo to a goose, and even became upset at a moth flying too close to a candle flame.

Mari decided that it was up to her to ask her father some pertinent questions. She was his eldest daughter, after all, and, surely, that gave her both a right and a duty to claim some position in the house, instead of dumbly being sent hither and yon at the will of just about everyone else. She had, at one time been able to run to her father freely and say almost anything.

She glanced at Miss Pardoe, hoping for support, but the governess stayed silent with a grave expression on her face.

A fresh spike of irritation reinforced Mari's resentment, and she opened her mouth to ask her father bluntly what plans he had for them, but was forestalled as the drawing room door swung open and Tamsin swayed into the room. Ignoring the girls, she crossed straight to Westin.

"Joseph – you have your seraglio here! Surely, I'm invited," she exclaimed.

She was arrayed in a loose house dress of blue silk lustring, with a froth of lace down the front of the petticoat, and her short, curly hair was unadorned, giving her an impish air. Her bright eyes were both merry and alluring, and claimed Westin's undivided attention.

He leaned back against a desk by the window and studied his mistress with a heavy-lidded, amused gaze, not saying anything.

"Aren't you coming to take tea with me before I dress? I need you to choose some adornments, my love."

She was standing close, and slanted a look up at him, and Mari saw that looped over her left wrist was an assortment of jewelry that Tamsin lazily swung to and fro for the stones to catch the light. One of the jewels, Mari saw was her mother's sapphire and diamond pendant.

Joseph Westin didn't seem to notice. Without bothering to look in his daughters' direction, he gave Miss Pardoe permission to withdraw and take the girls with her.

They would dine alone, and he would see them the next day, he said. The three of them rose, dropped a curtsey, and filed out like an unwanted Greek chorus, Mari, with her face flaming, Sophie, confused but relieved, and Miss Pardoe impassive.

In the days following their arrival, an uneasy pattern was gradually established. Joseph Westin seemed to be as restless in his town residence as at his country estate, and rarely dined with his daughters.

At first, though, he would instruct Miss Pardoe as to their activities. Miss Pardoe was to accompany them on a ride through the park, or she was to take them to view this or that place of interest, but he quickly ran out of ideas and interest regarding their entertainment.

Increasingly suggestions seemed to come from Tamsin Tallentire. Oddly enough, this was something of a relief. After the shock of meeting her, the girls did not feel the same degree of restraint with Mistress Tallentire as with their father.

Tamsin, herself, seemed not to give a fig for convention or formality. She could be generous and humorous, although often erratic and careless. Yet she did call in her dress-maker and ordered the girls new dresses.

She gained grudging approval from Mari in that she took as much interest in Sophie's appearance as she did in Mari's, and explained it was a scandal they were not attired in the finest available, given their father's position in society.

Mari and Sophie, trying to settle into the house routine, never knew from one day to the next whether they would be primped and arrayed for a fashionable display in the park, accompanying Tamsin, or would be confined indoors, bored by staid duties with Miss Pardoe and otherwise ignored.

A ride in the park with Tamsin was hardly a dull outing, although she pretended that she found London quite tedious these days. Mari soon realized that her father's lively mistress found the London scene dull when she felt herself neglected by Westin.

There was a circle of friends and acquaintances of Joseph Westin's that his Mistress Tallentire could never grace, and another set amongst whom she circulated freely, at least with Joseph at her side. When he was absent and she was left to her own devices she often had her own set of friends to visit her.

Miss Pardoe and Mrs. Pynchon, both, were disapproving of these visitors to the Westins' townhouse, but kept their opinions to themselves, not confident enough to be able to broach the subject of the suitability of Tallentire's friends in the same company as Westin's daughters.

The generally meek Miss Pardoe thought wistfully, and often, of Ravenhill. When Tamsin called for the girls' company to cheer up her spirits or to meet some acquaintance or other, housekeeper and governess would exchange looks and purse their lips.

The governess would sigh at interruptions of the girls' morning routine, but couldn't protest. For their part, Mari and Sophie found life at Conduit street a great novelty at first, if at times it was a strain to attend Tamsin on her jaunts.

Some of Tamsin's visitors were beautifully groomed and pampered ladies, attired in the latest fashions. They would step out of their coaches, bestowing smiles and shrewd glances all around. Feathered cockades in pompadour wigs seemed to be a favored headdress, and their silk panniered dresses and petticoats, with embroidered satin slippers peeping underneath, rustled over the polished floors of the Westins' townhouse as they drank tea or glasses of cordial, and nibbled marchpane and comfits with Miss Tallentire. Gentlemen friends were often as elaborately garbed and mannered.

It seemed to Mari a mockery of the times her mother entertained. Then, the ladies and gentlemen had come and gone with all due courtesies. They had supped and gossiped, admired each other, and flirted, and retired gracefully when the due time of a half or a full hour's attention had been given. Cards were routinely left and collected on a silver salver in the hallway.

Now that Tamsin Tallentire reigned, however, the courtesies were casual.

She amused herself occasionally by supervising the Westin daughters' toilette, and she would sometimes indulge a fancy, by having them attired in identical costumes, including matching pompadour wigs, with feathered brooches adorning their hair. They would step daintily, she insisted, a pace or two behind her, and accompany her on outings in the coach.

These outings were often in the mornings, and sent them bowling along the thoroughfares of the city to a salon, or a park. Tamsin would often order the coachman to stop for her to inspect the wares of vendors. She would often buy unnecessary gew-gaws, or sweetmeats, and hand them over for the girls to hold.

Mari felt they were treated rather in the way of pages, or servants. They were as bit-part players, trying out new roles: Sophie, innocent and confused but biddable; Mari ambivalent, a certain curiosity and fascination with Tamsim, holding a simmering resentment against her father and his mistress in check.

Escapades like running around in her brother's cast-off britches were history, while sitting on stiff couches with hated stays restricting natural movement was now the norm.

Uncomfortable with drawing room niceties and inconsequential chatter required on a daily basis, Mari raged inwardly with mounting frustration, wondering what on earth they were doing here. They were not allowed back to Ravenhill, but what purpose served their presence in London?

On their outings, Tamsin was vivacious and gay, and would offer a stream of commentary upon the scene around them, who was of consequence and who was not. The girls were dazzled and often bewildered into silence by her apparently inexhaustible insights and lurid gossip about almost everyone they encountered. Who liaised with whom, who was appearing at this or that event, or creating this or that scandal.

Tagging along with Tamsin Tallentire could be both entertaining and exhausting. Mari, exasperated, just wished for both her own and Sophie's sake that they need not be displayed so often as miniature ladies of fashion.

One fine morning, wheeling along with the horses at a smooth canter, she decided that sitting in the chaise was a form of purgatory. Her constricting stays were nipping her breasts and chafing her ribs underneath her petticoat. The need to hold her head stiffly to maintain an elegant profile, as Tamsin insisted, was so unnatural it made her head ache.

Poor little Sophie bore it all in quiet misery. Mari looked at her as she perched on the seat opposite Tamsin. The child sat rigidly with her dress puffed around her, small slippered feet dangling like a rag doll's. She clutched a posy of limp violets in one hand, and a packet of confection in the other. A small, pretty fan, a gift from Tallentire, was looped over her pudgy wrist. Beneath the powder and rouge Tamsin had inflicted on the little girl's own clear complexion, Sophie looked wretchedly uncomfortable.

Mari was put in mind of a sad little marionette in the wrong clothes and the wrong scene. Sophie couldn't even hold her balance on the cushions of the moving carriage because of the flowers and sweetmeats she held stiffly, as though ready to offer them to anyone who would relieve her of them.

Mari, chiding herself for not paying enough attention to the little girl, reached across the expanse of both their dresses and took the flowers and packet of sweets from Sophie's hands to place them on the seat. She consoled her sister.

"Hold on the side of the seat, but sit as straight as you can, Sophie. It's not comfortable being fashionably lady-like, is it little sister?

"I'd lean over and hug you, but my stays are digging in my belly and make me want to relieve myself. Hold hands though."

Sophie gave a small, painted-doll smile, and put a warm, sticky small hand in Mari's.

"Miss Pardoe said she is thinking of asking Papa to send us back to Ravenhill. I hope she does and he says yes. I want to wear an old dress, and help to collect eggs, and play with the puppies – Tess will have had her puppies by now – I hope they remember to save one for me – Do you think they will, Mari?"

"Surely they will, Sophie, don't fret so. Tess will have her puppies by her for weeks yet. We'll be back in plenty of time for you to choose one. "

"What's that, Poppet? You are pining for the country life?"

Tamsin fluttered her fan and smiled brightly to a gentleman friend who saluted her familiarly and spurred his horse away. She centered her attention once again on the two girls.

"I'm looking forward to acquainting myself with Ravenhill sometime, but not just yet, ladies. There are still sights to see in London."

She sighed in distracted, slightly impatient fashion.

"I get one of the best dress-makers in London to create you a wardrobe, and you still, both, look awkward and ill-fitted somehow."

"Mistress Tallentire!"

Tamsin turned, and her face lit up with delight and merriment as a carriage pulled up alongside, and two very pretty women waved at her and called for their coachman to stop.

"We are over to Ranelagh for a little diversion – will you come along?"

Tallentire hesitated, looking at Mari and Sophie. "I have charge here of Joseph's daughters. A whole day out will be too much, I expect, but…"

"Well, they have their coach. You can send them home in it. Do come Tami. We can carry you back this evening. We have missed you lately. Westin's not back 'til next week, is he?"

Tamsin made up her mind quickly, and nodded to the coachman.

"George, take Sir Joseph's daughters straight home for dinner. I shall attend my friends, who will bring me back later, so you are then free of waiting on me."

Whereupon, she snapped her fan shut, and stepped down quickly from the coach, hardly giving the groom time to hand her down.

"Don't go too fast, George, or the little one gets sickly and pale. I will see you later my poppets."

Turning to her friends, "Amelie, that hat is outrageous. Make some room for me."

There was much rustling of skirts and bursts of laughter, as the ladies' carriage pulled smartly off on the road to further diversion.

Henry the groom smirked and winked at the driver, who remained impassive. He looked back at Mari for assent, and she nodded briefly.

"Yes, George, make for Conduit Street. We've had enough of our ride in the park."

George showed a brief softening of expression, with a new respect on his face. He noted the set of her chin, and recognized a strong likeness to her mother in her.

"Home it is, Miss Westin."

He tipped his hat to her, and scowled at Henry to put him in his place, then wheeled the horses in a tight circle to return home. George took them back alongside Hyde Park, into Piccadilly, and turned smartly left up Old Bond Street, paying no mind to a couple of quarreling boys who had been taking turns sweeping horse-droppings from the road junction.

The boys scattered like startled cats out of the path of the Westin carriage, which turned right into Conduit Street. George found that he must pull up short of the house as a hired chaise was there delivering two passengers to the front door.

"Looks like Master Tom is home with a friend, Miss Westin," said George.

Mari stared at the unexpected sight of her brother Tom laughing with Bryce Hunter as they strode up the steps of the house. The American looked back and recognized the Westin coat-of-arms.

He touched Tom's arm and gestured, as George eased his horses forward to take the place of the hired carriage as it moved away. Tom ran back down the steps in time to hand Mari out of the carriage as soon as Henry dropped the carriage footrest. He laughed at her.

"My – aren't you the dainty lady, Mari? What a change a few days of city air can make – and who is that doll-child with you? Can't be little Sophie, can it? Look who has come to see you in your finery. We're just in from Chelmsford, and decided to come over and dine with you – you seem to have turned quite grand, though. Say hello to Bryce."

Mari stood fazed and mortified. She couldn't hold Bryce's gaze. He was staring at her with a smiling but startled expression on his face.

She didn't know what to say, but was saved by Sophie, who, delighted at the sight of Tom, nearly fell over as she tried to jump and hug him.

"Lord, Mari, what's Little Sis doing done up like this? You both look ready for a ball at court – and, at this time of day, where've you been Sis?"

"Oh, this...."

Mari affected nonchalance and waved her hand between herself and Sophie.

"We had to accompany Mistress Tallentire on her morning outing. She has been supervising our wardrobes. Let us get inside and change, and we'll join you downstairs."

She turned and mounted the steps, leaving Tom to hold Sophie's hand and lead her indoors, followed by Bryce.

"We're back early. Papa is still away. He won't be back until next week sometime, I think. He has a Miss Tallentire staying with him as a.....house guest. Find Mrs. Pynchon, and let her know you'll be in for dinner. Sophie, come with me."

She started up the stairs, cutting short Tom's questions by waving him toward the drawing room. She felt like fleeing upstairs, but forced herself to move carefully to maintain her footing in her unaccustomed finery.

By the time she and Sophie reached their shared chamber, she was thoroughly out of breath and countenance. She decided though it was the hated stays and not the effect of seeing the American again. She brought herself up sharply.

What could she be thinking? She had hardly greeted him properly. She regarded herself in the outfit dictated by Tamsin, and felt wretched. Her image in the mirror seemed like a stranger, dressed to pose for a formal portrait, primped and artificial. She felt as though her heart was in her throat, blocking the power of speech. Bryce had stood in the city street looking so vibrant and strong, and easy-mannered.

Mari mentally shook herself, and called for the maid to help her change. As the girl started to unlace her, she gazed at herself in the mirror, standing amongst rich folds of rose-colored satin pooled around her feet.

She was disgusted at herself for not resisting Tamsin when her father's mistress had insisted on painting and powdering her and

Sophie a la mode. Her flushed, agitated face looked unattractive to her as she started to scrub off the lead powder.

Miss Tallentire had insisted it would make her complexion like porcelain and hide "that unfortunate weathered look," as she had described the country tan that Mari had acquired.

Mari didn't care for the woman's comments, but realized that she grudgingly admired one thing about Tamsin, and that was the woman's flaunting of convention. She didn't think Tallentire aimed to shock deliberately. Tamsin simply did not care what others thought, and was entirely confident in her own talents and powers as a desirable woman. That was what Mari admired.

Focusing upon her image in the mirror again, she realized she was still wearing her wig. She pulled it off and threw it across the room, fretting at the maid' s nimble fingers not moving fast enough to help her disrobe.

"Fetch me some water to scrub this concoction off my face, Millie. Sophie, come here. Stop playing with your fan. Let's get you decently dressed for Miss Pardoe. She'll have a fit seeing you costumed so. We look like trollops. Master Hogarth would have enjoyed making us both silly images in one of his paintings."

She pulled on a plain silk day dress, and tried to pin her hair back in some sort of order. Millie, harassed and anxious, moved between the two girls, trying to help with ribbons and laces. She placed the detested wigs on stands, and took them down the corridor to the powder room. She hurried back with a small ball of lavender scented soap, claimed from Miss Pardoe, who came down the hall to see what the fuss was about.

The governess clicked her tongue and pursed her lips in disapproval. She looked even grimmer when apprised of the fact that Tamsin Tallentire had abandoned them to go off with her dubious friends. She immediately started in to clean up Sophie, seeing the frantic appeal for help in Millie's eyes.

Miss Pardoe frowned on the outings with Tamsin, and tried to discourage them, preferring the girls continue with their French lessons or go with her on an educational outing. She worried Mari seemed so curious about her father's mistress, and, although resenting the woman, was fascinated by her company.

The governess found herself brushing Sophie's hair too vigorously, and felt a rush of guilty affection when Sophie whimpered as her hair was snagged in the comb. Miss Pardoe gently stroked the soft brown waves of the little girl's hair to comfort her. They were both distressed.

This London visit was not going well, not at all, as far as she could see. The house was no home for Mari and Sophie. She determined to find some excuse for getting her youngest charge at least back to Ravenhill, and its quiet country pursuits.

Mari should really go too, she decided. Miss Pardoe felt instinctively that the eldest sister, bright as she was, bid fair to hold her own in the household, but was very naïve and, at fifteen years, was no age yet to cope with the city and what the governess considered its louche society.

Supervision and instruction at the house in London seemed erratic and ill thought out. She saw now that Mari was upset and harassed, and assumed it was due to Mistress Tallentire's lack of consideration.

"Settle yourself, Mari, and stop flitting all about the room. If your brother Tom has arrived with a guest, you should present yourself downstairs to be hostess. Straighten your cap first!"

This was said as Mari hastened to the door, pulling on a cap to cover her untidy hair. Miss Pardoe sighed, and resolved afresh to get the girls back to the calm of Ravenhill.

Mari paused before entering the drawing room. She was wearing a simple cream moiré silk dress, and a demure cap. She was the antithesis of the fashionable cartoon of the morning's outing, and was desperate that Bryce Hunter would approve. She opened the door and entered to find Bryce and Tom playing a game of chess by the window. Tom looked up first.

"Well, there you are, Countess, are you at home to visitors today? You seemed put out to see us – didn't you enjoy your morning's outing?"

"Yes, I am at home, and no, I didn't much."

She answered as she went forward to give him a hug to avoid looking at Bryce.

"Well, I thought we'd torment cook by having dinner with you, then later on we could take an outing to the tea rooms in Marylebone, if you fancy."

Without giving her chance to reply, Tom continued, 'Mind you – we really came over with an invitation for you to come and stay awhile and visit with Bryce's cousins at Gould Square. Bryce's aunt Alicia and uncle Daniel extend a warm invitation, and his cousins, Maybelle and Arabel, are desperate for your company. They wanted to come over with us, but the milliner woman arrived with more hats to add to their collection....in the attic, their father said."

Mari was pleased, and forgot her awkwardness, beaming at both of them.

"I would love to come – you know very well."

She turned to Bryce. "Your aunt and uncle are very kind. What shall I tell Miss Pardoe? Is Sophie invited, too? "

Bryce spoke for the first time.

"Yes, indeed – my cousins will make a complete pet of your little sister."

Tom interjected, "I'll be staying here tonight, and will take you both over tomorrow, with Miss Pardoe and Millie."

"Oh!" Mari's face fell. She remembered Tamsin Tallentire, and was thoroughly disconcerted.

"What about farther's...er... guest? I don't know what she'll think."

Tom exchanged glances with Bryce, and hunched his shoulders, hands in his pockets.

"I don't see that she should mind so much, Mari."

He paused, "I spoke to father yesterday in Chelmsford, and he intends returning earlier than intended to town, perhaps tomorrow. Your visiting the Hunters will be quite satisfactory to him."

They were interrupted by the footman announcing dinner, and Bryce extended his arm for Mari to take. She slipped a hand into the crook of his elbow as Tom went ahead to the dining room, teasing the maid and joking with the footman as he went.

She looked up at Bryce and the feeling of warm happiness she had found at Aunt Mat's ball in Chelmsford flooded back and lit up her expression as she gazed up at him. Observing her face, Bryce smiled back at her and squeezed her arm against his side.

The mid-day meal was a lively one. Mari, Sophie, and Miss Pardoe found themselves unconstrained without Tamsin Tallentire's overwhelming presence. Tom, who was a favorite with the governess, pressed her to take an extra glass of wine, and the two young men soon had everyone laughing with their exaggerated tales of hunting and fishing escapades.

Mari laughed the merrier, knowing well her brother's cheerful and irrepressible nature. He had always had a way of somehow getting himself into a fix and strolling out the other side unscathed. She taxed him with this, and said she hoped that Bryce hadn't to suffer anything because of Tom's behavior.

Tom immediately protested and opined that if he had, Bryce could exact revenge when Tom got around to visiting him in America, as he intended to.

This led to talk of Bryce's imminent return home, much to Mari's dismay. Bryce declared that he had not yet booked a passage back to the colonies, but would have to organize his affairs in the near future as his father would be expecting him.

Tom turned to Mari, "Mayhap you would like a trip with Bryce and me one day on the river before he leaves. We could go to Deptford or over to Spring Gardens. We could make a day out of it, and either take a carriage over London Bridge, or a wherry or a sculler from the Tower – there's always one to be had. We could pack a splendid picnic."

Bryce said it was a capital idea, and had thought of suggesting it himself, adding that Aunt Alicia had mentioned the possibility of attending one of Mr. Oliver Goldsmith's comedies at Covent Garden as an entertainment whilst they were visiting.

Mari was excited and delighted, and wished they could leave for Gould Square straight away. Tamsin Tallentire would be back later on in the evening, and if Tom had the right of it,

Sir Joseph Westin would be back in Conduit Street the next day. His daughter worried that either, or both, could over-rule the happy plans of the young folk. She mentioned this quietly to Tom as they left the dinner table and Bryce was engaged talking to Miss Pardoe.

"Don't fret, Sis. For some reason I seem to be well in with Pa these days. He seems to be letting me have my head. I even think if I did go for a commission in the Navy, he'd be all for it – he has many connections. He could help.

"I don't see playing the country farmer at Ravenhill as my future, not yet awhile, in any event. He'll be glad to see me on my way and off his hands. Though, I have to admit, the old codger has been fair with me and keeps me well supplied. I try to put in a word on behalf of you and Sophie when I can, you know. But on the subject of his females he seems to be distracted. He has taken up with his present lady, everyone knows all about her."

Seeing the concerned look on his sister's face, he quickly put in, "No, I know you didn't, but all London knows, and there are many folk in his set don't approve.

"It's one thing to keep a mistress, but to set her up in one's family home so blatantly is something else. Some friends don't mind, though – in fact, couldn't care less.

"Miss Pardoe, I know, will be glad to get back to Essex, and maybe you'll go back too – but enjoy what you can of the city round, and remember you are his eldest daughter, and you'll soon have the suitors coming by, that's for sure.

"As for visiting the Hunters, he already gave permission. I caught him in a good mood at Chelmsford. He turned up for dinner at Aunt Mat's and Uncle Fred's one evening, and between me and Aunt Mat was quite agreeable to our suggestion."

It was the most serious conversation Mari had had with Tom in a long while. She realized that his previous young boy's dream of going to sea would soon be realized.

The prospect of being left behind, either in the London house or Ravenhill, subject to the influence and authority of her father's mistress, appalled her. She had also a shrewd idea that Mistress Tallentire would not be enthused by the idea of competing for authority with the daughter of the house.

The threat of unwanted young suitors coming to pay court and carry off Joseph Westin's daughter might, in fact, fit Tamsin's plans, but not Mari's. She would find it difficult to gainsay anything her father planned, but she had some dreams of her own, and, surely, the wit and imagination enough to devise something for herself. Considering this, she became more cheerful.

III

"Tell me more about America," said Mari, taking hold of Bryce's arm. "It seems so far away and exciting."

"Tis very different," said Bryce. He smiled, yet his eyes were serious.

"In America there are so few of the things you enjoy so much here. Nearly everything has to be brought from England: our furniture, dishes, even clothes - at least if you want to be fashionable, and, of course, American ladies all want to be fashionable."

They had taken a chaise to Marylebone Gardens, passing by Tyburn with its grim but empty gibbet, and, further on, the outskirts of town with smoking brick kiln chimneys, and the dung heaps of city refuse.

Eventually the open fields, pressing pleasantly around the crowded city boundaries, provided some relief before they arrived at Marylebone and were able to enjoy a walk through the gardens and take tea.

Miss Pardoe, who had been reluctant at first to bring her charges on this excursion, finally relaxed and seemed to enjoy herself as she trod the pathways, but kept firm hold of Sophie's hand.

The prim governess found the gardens more decorous than she had imagined, and was relieved not to witness any of the scandalous behavior she had heard tell of occurring in the gardens' greenery. The place was not crowded, it being early season, and this, too, reassured her.

Tom, holding Sophie's other hand, was teasing her and making her laugh. Bryce and Mari were left to their own company, bringing up the rear. She held his arm with both hands, and he covered her hands with his.

"You seem to know so much, and you seem so like us," said Mari, nervous yet thrilled at the rare chance of being alongside the American.

"Well," said Bryce, "were you able to see America you'd find out just how different we are. There's even talk of us splitting from

England because of all the taxes we have to pay the King. But I'm not sure it will go that far."

"How I wish I could go there, but being a girl I suppose I'll never be allowed to have that kind of fun and adventure. My father is too strict," said Mari, adding wistfully, "Tom might get there. You know he's joining the Navy. I'll surely miss him when he takes to the sea."

"I know, and I'll be sailing myself soon," said Bryce.

"I came here to learn this end of the Atlantic shipping business. Uncle Dan has taught me a lot. I'd like to stay longer, but my father wants me back in his trading office to help in Virginia."

Mari went silent for some moments, then sighed.

"I had hoped you would be here for a good while. I've so enjoyed being with you," she said.

"Well," said Bryce cheerfully, "I'll be here for some days yet."

He shot her an amused glance, adding, "Maybe we can see more of each other before I leave."

The moment was suddenly broken by Sophie, who was jumping up and down between Miss Pardoe and Tom. Her wavy, brown hair was tumbled by the breeze as it caught against the brim of her bonnet. Detached for a moment from her focus on the American, Mari smiled at the contrast in Sophie's demeanor now to that of the wretchedly uncomfortable little girl in the park excursion that same morning.

"Mari, Tom says I can have as many sugar comfits as I please if I sit like a princess and sup tea daintily enough – let us find a table that is free."

"Mari, Sophie, come along!" Miss Pardoe's voice floated back to them. The governess had a a relaxed, complacent air.

"There's a pleasant bower here in the shrubbery – we just have to send for an attendant."

There was a sudden flush of breeze in the park, scattering loose blossoms in the air. Some brushed her face and Mari felt light and free. Releasing Bryce's arm, she caught at Sophie and twirled her in a merry circle. Sophie squealed, swept off her feet,

"You are almost flying, the both of you'"

Bryce caught Sophie and lifted her up, laughing at Mari's antics.

Mari was dazzled. He was handsome and seemed so full of confidence, strength and excitement. Mari felt a wild urge, a yearning to follow him anywhere, everywhere, to sail half a world away with him.

Miss Pardoe called to them again. They joined the others to sit down happily and drink tea daintily enough, whilst Sophie covered herself and Miss Pardoe in sugar comfit crumbs. Tom, suddenly quiet, munched more than his share of buns, occasionally casting an amused glance toward Bryce and his sister.

That same afternoon eventually turned blustery and dark with rain, so, in high spirits, the party hurried back to the waiting carriage and set off for home.

Mari was in her own rosy dream. Sophie cuddled and dozed against Miss Pardoe's comfortable form, but Tom and Bryce, in more serious mood, kept an eye on the roads as the rains came down. The coachman, though, held the team at a good clip, and there was no undue incident on the way back to town.

For the first time Conduit Street seemed welcoming to Mari. The lighted windows shone out on the darkening street as they pulled up to the door, and Mrs. Pynchon came out to see all was well. She had taken it upon herself to set out two trays loaded with refreshment, as though they couldn't possibly have had any sustenance on their afternoon's outing.

The trays were waiting in the upstairs parlor, where a fire was blazing against the evening chill. Amazingly, the young folk found themselves ready to tuck in again, and happily disposed of Abby's ginger parkin and fresh fragrant tea. Miss Pardoe smiled indulgently at them, but declined.

Mari worried from time to time whether their cozy party might be interrupted by Mistress Tallentire or Sir Joseph returning. But Tamsin did not return until late in the evening, by which time Bryce was back home, and everyone else was abed. Mistress Tallentire still slept when they set off next morning for the Hunters' house. There was no sign of Sir Joseph.

Mari was anxious to leave for Gould Square, and waited tensely as the coach was loaded with boxes and baggage. The coachman, George, was excrutiatingly slow and deliberate in his movements, and, then, when it seemed they were finally settled, Tom made Mari want to scream with impatience by telling George to hold the horses as he ambled back into the house to look for a medallion, or some such thing, that he had promised to search out and show to Bryce.

The morning was bright as a new penny after the rain storm, and there was a slight, fresh breeze.

Tom finally owned that he had everything that he needed, but then, to his sister's chagrin, delayed even further by having a discussion with the coachman as to the best route to take. He gave the nod to George, first insisting that Henry, the footman, as well as one of the grooms, should ride outside.

"Just in case of disturbances – or getting mired in a bad patch of road," he said.

"You never know these days when there might be some sort of mob protesting something, the silk weavers, or political crowds of some sort. John Wilkes' supporters have been piling out for him lately, and the poor apprentices, especially in the lower trades, are often so straightened at times they will cause affray at the drop of a hat."

At first Miss Pardoe looked alarmed at this, until Tom, swinging himself up into the carriage, ceased his seriousness and settled easily next to her, and, at last, they were off.

As the coach turned down Woodruffe Lane, leading to Gould Square, they found themselves a little north of the Tower of London fortress, and on the edge of some of the poorest parishes of the city. The area surrounding the Gould Square was very mixed, as to both buildings and people.

The square was something of an enclave, containing solid townhouses, a number of them occupied by respectable merchants. The well-built houses, however, were a contrast to the old, overhanging tenements in the surrounding streets and by-ways.

The Hunters lived at Number Ten, and also kept a country house in Putney, which they might visit later. The position of the Gould Square residence, though not in the most fashionable part of the city, was respectable enough, and certainly convenient for Mr. Hunter's business and the various activities of London's riverside.

Next door to the Hunters were the Nortons, friends and fellow merchants. They were, in fact, invited around to join the family for supper that evening. These neighbors had two little boys and a girl of Sophie's age, and during their visit Sophie spent more time over at the Norton house than with the Hunters. Miss Pardoe was also made most welcome there, and Mari was left to join Tom and Bryce and his cousins on their outings.

At supper that evening, Bryce and Tom persuaded every one of the pleasures of a river excursion, and so it was fixed to go on the Friday.

* * *

The Hunter household breakfasted early on the Friday morning, serving themselves from a sideboard loaded with kedgerees, slices of ham and beef, muffins and griddle cakes. Mari observed again how comfortable and merry the family were together on any occasion. There was an ease and informality in the house, both in their relations with each other, and with the servants.

She could not help but compare the atmosphere here with that at either Ravenhill or Conduit Street. In contrast with her father, who always seemed cold and dismissive with her, or irritated and distracted, Dan Hunter was jolly and approachable. He dealt with his staff in a humorous, shrewd way, and to Mari's mind afforded a warmth and courtesy to all.

His women folk, he obviously doted upon, and shamelessly indulged his two daughters with their whims and fancies. He exacted a form of payment by teasing and pretending to withhold permission for something or other, only to give ultimate assent accompanied by groans of mock horror at the expense of it all.

This morning, the master of the house gulped a final dish of coffee, sending compliments to his cook for the excellence of her spiced griddle cakes. He stood up, and, frowning at his daughters, told them to stir themselves and be ready as they were to conduct him to the wharf to go about his business before setting out on their river trip and the serious business of airing their parasols.

Maybelle and Arabel immediately jumped up, giggling in a fizz of excitement, and ran upstairs, changing their minds again as to what they would wear.

Mari followed after them, with Sophie and Miss Pardoe, who were invited over to the Nortons for the day. Sophie was unwilling to forego the delights of her new, young friends for the company of grown-ups, and Miss Pardoe was quite happy to resist an outing on the river – the

41

water had no appeal for her at the best of times. So, the party was to be six altogether as Alicia Hunter had decided to join them.

Mari herself was ready to set out. She had chosen a dress in the style of a riding habit. It had belonged to her mother, and Tamsin Tallentire's dressmaker had needed to alter it but slightly to accommodate the daughter. It was more simply styled than a day dress, and more comfortable for walking.

Mari surveyed herself in the looking-glass with satisfaction, seeing that her eyes reflected the color of the costume, appearing to be a darker shade of blue. Glancing down, she was aware of Sophie regarding her reflection alongside her.

"You look very pretty Mari, like a cornflower," said the little girl. "And your hair looks like sunshine. I wish I had hair like yours."

Mari hugged her, whispering, "I think I like your hair better, little sister – your hair is the color of sunshine on glossy chestnuts!"

Sophie gave a pleased smile and hugged her, and then remembered to be concerned.

"Don't fall in the river, will you?" she begged. "Though if you do, Mr. Bryce and Tom will jump in after you to save you."

The child perked up at this thought, and she skipped away to find the governess to chivvy and hurry with her over to the Nortons.

Bryce Hunter waited in the hallway of Gould Square, restless and impatient to be off. He intermittently paced the tiled floor, pausing at the foot of the stairs sometimes to listen for signs of readiness from the rest of the party.

There were sounds of footsteps going quickly to and fro as the Hunter girls twittered afresh, passing between their bedrooms. He threw a look of despair at Mari, who, thoroughly amused, gazed back at him. In contrast to Bryce, she was quite composed, happy and content to be spending a whole day in his company whatever the occasion.

Bryce finally tossed his hands in the air, and suggested to Mari a turn around the square's central garden, but they had hardly set out, when they heard the quick steps of Tom, who caught up with them, laughing but looking a little sheepish and harassed. He declared he was desperate to dodge the duty of deciding between the merits of the sisters' bonnets. He grinned at Bryce. "I'm staying out here with you two until everyone's ready for the coach."

The girls eventually appeared, waving and halloing to Mari and her escorts to hurry from the far side of the square and not delay their departure any longer.

"Where are we going on the river? Are we going up to Spring Gardens? We've packed a picnic, though we could dine there. Where are we going Bryce?"

Bryce smiled, teasing them a little.

"You'll see, you'll see, you dillies. Come on Tom let's get these saucy, fashionable bundles into a boat. It's a beautiful day to be on the water."

He handed Mari into the coach, as Tom did his duty by Maybelle and Arabel, and with the two sisters chattering and giggling, they waited for the girls' parents to join them and set off down Tower Hill.

It was a short ride down to the river, and Mari thought they could have walked for the exercise, but Mrs. Hunter had insisted they use the carriage. She had no desire to break her neck, she said, tottering on pattens over the uneven cobbles.

Before venturing on the river, she said, they had to carry Mr. Hunter to the offices of Court and Dickinson at the wharf, and leave him there to toil on their behalf.

This, she pronounced, with total equanimity, while Daniel Hunter maintained an exaggerated expression of sorrow on his face that he could not accompany his women folk on their outing. His mock despair set off more merriment from Maybelle and Arabel.

They had just descended Tower Hill when the coach suddenly lurched to a stop, juddering on the cobble stones, and the coachman swore. He had to pull his team up short to avoid crashing into a recklessly driven phaeton, commanded by a young man dressed in the height of fashion and decidedly the worse for drink.

The vehicle looked spanking new and as prettily tricked out as its careless driver. It bounced and cracked over the cobbles, the beautifully matched horses flaring their nostrils and lunging with fear as the young buck handled them roughly on the verge of an upset.

"Wastrels! Out all night ransacking the chop shops and bawdy houses, and out of control amongst decent folk in the daytime as well."

The coachman swore again, as, starting the horses forward, he had to halt once more. This time a squad of soldiers, with an officer on horseback, turned out of Thames Street, marching a sorry band of

43

about fifty prisoners toward the Tower Stairs. The Hunter party stared at the prisoners. Trailing along after the soldiers, they were a rag-tag bunch of humanity, collected from London's jails to be loaded onto lighters for the transport ships, ready and waiting mid-river for their miserable cargo.

"King's passengers," murmured Dan Hunter, staring from the coach.

"King's passengers," he repeated, smiling grimly.

"Makes it sound as though they are privileged invitees going at the King's pleasure to some royal event."

Mari and the rest looked on as the prisoners passed. The greater number of them were men, though about a third women and children. Most of them looked wretched, filthy and ill-nourished, but there were one or two who looked like gentlefolk, well fed and well dressed.

One man was striding along, his back straight and his composure calm. He glanced toward the Hunter carriage, and caught Alicia Hunter's eye. He raised the nob of his cane, touching it to the curled brim of his hat in a gentleman's salute and passed on.

"Some prisoners have the means to buy themselves comfortable berths," said Alicia.

"They still have to serve out their time, though I hear the educated, better sort, often serve as tutors or clerks of some kind or other."

"Where would this lot be collected from, and where will they be bound for, I wonder?" asked Tom.

Dan Hunter's face was sardonic as he replied, "Oh, they're for Maryland or Virginia, I expect there's much feeling there against the transport. Why should the colonies serve as dumping grounds for England's jails? This lot may be from the Fleet, Clink, or Newgate. They usually load them at Blackfriars, but mayhap 'twas easier to march them down here than wait for an empty lighter, or perhaps the tide was running strong against them."

The mood in the carriage had turned somber. Alicia gazed after the soldiers and prisoners with compassion. Bryce and Tom looked serious and thoughtful. The sisters, too, were quiet for a change. Mari felt suddenly sad and inexplicably shamed.

The coach started up again, however, and Maybelle soon had everyone smiling once more at her chatter. By the time they arrived at the wharf, where Mr. Hunter was to be abandoned to work, their spirits had risen again in anticipation of the river trip.

As Dan Hunter dismounted from the coach, Bryce and Tom, conferring quickly, suggested that the women wait by the carriage whilst they secured a wherry.

Mari was pleased to descend and looked with interest at the activity by the wharf. The scene was a busy one, with merchants, agents, sailors, longshoremen, and all manner of people coming and going.

Mr. Hunter mounted the outer stairway of the warehouse to the offices above. His daughters, with Mari in tow, followed, the better for viewing the surrounding river scene.

Mari strolled along the upper gallery, reading with curiosity the notices posted there. These mainly concerned scheduled sailings, naming ships, tonnage and destinations, captains of the vessels, and listing fares for different classes of passengers.

She observed that all the ships under the control of Court and Dickinson were declared to be well equipped, fleet and sound, and had the most experienced commanders, outperforming those of other agents.

As she idly scanned the advertisements, a variety of clients pushed through the doorway. Some were apparently men of substance, well turned out, confident, and absorbed in their exchanges with a like companion. Mari assumed they would be merchants, perhaps an occasional banker.

She watched two seamen fingering through notices and lists of some kind on the other side of the doorway. One of them glanced her over quickly, and sketched a quick salute in the air with a merry grin on his ugly face. They wore clean, neat, sun-bleached clothes, and Mari had the impression they were making an effort to be spruce and up-to-the-mark.

Probably, she thought, they were looking for berths. They did not have the desperate, hollow look so often seen on London's streets, but seemed healthier, and had an air of exuberance. The man with his hair in a sailor's queue suddenly tapped on a list, and leaning sideways motioned with his head at someone inside the building. His shipmate nodded and they both moved inside the door.

Mari went over to see what had interested them. She saw that amongst the advertising notices there were listings of crew required on some of the vessels. She read the ships' names, *Aurora*, *North Star*, *Heron*, *Integrity*, *Wind Maiden*.

Mari thought that *Heron*, in the middle of the list, was the one of interest to the two sailors. She noticed that it was short a number of crew, and supposed the two men, with luck, would obtain positions aboard.

Moments later, confirming her impression, the two sailors exited the office with pleased expressions, one giving the other a punch on the shoulder as they ran down the stairs. Mari glanced at the list again, *Integrity* had a full complement of crew, it seemed, except for a cabin boy.

"Ladies! Ladies!" Tom was calling from below. "We have a boat ready. Come!"

Alicia Hunter emerged from the agent's office in time to lead the gaggle of young people down to their river wherry, leaving her husband content to be captive at work. They settled themselves nimbly enough, and the boatman raised sail and angled his craft mid-stream, taking an oblique course down river.

"Where are we going, Bryce? Where are we going? Stop your teasing and tell us. Are we going to Spring Gardens?" Maybelle asked brightly.

"Oh, no – somewhere more interesting than that," answered Tom, exchanging grins with Bryce.

Alicia Hunter, who knew of their plan, said nothing, but smiled, content to let the young men have their way. She thought the trip they proposed would be educational, and a pleasant picnic somewhere in the country afterwards suited quite well her idea of an outing for her flighty daughters. They could parade their latest outfits in Spring Gardens at Vauxhall another day.

Bryce Hunter had told his aunt and Tom that, going about his father's trading business in the docks, he had learned of a ship preparing for a particularly challenging voyage. It was to record a rare passage in the following summer of the planet Venus across the Sun from the newly-discovered island of Tahaiti, accurate observations and measurements of this rare event being vital to refining navigational techniques.

He told them that it was not so much this mission that had captured his imagination though, but the daring and ambitious second charge:

to proceed southward and then westward from Tahiti to search for a new continent, known as Terra Australis Incognita, a place first seen more than a century earlier by Dutch and Portuguese sailors. It was, they said, a land mass believed to be as large as Europe.

There had been little or nothing in the newspapers about this venture, but Bryce, from his many chats on and off the quays with tradesmen, shipping agents and sailors, was well aware of its scope and ambition.

He had learned that Lieutenant James Cook, a veteran of exploration of North America, had been appointed by the Admiralty to command the *Endeavour*, which was being fitted out for the voyage in the Navy's Deptford Yard.

He had become fascinated with the danger and romance of the voyage, regularly taking a wherry across the river to follow the progress of *Endeavour*'s preparations for the high seas.

"Bryce and I have a passion to see how far advanced they are in preparing the *Endeavour* for its historic voyage," said Tom, explaining to the girls just what Cook was planning to do.

Seeing his cousins look perplexed and doubtful, Bryce added hastily, "Don't worry there'll be plenty of action to entertain you, and then we'll enjoy a picnic somewhere along the river."

"And you might," broke in Tom, "even find some splendid naval uniforms to compare."

Mrs. Hunter leaned back against the wherry's shabby cushions, and closed her eyes under the shade of her bonnet. Her daughters had now passed from discussing their own fashions to expressing admiration for the different ships' officers they spotted on the embankment. Tom interrupted them from time to time to tell tall stories about the river - how the different stairs to landing stages came by their names. Some were self-explanatory, he said, but why "Frying Pan Stairs," or "Elephant Stairs," or "Puddle Dock" and "Bull Stairs?"

"And talking of stairs," said Bryce, pointing to the river bank, "there's 'Dog and Duck Stairs.' We're nearly at Deptford. Get ready to disembark."

The wherry, having swung them smoothly down the Thames, passing wharves and timber yards, dry docks, shipwrights and coopers' yards, now nudged gently up against the King's Yard landing stage.

47

"Follow me. I know the best vantage point," said Bryce, who could barely suppress his eagerness and impatience as he helped hand the females ashore.

From the viewing platform to which Bryce quickly led them, they all gazed across the Navy's dry dock. *Endeavour* loomed above them, her three masts appearing to scratch the sky, her heavy rigging stretched like a strong black spider's web from stem to stern.

A small army of workers swarmed over her plump, strong hull, busy about the challenge of converting her from a Whitby collier, built for nothing more ambitious than carrying coals along England's east coast or across the North Sea to Scandinavia, to a King's Barque fit to convey explorers, astronomers and scientists to the ends of the world, to complete experiments and attempt discoveries that could shape and enrich the very future

Bryce murmured to himself, "What an adventure. And a fine name for the ship, for it is to be a real endeavor."

Mari looked at him as his voice trailed off, and she saw excitement and longing in his eyes. He turned to her at last, with a self-deprecating smile.

"By the time the *Endeavour* is on her way, I'll be on my way home, Mari. I'll show you the ship I intend to take passage on, on the way back. It's anchored just along the river."

He reached over and hugged her impulsively. He looked about to say something more, but caught himself, and then shook his head at his thought.

"One thing is for sure, sweet Mari. I'll be home a whole lot sooner than brave Lieutenant Cook."

He looked at her, his eyes dark with concern, as though he had blundered.

"Bryce, Mari! Come on, it's time to eat." Arabel came tripping toward them, flirting her skirt around coils of rope, bollards and barrels.

"Mama says we ought to find an inn, or have the wherryman take us to a decent spot to find a good, grassy meadow to spread our picnic."

Bryce said nothing immediately but hesitated, reluctant to leave. Mari realized that left alone he would have stayed observing the

Endeavour, and trying to strike up conversation with anyone remotely connected to Cook's expedition.

"My cousins are soon bored," he said resignedly. "Come on then, Mari – time to organize the party again. Where's Tom?"

They strolled arm in arm away from the shipyard toward the moored wherry.

"The man here knows a good spot for us to refresh ourselves," Alicia said.

"Then we must away back over the river to carry Mr. Hunter home for supper. We shall have to leave a visit to Spring Gardens for another day. Where's Tom got to this time? I shouldn't be surprised if that brother of yours, Mari, would try to talk himself onto *Endeavour*'s crew. He'll get to sea soon, I don't doubt, come what may."

She turned to allow the wherryman to help her into the boat, and scolded her daughters for fidgeting and rocking the craft. Mari and Bryce stood contentedly holding hands as they smiled back at Tom, who ran to catch up with them, calling goodbye to a couple of sailors.

"Move over Hunter sisters, your skirts are taking up too much room as usual – what have we for the picnic? Some of that splendid cured ham we had yesterday, I hope."

So saying, he looked up at Mari and Bryce, still on the landing stage. "Come on then, slowpokes. You're delaying us. We're waiting to be off."

Everyone burst out laughing at his innocent indignation.

"Yes, Tom, certainly Tom," said Mari, blushing, as she allowed Bryce to help her step primly into the wherry.

They made swift progress up the river, passing craft, large and small, anchored off, or moored to the wharves that lined both banks of the Thames, along which ebbed and flowed a never-ending tide of trade in every imaginable type of cargo.

In his two years in London, Bryce had become a denizen of the docks. He had become a familiar figure on many of the Legal Quays, and knew the business conducted on most of them.

Now, he pointed out the wharves that specialized in tea from Asia, coffee from Arabia, and chocolate from South America, tobacco from North America, coal from the north of England, spices from tropical islands.

As he shared his knowledge with the others, the wherry would be wafted one minute by the dry but refreshing smell of the tea leaves, then the acrid, choking presence of fine coal dust, and next the pungent, aromatic scent of the spices from afar.

"Many of these boats are on the Atlantic passage to the colonies," said Bryce suddenly, his arm waving ahead as they rounded the river bend at Rotherhithe and approached Wapping.

Mari noted that the vessels were all anchored mid-stream and looked much bigger than many of the other boats they had seen moored alongside the wharves.

Bryce pointed to one of the ships with two tall masts, its dark hull glistening in the afternoon sun as if freshly painted. She noticed a lighter tied alongside, apparently unloading supplies.

"That's the one I'm planning to take home to Virginia," said Bryce, his voice urgent, his eyes sparkling.

Catching an anxious glance from Mari, he quickly assured her, "She's commanded by Captain Coward, who I know to be a most experienced sailor. She should be ready for sea inside the week, Mari." He turned his head again to gaze at the merchantman. "It would be wonderful to be going with friends," he murmured quietly.

Mari looked again at the vessel that would carry him away from her, and noted with surprise the name in gold letters on the stern – *Integrity*. It was the ship advertising at the agent's office for a cabin boy.

IV

Tamsin Tallentire was bored and restless.

She sprawled on her favorite couch, aimlessly ruffling through her hair with the fingers of one hand. The other hand was outstretched in front of her, fingers splayed, the better to display the rings adorning them. Looking at her, Maisie, her maid, relaxed.

There were mistresses aplenty, who, when bored and restless, Maisie well knew, would make a servant's life miserable. They would be carping and critical, peevish and never satisfied. Mistress Tallentire was not such a one.

When Tamsin was full of ennui, she was, for some reason, kind and generous to Maisie, albeit in an absent-minded way. She showed herself so now by saying, "Help yourself to the rest of the chocolate, Maisie, and finish those biscuits. Sit yourself down, wench!"

She gestured toward a silver tray set with a beautiful chocolate service, sighed, and turned back to contemplating the rings on her fingers.

Most of the jewelry she wore had belonged to Joseph Westin's wife, including the ring on Tamsin's middle finger, a large ruby surrounded by pearls. With a woman's eye, she decided that the ring, although her own favorite, would not have suited the taste of Lady Westin.

She turned her attention to survey the room, which was still decorated as Anna-Marie Westin had it. Tamsin tutted with impatience. She wanted it changed, would have it changed, but she knew she should not show haste. She should go warily. Sir Joseph could be difficult and unpredictable.

Tamsin was confident of having her own way, but clever enough to bide her time. She mentally replaced gray, watered silk on the walls with rose brocade, and nodded to herself with satisfaction. In her opinion, the Lady Westin had had insipid taste.

No, the ring would not have suited the former wife, but here Tamsin recognized her own dissatisfaction. There was ambiguity as to whether Sir Joseph had gifted her his dead wife's jewelry, or whether he meant merely to allow her to use it – "as long as I hold favor," thought Tamsin.

He had simply one evening indicated a small chest and said, "Wear some of the trinkets in there for a change. There may be something to suit."

Acknowledging to herself that men were fickle and easily distracted, Mistress Tallentire now tried to calculate finely whether to enjoy wearing the pieces she was most fond of, such as the ruby ring, or perhaps to put one or two items to one side and hope that Sir Joseph would forget their existence. Jewelry would provide a most convenient cache if his gallantry failed at a future time.

She sighed again – Westin could be difficult to read. They had met at Epsom races the year before. She and sisters-in-kind had been engaged to service the gaming tables in pavilions set aside for London's well-heeled gentry to while away the time between races.

She recalled how she had abandoned her place at the tables, and returned with Sir Joseph to the city and the Conduit Street house that same day. She had been stunned when he made clear to her that he wished her to set up residence there. No private rooms, or inns, or discreet lodgings, somewhere for assignations.

For a sporting lady, as she sometimes termed herself, she knew that her rise had been swift, from the back streets behind the Radcliffe Highway to a bawdy house in Covent Garden, and then to Mayfair. She blessed the day she went to the races. Her finery then was borrowed. Not so these days - now she could parade with the best of them in the latest fashions.

"The daughters are back!" Maisie's exclamation broke into her thoughts.

The maid sat on the window seat peering down at the street, taking a last satisfying gulp of the chocolate and munching the remains of a biscuit. Tamsin stirred herself and sauntered over to the window to see Bryce handing Mari down from the carriage.

"My, it looks as though Sir Joseph's fair beauty has had a successful cruise and brought back a handsome catch."

Lively interest replaced ennui as she picked up her fan and crossed to the door.

"Clear that tray, Maisie, and wipe the crumbs from your face. We're not still down the highway."

In the hallway, Mari was holding Bryce's hand, wanting to delay his departure as long as possible, leaving Tom to organize their baggage. She anxiously gazed at Bryce.

"I promise I'll try and come to bid you goodbye, but I don't know whether it will be possible. I'll try though, I'll try. I'm not even sure what's going to happen with us. We might remain in London for a while, or be sent back to Ravenhill very soon. When you've gone, I think I'd much prefer to be there anyway."

She flushed, annoyed with herself for prattling. Bryce smiled, surprised to feel touched by the young girl's dismay, but uncomfortable and bemused at her protests.

"Don't worry for me Mari. I can't reckon on being able to visit before I go as Uncle Dan has business for me to clear, but I can perhaps write you."

He hoped he was brisk without sounding dismissive. His expression was quizzical, but Mari beamed. He suddenly stopped talking to jerk his head up, and look sharply over Mari's shoulder. His eyes widened in recognition as he took in the sight of Tamsin Tallentire descending the stairs, with an arm trailing languorously along the banister.

Her bright eyes were fixed on the young American, a lazy smile touching her lips. She ignored everyone else as she deliberately and slowly paced toward him. She held a hand to him, and Bryce took it, bending to kiss it reflexively. Tamsin did not release his hand when he raised his head, but placed her other on the upper part of his sleeve and stroked it. Her smile widened, and her amused gaze took in the disconcerted expression on the face of Mari, and the attempt at nonchalance on that of Bryce.

"And who is this handsome new friend? You should introduce us, Mari."

Mari was mortified, and furious with Tamsin. The woman behaved as though every man had to fawn upon her. It was most likely the last glimpse she would have of Bryce for a long while, and now she found herself urgently wanting him out of the door and away from her father's mistress.

"Bryce cannot stay – can you, Bryce?" she stammered. "He has business to attend."

She looked desperately at Bryce, who seemed transfixed, saying nothing. He was holding Tamsin's gaze, but, flashing a guileless grin, managed to excuse himself smoothly, and turned to Mari. He kissed her hand briefly, and then, with relief, accepted Tom's farewell handshake and God speed.

As Tamsin watched him leave, she realized she had encountered Mari's handsome suitor before. She remembered it was the very day she had moved in with Sir Joseph. As usual, she had been working the tables in the gambling pavilion at the Epsom races, when a clutch of young men came strolling in.

They were boisterous and obviously excited to be amidst the fairground atmosphere, with gypsies and performing players moving through the crowd, selling wares, or clearing a pitch to do tumbling or juggling acts.

There were card sharps and other sleight-of-hand opportunists out to con the gullible and unwary, and food stalls aplenty to cater for all tastes. Between the races, the young men had ended up surveying the gaming tables.

She recalled playing the double-game of gambling and titillation, using her expressive hazel eyes and revealing costume of coral-colored satin brocade to attract the attention of the men passing to and fro, enticing them to try the action at the table, and beyond.

Assessing Bryce's party, she decided they were high on enthusiasm but low on wherewithal to pay for the diversion she offered. She almost smiled at the memory of Bryce looking mightily encouraged at the display of her swelling décolletage as she leaned toward him.

She had nodded toward Tyree, the table master who didn't miss a thing, and then, holding Bryce's gaze, she crooked her finger at him and called to a thin fair-haired girl in blue silk.

"Delphine – take over for a while, I need some air."

Delphine slid her eyes at Bryce and smirked, but sauntered over to the faro table.

Tamsin had already turned Tyree a good profit for the day, and in record time. She knew it and Tyree knew it. She also knew that Tyree was on the point of demanding she stay with the faro players, but she had stared him down.

Tyree growled, shrugged and gave way, shifting to one side as she left the table. She had decided on a spell of amusement to please herself, and had Tyree's measure enough to know he wouldn't make trouble to rein her in, either at the pavilion or later back at the house off Radcliffe Highway. Tyree was peevishly resigned, his frustration no doubt, slaked by the weight of coin in his coat-tail pocket.

She had ushered Bryce past the curtain shielding the alcove at the back of the pavilion, a dusty chamber attempting a boudoir atmosphere with drapes and a chaise longue. Faded covers of old velvet and worn brocade were rendered soft and acceptable by filtered light from the pavilion.

Tamsin poured them both wine with one hand as she unfastened the lace of her petticoat with the other, nodding her head in the direction of the couch. It seemed to her the scene played lazily as if time slowed.

With a rustle of silk, she had settled over him, engulfing him in female scent, and the soft pressure of breasts freed from their bodice.

His pleasing response quickly persuaded her that here was no novice to seduction. He carried her along with him as the roar of the crowd outside and the drum beat of hooves on the track came in amazing coincidence with the surge of pleasure they enjoyed together.

Then, a throaty chuckle, silk whisked and swirled into order, and with practiced hands she had helped him pull his shirt together. Tamsin had laughed, and, amazingly, refused his money.

"My choice, friend," and with a wicked smile, "Put a wager on Fire and Brimstone in the next contest"

Bryce shook his head, surprised but amused, then, with a shrug, had tucked the golden guinea back into his pocket.

She had watched him rejoin his friends until her focus had switched with intensity to someone behind them. She had smiled, looking down, casually smoothing a fold of her mantua, showing an amazing silhouette, as she raised her gleaming eyes straight at the man behind Bryce. Here was business quarry.

Joseph Westin was standing, hat tucked under his arm and hand slotted into his waistcoat, observing the play at the tables. His heavy-lidded gaze traveled over Tamsin's display with a smile of recognition and satisfaction. Then, with a pleased look, he advanced toward her.

She had turned slightly away from Joseph Westin as he approached, and, holding her fan low, had flicked it half open toward Bryce, as if briefly offering a glimpse of something on a dainty platter. So, food for thought. Now here he was again, in her house, with Joseph Westin's daughter.

Mari returned disconsolately to the drawing room with a sense of anti-climax. She stood and waved after the Hunters' carriage until it turned at the corner of the road. Tamsin was also looking out of the window.

"Well, Mari – what a pity your handsome blade could not stay for dinner. I should like to know more about him. You look taken by him. I'm not surprised."

Mari didn't answer, but sat forlornly on a chair, eyes down, fiddling with her sleeve.

Tamsin smiled to herself, "He's a man who would look attractive in any costume."

Enjoying herself, she slid a glance again at Mari.

"I especially approve of his green velvet coat, cut so well. I don't see why some of our young men about town make fun of the colonials."

She paused again, then slyly added, "Don't you think, Mari, that a gentleman's strong body shows so well under velvet?"

Mari looked up, outraged. Tamsin pretended not to notice.

"Yes, my poppet, you have a catch there, and he would make a very attractive addition to our circle. Your father might not approve of such a young man for you, but I have a number of acquaintances who would be delighted to entertain him and show him the town."

Again, she paused, wickedly observing Mari.

"Though he has such style, I can't think he has been wanting for attention. He has access, I don't doubt, to many a lady's salon. He would not have to traipse around the houses for companionship."

A warning was given kindly though with a sly smile.

"In any case, better not to take him seriously, Poppet. Like any young man about town he'll be spreading his favors around."

Tamsin laughed.

"And no doubt they will be well received."

She then, in sham sympathy, made a mischievous show of soothing the girl.

"Oh, but Mari, I forget, you are quietly raised and bred and know nothing really of the world."

She chuckled to herself as she walked toward the drawing room door, relishing her own affectation of matronly concern.

"Never mind – we have to educate you, beyond the scope of Miss Pardoe, and..." she added as a merry afterthought, "make sure you enjoy it."

Mari felt she would explode. She knew that she was lacking in experience, but she was not stupid. and understood Tallentire's train of thought very well. She calmed a little, knowing that Bryce would be out of the woman's sight and away in America, wishing that she could go too.

She was in a quandary, unable to appeal to her father. He was besotted by Tasmin, and apparently insensitive to the feelings of his eldest daughter. She eventually realized she had been fuming and twiddling her sleeve at least ten minutes in her frustration.

Collecting herself, she went upstairs to see how Sophie and Miss Pardoe were settling back in the townhouse. She found them unpacking some small mementos given by the Nortons and their youngsters. Sophie was happy and ran to hug her sister.

"Mari, Miss Pardoe has promised to try and get us back to Ravenhill as soon as she can. I want to hurry back, 'specially because the Nortons say Courtney and Tristan can visit for a while, and I said if Tess has any puppies to spare they may choose one."

Mari smiled and returned the hug. The atmosphere in the room calmed and comforted her after the encounter with Tamsin.

Would she be sent back to Essex with them, or would Tamsin insist she stay in London? Neither prospect appealed, though she would take loneliness at Ravenhill over Tallentire's taunts. She flung herself down on the bed she shared with Sarah and lay looking at the ceiling.

A fierce desire to be with Bryce swept over her again. She imagined him in a few days, boarding the ship in the Thames, waiting to take him down river, to the sea and America. She found herself daydreaming about turning up at the quay as though to say farewell to Bryce, then surprising him by announcing she was leaving with him. Then, as she mentally scolded herself for silly meanderings, something tugged at her memory – a notice, nailed to a rough wooden board, advertising a berth for a cabin boy on a ship called *Integrity*.

V

Bryce Hunter's friends were planning a send-off celebration, supposedly a surprise for him, but Freddy Marmian let the cat out of the bag.

Bryce had walked in on Freddy and a couple of others in the Old Devil Inn at Temple Bar. The others groaned at Marmian's gaffe, but Freddy, unfazed and in typically garrulous fashion, happily continued.

"We're set on scouring the town, Bryce, m'friend."

Bryce had to grin at the irrepressible spirit of the youngest member of the set, and affected a mock show of ennui, declaring a lack of enthusiasm for an indifferent supper at some shady tavern, with suspect doxies as entertainment. Marmian rose innocently to the bait.

"No, no, man. We have arranged a splendid entertainment at the Shakespeare's Head in Covent Garden. If there's appetite for a play, we may do that, and then we're to carry you to Athene's Place, where you'll have your choice of the fair ones, on the house."

Bryce was both amazed and skeptical at this, and reminded Freddie that the famed Athene never gave so much as a swallow of water on the house.

"Well – on your friends, at any rate," Freddy admitted. At this Bryce burst out laughing.

"Freddy! You know as well as I do, you're all strapped for cash. What do you aim to do? Set me up against some alley wall, ruffling the feathers of some drab-tailed wench whilst you try to think where porter can be had for a couple of pence?"

His young companion looked comically hurt.

"Not at all, not at all, Bryce. The dinner is set up and paid for, and so is the session at Athene's."

Freddy paused, and his face cleared.

"Mind you, I don't mind goin' down market a bit myself. We could perhaps fit in a half hour before hand at Dukeberry's on Russell Street, watching 'em fight. Sometimes a couple of the girls strip off and start on one of the men, there's a sight for sore eyes, as my old Pa would say."

* * *

Big Lilly landed a hefty smack to the side of the costermonger's head with a pudgy fist. He was a huge slab of a man and he grunted in disgust. The punch had weight behind it, but it was still a woman's fist. He shook his head and reached a hairy knuckled paw to grab and tear at her grimy camisole, or what was left of it.

A sweat-slicked breast already hung from one side of the tattered garment. Freed from bondage, its partner swung in unison over folds of fat as the two fought, staggering and scuffling over the uneven floorboards.

"Give us a hand Fanny - kick him in the bollocks."

Lilly swore and flailed as her friend and partner in the contest tried instead to jump on the man's back.

The crowd packed in a tight circle round the wrestlers, roaring and cheering them on, placing bets on the outcome. Mari, appalled but fascinated, had to duck and dodge to see the action as a solid wall of male backs blocked her view. Distracted by the action, she had lost sight of brother Tom and friends, and wondered where they could be, perhaps somewhere in a backroom gambling. She felt a brush of panic.

She had felt safe trailing after the young men through the London streets, as long as they were in sight. Now, though, they had vanished, and she was left wondering why on earth she had thought it such a lark to escape the house and spy on her brother at all. Here she was, in a disgusting dirty hole of a place, and her protectors, totally unconscious of their role, had gone.

Unnerved, she gave up trying to push through the spectators and edged back instead, aided by jostling shoulders until pressed against the slanted board of the inn's leaning post. The other half of the post was taken by an unconscious drunk, slung there to dry out by friends, or strangers.

He was propped over the board, arms dangling loosely to the floor either side of his head. She couldn't see his face and didn't want to. He reeked of ale vomit and filth.

Revolted and queasy, she turned to scramble for the door and collided with the solid form of a man pushing in the opposite direction.

Jerking her head up to apologize, she was horrified to lock her gaze with that of a stupefied Bryce Hunter.

"Mari? Mari! What in blazes are you doing here? Where's Tom?" his eyes scorched in disbelief over her ragged disguise, Tom's old britches again. Feeling a fool she fumbled an answer.

"I-um-I've lost him. I think he's maybe in a back room playing cards or something."

She was stammering, making a play for insouciance.

"Sh-shall we look for him?"

She made a vague movement as if to go but Bryce arrested her straightway.

"No! No, Mari."

He made a grab for her arm.

"Maybe they ain't playing cards exactly-come away-I'll get you home. What do you reckon you're playing at girl? I can't imagine. Did you even come with Tom? I can't believe you did."

She opened her mouth to offer some lame excuse but he cut her off, "No, don't bother to explain, this is beyond a prank"

He then hauled her without ceremony down the dark, pokey stairs, kicking past a couple of inert bodies at the bottom of the steps. Outside the night air was clammy but not as fetid as the inside of the building.

Bryce kept a vise like grip on her arm as he marched her down Drury Lane, his face a mask of exasperation. One look at him and she bit back any protest, and concentrated on keeping her footing on the sharp uneven cobbles as he towed her along. He fired questions at her hardly giving her a chance to answer. How did she leave the house? Did Tom or anyone else know? Had she been seen?

The simple answer was no, no, and no, though he didn't appear to listen as his eyes ranged over their surroundings. She was flummoxed anyway. How would she get back in the house again without notice?

She had thought to surprise Tom at some point and join up with him. He would treat all as a jape and a lark, just another escapade, and come up with some scheme to smuggle her back inside the Conduit street house - maybe by sweet-talking Abbey and the kitchen maids whilst she sneaked upstairs. They wouldn't have to worry about the housekeeper Mrs. Pynchon, she would have taken to her room early with a hefty dose of rum Punch.

Mari's gabbled explanations and excuses were stopped short as Bryce pulled up suddenly and yelled "Tom!" across the street.

Her brother and two companions were exiting yet another of Drury Lane's dubious drinking holes. Bryce yanked her over the street to Tom, announcing that they had a problem. Looking at Tom, Mari knew there would be no more fun and pranks

that evening. Freddy Marmian, the youngest of Tom's coterie of friends and already tipsy, beamed cheerily at her, but Tom's face went through the gamut of expressions from disbelief and dismay, to guilt and anger.

"Sister-do you want to get me whipped around the houses? Move! Let's get her back home. I'll have to think of something smartish."

Mari was mortified but had no choice but to go along with them, a bedraggled, decidedly unwanted guest at the party. Tom and Bryce each took an arm, and marched her along to the Strand where they hailed a chaise. The only member of the party in good spirits was Freddy, who prattled happily and inconsequentially about any stray thing entering his head.

Tom did manage to sweet-talk Abbey in the kitchen, after roping in Henry the footman as scout and watchdog for the stairs and hall. After Mari reached the safety of her room, her brother came up and stuck his head around the door.

"Don't ever do such a fool thing again Mari," he hissed. "We ain't at Ravenhill and I've other stuff to do than play nursemaid to a silly sister."

She heard his footsteps running down the stairs, an exchange with Henry and a burst of laughter. The front door was closed and bolts drawn. Going to the window, she was just in time to see the friends swing around the corner. Tom thumped Bryce on the back and they disappeared. So here she was again, wings clipped and enclosed in her room at home, whilst the men went off laughing to roam at will.

She fumed at her impotence, flinging Tom's old jacket and britches across the room. There was no doubt now, her jaunts with Tom and George at Ravenhill were children's games. She had been patronized by Tom and his friends. Beyond that she could not go, would not be allowed, and was not wanted. She was relegated to the world of the parlor with its games and gossip, and proscribed behavior.

She sighed and picked up the discarded clothes. She had enjoyed the streets, trailing after the young men. She had not been nervous or worried about getting lost, but, dodging nimbly through the crowds, was invigorated by the bustle and activity around her.

Standing before the looking glass she pulled on the soft worn cap again, stuffing her hair into it. She stared at her reflection. Tall for a girl and skinny. Not at all plump and curvy like the Hunter girls, she looked more like a lanky apprentice, and found the image pleasing, useful in fact.

* * *

At midday the next day, a jaded Bryce Hunter swung open the door of his uncle's house in Gould Square to surprise Toby Moffat, who had one hand raised, ready to knock, while in his other, Bryce noticed, he held a large document carrier.

Bryce was about to go down to the docks to settle his passage to America, but, finding Toby on the doorstep, he escorted him back to his Uncle Dan's study and remained to hear what brought his uncle's factor from Bristol to London.

There were problems, said Moffat, emptying his leather box for Dan Hunter to examine the papers. Hunter was needed in Bristol to settle affairs regarding a shipment to America.

After pacing his study and perusing the documents for a while, Dan Hunter made up his mind quickly. Bryce should accompany them back to Bristol. They would take a stage to Bristol that very day after dinner.

"We can take coach for Oxford, there's one at five this evening, if I don't mistake – we'll overnight at the Blue Bell Inn, and set off for Bath, and there change for Bristol. I had intended to go over there next month in any event. A couple of weeks early makes no difference."

Bryce had no thought to disagree with his Uncle Dan at the disruption of his own plans. He had been sent over in the first place to learn "both ends of the business,'' as his father put it, and be at Dan's disposal.

It was now more than two years since he first arrived in England, but although at times missing home, he was in no real hurry to go back.

The colonial boy enjoyed the lively variety of the London scene and accepted Dan Hunter's instruction with good grace.

His uncle's haste to make for Bristol, however, was rendered useless. They had not made good time at all. Stretches of the Oxford road were poor, rutted and ill-maintained.

The driver settled into a sour mood, probably at the prospect of meager tips for a slow run, but then, a few miles south of Oxford, the track improved and the team was able to pick up speed. The driver, Jervis, did not hold back when the road started to slope downhill.

A more cautious coachman would have used at least the drag chains, but many veteran drivers scorned this precaution, relying on skill alone to manage an equipage. Jervis was one such, reckoning himself second to none.

He set his team downhill, and they ran as though bolting from the carriage. The driver was planted squarely on his perch, eyes bad tempered slits, whiskered jowls sunk into a grimy muffler. His boots were splayed against footboards.

He totally disregarded the skinny guard who was hanging on for dear life, teeth clenched in fright, and the yelps of outraged passengers just served to light a savage grin under the muffler.

Their momentum was too much to survive the upcoming bend in the road, though the coach amazingly stayed upright as it lurched and slewed into the offside ditch, jerking and dragging the team around with it.

Apart from possible damage to the coach, Bryce reckoned they would be lucky if the wheeler horses, running behind the team leaders in the traces, were not lamed. One of them had been wrenched back on his haunches halfway into the ditch.

The tumbled passengers were shaken and bruised, and angry to varying degree. Two journeymen, riding up top with the baggage, had proved lively enough to jump clear and escape injury.

Jervis ordered the passengers, still clinging to their seats, to disembark whilst he regarded the mess and tried to assess the damage. He seemed more concerned about the horses than the passengers, not from any particular sympathy for the animals' plight but rather from a concern to make up time, and frustration that the vehicle had its front offside wheel up to the hubcap in heavy mud.

Getting back on the road would be a feat, and no doubt he had forfeited the gold guinea that Dan Hunter usually tossed him for a good run.

As he turned to untangle the traces, a coarse command rang out. "Stand and deliver!"

Out of sight, Bryce froze at the sound of the rough voice. The highwayman's demand came as he was trudging back to the coach with a stave of wood suitable for leverage against the coach's wheels.

He saw three thieves, one on horseback, two afoot. The mounted man threatened the passengers with a brace of cocked pistols. His partners were standing nearer the coach driver and guard.

The thieves' backs were toward Bryce. They were unaware of his presence. He eased himself lower into the cover of the thick grass and bushes. A sudden, quiet movement at his shoulder caused him to tense with further alarm until he recognized his uncle Dan, who had strolled away from the party to relieve himself.

Bryce saw that his uncle had with him an old and favorite cudgel. Even in the circumstances, Bryce had to smile. No gentleman's cane for Dan Hunter. He even took a cudgel with him on visits to the theater, Bryce recalled.

Dan Hunter silently motioned his nephew to take on one of the footpads while he aimed for the rider. They crept closer to the road. His uncle held up a hand in warning to be still, and Bryce saw him slowly move his arm back, taking aim with the heavy-knobbed weapon.

He thought that his uncle was going to throw it at the highwayman, but instead Dan hurled it in a vicious, short arc at the robber's horse, which blasted into the air, bucking and screaming with fright.

The highwayman dropped one pistol and discharged the other, but somehow managed to keep his seat on the animal. Dan leapt for the man's leg to unhorse him, and Moffat jumped to help from the other side, both of them in danger from the thrashing hooves.

Simultaneously, Bryce jumped the nearer of the two footpads, getting a chokehold on him and slamming a sledgehammer blow at his temple. The man slump to the ground easily, faring better in his oblivion than his companion.

The other thief was having the life choked out of him by a savage-tempered coach driver, who not only outweighed him by a good fifty pounds but had a death grip in callous fingers conditioned by years of controlling teams of dashing horse.

Surprised by the lack of resistance from his chosen prey, Bryce looked back at his uncle in time to see him kicked in the face by the desperate robber who had still managed to stay mounted.

Dan Hunter staggered back in pain and blundered into Bryce as the highwayman pulled the cavorting horse around and away from Moffat's clutching hands. He charged off into the deepening dusk.

"You 'ave him....You 'ave him, Jervis. Leave him lie. He'll not be going anywhere!"

The guard was trying to pull the massive coachman off the limp ruffian, who fell like a rag doll when the driver suddenly let him go. Jervis's jaw was clamped shut and he breathed tightly through his nose.

"You did for him, Jervis. I reckon he's dead."

They all stared down at the two limp figures. The coachman said nothing, but glared in contempt, curling and straightening his fingers as if they needed more exercise.

Dan Hunter mopped at a bloody cut on his brow, as Bryce knelt down to check the two thieves, who were both breathing short and shallow. Bryce was amazed that he had felled his man with a single blow. Either he was stronger than he realized, or the man had a thin skull. The other passengers stood in a terrified cluster, stunned by the turn of events.

"What'll we do with these two?" Bryce turned to his uncle Dan.

"Truss 'em up, and drown 'em in the ditch for all I care," sneered the driver, who turned back to his horses.

Bryce and the guard looked to Dan for advice.

"We should hand 'em over to the nearest watch," the guard offered. "They's no room in the coach, and I doubt Jervis would give 'em a free ride anyway."

Dan felt his tender scalp as if feeling for cracks.

"Well, I've no sympathy either. We're no distance from Oxford. Tie 'em to the nearest tree. The magistrate can send someone back for 'em if they want 'em."

Dan fished in his pocket for his travel flask and took a gulp of brandy, handing it to Bryce, who took his turn and passed it to Moffat, who was nursing a strained wrist.

"Let's get this contraption on the road before any other passing riff-raff decided we're easy pickings. Next time you'll mebbe modest enough to use the skid pan and chains going downhill," Dan growled at the driver, who was still fierce and stiff with temper but kept his own counsel when meeting Dan Hunter's eye.

Engrossed in righting the coach, the men reacted too slowly to the sound of pounding hooves.

Fired with revenge, the escaped highwayman was riding like a madman back down the hill. The travelers' faces showed a mixture of dismay and disbelief as he charged past. A single vindictive shot rang out. Bryce Hunter fell to the ground, his blood soaking the trampled earth, and Dan and Toby watched helplessly as the life in his eyes faded with the dusk.

VI

May 3, 1768 - Mari stood listening at her bed chamber door.

Sir Joseph and Tamsin were going out for the evening. Having her father back in their Conduit Street residence was a mixed blessing. It could mean unpredictable interference in any activities she planned, with or without Mistress Tallentire, but it could also afford her the advantage of being left to her own devices.

She heard some exchange between Mrs. Pynchon and Tamsin, followed by Sir Joseph's voice sounding impatient and exasperated. There was a flurry of footsteps, Mrs. Pynchon, she supposed, retiring to her quarters at the rear of the house.

The front door closed heavily, followed by the snap of the coach door and the crack of the coachman's whip. The sound of the departure of her father and his mistress faded, and Mari sighed with relief and stepped up to the long mirror to study her appearance.

She had pleaded fatigue and retired early, supposedly to her bed. Her father was too preoccupied lighting up his pipe to pay her much attention, and Tamsin flapped a hand toward her and looked bored as Mari left the room.

Mari had rummaged at the bottom of a clothes chest for a familiar bundle, and now stood in front of a mirror dressed in an outfit of Tom's again. She regarded her hair with approval. She had cropped it short that afternoon, like Tamsin's, without asking any kind of permission.

She had used Tamsin's own reason for having done so - it was so much more comfortable and convenient when wearing a wig. Indoors, her hair was covered decently by a cap anyway, and she had trusted to escape the notice of her father because of this.

Tamsin, however, had not missed noticing, but had laughed indulgently at Mari's excuse, and even appeared a little flattered at the implied compliment of the daughter imitating the mistress. Her pleasant mood forestalled comment from Sir Joseph, who looked keenly at his daughter for a change.

Nervous but finally determined to make her bid for freedom, Mari wondered how long to wait. She did not wish to leave it too late, as she was hoping it would not be too dark for her journey across London. She had a pretty close idea of the main geography of the streets by now. She knew that at any point, even keeping to the main thoroughfares, she would not be far from the River Thames.

She had some idea of walking part, or even all, the way down to the London docks, or, if it proved too far, she could hire a chaise, and there should be any number about on the streets, to take her down to one of the many landing stairs on the river.

She could then hire a boat to go down to *Integrity*. She knew, for instance, that Westminster and Temple stairs always had river transport waiting for hire, and supposed that many of the others did, too.

Even so, she was apprehensive at attempting passage of the city streets, given what she had witnessed during the day-time, let alone stories she had heard of night-life. Tagging along after Tom and his friends, she had felt safe. Striking out alone was another matter.

Her courage was bolstered by the fact that she was dressed again in the fashion of a poor apprentice, and she was surely not likely to be bothered much. If in doubt, and at this thought she smiled to herself, she could always run, and run fast according to Tom.

She settled for a while quietly on Sophie's side of the bed they had shared and fondly smoothed the pillow that had cradled her little sister's head. She was sad but relieved when Miss Pardoe had announced that Sir Joseph had acquiesced to the suggestion that his youngest daughter had seen enough of city life, and would be better off in the country.

Having gained his approval, the governess had wasted no time at all in arranging their departure from Conduit Street. Tom was commanded to accompany them back to Ravenhill, and Mari was to stay and keep Mistress Tallentire company.

It was as though fate had given a nudge to Mari to make up her mind to leave. She had no real regrets apart from that of leaving Sophie, though she knew that her sister would be totally safe and happy with Miss Pardoe, and, one day, she was certain, she would be back to see her again.

Her thoughts continued to whirl, jumping from imagining Bryce's reaction when he realized she had joined him to go to America, to the reaction of her father when he discovered her disappearance. No doubt he would be furious and consider himself betrayed. Her father was totally taken up by his many interests, including his mistress, and seemed relieved to be free of his daughters' presence after being with them for even a short length of time.

Sophie would be in Ravenhill with Miss Pardoe. Tom was set on entering the Navy soon, and that left Mari to, what? To be an attendant and dogs-body for Tamsin Tallentire? To be only a step above the long-suffering Maisie?

That was the picture Mari envisaged. She would either have to fall in with the household at Conduit Street as it was, or retire to Ravenhill and stay, frustrated and isolated but safe and confined, buried in the countryside until her father decided to marry her off to which ever suitor happened along to relieve him of his daughter's company.

Reluctantly, Mari recalled the event that had finally convinced her to leave.

On the afternoon of the day Sophie, Tom, and Miss Pardoe had set out for Ravenhill, she had been sitting morosely in her room, already lonely for them. She had half-wished, in fact, to return with them, but had held back from suggesting as much, as the idea of running away with Bryce was already forming in her mind. She found herself holding a pot of powder Sophie had been using on the hair of her favorite doll, and rose to carry it down to the powder room.

The house was in its quiet time just after the mid-day meal, and Mari padded down the hallway in stocking feet. Just outside the door of the powder room, as she was reaching for the handle, she noticed a crumpled, lace kerchief, and what seemed to be the end of a man's cravat trapped on the sill, as if dropped and caught by the closing of the door. She bent down to scoop them up as she pulled open the door, but jerked up her head at the scene exposed in the little room.

Tamsin Tallentire was leaning back on a brocade stool, braced against the small dressing table. Her eyes were closed, her robe falling away either side of her lush, pale body.

Joseph Westin's face was buried in her full, white breasts as he thrust vigorously into her.

He was oblivious of any observation, but Tamsin, sensing the movement of the door, opened her eyes wide and stared straight at Mari over his back. Not at all fazed, she said nothing but threw back her head and closed her eyes again, laughing silently, it seemed to Mari, in triumphant glee.

Appalled, Mari closed the door and ran back to her chamber, face flaming.

The vision of Tamsin and her father blazed in her mind. The strong elegant line of Tamsin's neck as it arched back, pushing her chestnut curls against the mirror on the wall and twinning them with their reflection, her creamy thighs wide around her father, Sir Joseph, half-dressed with crumpled silk shirt pulled out of his britches, going at Tamsin as though it was a labor of Hercules.

In her shocked daze, odd details stuck in Mari's memory. In the haste of their passion, Tamsin had planted herself on one of her own wigs, from which, squashed under her plump backside, two ringlets dangled, swinging and jiggling with the motion of the coupling.

Mari had not had a sight of her father's face. All she had seen, other than his straining back, had been his shaven head, with its bald spot at the back, making him appear vulnerable as well as ridiculous.

She had dreaded going down to supper that evening. She assumed that Tamsin would have made some remark to her father, but apparently she had not.

Sir Joseph was, as usual, oblivious and unconcerned, paying Mari no mind. Tamsin glanced occasionally at her with an amused expression, her fine eyes laughing.

Upon retiring that night, however, Mistress Tallentire made it her particular business to knock on Mari's bedroom door and talk to her. She had not prevaricated or minced words, and had stated that it would soon be time for Mari to gain some experience of society.

She had smiled archly and mentioned that she had a number of bright, young blades in her set who would be more than ready to be gallant to Mari, but first, of course, she hastened to add, Mari would have to secure a husband, be married and settled. She must do her duty as was expected of any daughter in her position.

Tamsin sauntered to the door, and added, "But then, my dear Mari, there's no reason for a married woman in fashionable society to stay at home and be dull – not at all. You should be able to dance to your own tune much of the time."

Mari shook off the memory. She had her own ideas as to whose tune she was about to dance, and any steps, she decided, she would improvise herself.

Mari again gazed into the mirror, smiling at herself. She fancied she looked quite well as a boy, tall enough and straight. She took a deep breath and stuck her hands in her pockets, in imitation of Tom. Her hand encountered a crumpled, grimy neckerchief in one of them, so she pulled it out and knotted it around her neck.

She listened intently to the house again. It was quiet. Mrs. Pynchon, Mari knew, would be in her back parlor. Henry, the footman, would be gossiping with Millie and Abby in the kitchen down below, and Mari had to decide quickly how to escape the house.

If she timed it well, the rest of the servants should be in their hall. She could slip out the back way, the rear passage leading past a small flight of stairs down to the kitchen and servants' quarters, or she could be bold and slip out the front door, trusting to be able to manage drawing back the bolts without too much noise.

She took a last look around the room. There was no feeling of nostalgia, just a sensation, part exhilaration and part fear, of taking a plunge into unknown waters.

She picked up a small bag containing a few items of clothing, an extra shirt and jacket of Tom's, spare hose, and a little food she had held back from her supper tray.

She started for the door. On the dressing table was a square, white letter, with her father's name written on the outside. It gleamed in the fading light as she closed the door quietly.

Moving to the top of the stairs, she was halted in her tracks by the sound of a sudden loud laugh in the lower hallway. Her heart jumped to her throat as Henry's footsteps marched up the corridor to the front door.

Mari crouched down, partially hidden by the curving banister railing, praying that Henry would not glance up. The footman whistled jauntily as he checked the locks and bolts on the front door. He held a jug of what was probably porter in one hand, and Mari realized he must have been out to some local ale house to supply them downstairs with something extra to sup. Satisfied that the door was secure, he turned and marched back down the hallway, and Mari waited until she heard him thump down the kitchen stairs, calling out jokingly to Millie and Abby as he reached the kitchen door.

She rose again and hesitated. Then, squaring her shoulders, she descended briskly and boldly and stepped with determination to the front door.

"Hang the idea of slipping out of the back door and sidling down back alleys," she thought.

She reached up, eased back the heavy bolts, and swung back the door, striding outside and pulling it to behind her. Across the road, passers-by moved toward Swallow Street, so Mari turned left and went the other way, toward Bond Street. She consciously lengthened her stride, mentally hearing Tom's voice telling her not to be girly, or she'd be discovered. It felt good to be in britches, free, though oddly undressed, at least when compared to wearing heavy panniered skirts.

She quickened her pace and strode toward Piccadilly. She would then have to go down by Haymarket and Cockspur Street to make her way to The Strand. She knew she would have to turn east, following a parallel course to the river to the docks, but had no real idea how long it would take to get there.

She suddenly felt more relaxed and confident. If she stayed close to the main thoroughfare, if she tired or it took too long, there was bound to be a Hackney cab she could hire. She had four half guinea pieces and some small silver in a pouch with her. She had already seen quite a few chaises passing by in both directions, and a number of people were walking quite comfortably in this part of town.

Mari turned into Piccadilly, feeling more and more at ease, and less conspicuous. No-one, in fact, paid her any mind.

She adjusted her brother's cap further down on her head though, making sure all her hair was covered. Just as she began to feel buoyed up, however, there sounded a commotion. It was mainly the noise of men shouting, and came from some distance behind her. Looking back toward Hyde Park, she saw a crowd of men and boys spread across the road.

It looked to be a band of about thirty men, and the leaders seemed to be carrying cudgels. They were most likely John Wilkes' supporters out again on the streets. Mari decided to hurry and stay ahead of them, but glancing back saw that they were advancing quickly toward her, and she looked for a side lane to take, though not relishing the idea of leaving the main thoroughfare.

"Wilkes and Liberty! Light your windows! Wilkes and Liberty!"

The cry was repeated in ragged fashion as they surged on, and Mari, soon engulfed, was swept along with them. She found it much easier to trot with the crowd than to resist, and, fortunately, it seemed to her that they were going in the direction she herself aimed to follow, and it struck her that this was as safe a way as any to pass through the city streets.

The men were not a rabble. They were certainly fired up, though, for John Wilkes. The man and his actions were a current topic of debate and angry confrontation over many a dinner table, as well as in the ale and coffee houses.

Mari had heard her father say that Wilkes had been thrown out of the Commons on more than one occasion, and had been charged with outlawry, but the courts had reversed this, and ordinary folk loved him. Most of those with power and authority, however, wished him anywhere but in England.

There had been a number of these demonstrations, with threats from his supporters to break any windows in the elite part of town of households who did not set light in the windows to show their support for Wilkes.

As they neared the end of Cockspur Street, Mari noticed another crowd in turmoil coming toward them down Whitehall from Westminster Bridge.

Glancing back as she stumbled along, she was amazed to make out a carriage minus its team of horses, being pulled along by men in the traces. It was a strange enough sight, but, perhaps, she reasoned, the coachman had refused to drive with them, and the protestors, unable to control the team, had released the horses to put their own shoulders to the task of pulling it.

The men she was with slowed to a stop, waiting for the mob to pull abreast, and, as it passed with cries of "Down The Strand to Temple!" they fell in laughing and cheering with the rest.

Mari now found herself standing in a small group with a few boys and men, as the carriage was pulled in jerky fashion past them.

"Who have they got in there? Where are they taking him?" she asked.

"You, a bumpkin fresh from up country, or summat?" This said in a scornful voice.

Mari looked down at the disbelieving face of a boy of about ten.

"That's Wilkes – who d'yer think it is? We won't let 'em keep 'im inside, he's for us, and we's for 'im!"

Mari had nothing to say to this, and, as she glanced up, encountered an assessing gaze from a youth about her own age or a little older.

"You an apprentice? What's your name?"

The smaller boy looked sturdy enough, but had a pinched face, hard beyond his years. He wore a battered hat, and ragged clothes. The older one looked to be about sixteen, or maybe seventeen, but was dressed a little better with ill-assorted jacket and britches. Mari realized that even in Tom's old cast-offs she was better clothed.

"My name? Er – Will, and…er…yes, I'm a 'prentice, at least I hope to be, for the sea. I mean to sign on tonight if I can get down to my ship in time."

Their exchange was cut short by shouts of "Lobsters! Horse Guards behind 'em. Run for it – make for Three Tuns, if yer can."

Mari and the boys started running with the crowd. By now they were in the middle of it, and, looking back over her shoulder, she could see several ranks of red-coated soldiers, or "lobsters" as sailors and watermen called them, trotting after them in formation.

She also had a glimpse of riders of some sort, but at a considerable distance behind the foot guards, way back toward Westminster.

A fleeting question crossed her mind as to why she was running. She hadn't done anything wrong, but a primal urge to go with the crowd kept her moving along. She then became aware that the tall youth kept turning and running backwards a few steps as he scanned the crowd looking for some-one.

"Where's Perisher? Tibbs – we've lost 'im."

"No, we ain't, Jinty. He's already in front – down there by Brewer's Yard. E's kept in front, not to be trampled, expect. "

By now they were already heading down The Strand, and the youth called Jinty looked back once more, turned forward with a look of disgust on his face, and started angling toward the edge of the mob.

"C'mon, Tibbs – let's get Perisher and away a'fore they catch up." He included Mari. "You as well, Will – you want to get down river don't yer?"

Mari followed them at this, not stopping to think what they had in mind. She and Jinty were soon matching strides, and without breaking pace he called to a nondescript little figure waiting against the side of the road – "C'mon Perisher, down by the market to the stairs!"

Mari had a brief impression of the small figure skipping and scuttling behind them, trying to keep up with Tibbs. On young legs, they had outrun the rear of the crowd, some of whom had stopped retreating and were milling in the middle of The Strand, jeering at the oncoming soldiers.

"Down this way, down to the water!" They ran down a side lane toward the river, and Jinty slowed as they reached some empty lean-tos.

"Where are we?" Mari asked. Jinty looked at her.

"You don't know yer way around much, do yer? Hungerford Market – stay with Perisher. We've lost Tibbs this time."

He stood still, listening for a minute or two at the hubbub from The Strand. There was a clatter of hooves and several riders flashed by the end of the lane. Jinty took a few steps back up the lane and was almost lost in the shadows, when he stopped at the patter of running feet, and Tibbs caught up with them.

"Fell down and nearly got trampled by a stupid hoss – twisted my knee a bit."

Whilst this exchange was going on, Mari felt a movement at her side, and looked down at the small figure next to her, quietly waiting for Jinty to take charge of their destinies again.

"Hello, Perisher," offered Mari, and felt a jolt as the child looked up at her. His face had been ravaged by disease. It appeared distorted as though bones had been corroded away. He was diminutive. He made no answer, but looked again at Jinty and Tibbs who rejoined them.

"Ain't up for fightin' with Lobsters tonight are we Perisher? Let's get down to the stairs." Without any questions, they followed behind Jinty to the river.

Mari finally found wit enough to ask how she could get down river, only to receive yet another scornful look from Jinty.

"I'm a waterman, ain't I? Boat's here at the stairs. You got the fare?"

Mari said she had, and promised a half guinea to get her past London Bridge, down to the ship *Integrity*.

"We know where the docks are, don't we Tibbs?" he said dismissively "C'mon – a half guinea'll get you down river in no time, more ways than one, come to think of it. Wait while I check for my Pa's boat."

He left the three of them squatting at the top of Hungerford Stairs, listening to the furor still coming from The Strand, as he disappeared, swallowed in the black well of shadows at the bottom of the steps.

The smells of the river wafted up to them, and there was a sense of space stretching over the smooth, glassy surface of the swift-moving Thames. The air was chillier down by the water, and Mari pulled Tom's jacket closer round her as she studied the small, squatting figure on the top step.

"Why do they call you Perisher? That can't be your real name," Mari asked, as much for something to say as anything. The strange little boy had not said a word, but seemed to follow Jinty and Tibbs like a puppy.

"That's the only name he's got – and it suits 'im 'cos that's what's goin' to 'appen," Tibbs answered for him.

"What do you mean?"

"Look at 'im – 'e was born riddled with pox and was weaned on gin – 'e won't make old bones, will he?" This was said matter of factly with no apparent peevish intent from Tibbs. He shrugged. "Me an' Jinty look after 'im." He regarded Perisher. "Best we can, at any rate."

Mari stared at the boys through the gloom, and found nothing to counter Tibbs' laconic attitude to Perisher's condition.

"Why do we have to wait? What's Jinty doing?" Tibbs shrugged again, and rubbed absently at his knee.

"Wants to see if 'is boat's there. 'E sometimes lets it out to his cous'n, and a coupl'a mudlarks doing shifty business."

Mari was puzzled by this at first, but quickly realized Tibbs' meaning. The river was rife with all kinds of dubious activities, and many a ship's hold leaked cargo mysteriously, under the cover of darkness, to the so-called mudlarks.

Small craft of all descriptions, hiring out under legal trade during the day, ferrying people and goods to and fro on the water, did double-duty at night re-distributing all manner of pilfered items to all manner of destinations.

The sheer volume of shipping from around the world ensured that Customs and Excise officers, be they ever so energetic, simply could not police the scene. However many eyes authority had on the Thames observing the comings and goings, they were more than matched in number by those looking to spot an opening for illicit business. There was outright thievery, or, with the connivance of captains and crew, deliberate offloading of merchandize to avoid duties.

"'Ere he comes." Tibbs stood up as Jinty reappeared. Almost at the same moment, there were more shouts from the end of the lane. They could see a jumble of men fighting with a blur of red coats. Jinty didn't pause.

"Let's be out on the river, lads. C'mon, c'mon!"

Mari breathed with relief. His boat must be there. In the waning light, a number of craft were plying the Thames. Jinty led the way, scrambling down the stairs to the mooring of his father's wherry. His own sculler was tied up to it.

"'Ere, Perisher, get into Pa's boat and stay there 'til we come back. Tibbs, hop in with us."

Perisher clambered crabwise down the stairs and scrambled into the wherry. Mari followed, transferring over into Jinty's row boat. Tibbs climbed over like a nimble monkey. Mari was more ungainly and uncertain on the shifting boats.

"Not used ter boats either, are yer, Lanky," muttered Jinty. As he untied the lines to his father's boat, he repeated his instructions to Perisher not to leave the wherry, and reached for the oars to pull away.

"Wait!" Mari demanded on impulse, and leaned over to grab the side of the wherry to keep Jinty's sculler alongside. She rummaged in her bag and pulled out a napkin-wrapped package of meat slices and a small loaf. She thrust it at Perisher, who took it after hesitating and clutched it against his chest. The fragrant smell of Abby's new-baked bread wafted back at Mari, but stirred no appetite, she was too excited.

"Take this, as well, Perisher," she said as she put a small piece of silver change in his hand.

"Try to keep warm," she added, feeling it was a useless thing to say to him. The little boy sat hunched over submissively, and ducked his head in a gesture of acceptance.

As they pushed off, he peered up at her. He seemed to be grimacing, his mouth distorted, and it was only by looking into his eyes she was able to recognize the child's tentative smile, the disease he was born with robbing his face of its true expression.

Looking at Perisher for the last time, Mari was distracted again from the urgency of her own situation. She felt a mix of strong emotions. She was repelled by him as well as wrenched with compassion.

Memories of London and Ravenhill whirled through her head, but uppermost were the extremes. She thought of the grotesqueries of fashion. How Sophie and she had been dressed like painted dolls, parading around in carriages in the parks, eating sweetmeats. Seeing and being seen, but to what purpose? And whilst Tibbs and Perisher had been all the while scurrying around the city's dark side, scrambling for a living any way they could.

"See yer, Perisher. Enjoy yer supper!"

They were away in a few strokes as Jinty settled into a rhythm with the oars, sculling them in no time midstream, where the River Thames swung them on its back, carrying them downstream toward London Bridge. The current was much swifter than was apparent from the banks, and Jinty, dipping the oars and pulling full-stretch, had the boat skimming along.

Mari breathed deeply and relaxed again a little, although she was still tense with excitement. She felt it was fate that she had fallen in with the likes of Jinty and Tibbs. Jinty was obviously a skilled waterman. Tibbs, young as he was, looked perfectly comfortable on the tiller, his tattered hat brim lifting a little in the breeze over the water, his grubby face seriously set to the business of keeping the craft straight. Mari remarked on their apparent easy progress.

"It's just about slack tide, river current's carrying. Soon as tide turns, we'll really be moving down. If'n your ship's due away this night, though, they'll be ready'n for the tide now. We've no time to spare," said Jinty, then went silent for a while.

"Mind – when the tide turns…," he paused for breath, bending and bracing smoothly against the oars… "When it turns – even if she's underway – we stand a chance of coming up to her at this rate…least ways, first off."

He continued to pull, and the banks slid by. In the increasing gloom, Mari could see sporadic lights from buildings on each bank. Smells and sounds from the river floated out to them. Every so often there were cries and hullabaloos.

On one stretch a foul stink suddenly blanketed them as they swept past some ditch disgorging into the river. Perhaps, the discharge from the Fleet Ditch, because, soon after, Mari saw the dome of St. Paul's Cathedral against the sky.

Then, pleasantly, the fragrance of meadow grass came from the south side of the river, mingled with that of silk drying on the tenter grounds, and new-sawn wood smells from the many timber yards. She had the sensation of being in a dream. Conduit Street seemed far away already, and Ravenhill even more distant.

The relative quiet on the river was disorienting after the tumult of the mob on land. There were many water-craft moored by the banks, especially by the landings or stairs, where the wherries waited for hire.

The river was a highway with its own life, apart from but connected to the city gliding by on either side. A number of vessels of different kinds were still working on the water, but Mari knew Jinty had to get them below London Bridge to be amongst the big ships, where *Integrity* lay.

Amazingly soon, the bridge's span came into view as the broad waters of the Thames swung their little boat around the curve of its banks. Mari felt apprehensive as they passed under the bridge's gloomy arches. A sudden racket of horse hooves and carriage wheels echoed from above, briefly masking the water's sound until they emerged on the other side and found themselves among the imposing, dark shapes of the many trading ships riding at anchor.

Splashes of light were cast from the lanterns hung fore and aft on many of the vessels. Mari had an idea of the position of *Integrity*, but Jinty didn't appear to pay much attention to any suggestion she gave him.

"Ships for th'Americas are found by Rotherhithe and Wapping," he said, continuing to pull on the oars

From their position, low to the water, the ships towered above them. A few were quiet and dark, but some were busy, with lighters and wherries loading and unloading them in the dusk.

Several times Mari thought they would collide with one of the shuttling craft. Jinty occasionally called out to other watermen, asking where *Integrity* was anchored. Mari knew that the ship was mid-stream, not berthed at a dock, and worried that it might already have sailed. She wasn't sure whether she was more anxious about the necessity of getting aboard, or her story once she did.

It was confusing maneuvering among the ships, with their forest of masts and rigging silhouetted against the evening sky, like so many denuded trees in winter. They passed under the forbidding walls of the Tower of London, rising implacable and monstrous on the northern bank, and Mari remembered wretched prisoners being loaded onto a transport at the stairs there.

She couldn't imagine how sailors managed to crowd so many vessels so close without collision and damage. She peered around, trying to work out which of the dark shapes would most likely be the one she sought, when Jinty startled her by hollering loudly, "Ahoy, *Integrity*, permission to come aboard."

He swirled an oar strongly, backing his small boat and sliding it around the belly and square stern of a well-lit ship. He voiced grudging approval, "Looks pretty new-built to me."

Mari was fascinated at being so near she could almost touch the sides of this vessel that she hoped to carry her to a new life.

"What fine crew's that's causing a ruckus?"

A voice came down to them, as the head and shoulders of a sailor appeared, foreshortened in a lantern's glow, over the rail of the ship.

"Shipmate for yer," answered Jinty.

"Who is it? Styles? Yer cuttin' it fine, lad. Get yer arse aboard."

With this brusque comment, a rope ladder was thrown down. Jinty grabbed the ladder to hold his craft snug in for Mari to climb up.

"What'yer waiting for? Up y'go – go. They ain't going' t'haul yer up. Where's that half guinea yer promised?"

Mari handed him the coin, knowing it was far too much. She was trembling with nervousness and hesitated, holding onto the seat of Jinty's boat.

Climbing the ship's ladder was a first test, as, one moment, it clung to the bulge of the ship's side and, the next, it swung in space down to the sculler.

Tibbs unexpectedly piped up, "Go on – young gent. Yer going ter sea. It's adventure yer after."

It was now or never, thought Mari. She crouched to keep balance while reaching for the ladder, and somehow managed to gain some purchase for her feet and started to climb, scraping and bruising her knees and knuckles against *Integrity*'s side.

Half way up, she looked down at the face of Jinty and Tibbs to say goodbye. Their craft had already drifted clear. Jinty was leaning still on his oars, and they were both gazing up at her. She tried to hold on with one hand and wave, and caused her shoulder to thump painfully against the ship. Tibbs gave a brief wave in reply, as Jinty dug his oars in the water against the drift of the current.

Screwing up her courage, Mari gulped in a breath and scrambled up to the top of the ladder to heave herself over the rail. It had been much more difficult than she had thought, pulling herself straight up the swelling side of the ship, and she was breathless and put out, knowing she looked very much a land-lubber.

"Well, Styles you ain't – unless he's all of a tumble turned pretty on us. Who be you, lad?"

The seaman facing her stood holding a lantern, casually propped on the edge of the rail, his other hand on hip. He had a seamed, tanned face in the lamp's glow, and it registered both amazement and amusement. Mari gulped and tried to get her voice under control.

"I heard the captain needs a cabin boy – I came out to sign on, if he'll take me."

"Cabin lad, eh?" The man tilted his head back and scrutinized her.

"Mister Lewis. Y'there? Young sprog's here, offering for cabin lad. Looks like a poncy little gent on 'ard times – an' a landlubber if there ever was one – but 'e's clean an' spritely lookin' – better than some of the sickly lookin' scraps you've turned down. Mr. Lewis! Y'there?"

Footsteps sounded, and a sturdy, pleasant-faced mate materialized from somewhere below decks. He strode up, and lifted the lantern to study Mari better.

"What's your name, shaver?" he asked.

"W…William,…er, Herrion, " she answered, plucking a last name she remembered from a theater notice.

Lewis studied her. He saw a young stripling, with features sweet for a boy, but healthy looking, with a straight gaze, nervous but determined.

"Let's take you to the captain – not sure whether he still wants a lad, but we'll ask. He'll most likely leave it to Allard. Follow me!"

The mate turned on his heel and marched aft toward the captain's cabin. He knocked on the door of the state room, and, answering the summons, he went in, jerking his head for new-found Will Herrion to follow.

Captain Coward, of *Integrity* was scanning his ship's manifest. The would-be cabin boy saw a strongly built, serious faced man, with graying hair, waiting with a questioning gaze.

"Pardon, Sir, youngster here came out on a wherry to try for cabin lad."

The captain sighed and shook his head. He released the papers he had been holding and leaned back in his chair, assessing Mari.

"Where are you from lad, and why do you want to sail with us?"

Mari was then put to the test to make up a story of wanting to go to sea, and recently finding herself alone with no family or friends, having to strike out by herself to essay her prospects. She was not encouraged during her rigmarole by the ship's captain, as he punctuated her words by continuing to shake his head.

"Get Allard. See what he thinks," he said to Lewis.

The mate disappeared, and whilst they were waiting for the steward, Coward informed her he was not sure at all that he still wanted extra help, especially in the form of an ignorant novice.

This set Mari's mind racing. What could she do to stay on board? Where was Bryce Hunter? She had not seen him on the deck. There had been a few passengers moving around, and sailors carrying out duties, but he was not amongst them. She had no idea yet of how to find him, or make mention of him. Perhaps he wasn't aboard yet. She was not even sure the ship was cleared and ready to sail. Maybe it would wait for a later tide.

She ought to have let Bryce know what she intended to do, instead of trying to surprise him. Here she was, talking to a captain of a sea-going vessel and the men who worked for him, and they were taking her seriously at her word. She mentally castigated herself for not thinking her action through to a logical conclusion.

But, so far, she was being accepted as a boy. That was both a relief and a triumph. But where was Bryce? If only he were here to explain and ease the way for her, but he wasn't. She was going to have to shift for herself until he arrived. There was a sudden rap on the state room door. It opened and another sailor came in.

"Allard, what idea do you have of this young'un. Wants a berth as a cabin boy. I'm not at all sure whether to take him on – never been to sea, of course."

The man called Allard studied her hard for a minute, then asked if she could read and write, nodding at her affirmation as if he had expected it. He asked whether the agent had sent her, and Mari said no, but she had seen a notice outside the agent's office on the dockside that evening and decided to try for it. Allard smiled and turned to Captain Coward.

"Oh – he'll do, I think. A lad has to start somewhere, and a fair run across the Atlantic, that'll set him up for a sailor on his sea legs. I'll soon have him schooled as to what's what. You, lad, quick on your feet and a fast learner, are you?"

"You'd better be," interjected the captain. "We don't take slackers on *Integrity*."

Mari nodded vigorously at both men. She had placed herself in a pickle, and had to work out a way to deal with it.

Coward looked down at the papers on his desk. He had one hand placed over them, drumming his fingers. He looked searchingly, once more, at Will Herrion, and finally nodded brusquely, and told Allard to draw up an indenture, then, turning sternly to Mari, "Two years in my service, William Herrion. Allard will explain the terms, and you can sign if you are of such a mind to sail with us."

He looked at Allard again.

"Get Lewis to show him where to berth. We are all set to catch the tide. Any hand not on board, still drunk in the whorehouses on Radcliffe Highway, won't sail with me again."

BOOK TWO

COLONIAL AWAKENING

VII

June 20, 1768 - "Break out the grog, Mr. Lewis – a toast to home waters," Coward ordered.

He looked over the shimmering water at the familiar shoreline of the Chesapeake Bay, flat, green and reassuring after so many long weeks amidst the heaving, gray uncertainties of the ocean. He had passed between Virginia's two welcoming capes, Henry to port, Charles to starboard, and was finally sheltered from the sea's full force.

Confident that *Integrity* was firmly anchored and with a fiddler striking up a sea shanty, he retired to his cabin in pleasant anticipation of return to Plinhimmon, his Maryland home, where Bridget, his wife, would be waiting.

He settled tiredly but at ease at his desk, log books and trade invoices set out neatly by Allard, his cabin steward and man-of-all-works.

As usual, the paperwork was up to date, and he barely glanced at it. Allard placed a decanter of wine and an empty glass in front of him, but, waved away, let the taciturn captain pour his own drink. Coward supped the wine, judged it on the verge of spoiling after so long at sea but actually savored its sharpness while he thought of Bridget.

In his sea chest he had a pair of pink satin shoes, as pretty as any he had ever seen, which had caught his eye as he wandered on an idle day through London's bustling Cheapside. They were of the latest fashion, with laced fronts, on which Bridget could sew decorative bows or gilded buckles if so minded, and they had upturned, pointed toes, with elevated heels that narrowed at the shank and flared wider at the bottom, the sort to grace the most elegant of soirees.

He was sure Bridget would be delighted with such a fashionable addition to her wardrobe. They were made by John Hose, a favorite shoemaker for the ladies of London whose styles were seen in all the best salons. He knew she would exclaim at the expense and luxury of satin slippers. He could already hear her asking where would she wear them and with what? They were a frivolity, but she would love them nevertheless.

He looked forward to facing Bridget again across the table, and enjoying fresh-baked fare instead of the tired victuals served aboard *Integrity* toward the end of a long voyage. He smiled to himself.

She always urged variations of her grandmother's receipt for ratafia biscuits upon any visitor taking a glass of wine for refreshment. Generally, the men refused the offering, albeit politely, though her matronly friends and neighbors accepted as a matter of course. The only males who chomped on her biscuits, when he came to think of it, were his ship's crew, who, being sailors, had a stomach for anything.

Not that he often entertained any of them at his estate, the occasion of the rare invitation being not so much to socialize as to review shipboard matters, maintenance, and the next voyage.

Coward had inherited Plinhimmon from his father. It was a small, beautifully situated estate on a bend of a creek off the Tred Haven River, with water on two sides of the land. Apple orchards, lawn and shade trees stretched around the house to the water's edge, with the tobacco fields cast mainly to its north and the port of Oxford to the south. A straight-as-an-arrow drive, also pleasantly shaded by an avenue of trees, led from the Oxford road to the house.

Any time arriving home, having cleared port officialdom, Coward could follow the Easton road for a mile or so out of Oxford and turn up Plinhimmon's drive, or, more usually, simply take one of *Integrity*'s long-boats and sail round the creek to his own landing.

While his thoughts meandered, the noise from the crew gradually became more boisterous, the flow of drink loosening their tongues. A tin whistle had joined the fiddle, and together they encouraged a growing burst of mirth. Shouts and laughter swept like a wave across *Integrity*'s deck. Coward remained seated, listening indulgently to the increasing buzz of joviality.

As they ran through their repertoire of jigs and frolics, sailors, clumsy and nimble, clattered to and fro on the deck like manic, jerking marionettes, anxious to partner a couple of the bondswomen passengers who had joined in.

Two of the crew, Ted Horrocks and Tom Jakes, were backing and advancing in a parody of a tarantella with the two women who were happy to sup rum, and grace the sailors' attempts to dance. A third

88

sailor, Jim Chase, stumbled across the deck, causing a collision among the rum-wreathed jumble of merrymakers.

"T'aint right having ter dance with such ugly partners," he complained.

"Why ain't I got a proper partner? Tom and Horrocks is set up for a pinch and a cuddle. Where's pretty Will? He'll do. He's been treating us to an air or two. How's your dancing Will? Let's see how you would look like my sweetheart, matey? Come over here and be winsome. T'aint no use trying to make yourself scarce."

He had pushed through to the edge of the bunch of sailors, to where the cabin boy was trying to fade into the background, shrinking against the ship's rail and protesting to no effect. Chase dragged him by the wrist and swung him against his chest, leering down at him.

"Hey – you don't feel half bad for a lad!"

Chase was raucous. He grinned lecherously at the surrounding crew and suddenly bent and planted a rough kiss on Mari's mouth. Everybody roared, including Chase, bending over in merriment and loosening his hold on the cabin boy. Mari took her chance and ran.

"Wait, sweet Will," yelled Tom Jakes. "If you're spreading your favors, how about some for me and Horrocks?"

The three of them surged after her, laughing and shoving each other. Panic-stricken, Mari fled in the only direction she could think of for help. She scrambled, with their hands trying to capture her, through the rest of the merry crew along the deck toward the captain's cabin.

The sun had almost set, its last rays setting a pathway of dazzling gold across the darkening water as they slanted through the cabin windows, when the sudden, extra commotion broke through the captain's reverie. Coward heard racing, stumbling footsteps, a high-pitched screech and coarse yells coming from the deck. Rising with a grimace of irritation, he strode to the cabin door, only to have it burst open toward him.

He saw Will Herrion fall in a heap at his feet.

Coward glared, astounded at the intrusion as the cabin boy tried to scramble upright, only to stumble against him, grabbing hold of his stockinged leg and cowering in fright.

"Lewis! What the hell fire's going on? I said break out the grog, not start a riot. What's the blasted matter with this milk-sop lad? Stand up Will Herrion, and stop clutching my damned legs."

Mari, pulling her shirt tails around her, unaccountably stayed put, curled up at Coward's feet. The three men chasing her had already backed away from their captain's outrage. Flushed with alcohol, they looked foolish and made sheepish gestures.

"We meant 'im no 'arm, Cap'n," Harry Chase spoke up.

"We be having a bit of fun with t'lad. 'E being so dainty seeming. 'T'were just a prank, and a bit of fun."

Chase's ugly face contorted to a semblance of apology as he spoke, his hands nervously mangling the cabin boy's coat, dragged off in the scuffle. Tom Jakes, next to him, had a crafty, dissembling look. Ted Horrocks, the last of the trio, was trying to appear small behind the other two and just stared at the deck, resigned to accepting whatever Coward dished out.

The captain was tired. A feeling of intense irritation was more from the necessity of having to deal with the rowdiness of his sailors than from the actual cause of it, whatever that was.

He could imagine, though. Will Herrion had always struck him as a sweet-faced youth, and, in fact, improbably delicate-looking for a sea-faring life. Coward had had his doubts about taking the lad on the crew roll the last hour before sailing from England, but he had needed a cabin boy, and the child had proved a fair asset, all in all, to the ship's company.

Will had proved popular, helpful, and willing to learn any task set him, particularly regarding Coward's own comfort. He proved not only meticulous in carrying out his duties, but after an initial period of gloom and apparent anxiety while still in sight of England's shores, once fair out to sea had snapped to and showed a merry, generous nature.

Will was always ready to run with drinks of water to a sweating watch hand, or to sweep clear the cabin, clean the livestock pens, or help the cook. Many a time, he would entertain the crew, singing in a clear, sweet voice. He had, Coward appreciated, quite a repertoire. The cabin boy was equally accomplished at happy country ditties or plaintiff love songs, and even knew some of the songs of the current London stage.

What the lad's background was, no-one knew, but Coward agreed with Allard that the cabin boy behaved like a well-bred, fairly educated youngster. They surmised between them that he had absconded from some family situation. A young shaver running away to sea was hardly unusual. Some ships, naval vessels included, took them aboard even as young as eight or ten years old.

Coward frowned down at Herrion. The crew waited with varied expressions of wariness on their faces, Lewis trying unsuccessfully to look deadpan to cover apprehension at the captain's temper. For a moment, Coward was not quite sure what to do with the cabin boy and his tormentors. Finally, with an impatient, tetchy sigh, he reached down and grabbed the boy by the scruff of the neck, hauling him to his feet.

Mari was no longer whimpering, but stood silently with her fists pressed to her eyes, head down. Coward, towering over her, regarded the thin shoulders below with exasperation.

"Well, Will? Why so afraid? Speak up for yourself, boy. You're a sailor at sea, show some gumption lad."

"I'm not, Captain."

"What? What do you say? I can't make you out."

"I'm not, Captain."

"Not what, Will? Speak up."

"Not a lad, Captain." This was said almost inaudibly. But the men nearest made it out and looked totally mystified at each other.

"What's he talking about?" muttered Lewis, easing the collar of his sweat-soaked shirt. Captain Coward's temper was rising.

"What do you mean? Make sense, Will."

Mari lowered her fists and clutched the shirt again.

"I'm a …I'm a girl, Captain."

This, again, said low, but clear.

There was a stupefied silence. Lewis looked dumb and uncomprehending. The three tormentors were heads up, instantly alert, Chase, with a calculating focus on his face, Tom Jakes looking slightly smug and knowing. Horrocks had a sudden expression of keen compassion.

Coward was a picture of disbelief.

"You what?" he roared, grabbing Mari's shoulder and shaking her.

"I'm a girl. A girl. I'm a GIRL!"

91

Allard, having until now stood quietly in the background, stepped forward. He had been staring at the figure crouched at the captain's feet. As Mari stood up and pulled the loose shirt tightly round her body, he recognized gently rounded hips flaring from a slender waist. He took Mari firmly by the shoulders and turned her face-to-face. He pulled the shirt down tightly by spanning her waist with his hands, and the gentle swell of young, firm breasts was there, pressing against the cotton, but previously hidden by the baggy, ruched, sailor's shirt, and further concealed by a shabby oversized jacket.

"No wonder," thought Allard ruefully, "we were all beguiled by the young cabin boy."

Coward took hold of the abject figure, and marched toward the cabin's main window. In its light, a reddening of anger spread steadily from below the buttoned collar of his shirt, up his bulging neck, bringing a flush to his crevassed cheeks and settling into a scarlet band stretching from temple to temple.

He pulled off the sailor's woolen cap, and saw a young woman's soft, short tresses, beginning to grow again after being shorn in London.

He looked closer than he ever had at the familiar face, which he turned upwards to the light for better scrutiny, and remarked its smoothness, the gloss of fine skin, now blushed with emotion and exertion, the neatness of the nose, the fullness of the lips, and the softness of the eyes.

He wondered what was going on behind those eyes. The hands that so often served at his table had struck him previously as unusually delicate, but he had put that down to this being the lad's maiden voyage. A few more ocean crossings and they would be hard and calloused, like all seamen's.

Allard, giving a sigh, cast a quizzical glance at Coward. Lewis still looked vacantly dumbstruck. The two of them, and the three sailors, all gazed with interest at John Coward, anticipating the next outburst. He stood transfixed, disbelief, outrage and mortification playing over his face.

"Blast and damnation," he got out through clenched teeth.

He wanted badly to round on his men and bawl them out for idiots and lame-brains, but could hardly blame them for missing a deception he had failed to spot himself. Grown men, they had all been gulled by a naïve, young wench, or was she so naïve? Looking keenly at the three crewmen, he wasn't so sure about their own gullibility.

He regarded all three as knowing coves. How could they have not spotted the girlish Will Herrion for what he really was. Thecrew, after all, lived in close quarters.

Though, again, the lad had been in and out of his cabin often enough for him to have seen what was now obvious, but he had not paid Herrion much mind.

Allard had dealt more directly with Will. Staid Allard, sober and proper enough much of the time, or, when he chose to be, charming enough for a lady's parlor. He flicked a scorching glance at his steward. Allard gazed steadily back and gave a slight shrug.

John Coward felt weariness well up in him. He had to decide what to do with the wench and wrest some sense of control and dignity from the situation. He was not a man accustomed to feeling flummoxed.

He jerked his head, signaling Allard to stay behind in the cabin with the girl, and ordered Lewis to carry on. He threatened chastisement of the three sailors later.

Hesitating as he turned back into the cabin, he spun round and called to Lewis, "Get me one of the bondswomen, the one called Betsy. She'll do. Fetch her."

He slammed the door on the crowd of faces, now gazing with avid curiosity from the deck, where the music and merriment had stopped. Inside the cabin, Allard and the erstwhile Will stood silently waiting, the girl, with downcast eyes, aimlessly pleating her shirt front.

Coward went to the cabin window and looked west into the darkening sky. They had three women on board, amidst a gaggle of would-be colonists. All three were bonded to him for their passage, and he would make a profit on them when they were indentured for service as soon as possible after landing. Two of them he had prospective masters for. The third, Betsy Murphy, he intended to take home to help Bridget.

Betsy had made a more favorable impression upon him than some of the poorer transients putting themselves in bondage to travel west. She had appeared sensible and practical and realistic about the role that would be hers for at least four years.

Now, it occurred to him, instead of using Betsy himself, he could use the distraught girl in front of him, though there was a nice point to think on.

The lass, posing as Will Herrion, had indentured to him as cabin boy for two years, and had, in fact, satisfactorily worked this passage.

Coward felt a slash of renewed irritation. He did not feel like paying her off, even a cabin lad's pittance, for her deception. He could withhold pay for her ploy. She could be put to work by his wife, maybe as a maid, or tutor for his daughters, to work off the rest of her indenture.

Underneath his anger and mortification, Coward felt a conflicting mixture of conscience at abandoning the girl without means of support, and a feeling of peevishness coupled with a desire to punish her for her temerity.

He straightened up and drew in a long, deep breath. He would punish her by withholding pay and take her home for Bridget to deal with. This salved his conscience at her plight and satisfied his need for retribution.

He turned again to Allard and the girl.

"Alright, lass, first things first. What's your name? And why the devil did you come to my ship? Why would a seemingly well-bred young maid disguise herself as a scamp and run away to America? And what of your people – your family back home? Speak up."

He spoke forcefully as the youngster stood, opening and closing her mouth as if desperate for air.

"I can't. I'd rather not say my name. Can't I just stay Will?"

"What's the difficulty saying your own name girl? No, you can't be Will. Is your name even Herrion?"

"No, no, 'twas just a name I heard that took my fancy." This mumbled nervously and quickly.

John Coward gazed at the roof of the cabin and held his temper again.

"Why cannot you tell me your name, child?"

He asked the question with studied calm. The girl hesitated infuriatingly again, but then suddenly stopped fidgeting with her shirt, stood straight-backed with her head up, and looked Coward directly in the eye. Her eyes were dark and enormous like those of a startled calf, and she had gone pale, but was resolved.

94

"I'd rather not say for my family's shame," she replied in a wavering voice, at variance with her steady posture.

Coward and Allard looked at each other and back at the girl. She stood there, frail and unkempt, but with an air of desperate dignity backing her words.

"I've been foolish, and I know you should, indeed, be impatient and angry with me, Captain. But I don't wish at all to attach Papa's name to my behavior. At least I believe I owe him that."

Allard and the captain exchanged another look. If there was a common occurrence aboard ship, it was that of a sailor signing on under an assumed name. Usually it was a simple ruse to hide identity, and most were unable to sign their name anyway. Some came from childhoods on mean streets and grew up with nicknames, often little more than an epithet thrown at them. Some just simply accepted and used names given them by shipmates, as good as forgetting the original ones given at birth. Coward sighed in exasperation again.

"Well I must call you something," he said. "You are from a good family, I take it."

She nodded, "A fine family, Sir."

"Are we yet to know then, Missee, why you played this subterfuge on us to careen around as a lad and go to sea?"

She flushed and hesitated.

"Come on, come on. Out with it," broke in Allard. "We are all shipmates, Will. You can tell us."

The girl kept her face decorously deadpan.

"I – I had in mind to find my young Virginian gentleman aboard. He promised to take me to America with him."

Coward stared at her, arms akimbo.

"Holy Mary, lovelorn into the bargain," he thought.

"Virginian gentleman, eh? Well, what kind of gentleman offering for a fine maid expects her to work passage as a cabin lad? Tell me that."

Giving her no time to reply, he roared: "Which one is it? There are no Virginian gentlemen among the passengers on this trip. We have samplings of London's flotsam and jetsam. One of those fed you a story did he? Whose lies did you swallow, lass?"

The girl looked both startled and wretched.

"No, no, no-one on board, Captain. He wasn't here. He didn't come. I thought he might at least try, even at Gravesend, but he didn't come."

She dropped her eyes again, unable to meet the Captain's gaze, which was diamond hard. His words let loose a tide of anguish and mortification at her memory of her first hours aboard *Integrity*.

Her initial disbelief and dismay at finding no Bryce Hunter to welcome her, scored her again like a sharp blade. The strength of his words and his ardor describing his home had so caught her imagination that she had felt a sense of euphoria, fantasizing the idea of life with him. He had seemed part of a world of liberty and adventure. By contrast her own daily existence was oppressively constrained and limited.

Many nights at sea, she had tried to think what could have happened. Why had he not come? What had made her plan go so badly wrong? She could not accept that she had been abandoned. But could Tamsin have been right after all? Had Bryce simply played with her feelings as a passing distraction?

She had, after all, left her family, and the only life she had known, for him. Her father would likely disown her.

She felt she had jumped into a rushing river without hesitation, and was amazed at how well she had coped. Though at times intimidated and anxious in her role as cabin boy, she had also been able to savor the freedom of it. She had been fascinated and eager to learn, and she had become surprisingly comfortable in the company of sailors, men for whom she previously would have had no time.

She looked at the captain, but, quailing under his gaze, mumbled inadequately, "It was not supposed to be so Captain. I expected my gentleman to negotiate with you my passage under his protection and care once we had set sail, and I fear some terrible event occurred to prevent him."

Her explanation faltered to a stop, and she mentally berated herself for her naïve statement. How could she have been so stupid? Her voice had sounded stilted even to her own ears.

Coward stood there, grim and domineering. Distracted as she was, she noticed his clothes. Though of good quality, they were salt-stained and tired-looking, as well they might be after an ocean crossing. The blue of his jacket especially was sun-faded over his shoulders, and his cravat was clean but creased from use, and ill-folded, not fashionably so. His beard was untrimmed, but the man was nevertheless impressive.

She lowered her eyes to her hands, still nervously kneading her shirt, and abruptly realized that her tight clutch was accentuating the curve of her breasts. She quickly let go the cloth, and dropped her hands at her side.

Allard was gazing thoughtfully at the floor, and then looked up and nodded at John Coward. Her story fit. He believed she was telling the truth. He recalled how distrait and worried she had been until they were well beyond England's coast and out to sea. They had all thought it was a young lad's anxiety on setting sail for the first time and leaving behind family and friends.

The crew had taken to Will Herrion. In their rough and ready way, they had seen his distress, had sympathized and tried to jolly him along. Before any more could be said, there was a tap at the cabin door.

"Enter," barked the captain.

The door was pushed open quietly, and Betsy Murphy, the bondswoman, stepped carefully through. She seemed to lift her feet precisely, almost like a stalking cat testing the boards underfoot for creaks. She bobbed a half curtsey to the captain, and started to speak, but Coward cut her off.

"Seems we have a conundrum on our hands, Betsy."

The woman flitted a glance at the cabin boy and back at the captain.

"How can I help, Captain?" she asked.

Coward looked at her with some approval, feeling his temper ease. The woman had an air of respectability and reliability. She'd do well as a servant, no silliness, no airs and graces, no requiring long explanations.

"We've a silly snippet here, turns out to be a lass, not a lad. We've a couple of days to port, and I want her out from under my feet, out from under everyone's feet. Take her down to steerage, keep her by you, and don't mix with the crew. We'll have to sort out something on land."

Betsy seemed curious rather than surprised.

"What's your name?" she asked, turning to the girl.

The captain put in abruptly, "Oh, she's not telling the likes of us who she is. But then, now, we must call her something."

Perversely, in the midst of all this upset, he found his mind recalling a pleasant night in London. Whenever anchored in the Thames, he would occasionally leave the boat for an evening in the city. He had been pleased one night to attend a revival by David Garrick, the most remarked actor of the day, of Shakespeare's "The Winter's Tale" at the Drury Lane Theater. So much had he enjoyed the performance that he had taken pains to purchase, at no small cost, a leather-bound copy of the play, and its pages had been well-turned during quieter moments on his many voyages since.

As he looked at the distressed girl before him with her air of refinement apparent in spite of her predicament, he recalled the shepherdess in the play who turned out to be a princess. In spite of his anger, Coward's mind conjured up Shakespeare's description, committed, along with several others, to memory: "This is the prettiest low-born lass that ever ran on the green sward; nothing she does or seems but smacks of something greater than herself, too noble for this place."

"Perdita," Coward told the hapless and disheveled young woman. "That's it. You will be Perdita." If the girl's protestations of being well-bred were well-founded, it was, he decided, a most appropriate name.

She seemed not displeased, though a little startled by the captain's choice. She made as if to speak, but then quickly nodded in acceptance with a tentative smile. In fact, she accepted her new name as readily as, with the seasons, she changed her summer cottons for winter's wools. To her, as to Coward, Perdita seemed simply to fit her situation.

Bringing the confrontation to a merciful end, Coward told her to confine herself to the quarters of the three bondswomen for the rest of the voyage.

"'Tis at least more seemly," he frowned at her, inviting as much as commanding Betsy Murphy to take charge of the young woman.

"I'll stay by the maid," Murphy murmured, and bobbing her head toward the captain, she plucked the girl's sleeve and urged her toward the cabin door.

VIII

Betsy nudged the girl ahead of her down the gangway, pushing past the sailors standing around the deck and looking speculatively at the former cabin boy, who kept her eyes down and scrambled to the lower deck.

"My, but you're a one, Missie – I wondered when you'd be found out. Sit over there," said Betsy, pointing a corner by the bulkhead.

"You'll have to berth with us, and there's no room to spare as it is. Mr. Allard said to see if we could find you some spare clothes. Where in heavens name does he think the likes of us have anything to spare? I'm the only one with so much as a spare shawl, the others have what's on their backs. Anything else was bartered for extra bread weeks ago."

The girl looked at Betsy sharply for the first time. Betsy gave her a knowing look back.

"Oh yes, Missie, I spotted you from the first. I know you, Mari Westin, and your little sister, Sophie, and brother Tom. Oft' times I've seen the three of you together. I recognized you right away, even in your brother's borrowed clothes.

She smiled at the girl's look of startled concern.

"You won't remember me, little lady, although your Aunt Matty would."

"How do you know me?"

"Oh, never you mind."

Betsy was deliberately off-hand. Then, glancing at the girl's crestfallen face, she relented.

"I quite often did seamstress work for your aunt in Chelmsford, not dress-making but mending linens and such. I helped out Annie Maitland, who did stuff for your mother, too. She recommended me to your Aunt Matty. I sometimes carried work over from Annie's to the big hall," said Betsy.

"I often saw you romping in the fields with Tom. From a distance, I never thought you were any other than another young lad. Then, one day, I saw you dodge through the bushes by the backyard privy in a dress and push a bundle of clothes for Tom to carry. I was waiting by the scullery door to be paid by Mrs. Trant, that sour-faced housekeeper of your parents.

"I remember envying you your lovely gold curls as they tumbled over your shoulders. Lordy, whatever happened to them? To me, you were just a couple of young 'uns having a merry time. I never mentioned it to anyone. I like to mind my own business, anyways," she added, offering her charge a beaker of rum and water.

Mari Westin sat there, silently considering Betsy's words, then asked aloud, "If you had good work at the hall and Chelmsford, why are you here? Why offer yourself as a bondswoman and take off to the colonies?"

Betsy cradled her drink between both hands and studied it before she answered, as though half-listening to the sounds on deck, the last chickens pecking and scratching at the planks above her.

"Well might you ask – I doubt you've time for my long story, though. I'm for following my brother, Liam. He's the only family I have left, and he's younger by a good 12 years or so. He's outward bound as a king's passenger."

Betsy shot a defiant look at the girl.

"And I'm worried whether he'll make it, though he's young and strong, that's for sure."

"Why should he not?" Mari asked innocently.

"We've made it – our crossing was really not so bad, and we're women after all."

The fiddle had started up again, and there was the buzz of genial exchanges between the crew and passengers, though things were at a quieter tempo than before. A crewman's voice called out the watch, and first-mate Lewis could be heard giving orders. The motion of the ship at anchor was easy and gentle.

Betsy fell silent. Her face softened as she thought of her brother.

"But, my, he's a handsome one. I always hoped he would take up with one of my friend's daughters."

Betsy smiled again, going over an old fantasy, or dream, in her head.

She gave Mari an exasperated look that turned grim, thinking of the prison ships carrying their human cargo from England's jails to the new world.

"Those sellers of souls, don't care too much when they lose some of their cargo in the crossing. They've already collected the passage fee for the prisoners from London, but then I suppose they stand to make that much extra for those they keep alive to sell on the auction block. I'm trusting and hoping he'll be alright.

"He'll have been sold for labor and will have to serve out his term. I hope to be free a bit sooner, and then we can make some kind of life of our own in the colonies."

She paused, thoughtful again, and continued quietly, anxiety edging her voice.

"Trouble is, Liam, is, he's...well, not simple exactly, but not too sharp either. He's willing and good tempered and easily led, thoughtless for his own account."

"But how did he come to be a king's passenger, then?" asked Mari.

In the deepening twilight of steerage, her eyes looked large and beautiful, like velvet pansies, thought Betsy. Her curiosity about Betsy and her brother had distracted the girl from her own plight.

"What did he do to be sent to the colonies?"

Betsy's voice came through the dusk. She sounded tired and resigned.

"What did he do? Well – truth is it's pitiful really. He wanted to learn to read, so he stole, or so they said, a book. He said he just borrowed it."

This was incomprehensible to Mari Westin, who thought immediately of her father's library, with how many books on the shelves she didn't know, and couldn't guess. "But how did he come to get it?"

"Oh, he was helping with some pointing work on the masonry of the rector's house and saw it on a table by the window. It was in the same place for a couple of days, so he convinced himself, no-one would mind if he took it away for a while. It was bound in pretty green leather with gold lettering. He asked me to teach him, but I knew he shouldn't have had a book like that. I told him to take it to the rector and tell him he had found it somewhere, but he made a pig's ear of that.

"The rector wasn't in, and the rector's wife is buttoned-up and mean. She, of course, recognized it, and accused him of stealing it, and he's no wit to sort himself out on his feet. He mumbled and stumbled, saying he wanted to read, but she poured scorn on that, saying why should a clumsy oaf like him want learning.

"He wasn't fit, and anyway, long and short of it was they arrested him, and tried him as a common thief at the Assizes. The magistrate sized him up for what he was, I reckon though, and put him for deporting to the colonies."

The harshness of it all was beyond Mari. She remembered getting a reprimand herself once for taking an old book on gardening to show Sophie some pictures of flowers to copy. The pictures folded out into quite a large sheet from the pages of the book, and she recalled she had remarked to her father how much prettier they would be if colored, and, turned aside from chastising her, her father had agreed, but reminded her to ask first before taking books.

This was so far removed from the idea of sending a man to jail and then deporting him for borrowing such a thing as a book – it stunned her.

Still not able to understand what Betsy was telling her, Mari asked, "But couldn't you have explained to the rector and his wife, or in the court, what had happened, and that Liam wasn't responsible?"

Betsy looked through her at that.

"Rector does what the wife says, and folks like us – situation's useless, unless there's some important body to speak out and take a stand for you. The only one I could have approached, maybe, was your Aunt Mat, but the family was away at the time, somewhere, and one way or another it became too late.

"Liam, he'll always need someone to look out for him. Colonies is better than hanging, so I made up my mind to follow him as soon as I could and link up with him over here. His ship sailed a month before us, and I'm hoping he made it safe and is serving his time somewhere local to where I'll be."

She subsided into silence again, and absently sipped rum and water, grimacing a little at the taste. The sounds from above had quieted down by now. Off-watch sailors had claimed hammocks or settled down in corners on deck, easing their bodies from the day's toil and lulled to sleep by the rum.

The two bondswomen, who had been treading the light fantastic, had been persuaded by drink and attentive tars that they'd be more comfortable in a sailor's hammock than in steerage, and had not returned to bunk down with Mari and Betsy. No-one had bothered them since they had been sent below.

The dim glow of the lamp swinging from the bulkhead to the ship's movement slid over the heads of the two women, catching the expressions on their faces by turn. The ship creaked comfortingly as it rocked to the steady motion of the bay water. Other steerage passengers were curled up, sleeping off the rum, lying in dark indeterminate bundles in the shadows beyond the lamp's glow

"Oh, lie down lass, and get some sleep. We'll both be facing the auction block soon. You're bound to be cherry-picked, m'dear, though most likely not for scrubbing floors. Whatever morning brings, at least we're safe over the ocean. Here, take this old shawl – the night's mild but early hours might be chill."

They settled down on the boards. Mari, wishing she could have claimed her own hammock, tried to get comfortable, curled on her side behind Betsy's back. There was silence for a while and she thought her guardian had gone to sleep, but then Betsy spoke again.

"I've been going on about Liam. But what, may I ask you, persuaded you to run away from that fine family of yours to be a cabin boy of all things? What kind of a fine lady does that?

"I know you fed the captain a story about a young gent from Virginia, but even if that's true, why didn't your parents put a stop to that? It doesn't make sense. Me, the likes of me – well, I've always had to make my own way, but the likes of you – you can't know you're born, you silly, young flipperty-gibbet."

Mari lay in the dark not answering, not knowing how to answer. Her eyes smarted with tears, suddenly remembering the last time she had seen her mother. Strangely, though, there was no intense grief. Her mother had seemed to retreat from her family long before she had actually died, taking less and less interest, and her father had also become more and more remote.

Betsy's voice broke into her thoughts.

"What was this gentleman of yours like, then Missie." Her voice sounded gentle in the dark as though she realized Mari's sadness and confusion. "Was he as beautiful as my Liam."

Mari smiled ruefully into the dark.

"Oh yes, I think so, I'm troubled though that something terrible happened to prevent him from joining me on the boat. I still cannot really believe he would desert me so without some serious cause."

Unseen, Betsy rolled her eyes to heaven.

"Where did you meet him, then, anyhow?"

"At Aunt Matty's and Uncle Frederick's house. Aunt Mat was over on a visit and took us back with them to Chelmsford for a change of scene. She said a little socializing would do us good. Pa, for once, agreed. Bryce was there, then."

She paused, in a reverie again. Betsy frowned, then asked, "I wonder why he didn't turn up, though, this young maid's dream of yours."

"I don't know. I don't know," Mari whispered into the dark.

She wanted to stop the conversation and be quiet with her churning thoughts.

"Well," finished the bondswoman. "However much of a fool you are, you at least had the courage to fly your colors, little miss. More than he did, seems to me."

* * *

With the dawn blushing a clear eastern sky, *Integrity* slowly started up the bay on the last leg home. Captain Coward's focus was once again on command of his ship and preparing the vessel for its arrival in port. He would be judged by the ship's owners on the speed of his passage and the condition of his cargo when it was unloaded.

He ordered a last thorough inspection of the hold. Hatches were prized open by an enthusiastic crew, who swarmed about their business, laughing and joking, spirits up at the thought of the comforts of home port. First-mate Lewis led the inspection, reporting back as Coward hoped: no apparent damage to any of the goods he was charged with delivering safely.

Coward viewed the familiar approach to Oxford, which lay across the Choptank River, with equanimity. On a day as fine as this, it presented the simplest of passages for a practised skipper across clear, deep waters.

Once round Benoni Point and into the Tred Haven River with Robert Morris's white shingle house a beckoning beacon, he would fire a single canon shot to simultaneously herald *Integrity*'s arrival and salute the townsfolk, who would assemble on the Strand, which curved gradually and gracefully around the waterfront.

He was confident that some of the wealthiest families in Oxford and surrounding Talbot County, who already owned items he had shipped, would appreciate the fine furniture, china, silverware, and textiles in his holds so that their homes could stand comparison with those of the English gentry.

The captain ordered Lewis to bring the girl back to his cabin. He was still in conflict over the problem posed by her deceit. He barked a gruff command to "enter" when Lewis rapped sharply on the cabin door, and saw she was still attired as a cabin boy.

"Well, now, Miss Perdita," Coward said, his eyes assessing her. "You must be a mite fearful, I suppose, of what awaits you. What in the name of Heaven had you thought to do, once landed in America, your Virginian…er…gentleman, having let you down?"

She stood there, hesitant and uncertain, chafing her jacket sleeve against one arm as though to make it longer.

"Presumptuous chit, silly girl – spoiled, no doubt," thought Coward.

Her blue-eyed gaze flicked away from his cold stare.

"I had thought I might make my way to his family estate after I was paid off," she finally muttered.

"But, I know, I could hardly do that, dressed as a boy and with no introduction at all. Then, maybe, I thought, I could just work a passage back to England. I didn't think to be discovered as a girl. I was quite able as a cabin help, wasn't I, Captain? Couldn't I still just do that?"

Coward's stare shriveled the hope in her face.

"No, no. You certainly cannot. I'd hardly keep a decent reputation, palming you off as cabin lad to one of my brother captains. Impossible, even were I of a mind.

"You don't seriously think, girl, that the crew of every vessel in Oxford won't know of you in days if not hours, perhaps even before you're ashore. The whole town will know.

"What a feather-brain. How, in any case, would you maintain yourself waiting for a berth? Singing and dancing for the sailors ashore, most likely, eh?"

Mari flushed at his scorn, and said nothing.

"No, no, my lass, I don't know why I bothered to ask you. No, there's nothing for it, but you must to Plinhimmon. I have decided to take you home with me. I have a wife and three daughters. They can maybe do something with you. You can read, can't you, girl?"

This last asked suddenly as though an afterthought. She was startled.

"Yes – yes. I can."

She seemed about to offer more, but stayed silent.

Coward looked out over the water again before informing her sternly, "There's much work to do at Plinhimmon. You could perhaps help some in the house, or coach young Hannah, Bridget and Penelope. They're none too forward in their learning.

"They'd maybe like to know something of London ways and fashion, though why I should encourage that, I can't think.

"At any rate, lass, you're in a pickle of your own making, and must make shift as best you can. I've given my best offer, and I'll be damned if I'll pay you off as cabin lad and leave you to your devices. I'd be a laughing stock on the bay."

He paused, surveying her sternly.

"What do you say, miss?"

The thought of going ashore in this new country and fending for herself appalled her. The captain intimidated and unnerved her, but she also looked to him for protection. The prospect of further servitude ashore was bitter medicine, but, having no other choice, she gave in with a show of compliance she did not feel.

"You are most kind, Captain."

IX

Integrity settled at anchor off Oxford's Strand, and casks, barrels and crates were readied for the wherries to take ashore to the carters, waiting under the watchful eyes of local factors on the quay.

As one of the boats coasted alongside, Mari's heart jumped in her chest, hearing Lewis call out, "The gentlemen from Virginia, captain."

For a wild moment, she actually thought that Bryce might be coming for her. Could he have arrived ahead of her somehow and been waiting for her, or had he gotten word to his family to meet her? She and Betsy were still below on orders from Captain Coward. She could hardly breathe.

Her hopes were shattered when they were herded up roughly onto the deck and lined up with the others to be inspected by a group of strangers.

Betsy looked stolid and serious, and was silent. Mari opened her mouth to ask a flood of questions, but quickly closed it again and stood quietly with the rest of Captain Coward's flotsam and jetsam. They had all been told to tidy themselves up, to take care to appear as neat and nice as possible. It was apparent now they were to be bid for right there on the deck, without even setting foot ashore.

Mari was aghast at the thought that she was to be disposed of with the rest of the bond passengers. Wasn't she supposed to go with John Coward? She must have misunderstood.

There were about a half dozen buyers strolling the deck, sizing up the line of hapless humanity, combed and primped at the captain's behest as best could be managed after weeks at sea. The motley bunch of redemptioners stood there outwardly meek enough. A few seemed confident, a few apprehensive, others just bewildered, but Mari felt her blood boil as the colonial men, with their rough, homespun clothes and manners, looked them over with hard, calculating eyes and indifference to their feelings.

Captain Coward stayed in his cabin as the buyers took turns judging the rag-tag group's suitabilities, remarking callously on the appearance of this or that man or woman, the height, the strength, the comeliness, or not, of each. Their questions probed knowledge of this or that craft or trade, or, indeed, any kind of skills possessed. The width of a man's shoulders, the straightness of a woman's back, the firmness of her body, good or bad teeth, all came under consideration.

Mari's face flamed with mortification and shame. She wondered, not for the first time, what on earth she had done. How would her brother, Tom, advise her now? Three of the buyers took obvious fancy to Betsy, and they all seemed to take note of the bright-eyed girl standing nearby, but asked her nothing.

Then, one of them, a very tall, grim and forbidding looking man, came close in front of Mari, staring down intently at her. She noticed he had a large, unshapely nose at odds with his face, and a mean gaze. He reached forward and grasped her shoulder hard with long, strong, bony fingers, and leered with eyes like cold, gray pebbles.

"What's this pretty urchin good for, then?" he said, appearing to enjoy his moment of domination.

She felt his fingers digging into her shoulder, sending a nerve pain through her neck, and then fear suddenly quelled and her temper rose. How dare he? Whoever he was, or thought he was, he was an uncouth lout, and would have been whipped off her father's estate or thrown in jail for daring to handle her so.

Betsy, standing next to Mari, sensed the tumult of the girl's feelings. The older woman's hand moved slightly as though to check anything Mari might do or say.

Then - "Allard! What are Will...er, dammit, Perdita and Betsy in the line for? They're indented already to me. Send them below."

Captain Coward's voice cut down from the poop deck. Everyone looked up to where he stood frowning down, both hands grasping the rail.

"Be with you in an instant, gentlemen," he shouted to the buyers as he hopped down the gangway.

Mari glanced at Betsy, who seemed startled and confused, but relieved.

"Mr. Thorberry – my compliments." Coward reached out his hand to the ogre of a man who reluctantly loosened his grip on Mari's shoulder to return the captain's courtesy. Allard and Lewis tugged her and Betsy away, taking each by an arm.

"Go wait below a while," said Allard. "Cap'n will send for you when you're wanted."

He was looking back at Thorberry when he spoke, then abruptly nodded at Lewis to take the two women away, and went after the captain as he progressed down the line of redemptioners with his prospective buyers.

Mari instinctively huddled next to Betsy as she set herself down in their old place below deck, against the bulkhead. Betsy looked suddenly gray and unwell, and Mari was concerned. She reached over and pulled Betsy's shawl close around her, and took one of her cold hands in her own.

"I hadn't really realized," Betsy said in a low voice. "How – how – difficult it could be."

She had leant her head back against the side of the ship and closed her eyes.

"To stand there and be bought! Looked over like cattle. I know they do it at labor fairs back home, but I never did that. I always found recommendation and dealt with ladies in their own drawing rooms or proper house-keepers interviewing for an honest, reliable worker. And then, even laborers at fairs can bargain for their positions.

"They just were looking at us like – things – farm animals – a cart – a chattel. Oh Liam, what did you do to us? We could have been happy and settled at Meg's."

Mari was anxious to comfort her, and worried too, suddenly realizing that, already, she looked on Betsy as an ally and friend, older, more experienced in the world and stronger too.

"Don't fret yourself, Betsy, please. It was obviously a mistake we were sent up with the others. The captain made clear we are both going to his house with him. I'm glad, too. I was dreading being all alone. But we are neither of us now.

"We have each other for company, and we can give each other support, and, one way or another, we can find out about Liam and find a way to work out our futures."

Betsy's eyes remained closed for a moment, then she took a deep breath and let it out in a sigh. She opened her eyes and turned her head toward the girl and gave a smile. She already looked better.

"Yes, little miss, you are right. We can do just that. I don't know why I suddenly felt so overcome. It's not as if I don't know the ways of the world, and how hard it can be, especially for folks like me.

"You though – you've been a silly young thing – but you have spirit. I think you may win through in the end, little one, but you're for certain in for some lessons about the rough side of life."

Mari felt piqued at that. She had, after all, run away to sea. She had completed a sea voyage, and felt she had proved a pretty able cabin-boy. It had been something of an adventure, in which she had acquitted herself well. She thought of her brother, Tom, again. She would have loved to dazzle him with her exploits. Betsy's voice interrupted her silent self-congratulations.

"Don't look so smug miss, you have been fortunate so far, but a woman alone in this world, without money or friends, or any means of support and influence is in a dangerous state."

She gave a wry look.

"Like dancing along the edge of a cliff."

She studied her young companion some more, and then gazed upwards, thinking, "Oh Lord, feathery gold curls and eyes like blue lakes – she surely has some sorely-tried guardian-angel."

Mari turned to Betsy.

"Surely helping out in the house can't be harder than managing on board ship? I think I found myself quite well as a cabin boy."

"Oh well, I grant you that," said Betsy. "But on land there are different possibilities. You might think you'll be working under the captain's authority in his house, but you won't. It'll be the mistress's domain, and when she's not there, housekeepers, daughters, cousins or other servants over you.

"You'll not like it miss, not at all, considering where you came from."

At this, Mari was anxious again, not with the idea of fitting into the household, but at Betsy's reminder of her own family.

"Betsy, please don't tell anyone you know me, and don't call me Mari. I don't want anyone to know my real name."

"Oh, don't bother yourself. Perdita you shall remain. I know how to keep my own counsel, missie. All I owe anyone in the world is work for my passage to the captain, and, no doubt, he'll extract every penny's worth and more if he can. They all do.

"There's many a fine family – when it comes down to it – maintains itself on the backs of lesser folk, and doesn't think even paying a living pittance is due."

Mari sat there distracted and dismayed at the bitterness in Betsy's voice, and the bondswoman must have seen it in her face because she softened and reached over to pat her hand.

"Oh, I must own, your mother, and your aunt Mathilda in particular, were always true, fine ladies with me, and always did their best for their people."

She fell silent for a moment.

"Even fine ladies, though, you know, are fettered by what they can't do. Comes down to the men, Perdita. We all have to knuckle under and keep our place, though you, with your looks and position, could have had a deal of your own way. Whatever possessed you to be a cabin boy?"

She shook her head.

"Words fail me – you don't look so brainless and empty-headed. I've watched you. You have your wits about you – most of the time at least."

She gazed at Mari again.

"There must be a wild streak somewhere in your family – came out in you."

Mari started to answer, but was cut short by a shout down the companion way from Horrocks.

"On deck you two. Cap'n's ready for shore and Plinhimmon. Deal's done with the bond folk. Most of them off to Virginny. A couple for locals."

They clambered back up on deck into the fine morning again. The view of the shore was low and lush, with a sweet offshore breeze playing over the sparkling water.

Several different craft were plying the river, ferrying goods and people. A couple of them were sailing steadily back toward the Chesapeake Bay, and, in one of them, Mari could just make out the tall hat and dark-clothed form of the man who had troubled her in the line-up. There seemed to be at least three of the indentured passengers with him.

She found herself shivering, the thought of being bound to a man so repugnant to her. All in all, if she had to be beholden to a master for a while, she felt Coward would be preferable to that one.

The sailors had lowered the long-boat, and Lewis and Horrocks were there to hurry them into it. Mari swung down first and climbed down past the oarsmen, getting a smirk and knowing glance from Cahill. Betsy came after, and almost fell into the water, her knuckles white clutching the rope ladder with her skirts hampering her. She obviously hated the business, and gasped with relief when she was finally bundled next to some supplies.

In short order, Captain Coward came over the side of his ship, giving instructions of some kind to Lewis before swinging easily down. Allard came with him, and they settled aft as the crew, casually expert, pushed off and headed for the Oxford waterfront.

X

The general mood on shore was merry, and the sailors seemed to do everything with a special flourish as though they were flaunting their skills to entertain the crowd looking on from the Strand. They shipped the oars smartly as the longboat swung smoothly against the dock.

Betsy and Mari moved aside as Captain Coward greeted several people at the dockside. He paid the two women no heed, jumped easily ashore, and strode quickly toward the Customs House to complete his paperwork

Betsy and Mari watched as a young woman ran forward from the crowd and flung herself into Coward's arms. One of the crew said it was the captain's daughter, Hannah. She was a good-looking girl, younger than Mari, with a slight figure.

After exchanging some words with his daughter, Captain Coward handed her into a waiting pony trap, driven by a slave, and waved her off. Allard, glancing back, signaled for Betsy and Mari to stay where they were, so they did, each with a pathetic bundle, trying to take in their surroundings.

The activity at the waterside had a comforting familiarity. There was one other ship in the river anchorage, and there was quite a business of loading and unloading. Jolly boats were shuttling about, already unloading *Integrity*, and others were ferrying provisions over to the other boat.

Mari wondered whether this was where Bryce would have landed, but then remembered that the Virginia men, settling for servants, had immediately taken boats back into the big bay. They had not landed anywhere, so she supposed that the water route was the quicker, wherever they wished to go.

Horrocks's voice broke in.

"Why don't you two promenade a bit? Get your land legs under you. Stay in sight of the Customs House so you can mark when the Cap'n comes out and is ready to go."

It was strange feeling firm land underfoot again. When Mari first stepped ashore, it was as though the earth was tilting to and fro. She

113

found herself staggering, and noticed Betsy was equally unsteady. The sailors all grinned.

"Hey, Will, you should have taken it easy with the grog," called someone, and they all laughed.

The two set off, a little hesitantly, the same way down the Oxford Strand that the captain had taken. The town itself appeared a pleasant place, with comfortable manses, their shingles painted white, black and green, set out on orderly streets. The lay of the land was flat, with cultivated fields of some kind in the distance, and mature, tall trees shading the streets in the town. They took a couple of turns on The Strand,

Betsy decided she wanted to sit down again, so they did so beside the longboat. Before long, Captain Coward and Allard emerged from the Customs House, and the others hurried to get back into the boat, anxious not to delay the captain. Betsy bit her lip again as she stumbled aboard. Allard and the captain climbed down and settled aft, ordering the crew to set for Plinhimmon over the smooth water.

As the boat, with the tars pulling easily on the oars, turned into the home creek, it disturbed a small flock of wild geese. They honked and took flight, swinging in a wide, noisy circle overhead before skimming back down to the water, their feet splayed forward to stop them in a cascade of dazzling spray.

Hearing calls and laughter from a landing stage on shore, Mari pulled her gaze from the birds' performance to take in the aspect of a comfortable house standing in a copse.

The house was surrounded by grass that ran down to the small jetty, where they were headed. Tall trees dappled the sunlit property with shade, like a black Spanish veil over a pale face, making it look invitingly cool. All around it were fields of uniform plants, their broad, green leaves hanging heavy and still, languid even, over the dark earth, adding to the overall sense of serenity, although at that moment Mari was feeling far from tranquil.

Captain Coward sat looking intently at his home, and its surroundings as he neared the jetty. It was as though he was impressing the prospect afresh on his memory. He had a look of deep pleasure and satisfaction at the sight of his family hurrying across the grass to greet him.

Mari saw a small, plump woman trying vainly to keep up with her children, who were racing ahead to greet their father. Skipping and jumping, the youngsters dashed onto the jetty, waving all the time at the approaching boat.

Behind them, the dark figures of two men and a woman emerged quietly from a small hut aback the house with smoke curling from its chimney stack. They observed the longboat's arrival with interest rather than excitement.

Mari took them to be slaves, although she had never in her life met one, and had only rarely seen a black person. They stayed where they were beside the hut, apparently waiting to be summoned, still, watchful figures in the backdrop of Plinhimmon's landscape.

While the sailors tied up to the dock, Mari scanned the family group with interest. Of the three daughters, one looked to be about her own age and this heartened her. All three wore simple dresses of gingham, or perhaps cherryderry, ornamented by collars of fine lawn.

She noticed that they seemed lightly corseted, if at all, judging by the way the younger two gamboled and jumped around in their excitement at greeting their father. The elder sister stood a little stiffly apart from her siblings, affecting nonchalance. She was called Bridget, Mari learned, after her mother.

Mrs. Coward, too, was dressed plainly in a figured dimity dress of dark blue with a lace bib. She wore a lace-trimmed cap, and her dress was unhooped.

The boys, also dressed for ease in their shirt-sleeves and loose waistcoats, stood behind their mother. The whole family displayed a happy, informal welcome. Glancing across at Betsy, Mari saw that her mood, too, had lightened, and she smiled with relief.

* * *

A month had passed since the two English women arrived at the Coward estate, and Mari had grown used to being called Perdita.

She quickly came to understand what Betsy meant about how different working in a household would be to serving onboard ship. Mari did not feel welcome in the household. Betsy clearly was.

Betsy could turn her hand to most things. She mended linen, helped make dresses. She knew to help in the kitchen, and to put-up preserves and cordials against the winter. She even learned a new skill, making candles from the tallow bought from whaler-merchants up north. She didn't scorn any work, and set to help where help was needed.

The mistress of the house was clearly dismayed at Mari, even her appearance. She had no clothes of her own, apart from Tom's old shirt and britches, so she was given a hand-me-down dress from one of the Coward daughters. It was ill-fitting, but served the purpose of getting her out of boy's clothes. Wearing a small muslin cap covered the fact that her hair was cropped.

The daughters didn't quite know what to make of her either. Mari knew they were intrigued as they questioned her about her adventures. The eldest daughter, Bridget, was the first one at Plinhimmon to be severe with Mari. Mari thought that, under other circumstances, they could have been friends, but it was as though Bridget was delighted to exercise her superiority over the new house help

The captain suggested to his wife that as the newcomer seemed to have a certain education, she could help school their daughters, in effect be a sort of governess. Mari could read, write, draw, and even paint a little, as well as sew, all a lady's accomplishments, and even knew to speak some French.

Some attempt was made at tutoring, but it did not turn out well. Mari was not old enough to have any sway over the girls, and, knowing what she had done, they had no real respect for her.

They would be entertained and amused whilst she told them what they wished to know about English fashions and which plays she had seen on the London stage, but they tried her to the utmost whilst they were supposedly having lessons.

Hannah, the youngest, could be enjoyable company, and when bested by wit, she would hoot with laughter and collapse on the window seat with her arms around her would-be governess, begging to be told some diverting story or other.

Bridget, the oldest, was more difficult. She told Mari one day that she would ask Betsy to make over one of her better dresses, but, a week later, when reminded, she airily announced that Sarah, the slave, who cooked for the household, deserved it much more than a London trollop.

The insult stung. But when Mari replied that any lady worthy of the title would never demean herself by using such language and displaying such spleen, matters went from bad to worse.

In the weeks following there happened to be quite a flurry of visitors to the house, and a pattern of behavior became apparent. It dawned upon Mari that she had become an object of local curiosity.

Sometimes a party would arrive, and she would be summoned to be inspected. She would be questioned and then spoken of as though she were part of the furniture. She hated this discourtesy, the more as it reminded her of being inspected for sale on the ship.

Other times, when Mari thought she might be expected to help serve, she was hurriedly banned to the kitchen, out of sight of any guests as someone not fit to be in good company.

Betsy was right. They actually saw very little of Captain Coward as he went about his business in town and at his warehouse. They knew also that he could be sailing again soon. It was therefore clear that the comfort of Mari's own position relied primarily upon his wife's goodwill and care, and Mrs. Coward appeared more distracted and doubtful as to what to do with her as time went on. She doted upon her daughters, and they constantly played upon her feelings.

It soon became apparent that the idea of playing teacher to Bridget and Penelope in particular, was to be forgotten. Mari's career as a governess would have lapsed altogether except for occasional mornings with Hannah, who actually sought her out sometimes and claimed her services and attention for whichever activity took her fancy at the time.

Mari made a show of teaching her French, and, with amusement, thought of Miss Pardoe, who would have had some comment about that presumption. She also made a grim effort to help Hannah with a sampler she was supposed to finish by Christmas.

Teaching the youngest Coward daughter was a very haphazard business, however, given the ease with which she became distracted, abandoning Mari's company at whim for something or someone else. And, in any case, Mrs. Coward would increasingly set tasks helping in the kitchen or vegetable garden.

The Mari rebellious at dancing attendance in London society was reduced to scullery maid at Plinhimmon, and an afternoon of helping Robin hoe weeds taught her the woes of an aching back. The chafing

117

of a stiff corset and formal dress while sitting for an hour on a parlor couch was a distant memory

Robin seemed perplexed at her presence at Plinhimmon. He appeared to regard her as an oddity who didn't fit in anywhere in the household. Robin and Peter, the other male slave, did most of the outside work at Plinhimmon.

As a slave, Robin was not actually servile, but was quiet and respectful to the family. It was very difficult to know what he thought about anything. Betsy could have taken lessons from him at keeping her own counsel.

* * *

One late summer afternoon, Mari tried without much success to engage Robin in conversation as they were shucking some corn, gathered out in the fields. She was curious as to how he ended up with the Cowards. She wondered whether the three slaves had been passed on to Captain Coward from his own father.

How long ago? Had Robin been born at Plinhimmon? Mari thought, at first, he had, but was proved mistaken. She wasn't a good judge of age, but she surmised he might be about forty years. She started prattling on about the discomfort of ship-board life below decks, and the stifling heat there, once the sea route passed into the warmer southern latitudes.

She suddenly realized that Robin was totally silent. Instead of fending off her questions by directing her efforts at shucking the corn, he had become still and morose.

Mari finished stripping an ear of corn of its fresh, green sheath, and the scent of the broken green washed back as she took pleasure in rubbing off the remnant of the shiny tassels of corn silk. She turned to him to ask whether he was married, but was struck silent herself by his stare, and her questions stumbled to a stop.

His stillness heightened an air of brooding strength about him, and, suddenly, she felt a chill brush of fear, which, however, was transformed into something else as she met his eyes, and compassion flooded through her.

Even kneeling next to her, he seemed to tower over her, and she felt an aura of tremendous strength and tension, and a deep sorrow, mixed perhaps with – what?

She couldn't read the turmoil in his brown, brooding eyes. She had been chattering on, even boasting a little of her adventures traveling the ocean, and they suddenly seemed puny. She felt silly, and young, and appalled.

What was she thinking? Why should a grown man, a slave, who had been bought and sold, perhaps many times, want to respond to her inconsequential prattle?

This man had no right to dispose of his time, or his labor, to see to his own needs or those of his family, if he had one. He was a man who could not even say No to any demands upon him for the rest of his natural life. He could not, even with a kindly master, count on any kind of security or dignity.

Mari had learned to sympathize with Betsy and others of her class who work all their lives for next to nothing, and who could expect little consideration if they became ill, or old, or useless. Betsy and she had suffered the hot, humiliation of being lined up and looked over like cattle for sale at a fair, to be eyed and judged by dispassionate, calculating men – who knew? – men who might be cruel masters.

She remembered exactly how the heat of anger had risen, burning out fear and shame.

The turmoil in this man Robin must be fueled by a deeper rage. He was owned, nothing more than a chattel possession. How much more must his feelings have been lacerated by experience?

Staring at him, Mari felt suddenly on the edge of an abyss. For some reason, she became acutely aware of the warm, gritty earth beneath her knees, and the hot sun on her neck. She fiercely wished she was back home in England, doing something, anything very ordinary, perhaps teasing Abby at her kitchen table, or arguing with George or Tom over some game or other.

Robin must have read the consternation in her because his eyes focused and softened, and he released her gaze. He reached over to gently take her hand, which was holding the ear of corn. The back of her hand in his work-hardened palm felt as though it was resting on warm leather, as he slowly traced with his other hand the rows of close-packed corn kernels pressed together like so many creamy, yellow pearls, with no space between.

"Bodies like that, Perdita, Missie."

His voice was low, as he stroked his finger along the corn.

"No room to turn, breathe, ease a poor body, look t'see who's cryin', dyin', no water, food – all filth…pain…fearful. Dark…chokin' dark. Slavin' boat's from hell, Miss Perdita, from hell!"

She stared mesmerized at the neatly packed, perfect ear of corn, not really able to comprehend what he was saying. The corn looked pristine and fresh in the bright sunlight, but Robin stayed absent-mindedly still, stroking along the nubby rows, seeing scenes Mari couldn't even imagine. She watched and waited for him to speak again, but he was lost in memory.

As if it were yesterday, Robin could see himself standing trembling on the auction block in Annapolis harbor. He wasn't sure how old he was then, or now, but thought he must have been ten or twelve at the time.

A coarse rope had chafed his neck as he was herded to the auction block with the few other children who had survived the crossing. The adults were shuffling and staggering in chains. He hadn't been able to stop his knees shaking from fear and the effort of holding himself upright on land after the disorienting time at sea.

The Annapolis dock scene had been full of brightness and noise after the squalor and claustrophobic darkness of the slave ship's hold.

The slaves had been roughly sluiced down with sea water by the sailors before being hauled ashore to be sold to buyers already waiting and anxious to bid. There were mostly men to be sold, with a few women and children.

Robin remembered that some of the women wore little but the body and hair ornaments that they had on when first captured far away in their homelands. Some of them had scarification patterns tattooed and raised on their skin in beautiful, elaborate designs, displaying tribal origins and status.

He, himself, had been naked, standing exposed on the block, the confusing hubbub of the port all about him. He had looked wildly around the crowd of strange faces, and, finally, focused on a black woman standing toward the front.

She was wearing a plain, homespun gown, and was staring gravely back at him. She was with a man who was sizing up the bodies on offer. The woman, for it was Sarah, said something and gestured to the boy.

Though he had seemed dubious at first, John Coward nodded and bought Robin for fifteen pounds.

Sarah led Robin to a cart, the tether still around his neck. Then, watching the captain, who had stopped to greet some acquaintances, she slowly started to ease the rope from his raw throat. She stood still, the noose halfway over his head, as John Coward glanced over at them, obviously discussing his purchase.

Coward stared at Sarah for a moment, then gave a slight, abrupt nod of the head. She smiled and threw the rope into the gutter.

"You – a fine boy – I'll put some salve on that neck, and feed you up. You'll be good in no time. Plinhimmon – living's good as any, better than most in these parts."

Sarah had switched from English to Bantu and back again. He had not understood all of her words then, but had latched on to her good intent. She had spoken the truth, life at Plinhimmon was better than many other places for a slave, or a servant. It was some time before Robin came to know how harsh it could be elsewhere, and that others of his kind stepped from the nightmare of the sea crossing to another, just as awful, on land.

"Perdita! Perdita!"

Bridget's petulant voice pierced the sun-filled air. It took Mari, still mesmerized by the ear of corn, and Robin, deep in thought, a few moments to react.

Robin was in a reverie, staring down at the earth, his old broken straw hat shading his face. When he looked up, his expression was blank and calm again. They were momentarily shielded by the tall corn stalks, but heard the crackle and swish as Bridget pushed through the field toward them.

Mari had an almost unbearable urge to panic, grab Robin's strong hand and yell "Run! Run like the devil!"

As though he divined the impulse in her, Robin suddenly laughed out loud and stood up, hauling the basket of corn with him, and started for the kitchen.

Mari was still on her knees stuffing corn sheaths into her apron for drying when Bridget reached her. Sarah used the dry sheaths in all kinds of ways, making mats, hats, and baskets, and even stuffing mattresses with them.

Bridget stood over Mari, looking discontented and suspicious.

"Having yourself a fine time in the fields with Robin were you, Lady Perdita?" she sneered.

Mari stood up and stared back at Bridget's pinched face, reading in it the threat of a beating at the slightest excuse, and silently thanking fortune that the parents had authority over the servants' disposition.

"Mama wants you at the house," Bridget said abruptly, and stiffly turned away.

Mari bunched up her apron and hurried after Robin, hearing "Trollop" hissed in her wake.

In the parlor, the captain's wife considered her hapless kitchen maid. Mrs. Coward looked harassed again. Mari had the usual sensation she experienced in her mistress's company. Mrs. Coward was not actually hostile, but the maid, clearly, was a problem she felt she could do without, an unwanted bother.

Captain Coward was in the room as well. He had been away for some time, and Mari had hardly had any kind of exchange with him for some weeks. He came over, and examined her in her untidy state.

"Heavens, Perdita! You looked more presentable as Will."

He turned to his wife.

"She will have to be cleaned up to make a better appearance than that, if she's to play the part of a lady's maid in an Annapolis house."

Mari looked down at her clothes, bits of corn silk clinging to a patched apron which half covered her hand-me-down dress. She was dusty and crumpled.

She had been sharing the attic space over the kitchen with Betsy and Sarah for their sleeping quarters. Bridget thought they ought to be outside in the lean-to. She complained that other folks' servants bedded down with the animals – why shouldn't they? She did not aim her spleen so much at Betsy or Sarah, but rather at Mari.

Mari looked from the captain to his wife without saying anything. Mrs.Coward sighed resignedly,

"I'll find something of Penelope's, I suppose. She could look fine as a lady's maid, if only she would act the part. John, you might whilst you're about it, have a word with the girls."

She gave him a significant look as she called Penelope, who was to be persuaded to give up a decent dress for once. Mari was pleased at the thought and cast Penelope an innocent smile.

They were to go to Annapolis for the races! The girls were full of it – what sights they would see, the visits they would make. Annapolis was the metropolis.

Mari had no idea what the town was like. Her impression, from overhearing talk at Plinhimmon, was that it was a hub of social activity, commerce and politics. She had heard of growing feelings in Annapolis, and elsewhere, against the British government, of harsh taxes, and efforts to have them repealed, but she knew little of such things and cared less.

XI

"Perdita, go with Mr. Thorberry's man down to Middleton Tavern. Leave whatever you're doing, girl!"

Mrs. Coward sounded irritable and perplexed, as she summoned her help. Mari hurried from the back scullery to join her in the front room of Tuckett's Tavern. Mrs. Coward turned to her impatiently, and waved a hand toward a young man standing in the middle of the room, as though to shoo him away.

"Liam's master has stepped out with the captain on some business – but Mr. Thorberry is needed down at the docks it seems. Go with Liam to find them. I want you, anyway, to tell the captain to call back here for me before he goes about his other affairs."

Mrs. Coward stepped to the window and surveyed the street fretfully.

"I know he's a mind to call on Mr. Farris, the clock-maker, and I mean to go with him, so off you go, girl. You should catch them at Middleton's. Why his man didn't try there in the first place, I don't know. I think he must be simple," she added.

She frowned at Mr. Thorberry's servant, who gazed equably back but said nothing.

"Off you go – off you go. I'll help Mrs. Tuckett the while."

Mari wondered why the man couldn't deliver both messages himself, but offered no complaint, being happy to accept relief from chores and some brief liberty. She and Liam stepped out into the clear May day, blinking in bright sunshine after the gloom of the tavern.

Her spirits rose as she gazed down the hill toward the busy Annapolis dock scene. The washed blue of the sky joined the deeper blue of bay and river that glinted and sparkled as a fresh breeze ruffled over the water.

Sea-going vessels rode at anchor offshore, waiting, loading or unloading, and a variety of smaller craft ducked and dipped in a concert of rhythm between wind and wave. Wisps of white cloud drifted high above.

Mari glanced at her escort as he padded silently at her side, averting shy, gentle eyes when encountering hers. He looked immensely strong, with a well-muscled body filling out shabby, worn, homespun shirt and britches.

"I believe Mrs. Coward said your name is Liam," Mari said.

His face was bland as he nodded his head in assent, and this was all the reaction she elicited from him, though she made several attempts to engage him as they made their way. It seemed to be an effort for him to say anything, as he met her attempts at conversation with a vague smile, and slightly puzzled expression. She became exasperated, but a little intrigued.

They reached the entrance to Middleton Tavern, and, pushed through the heavy oak door into the hallway. Mari suddenly stopped in her tracks, causing Liam to stumble into her. She turned and stared at him.

"You're not Liam Murphy, by any chance, are you, man?"

Again, he said nothing, but a look of consternation passed over his face as though she were criticizing him. He nodded.

"You have a sister, Betsy?"

The man seemed finally to focus properly on her face, and stood still and solemn. Yet another nod of the head.

"She's over the bay at Oxford, working for Captain Coward's family, as I do. She came over to America, on the same ship as I did, to find you. Where are you now, Liam, with that man Thorberry?"

He was so slow to respond, she felt she could have shaken him. Then, a sudden blaze of joy spread over his face.

"Betsy…Betsy…over here for me?"

His face fell again.

"Master Thorberry, we go back down to Virginia soon."

They were suddenly interrupted as the inn door swung open and a sailor maneuvered past them. He was a stocky, vigorous-looking young man, and his direct, appreciative stare flicked over Mari as he went through to the tap room.

She turned back to Liam, disconcerted, to find him sawing at a hank of his unkempt hair with an old knife, and stood at a loss as he presented her with the result of his efforts.

"Give that to my Bets when you see her. Tell her I'm with Master Thorberry in Norfolk, but he might be handin' me on soon."

125

Liam lapsed into vagueness after this essay. Mari stared in dismay at the tufts of hair he had thrust into her hand.

"Put it in your pocket, mistress. Keep it by you, and give it Bets. Tell her to come find me when she can. I'll look for her."

Mari was bested by his simplicity. She knew he must have years to go before being free again, and Betsy had her bond to serve as well. Anything could happen to either of them in the years ahead, but she saw sweet, childish hope in the man's face, and couldn't deny him.

"Yes – oh – Yes, of course, I'll tell her where we met…and…and…where you are, and she can keep track of you till you're able to get together again."

Feeling confounded and silly, she fumbled, and stuffed the bits of hair into her pocket.

"Now, we have to find Captain Coward and Mr. Thorberry to give them Mrs. Coward's message."

The big man nodded, pleased and happy to accept her direction.

Captain Coward wasn't hard to find. He was in the tap room, off the passageway, laughing heartily at some remark of Captain Tuckett. The recently arrived sailor had joined them. There was no Thorberry, though both Liam and Mari scanned the crowd anxiously for him.

The place had an overwhelming masculine atmosphere, with a motley mix of gentlemen, merchants, and seamen of all stations, drinking, eating, and gambling. A few were reading the *Gazette*, or enquiring after letters or packets left for them, or arranging to leave some such in their turn.

Mari received a number of curious looks as she approached Captain Coward and delivered her message. Coward was in a good mood, inspired by the company and a generous measure or two of brandy.

Liam was directed to the White Hart Tavern, across the dock, where Thorberry had returned. He shuffled his feet, mumbled his respects to Coward, and, giving Mari another of his innocent smiles, he lumbered out into the street.

Captain Tuckett turned a snub-nosed, ruddy countenance to Mari, after clucking with disapproval and pursing his lips at some move on a backgammon board at a nearby table.

"Well – this is a fine lass you have for help, John. Mrs. Tuckett has been most impressed and pleased with her assistance. Treat the girl to a noggin of something."

Coward looked at first askance, and hesitated, but then shrugged and gave in to his friend's suggestion, ordering a small cordial for Mari, who took the delivered cup in her hands and stared at it, speechless.

"Well, go on – drink it. Will Herrion used to like an occasional taste of grog, as I remember."

Captain Coward directed an amused gaze and slightly savage grin at the young sailor standing with them. Stewart Dean shot a quick, surprised look back at him, and then at Mari, who dutifully kept her eyes down and supped a cordial she didn't want.

Her blushing discomfort under the close scrutiny of Coward and Dean was only partly assuaged by the benign disregard of Captain Tuckett, who patted and smoothed his doeskin waistcoat as though reassuring his paunch. Tuckett then surveyed the busy scene in the tap room with good humor, not begrudging a fellow tavern-keeper his clientele. He well knew his own establishment to be bulging with custom.

"Well, Mr. Dean, as I was saying, it is good to hear of Captain Coxen - and we look forward to seeing him when he calls in on his way down from Baltimore.

"All and any news is grist for an innkeeper's mill, and though our city here is in thriving times, it seems, nonetheless, there are always rumors and grumbles, and disaffections and such with government and taxes. Men these days do well to keep abreast of things – indeed, a step or two ahead of things, at that."

Tuckett nodded to himself, his bright eyes darting around the room.

"I confess I, for one, am curious as to whether the good merchants of Baltimore are standing by their guns against imports from the mother country, and where it may all lead." He paused reflectively again, and smiled at Stewart Dean.

"I envy you something, young man – your life ahead at sea. What adventure it can bring."

He gave a self-deprecating chuckle.

127

"Mind ye, I've developed a fondness for my comfortable berth here in dry-dock, with a feather bed and a good woman to warm it, not to mention my garden vegetables."

The others looked slightly confused at this.

"I'm pleased to grow them myself, and keep us well supplied," Tuckett added with some self-satisfaction.

"So, Mr. Dean, we should be most obliged if you would join us on Thursday evening, when Mrs. Tuckett is herding us all to the Assembly Rooms for an entertainment on her anniversary."

The young sailor made a brisk appreciative acceptance, whilst gazing warmly at Mari. With Captain Coxen off to Baltimore, Dean had a couple of days to cool his heels. He smiled his thanks again, and took his leave, delaying a moment in the tavern doorway for a swift glance back at the Coward's maid-of-all-work.

Mari, looking after him, encountered his warm but unfathomable regard. She annoyed herself by blushing at the attention and a sudden fantasy she had of promenading on his arm in the spring sunshine, free as a bird.

Stewart Dean's face crinkled into a quizzical grin as though he read her mind, and she dropped her eyes as he turned away, the door swinging to after him.

"Good lad – good lad," Tuckett enthused, looking after Dean.

"Sails with Coxen – 'prentice to the merchant Lowes. Had an eye for the lass here, didn't he? Wouldn't mind him for one of my girls when I think on't. 'Bout time I got 'em settled."

He paused and changed his mind.

"Bit early yet, perhaps."

With this, Tuckett, in his mellow mood, settled back, sipped his wine, smacked his lips, and, after another moment's silence, said, "Ah, we've been hearing of scandal in high places no less. You may have caught word of it in London, John. Our Lord Proprietary himself has been caught out, forcibly pressing his favor on a young woman. Always struck me as a tawdry man, not fit for his title. They say he's gone into hiding, or fled England to the Continent."

"Caught word of it! It was the talk of the town while I was there," said Coward, who shared the Tuckett's scant regard for Lord Baltimore.

"But he's not missing. He's been on trial for his life – and been acquitted."

"Acquitted! How's that? He's such a lothario. Everyone knows of his dalliances. We've all heard of his seraglio in Turkey."

"True, but there was doubt about the woman's story as well. Leastways, the jury obviously thought so."

"A seamstress, wasn't she?"

"No, a milliner, from a middling family. Sarah Woodcock, a name now on everyone's lips in London. Pretty enough from the drawings I have seen, a nice turn of ankle, a jaunty little thing with a twinkle in her eye.

"She said she was lured to Baltimore's house in Southampton Row by a woman retainer on the notion of selling some ruffles and hats to fine ladies. She testified she was kept there, and for several days she resisted his advances until, finally, he forced himself upon her."

"Thought he'd exercise *droit de seigneur,* did he?" interjected Tuckett.

Coward shrugged. No Marylander had set eyes on their Lord Proprietor, but rumors of his dissolute ways had crossed the ocean as regularly as the trade winds, and, if anything, simply added contempt to the mounting anger and resentment toward British authority.

"There were weaknesses in her story," he said.

"Twit of a girl even admitted getting back into his bed at one point, and he had witnesses enough on his side – genuine or bought, who knows? It was all dragged out in public, detractors and apologists arguing it out."

Coward shrugged again.

"It's done him no good, but, then, he's in little need of anything with all he takes from us."

"That's for sure," agreed Tuckett.

"Even the legislature complains about the twelve shillings he gets on every hogshead of 'bacco, and he's never even set foot in this colony. Some Lord Proprietor! They should have strung him up."

Tuckett's was the last word on the subject as the two men reluctantly recalled it was past time to return to their wives.

"Better the both of us get back to domestic bliss, John, though I've enjoyed our little sortie. Come on, lass, back to the chores. You can tell the mistresses that we've been held up hard bargaining in the market," said Tuckett.

Mari smiled as she traipsed after the two men, starting back up the hill, avoiding handcarts, someone's cow, and a stray pig snuffling in the sandy road for waste.

Ben Tuckett was an old friend of Coward's. He ran the tavern on Church Street, where the Cowards usually enjoyed his hospitality when in Annapolis. The Tuckett daughters reminded her of Maybelle and Arabel Hunter. They were carefree and coquettish, and obviously doted on by their parents. She sighed, and thought of the seaman Captain Tuckett had invited to his house.

She had sensed both sympathy and curiosity from him, and had noticed that he had fastened upon Captain Coward's reference to Will Herrion. If the man sailed out of Oxford, he might well know of the girl who had played cabin-boy on Coward's ship.

Her thoughts then wandered back to Liam. She wondered whether she should try and see him again before the Cowards returned home and Thorberry took his goods and chattels south with him. She envisaged Betsy's face.

Betsy would be so relieved and happy to know her brother was safe and sound at least, even though with a miserable master.

The two sea captains slowly stalked along Church Street, talking politics, unrest in the colony, which horse was a good bet on the morrow, and problems they had in common with daughters.

"It's quite clear Annapolis is on the upswing," said Coward, glancing back down the hill at the forest of masts bobbing in the crowded harbor.

"Baltimore, too. Just wish the same could be said of Oxford. Our business is all going west, and not much we can do about it. Geography's against us on the eastern shore, that's for sure. Sometimes, I think I should move to this side of the bay."

"Maybe you should," said Tuckett. "We have all kinds of business, cabinet makers, clock makers, silversmiths, hosiers and cobblers. They're all opening up shop here or in Baltimore, but, you know, John, there's more worrying moves against British trade in the offing."

The clear anxiety in his voice sharpened Mari's interest. Coward, too, picked up the change of tone. His best guess was that there must be some new independence-inspired move from Massachusetts or

Virginia, the usual sources of political protest, that was testing Tuckett, whom he considered a royalist at heart, despite his apparent disdain for Lord Baltimore.

"What's afoot?" asked Coward.

"Is it the Townshend Acts? Wouldn't surprise me. Can't for the life of me grasp the distinction they've been trying to make between these new taxes and the old Stamp Act. They seem to think these new levies should be more palatable, but it's beyond me why that should be. It's still our money they're taking."

"The point," Tuckett said in a low, firm voice meant to signal defense of his corner, "is that this levy is on imports that we buy, and it will be used for our own protection. The Stamp Act was aimed at enriching the Treasury in London.

"Don't you see? The new taxes will be raised here and spent here, not raised here and spent there. Surely, there's a true difference in that."

"If you say so, Ben, but to me it's more of the same. The difference will be lost on most of us expected to pay. It's going to cause trouble. Mark my words."

Both men looked ponderous.

"You may well be right. There's new calls for us to ban all taxable imports from England," said the publican, warming to his subject.

"Won't help either of us. There's talk of forming an association against importation. It's already taken hold in the north, and it's gaining strength here. Just like the Sons of Liberty last time round with the Stamp Act. "

"What's their cry?" asked Coward.

"Frugality – that's their battle-cry. As if life isn't hard enough already. Frugality – and self-reliance. They've got the attention of Annapolis.

"Certainly, it won't advantage the likes of you or me, and Mrs. Tuckett will not be best pleased when her dresses and shoes wear out and she can't buy new ones from London, or when she wants something new for the house. I doubt that Bridget will be any more pleased about it."

"Well," said Coward, "judging by the folk who turned out to see what *Integrity* was carrying, it doesn't seem to be getting much popular support yet. I hardly needed put a notice of sale in the *Gazette*.

"Of course, no-one likes taxes, but the parliament keeps putting them on us. We're not a conquered people, are we? Our fathers came here at their own expense and of their own free will. We can't just keep accepting it, particularly since we are allowed no voice in the business. Besides, we have our own representatives here to decide these things."

"Aye, as you say, but we owe allegiance to the King, do we not?" responded Tuckett.

"And we'd best not cut off our nose to spite our face. What good would come of that? I fear the day when we'll be dressed in little more than sackcloth or homespun, and our houses will go unpainted for want of a spot of lead coloring.

"Still, we must be careful what we do about it. George is still our king."

Coward was conciliatory.

"Perhaps, but something has to be done, or, one day, our loyalty to the Crown may be tested too much."

His voice was low and mild, at odds with the sharp sideways look he gave his friend.

It occurred to Mari that should relations with England become strained to breaking point, these two old sea dogs could find themselves on opposite sides.

Captain Tuckett put an end to the interlude by opening the door of the inn, exclaiming, "Land problems, my friend, land problems, Takes an ocean to clear the head of 'em."

* * *

Race day dawned, bright and clear.

"A gem of a day," Ben Tuckett declared.

He sat at the head of his breakfast table, surrounded by his own and the Coward family in an upstairs room of The Flag and Anchor tavern. A huge, snowy napkin was tucked into his shirt, and in between demolishing fat slices of ham and generous helpings of kedgeree, he regaled his captive audience with racing tales, and enjoyed airing his knowledge and enthusiasm for horses.

Mrs. Tuckett and Mrs. Coward were engrossed in a discussion of the curing of ham and different seasonings to add to salt petre and molasses, finding themselves in easy agreement.

Mari, waiting on the breakfast party, was hopeful that she would somehow be included in their day's outing, even if only to carry cloaks and picnic baskets.

Her hopes received a blow when Mrs. Tuckett announced that she would rather go to the races by horse and buggy than by foot, but fretted that they could not all fit in to the conveyance and would have to make two journeys, which was awkward, given the crowds there were bound to be.

The younger women were immediately enthusiastic to ride rather than walk, thinking to show off some newly acquired finery, sitting prettily above the heads of the crowd, rather than buffeting along with their parasols at street level.

Since their arrival in Annapolis, the Coward daughters had linked up firmly with the Tuckett girls. They had sashayed abroad, taking tea, and gossiping with friends and acquaintances. They had spent hours pretending they could afford numberless new hats and gowns, and fantasizing equally about social events they would grace with their presence.

Mari was satisfied to find that she had little to do with them, or for them. Two quiet house slaves, women in prim dimity dresses and starched caps, attended to their needs, and took turns following after them as chaperone on their outings.

Mrs. Coward usually kept her maid close by her, part companion and part parcel-carrier. It seemed to Mari that her mistress managed to visit just about every commercial establishment in town. Milliners, dress-makers, silversmiths and locksmiths, shoe-makers and even a wig-maker, all received their share of attention.

Mrs. Coward's voice broke into Mari's wandering thoughts.

"Yes – as Captain Tuckett and Captain Coward intend stopping by the Treasury on some business before going on, Perdita shall accompany Hannah and me, and we'll set out with them. It is not so very far to promenade, and the exercise shall do me good."

This being settled, as far as she was concerned, she smiled around the table as though conferring a favor.

"We'll walk and see a little more of the shops on this fine morning. It won't be long before we are back in the quiet of Plinhimmon," she added.

Mari hid a pleased smile, and scurried to clear dishes away to the kitchen, anxious to stay in favor with both matrons.

Mrs. Coward had avoided her husband's eye while arranging to accompany him on the walk to the race meeting. He would have preferred to go alone with his friend, leaving the women to "fuss and froth," as he put it, to get themselves under way, whilst their menfolk idled along at their own leisurely pace.

Being included in the Coward party for the outing to Annapolis, even as a general dog's body without a penny in her pocket, was an unexpected treat. Mari had never attended a horse race before, though her father, she well knew, had long been an afficionado of the sport.

On this race day, the women and the two captains, had perhaps a mile to walk to the race-course, just outside the city gate. They made a leisurely progression, initially to the Treasury building on Public Circle for Tuckett to conclude some business he had with the proprietor of the coffee house opposite his tavern.

Mari followed Mrs. Coward and Hannah strolling down North East Street with Captain Coward, admiring a few of the grander houses.

.By this time there was a steady stream of people, making their way toward the city gate, where Mrs. Tuckett and her daughters were to wait for the others. Mari observed one or two fine-looking carriages moving along quite smoothly as the crowd parted and fell back with good humor to cede passage to the gentry.

It was evident that a significant number of Annapolis citizens prided themselves on being second-to-none when it came to sporting the latest in fashion. The well-appointed carriages contained elegantly-dressed parties, and there were several sedan chairs with equally well turned out occupants, relaxing in comfort and entertaining themselves by eyeing the throng.

All the world and his uncle, it seemed, was set on parading with the rest of the town's society to chance a few pistoles on competing horse flesh, and to enjoy whatever other contests might be offered as diversion between the races.

The small party, with Mari trailing after, moved on toward the race course, negotiating Church Circle, where St. Anne's beckoned all to prayer from its hill-top perch. They proceeded along West Street where the press of people increased until it was quite a challenge for Mari to keep up with the Cowards and their host.

Eventually passing the town gate, they found themselves at the edge of a large, flat meadow, with a series of posts marking out a huge track, over the far side of which bubbled a clear fountain.

It was a festive sight, with a motley crowd pressing around the track, making and taking wagers, setting out picnics, gossiping and arguing about everything under the sun.

The fashionable set entertained and scandalized, sitting in their smart equipages to have a better view of the races. Mrs. Tuckett and her gaggle of girls, did the same, not to emulate their betters, as Mrs. Tuckett put it, but to ease her legs, which would surely give out if she had to stand for long. It was simply practical, and afforded a better view, anyway.

The only unpleasantness was an odious smell from the belching tannery nearby, but a brisk breeze from the Chesapeake dispersed it enough to prevent it from marring the enjoyment.

"It's so much better these days," Mrs. Tuckett was saying to her husband.

"Do you remember, when they used to run the races straight, right along West Street, all the way to Three Mile Oak? Couldn't see anything. They were gone in a flash, and that's all you saw. Don't know whose idea it was to make them go around a track, but you can watch it from beginning to end now. It's much more satisfactory."

Ben Tuckett was surveying the crowd with interest, nodding automatically as his wife chattered on. His daughters giggled and preened, as though every unattached young man passing by were ogling them.

"Much better," agreed Coward, doing his duty by his hostess.

"If I'm right, they had use of a circle track in New York years ago. In England, horse racing's been called 'the sport of Kings,' and His Majesty and his friends have shown little interest in sharing the enjoyment with lesser folk.

"But here, it seems, everyone likes to have a good time, and so they introduced the round tracks at which the crowd can see everything, and get their money's worth."

135

Then, laughing, "At least now you know immediately whether you've lost the farm!"

Mrs. Tuckett's face mimed shock and horror at the thought, though she indulged in a fit of the giggles.

Unregarded and ignored, Mari had wandered a distance from the back of the phaeton. She looked around her to take in the setting and all the activity. She could see the spire of St. Anne's and the roofs of some of the finest buildings in Maryland, and, across the track, a company of militia, bivouacked. Around her, everyone was assessing the horses that were about to be off on the first of their two three-mile heats.

Mari liked the look of a large bay horse with a dark mane, and a white flash down his face. He was a handsome beast. She was struck by the muscles glistening on his haunches and the depth of his great, brown chest.

He was lined up in the middle of the five horses, nervously waiting for the start of the race, his ears twitching back and forth. The bay was scratching the earth with his forefoot, arching his neck, then bucking and backing energetically, making his rider, a small black youth, work hard to stay in his saddle and keep his mount pointing down the course. He had about him an air of alertness, almost anxiety, suggesting to Perdita, who knew little about horses or racing, that he was simply raring to go.

She noticed Captain Tuckett, also, was looking admiringly at the beast.

"Selim," she heard him say to Captain Coward. "Terrible Selim, they call him. And you can see why."

"Strange name," said Coward. "Where's that from?"

"He was a foal of Selima, perhaps the greatest horse ever to come here from England. But you can tell from their names, of course, that they are of Arabian blood.

"All the best horses are from England I reckon, though there are those who would disagree and say we now have some splendid home-bred animals, fit to take on any import."

Tuckett was warming to his subject.

"If we don't yet, we are certain to make up the difference soon."

He beamed at the scene around him with great satisfaction. Since being on land, he had found a considerable knowledge of horses useful and entertaining for the guests at his tavern during the town's spring and fall race meetings, which attracted visitors from throughout the region and as far afield as New York and the Carolinas.

He took particular pleasure of a Sunday in walking up the hill to St. Anne's to study the horses tied up outside the church, some of them fine thoroughbreds belonging to local gentry.

He found the scene outside more interesting than the sermons inside, although he never admitted such to Mrs. Tuckett, who, herself, for all her professed piety, often found herself paying more attention to the fashions and bonnets around her than the ministrations from the pulpit.

Occasionally, after the service, an impromptu sporting challenge would send two or more owners to the track to settle a wager, and he never missed these spectacles.

"Selim's a horse of Samuel Galloway," he continued, pausing to look admiringly again at the excited horse.

"Isn't a one here today that can beat 'im, I'll wager. Hardly lost a race yet, and he's been running nine years. Takes a good horse to best him. Believe only Figure did so at Marlboro' last year."

Captain Tuckett's musings were cut short by a sudden roar from the crowd as the crack of a pistol sent the skittering group of horses thundering away, their hooves digging hard into the ground and throwing up small clouds of dust with every powerful stride.

Caught up in the air of excitement, Mari watched the big bay take the lead quickly as he sped round the posts, streaking past the town's skyline, the army tents, then the fountain, and finally, chest heaving and legs pounding so that the thick veins bulging from his muscles seemed likely to burst, make the last, winning effort up the slight incline to the finish line.

If he could do the same in the next heat, he would win his owner a pretty sum and a silver plate, she had heard.

As she quietly congratulated herself on picking the winner of the first race, she was startled when a small black pig suddenly sped by her, chased by a dozen or more youths, shouting and laughing, who took turns in diving on the squealing animal, which repeatedly squirmed its way out of their arms without too much trouble.

"It's greased."

A voice she recognized came over her shoulder, and she turned to find the sailor Stewart Dean smiling at her fascination with the scene. "If one of' them can hang onto it, it's his to take home. His supper will be served!" added the young man as he grasped her arm and tugged her out of the way of the lively, squealing pig, which had doubled back through the crowd to hurtle past them again.

They laughed as the noisy little group moved off, still in pursuit of the slippery prey.

"Would you believe, I favored the winner in the first race," she boasted in an attempt to keep the conversation with this young man going.

"If you could do that regularly, you'd be a rich woman quite quickly, well..if you could afford the wager," said Stewart Dean.

"But it isn't so easy. It can be a fool's game. You had a lucky choice maybe, beginner's luck. That's all."

He was brought up short by a pert look from her, and hastened to add, mock seriously, "Or, then again, Mistress, I expect you're a fine judge of horse flesh. We sailors size up boats better."

"Oh, don't put a damper on it. It's just so much fun."

"Well, it's fine for the rich and dandy. They can afford it all, but more ordinary folk, perhaps, should watch their pennies."

"And enjoy," said Mari. "It's an occasion for a holiday, and good times."

She wanted to keep the warmth of the moment alive.

"For the likes of me, it's just a chance to make a modest wager," said Dean. Unfortunately, my money wasn't on your horse."

"I'm sorry about that. But, maybe, your horse will do better in the next run. That, likely, would put a smile on your face."

"Not this time, it won't. My horse didn't make the distance."

"What's that?"

"Well, if a horse is too far behind when the winner crosses the line, it is eliminated. Look down the course. See that red flag. There, just after the bend."

Her gaze followed his gesture and she saw the small marker beside the track.

"To qualify for the next heat, a horse must have passed that flag when the winner crosses the finish line," said Dean.

"And yours hadn't reached it?"

He managed to look gloomy and comical at the same time.

"That's right. So it was eliminated. The flag's position is set, depending on the length of the race. In a two-mile race like this, it's around 100 yards. But it would be further away for a longer race."

Gazing around, Mari noticed a crowd forming along one side of the course. She saw they were watching two slave girls line up, apparently to run against each other.

"All sorts of contests go on at the races," said Dean. "There's lots of time to fill between the heats. There's always a break to let the horses rest."

"How long does it last?" asked Mari..

"Depends," said Dean. "Short races it might be fifteen minutes, but it can be up to thirty minutes for longer runs."

"What are those girls going to race for?"

"Don't know. I doubt it will be for much, maybe for a new cap, or a shift. But there'll be some prize for the winners of all the events. Maybe a saddle and bridle, a tankard, silver spoons or a sword. For the actual races, also money. Sometimes, quite a lot of it.

"There'll probably be some wrestling and boxing. Maybe a cudgel fight. Often there's dancing competitions, fiddling, singing and whistling, too. The winners could get a new shirt, or a bolt of cloth, or a hat with a ribbon. Dancing could be for a pair of shoes or silver buckles."

He turned a roguish look on her before saying, "How about a pair o' fine silk stockings for the fairest maid in the crowd? You could win that. It's mostly fun, with all sorts of diversions. It's like a big party, really. Those girls over there, they're going to run against each other for something. "

"Is that why those girls are racing – for the prize?"

Dean shook his head.

"Not only that. They mayn't have any option. Their masters could have ordered them to run, as excuse for a wager, knowing they're fleet of foot. It's just another diversion for the gentry between horse races. Entering a slave in a race isn't any different for them than entering a horse."

Mari noticed that one of the girls was taller and slimmer, with longer legs, and fancied her the likely winner, but it was the short sturdy one who tore away to cross the line first, her skirts flying, her bare feet barely touching the ground.

Her white teeth sparkled as, breathlessly, she accepted her reward - a new, white cotton shift, which she rolled up neatly and tucked firmly under her arm. It seemed to Mari that, whether she was a willing runner or not, she was quite pleased with her prize.

"Are you of these parts?" asked Mari, starting to feel easy with her new acquaintance.

"No. I'm off a ship that's in Oxford, down the bay. Cap'n wanted to come to the races, but had to go to Baltimore and left me here, anyway. Captain Tuckett was kind enough to invite me to supper tonight, so I'm able to fill my time nicely until Coxen gets back."

"There's a coincidence now," said Mari. "You know Captain Coward, of Plinhimmon, in Oxford, brought me here. You met him at the tavern yesterday."

"Yes, I know. He's a good reputation, a fair and regarded skipper."

"Maybe, but he takes no nonsense from anyone."

"There's talk of him bringing a girl over as a cabin boy on his last voyage," Dean teased her.

"Everyone's fascinated of it. Strangest thing, eh? They say he's put her to work on his estate. I'd love to hear her tell her story. And so would everyone else."

He looked at her with an amused, expectant gaze, but she avoided the hopeful enquiry in his eyes.

"We weren't really introduced," she said, and gave a deprecating shrug.

In her discomfort, she looked around the crowd, and noticed Captain Coward talking to a familiar, ominous and stooping figure. After gazing for a few seconds, she realized that Coward's companion was the same character who had prodded and scrutinized her on the deck of *Integrity*, when she had arrived in Oxford. She stiffened in disgust at the thought of him.

Stewart Dean noted her reaction and was puzzled.

"What's the matter? Do you know that gentleman? He looks a sober enough type to me from the cut of his cloth."

"Sober or not, he's no gentleman at all, I'll warrant."

She felt herself hot and tense, but her voice became cool and arrogant. Seeing Dean's startled expression, she realized that such a tone must sound strange coming from a mere servant.

She faltered, "I don't know him really, but he appalls me."

It sounded inadequate, but she could hardly explain her instinctive revulsion against Thorberry. The memory of cold, greedy eyes, and hard fingers twisting her shoulder came fresh in her mind.

She made a dismissive gesture toward the two men, and was about to speak to Dean, when she saw Thorberry suddenly turn toward her to stare. Again, she felt herself under the penetrating scrutiny of those hard eyes.

With a nod of his head, Thorberry shook Coward's hand, gave a slight bow, and walked toward the track where the horses were lining up for the second heat.

Mari felt a sense of dread descend on her.

Stewart studied her, a frown on his face, then offered her his arm to return to where the Tuckett and Coward daughters were hooting with amusement around their carriage.

Mari hesitated, then declined his arm. Her stomach was still tight with anxiety, and she didn't want to provoke comment from young Bridget. She wished she could just disappear into the crowd. A puzzled Dean followed her back to her party.

The next few days were a buzz of activity as the return to the backwater of Plinhimmon drew near. The Assembly Room ball was a highlight for the girls, but Mari's role was limited to hustling about helping to primp hair and prepare dresses.

Stewart Dean had accepted the Tucketts' invitation to supper after the races and had indicated to Mari that he hoped she would be able to accompany the families to the ball. Mari knew there was no question of her attending, but was warmed by his attention.

The day after the ball the Cowards set out for home. It seemed as though they were all out of sorts, the girls sullen at leaving both their friends and the town's attractions, and Mrs. Coward professing fatigue and a readiness to return home to her own hearth. Captain Coward endured the fuss of departure in an abstracted fashion, and spent a good while gazing at the Annapolis shoreline until it faded from view.

XII

Back at Plinhimmon, Mari sought out Betsy to give her the news of her brother. She found her hanging laundry behind the house.

"Betsy, you won't believe this," she called. "I've met Liam."

Betsy stopped pegging the sheets, turned toward her, and looked dumb-founded.

"What?" she asked. "What did you just say?"

"I've found Liam, met him, and talked to him," said Mari.

Betsy could hardly grasp the words.

"Where? How? Are you serious?" she said.

"He's with Mr. Thorberry. You remember that horrible man on the boat. He's now working for him in Virginia."

The words stopped Betsy dead. She stood, gasping for breath.

"Are you sure?" she asked. "Are you sure it was him?"

Mari took the crumpled paper package from her pocket and handed it to Betsy.

"He asked me to give you this," she said.

Betsy opened it, saw the snippets of Liam's brown hair, and tears started to trickle down her cheeks.

"He said he would look for you, and, if necessary, wait for you," said Mari, who then, called to task by Mrs. Coward, had to leave her friend standing tear-stained and bemused, but smiling with hope and unspoken thoughts.

Later, with the hot, sultry days of summer overlaying their quiet routine, Betsy extracted every detail of Mari's meeting with Liam. For her it meant that her selfless odyssey would likely prove worthwhile.

"He will always be my Liam," said Betsy, more than once.

* * *

Mrs. Coward relished the homecoming. Her daughters were restless and fretful, wishing themselves back in Annapolis gossiping with the Tuckett sisters.

Bridget was particularly discontented, but was partly mollified by the prospect of a trip over the creek to the Chamberlaine family at their Plaindealing estate.

John Coward, mind on his next Atlantic run, was easy and indulgent with his women folk, compliant with any suggestion for neighborly visits. He knew that whilst away with *Integrity,* his family would be pretty well isolated at Plinhimmon. He was resigned to go with them to the Chamberlaines, and told Mrs. Coward to set the date promptly. He would do his social duty.

For Mari, the Annapolis excursion had at least provided some variety. Now she was back again as general dog's body, dragging through the desultory heat of late summer. The only pleasing event on the horizon was the absence of the Coward family for a week or so.

She would be glad to see the back of them all. She was sick of Plinhimmon and its folk. The day of their departure she was relegated to doing more laundry.

It was heavy, tiring work in the August humidity. Mari wiped her face with a piece of flour sack as sweat ran in itchy trickles down her back. She found herself clenching her teeth as snatches of excited chatter and giggles sounded from upstairs.

She poked away grimly with a laundry stick at the sodden, heaving mass in the huge boiling kettle, and cast a sour look over her shoulder at a fresh burst of merriment from the Coward girls.

She glanced over to where Sarah was humming quietly to herself as she put-up peaches at the kitchen table. The smell of fruit, spices and raw brandy, scented the heavy air. Betsy was a picture of composure, sitting by the window mending shirts with fine, painstaking stitches. She looked unusually content.

Mari reflected bitterly that when the laden lines of laundry were finally dry, she and Sarah had the drudgery of ironing it to look forward to. She could gauge the heat of the stubby, flat irons lined up on trivets over the fireplace. Betsy said to lift the iron and spit on it to see if it was ready. If the spit sizzled and dried up but didn't explode back at you, it was alright. Mari was disgusted but didn't say so. Spit on the iron! Her throat felt dry and choked with dust. She longed for a cool drink.

Her mood swung between building resentment and enduring self-pity. Both Betsy and Sarah did a fine job of ignoring her. Relief came, finally, when Mrs. Coward called her away from the detested wash tub to go and help the girls sort out the upstairs linen press.

Mari fled to the upper landing where open windows afforded a slight but welcome breeze. Penelope was sitting on the floor, daydreaming and idly brushing through broken tobacco leaves. Mixed with dried herbs they were strewn in the press to freshen it and repel moths and other pests.

As Mari knelt beside her, they were distracted by the sounds of a spat coming from the girls' bedroom. Suddenly the door crashed open and the other two sisters spilled out into the hall. Bridget was red-faced and furious.

"Hannah, you should be slapped and locked in the cellar. None of that's true. Everyone's just jealous of me," she snapped.

She swung round on Mari.

"What are you smiling about, scullery maid? You won't be so merry when Papa sells you on to Mr. Thorberry, which he'll do soon as we are back from visiting the Chamberlaines. Mr. Thorberry is to take you to Virginia next time he's in town – and good riddance."

Mari's face flushed with agitation. The thought of Thorberrry brought back the memory of his cold gaze and grasping fingers on *Integrity*, and of that brusque nod of the head and hand-shake with Captain Coward at the Annapolis races. It unnerved her.

She pretended indifference, but found her hands shaking as she folded sheets for the press. She believed Bridget was telling the truth this time, and not just peevishly tormenting her.

Fortunately, Betsy appeared at the door just then to direct the sisters down to their mother and friends in the parlor, and Bridget flounced off, a meek Penelope in tow. Betsy noticed her young friend's distress.

"What's the matter? You look flustered."

She stood there, regarding Mari closely and looking more like a respectable governess than a bonded housemaid in her simple, brown dress, enlivened by a crisp snowy collar and flounced sleeves, old fashioned but attractive in its way.

She didn't smile, but continued to study Mari, who was choked with emotion and anxiety about ever having a prospect of escape. They had had very little chance to talk to each other in recent days.

"What is it, chuck – are you down in the mouth at being left behind this trip?" Betsy asked.

Mari ceased folding and re-folding linen, and blurted out, "Betsy! Bridget says that the Captain intends to sell me to that man, Thorberry, as soon as maybe. Say it's not so, Betsy!"

Betsy looked taken aback. She looked away from Mari, standing silent and thoughtful for a moment. Mari thought she was evading an answer.

"Girl, how would I know?"

She turned to leave, but then hesitated.

"I have to say, though, I think Mrs. Coward is of a mind to pass one of us on."

She paused again, and seeing the other's look of despair, offered quickly, "Maybe it will be me. Thorberry wouldn't be my choice for a master, but at least I could find myself with Liam."

She directed a tentative smile at Mari, who was unconvinced and fumbled awkwardly with the contents of the press. If anyone were to be let go, Mari knew it would be her. Betsy was valued, whereas she herself had never really suited.

There was little chance of mulling it over further, however, as the rest of the morning was taken up with getting the family on their way.

Mari helped Sarah and Betsy fit out baskets of food, including some peaches and preserves to take as gifts. Mrs. Coward directed last minute instructions and a farewell to Sarah, who waved them off from the small dock.

Watching the boat carrying the Cowards and Betsy move slowly round the point, Mari felt some relief, knowing that the house would be quiet and relaxed for a few days. She turned to walk amongst the apple trees. She was tired, and contrasted the laughing, care-free departure of the Coward girls to her own sorry plight. Her mood sank. How had she come to this pass?

Oddly, she felt no particular longing for the luxury of her old home. She had thought mistakenly that she was fleeing that house for love and adventure, and freedom to live as she chose.

Instead, she had traveled ignorantly into a trap, and could not now see how to escape it. She furiously berated herself for her naivety. Her thoughts were bitter. Here she was, indentured and fit only to be left with the slaves, bound to do her master's bidding with no reward and no hope for betterment.

She studied her work-scoured hands. Her fair hair, she knew, was bleached to straw from being out in the fields so much helping Robin and Peter. It poked out in all directions from her hand-me-down cap. Her complexion and arms were brown as berries, much to the amusement of the Coward girls.

Even the slaves regarded her as some kind of oddity, although Robin had at least shown friendship. Sarah was not unkind or hostile, but sometimes, behind her usually calm, impassive face, Mari detected exasperation and a distinct lack of sympathy.

Mari Westin had had advantages denied to most, and had squandered them. Why should she deserve the friendship and goodwill of such as Sarah?

Her thoughts turned heavily to Thorberry. Even if Bridget had merely been taunting her, the idea of being sold to him left Mari sick and hollow inside.

In the back of her mind there was also another worry - the imminent return of the Coward sons from school in Philadelphia. She recalled their behavior on their last visit home. They had surprised her out in the fields one day, at the back of the Plinhimmon estate.

She had not slept well in the heat of the attic, and so had risen early and slipped out to wander restlessly in the fresh early morning air. She had trudged aimlessly to the far land boundary of Captain Coward's holdings, ending up back by the shore line after circling the fields.

Passing a stretch of woodland, just out of sight of the house, she stood, wondering for the thousandth time how she could possibly make shift for herself and get back to England.

She toyed with the idea of playing the cabin boy again. That trick would not get by in Oxford, but if she could make her way to Annapolis, or, better, Philadelphia, it might be possible. The larger and busier the port, the better, she reasoned.

She was suddenly startled out of her reverie by the noisy rush of a flock of red-winged blackbirds taking scattered flight over her head. They had been flushed from the woods by some disturbance, but, even as she turned to look, an arm came around her neck from behind, and her legs were kicked from under her.

A hot, damp hand clamped her mouth, stifling her breathing as she tried to cry out. She fell awkwardly twisting to the ground, tangled with her attacker. She confusedly caught the smell of fish mixed with that of applejack and male sweat, and heard hoots and shouts of laughter.

The Coward boys and a visiting friend had decided to have some fun.

Her attacker lay splayed over her, grunting and pinning her to the ground. She grasped the hand over her mouth in an effort to wrench it away. Twisting and turning to get free, but, although not a full- grown man, he was surprisingly strong and enjoyed the struggle, laughing at her until she bit hard on his hand and drew blood. That stopped him for a moment as he yelped and regarded his hand in stupefied amazement.

"Savage little slut!"

His face went dull red with ugly temper, and he brought back his fist, arching his body to put some force behind it.

"No – Harry, stop!"

The youngest Coward son, Richard, grabbed the friend's wrist and hauled back on it.

"I can hear some-one coming," said Richard.

"Don't be an ass, Rich." William, the elder brother curled a contemptuous lip.

"Better not spoil her face, though, Harry," he leered. "It won't go unnoticed. Move yer knee man, and I'll get her skirt out of the way."

Harry leaned an arm across her throat, nearly choking her, and quickly rammed his knee back between hers as William wrenched her dress up around her hips.

His friend was fumbling at his britches, when Richard, looking frightened and horrified, called in a hoarse voice, "Stop it – stop it, you two. Pa's coming. Pa's coming. William! Harry!"

William froze, looking up, his leer wiped from his face.

"Harry git down to the boat."

As quickly as they had ambushed Mari, the three of them jumped up, and fled, stumbling through the trees toward the water.

Scrambling to her knees and trying to pull her clothes into some sort of order, the last Mari saw of them was Richard's young, distressed face looking desperately back at her as he followed the other two. She was panting, and realized that the sound coming from her was made by dry sobs in her throat.

Trembling in the rough grass, she listened, and realized there was, indeed, someone approaching from the other side of the slope in the direction of the orchard. She recognized Captain Coward's voice, rumbling in a monologue interspersed with an occasional murmur from some-one else.

Standing up hastily, she snatched her cap from the grass, and, pulling it on, set off for the house. She tried to walk briskly, though her legs felt weak and unsteady. The men didn't notice her.

When she gained the crest of the slope down to the orchard, they had turned off at an angle over the fields, leaving her able to scurry back to the safety of the kitchen.

There, she set to, meekly and swiftly going about the morning chores, still trembling in reaction, her feelings a mixture of fright, fury and mortification. She said nothing to anyone.

Remembering the boys' behavior that day, Mari knew that it was only a matter of time before such a scene would be repeated. Away from them, she knew they were stupid, inexperienced young men she could normally best with wit, but the mood claiming them that morning had been ugly, and she could not rely on being so fortunate again in dodging their clutches.

Her mind fretted anew at the idea of escape. How could she hope to get away from Plinhimmon? She had nothing to sustain her, no clothes, no money, no friends. Where would she go anyway? As Perdita, she was something of a local curiosity, so even if she did run away, everyone in the area knew she was bonded to Captain Coward. She would be hauled back and punished.

She thought of the slave, Peter, with his wiry strength and knowledge of the land and waterways. He had been brought back twice after running away, according to Betsy, and had the marks on his back to prove it.

Her spirits spiraled down and hot tears welled up. She did not usually cry, but the tears seemed to come of their own accord. Sinking to her knees under one of the trees, she gave in to self-pity, oblivious to the tranquility and beauty of the water scene.

* * *

148

"Perdita, Perdita! What's this? Are things so bad? What has happened? You're sunk in grief, girl. Ssh-ssh- ease yourself, calm a little, please. Tell me what's wrong."

Curled up under the apple trees, Mari was horrified to hear the warm, kind tones of Stewart Dean's voice. She recognized it straight away, and was ashamed to look him in the face.

She stared, instead, at his boots, planted in the grass next to her, as she gulped back sobs, and scrubbed her face with her apron. She sat, backed up against a tree trunk, unable to say a thing in explanation.

Of all the people she had met since arriving in America, Stewart Dean had made a singular impression, though from force of circumstance they had had little enough acquaintance.

Nevertheless, on occasions out with the Coward women, she had encountered him. He had been civil, humorous and kind, and had seemed to try to extend civility to the Cowards' maid-of-all-work. He put Mari in mind of her brother. A natural good humor lay beneath an alert but grave countenance.

"You're surely not so depressed because you've not been included on an outing?"

She ignored his question, to ask, "What are you doing here, Mr. Dean? The family left not so long since to go visiting. You've just missed them."

"I know, I know. We've brought some casks over for Captain Coward. We had the impression that the captain and his ladies were not leaving until tomorrow, but we passed them on the water. We'll leave the stuff anyhow. You haven't said, though, what is the matter. Why so desolate?"

She looked at his face. He had shifted to crouch down beside her. He was in trim sailor's dress, and the blue cloth of his coat pulled tight across his shoulder as he propped one arm against the tree to steady himself, the other elbow resting on his knee.

His gray eyes were direct and concerned, and Mari thought she could detect a faint scent of orris root powder about him, mingling with the smell of apple wood. She looked toward the kitchen. There was no sign of anyone else.

"Tell me how I can help you, Perdita? I insist. I've heard the story – not to say rumors – of how you came to be here at Plinhimmon, but I have not heard your version of the adventure. Tell me."

149

His voice was insistent, and his gaze focused on her.

She was suddenly overwhelmed by an urge to confide in him. She started, awkward and embarrassed, but found herself pouring out her woes and feelings as she had never confided in anyone before, not to her father, not to Miss Pardoe or even Aunt Matty, and not to anyone at Plinhimmon – that was for certain.

He heard her out in silence until she finally ran out of words. Embarrassment and uncertainty flooded back as she waited for him to speak. He sat for a while, staring out over the water, whilst she wondered what was going on in his head.

Was he dismayed at her litany of distress? Why hadn't she kept her sorrows private and not rushed to unburden herself?

"Coxen will be taking *Hazard* down the bay at the end of next week. We should be well stocked and loaded by then."

Dean paused, and chewed on a grass stem.

"It will be my last voyage with him as 'prentice seaman."

Again, a contemplative pause. Then, suddenly, he leaned forward to give an assessing stare.

"You're not the usual kind of kitchen maid, and you're not any usual kind of lady, are you, Perdita? I don't suppose you still have your brother's clothes do you?"

Tears forgotten, Mari stared back, speechless. What was he saying?

"Well? You managed the passage over here under your own initiative, girl. Do you think you could manage it back with some help?"

She was dumbfounded, but had sense enough to scramble a reply.

"What do you mean? Work again as a cabin boy? Your captain wouldn't take me. I'd be hauled back to Plinhimmon in no time."

Her voice sounded squeaky and wavering to her ears.

"No, no. That's just not possible."

He chewed some more on the grass.

"But we might smuggle you aboard, and stow you somewhere. *Hazard* is not so roomy a vessel, but I think it could be done. Not comfortable. But possible."

She held her breath. Her heart was hammering. Hope shot through her. Could it be done? Was he serious? She could hardly believe her ears.

"What do I have to do?"

She realized grimly that she didn't care what had to be done – she would go.

"What about the other crew?"

Her hopes pitched down as he frowned.

"The only problem I would anticipate would be with the first mate. Captain Coxen stays on his deck, aft, doles out his orders, and trusts us to do the rest. We've a good crew.

"There are a couple of them from Captain Coward's *Integrity*. Horrocks is one. They don't want to wait around for Coward's next sailing, but are signed on with Coxen to go back to England. They would assist us, if I ask, I'm sure. They can then pretend no knowledge if you're discovered, so their pay would be safe."

He leaned back on his elbow, contemplating his boots as if to decide whether they were worth the money he had paid for them.

"What about you though, Stewart Dean? What would happen if I were to be discovered?"

Mari already knew. He would be stripped of his position, probably flogged into the bargain, and docked pay. He looked back up at her.

"You won't be discovered. Don't fret. I'll take care for both our sakes."

"But, Mr. Dean, why do this for me? You hardly know me at all, and it would be a serious enough business."

His eyes roamed over the water.

"I have, if I don't mistake me, a certain standing in Captain Coxen's eyes. He's a tough old customer, but never fear."

He glanced back up at her.

"He won't pitch you overboard in the middle of the Atlantic, and he values me as a sailor. I've put in a hearty apprenticeship with him, and earned his special esteem on a couple of occasions."

He sat up again, and plucked another blade of grass to chew.

"I'll come for you on the night of the thirtieth, after moonrise. Look for me by the dock. You have the courage, Perdita?"

She nodded vigorously.

"But – why are you so willing to help me, Stewart Dean? You haven't answered."

He rose to his feet, dusted his britches, and extended a hand to raise her up, then cradled her hand in both of his, looking into her face. He was broad shouldered and vigorous looking, though not overly handsome.

She felt total trust in him, and did not doubt his intentions, but had to give him the opportunity to state his bargain if there was one. She kept her own gaze, unwavering, and saw his eyes soften. He put up a hand and traced her jaw-line with his fingers.

"No conditions, Perdita. You simply don't belong here. You're like a captive bird, unable to fly. I think you are meant for a different life, though, I have to say, your gentleman from Virginia has let his countrymen down. The man must be a complete fool, if he's still living and breathing."

A smile transformed his face.

"You won't have to worry about meeting me aboard. I'm coming to fetch you myself."

She felt a wave of relief as he pressed her hand.

He paused and added, "In fact, it may be a better thing if I visit you a couple of times before the thirtieth. That way I'll be accepted as a smitten sailor, and your inclination to tarry by the dock won't be remarked. Keep your spirits up. I shan't let you down, Perdita."

He gave a salute, smiled again, and jogged off to the dock, where Horrocks waited.

Mari stayed amidst the apple trees, and watched him go. Her spirits soared. When she went back to the kitchen, Sarah gave a knowing look and smile. Dean, Mari thought, was already accepted.

He came three times over the following week, as though paying court to her. There were no Coward family members to interfere or chide her, though when she thought of it, her heart baulked at the very idea of Captain John Coward casting his gimlet eye over the situation. She pushed that thought away.

On his third visit Dean asked Mari her real name, and she almost blurted it out but checked herself in time. She imagined her father thundering his anger at his daughter's temerity, outrage and disbelief on his face.

"No, Stewart Dean. I can't tell even you. No-one must know my name. It must remain secret."

Her voice sounded like that of a stubborn, silly child to her ears.

"I'm sorry – forgive me. I must seem churlish, and ungrateful."

Now she was stiff and formal, and turned anxiously to him, hoping he was not offended. He gave a rueful, sideways look she recognized.

"No, don't apologize."

He looked away.

"I think I understand. The least you feel you can do is protect your father's name from something of a catastrophe. I shan't ask you again."

He frowned.

Mari was contrite and upset at hurting his feelings. Why had she always withheld her name, anyway? Perhaps, he was right. It was something of a salvage operation. To say that she had made a fool of herself, didn't allow for the half of it. But, no, Will Herrion and Perdita must remain forever separate from Mari Westin.

She became aware that Stewart was brushing his coat, preparing to leave again.

"Remember – look for me an hour after moonrise tomorrow, Perdita."

Mari nodded dumbly, and walked him to his horse. He had arrived by road this time. He mounted, looked down, gave a final salute, and was gone. Mari could hardly wait for the next day when he would come by boat to take her home at last.

XIII

August 30, 1769 - Tonight she would be gone from this place, Plinhimmon, that John Coward called home but to her was little more than a prison.

Mari knew that Stewart would not come for her until after sunset, but she had a surging impatience to be off, and forced herself to stay away from the orchards and fields of the estate to avoid suspicion.

The family were due back in two days, and Sarah had fussed some, keeping everyone about their business so that everything would be in good order.

Mari made no complaint, dutifully occupying herself around the house until the Maryland dusk settled its humid hush on Plinhimmon and only the lapping waters of the Chesapeake Bay disturbed the evening quiet.

She looked over to where Sarah was mending a shirt. The slave woman sat in a rocking chair by the fire place, the flames reflecting from the planes of her dark face like moonlight off mahogany. She wore a simple brown homespun dress with an old, clean, and patched apron over it. Underneath a muslin cap, her hair was close cropped and flecked with gray.

Mari was almost stifled with anxiety, wishing that the woman would go up to bed. As though she had picked up the thought from the girl's head, Sarah suddenly dropped her hands into her lap. Holding a cambric shirt, with needle and thread still attached, she leaned back and closed her eyes with weariness. The chair rocked with small movements, to and fro, to and fro.

Fiercely, Mari willed her not to doze off in front of the fire as the minutes ground by. Then, Sarah sighed and shook her head, bending over stiffly to place the unfinished shirt in a work basket by her feet.

"Can wait 'til mornin'. No rush – nobody here short of a mended shirt."

She straightened up and stood looking out at the darkening evening.

"I go and rest my body, Perdita."

Sarah made for the back steps to the loft, but paused with a hand on the knob of the rail, and looked back quizzically at the scullery maid.

"Your sailor man – he come callin' tonight?"

Mari tensed, not daring to reply or look up, giving an exaggerated shrug instead.

Sarah smiled, muttering, "Secrets hard to keep, girl – watch your way, watch your way."

She paused as if about to say more, but shook her head again, smile gone, and started up the steps. Perversely, Mari suddenly wanted to call after her to stay and talk. She felt a desperate need to confide in someone, but Stewart had warned to let no-one know of their plan.

She was, anyway, prevented from saying anything by Robin, who suddenly swung open the kitchen door and came clumping in with a bucket of clean beach sand to strew on the kitchen floor in the morning after sweeping-out and the main chores were done. He looked over at Sarah, paused on the stairs.

"You alright, Sarah, momma? You lookin' weary, old woman."

Sarah flashed a smile at her favorite, and waved her hand dismissively at him.

"I just a mite tired, man, a mite tired. You'll see t'door and winders?"

"Surely, momma, get your body to rest."

The big man put the bucket in a corner, and turned to leave, taking an apple from the barrel on his way out.

"Things be easy, fer a couple days more, mebbe," he chuckled, closing the door behind him.

Left alone, Mari ceased the pretense of knitting spare potholders, and, dropping the thick wooden needles with her crude attempt into Sarah's work basket, she sat listening.

A few creaks and sighs came from above as Sarah settled down. She hoped Sarah would drop off quickly and sleep deeply. The last thing she wanted was her calling that it was time for the kitchen help to be abed.

Restless, she crossed to the scullery window to peer out. All was quiet inside and outside the house. The moon was rising, a full and shining orb. Stewart should soon be coming, and she imagined him

155

sculling quietly over the water. She wondered whether Sarah could possibly have guessed something.

In her time at Plinhimmon Mari had not had a close relationship with the slave woman, and had no confidence in reading her mind. Sarah went about her daily rounds with an inscrutable air. She had a serious, quiet demeanor, and, like Robin, seemed practiced in a passive rather than servile attitude

Now that she was about to take her chance at freedom, Mari found herself with the same mixed feelings she experienced when she had run away from home in London.

There was the same tension, the same waiting, the same pulsing hope and urge to flee, and the same fear of failure.

When she had fled her father's house in Conduit Street more than a year earlier, she had stupidly thought nothing through, but had reacted to the situation according to her needs and desires. She had trusted in her own quickness of wit and ability, her girlish guile, to get by.

She listened again.

The silence in the kitchen was punctuated only by the sound of ashes shifting in the fire grate. She thought it best to wait in the darkness downstairs so as not to risk making a noise going up to the loft and down again.

She felt confident that Sarah would sleep soundly, and there would be no problem from the men, who had trudged across the yard to their cabin for a taste of corn liquor which would put them safely asleep.

Settling in the fireside chair, Mari leaned back and closed her eyes, as Sarah had, her nerves taut. Finally, she rose and went over to the kitchen window to check the yard once more. There was a dim light in the men's cabin, but no sound. She returned to the rocking chair.

The days without the family had skimmed by. The house had been calm and easy, the men carrying out their usual duties, Mari doing Sarah's bidding. They had all eaten together in the kitchen, and it had been comfortable not to be constantly at the family's beck and call.

She tried to guess the family's reaction to her disappearance. Mrs. Coward might be relieved to have her gone. Her daughters, no doubt, would kick up a fuss for the sake of something to fuss about. She wondered whether Captain Coward would put a notice of a runaway in the *Gazette*. It was the usual practice.

156

Mari had read notices, offering rewards for the return of absconded slaves and servants. More often than not, it seemed they were caught, and paid a high price for a few days of freedom – the cord pattern of the lash on their backs as a decoration for life, or increased time in servitude if a bondservant. Some masters had runaway slaves branded, and others boasted of mutilating ears as constant reminders of the cost of freedom's lure.

She shuddered, and wondered what reward would be offered for a runaway scullery maid. Would it be more or less than the fifteen or twenty dollars they usually offered? What would the notice say?

"Absconded. Female Bond Servant, known as Perdita. No household skills. Reads and writes, and answers back impertinently!" She smiled sourly.

Would Captain Coward accuse her of stealing the clothes she wore? The thought of the notices of runaways caused her to stiffen with contempt at the pathetic description of the rags they had taken. Mari scornfully catalogued what she was wearing – one patched, ill-fitting, worn-to-death-hand-me-down dress, and a dingy, stringy cap.

She had been able to sneak occasional, quick looks at the newspaper while cleaning Captain Coward's office, ever wishing to find some mention of Bryce Hunter on one of the arriving ships. It was not likely, she now knew, but she had for a while stubbornly hoped.

Her thoughts were disturbed by the cinders shifting again in the hearth. Standing, she moved to the loft stairs to listen, realizing it would be necessary to creep up after all. She had left the bundle of her brother Tom's clothes wrapped in an old kerchief, by her sleeping mat.

She didn't wish to wake Sarah, but had to get the clothes now. They could keep the decrepit dress. Mari was going to wear her old cabin boy's outfit again, and hoped it would still fit.

Holding the stair rail with one hand, and her skirt out of the way with the other, she crept up the steps until her head was just above the loft floor. Through the shadows, it was just possible to make out Sarah's shape, lying huddled on her side on her thin palliasse like a bundle of laundry. The woman hardly seemed to breathe, she lay so still and silent.

The moon shone through the low windows with their sills almost at floor level. Old netting was hung over the opening to keep out mosquitoes, but one whined past Mari's ear. Dust tickled her nose.

157

Easing up from the narrow loft steps to sit on the floor, she could just reach her bundle by lying down and stretching her hand to them. As silently as she could, she crept back down the ladder.

The air of the kitchen seemed suddenly too close and heavy, and a sense of suffocation and a desperation to be outside gripped her.

Whatever happened, she would go now and wait by the water.

Stewart had said he would come an hour after dark. His ship was due to sail for England just before dawn. He had to get her aboard secretly. Mari had no idea how he would manage it, but she had to trust him.

At the bottom of the steps, she pulled off the hated scullion's dress, and quickly changed into britches and shirt. They still fit. The dress she bundled and dropped into the work basket, over the despised knitting attempt.

She listened again. All was still quiet. A feeling of lightness, almost euphoria, bubbled up in her. The urge to laugh aloud was almost irresistible. She had no possessions at all now to burden her. Crossing to the kitchen door, with her hand on the latch, she gave one last look around the room. There was no nostalgia, just her heart racing at the thought of fleeing.

Then, she suddenly froze, paralyzed with fear, feeling as though the hair on her head stood on end. The door latch was moving, lifting under her hand.

She started back, heart pounding in her throat as the heavy door swung inwards to reveal Robin's towering form blocking her. His eyes gleamed in the light from the kitchen embers, and she could smell his musky body odor and the liquor. Before she could move or make a sound, his hand shot out and grabbed her by the neck. He took in her appearance in a swift glance, and glared at her, head dipped slightly to one side.

"Well now, Perdita, Missee, where be we goin,' and all dressed like that?" he said.

Mari was devastated. There was no way she could get past this giant of a man. If he let her go, he would be blamed and punished for aiding and abetting her escape. Words choked in her throat.

"Please, Robin! Please, Robin!" she whispered hoarsely.

She looked behind him toward the dark water, marked out from the land by the silver gleam of reflected moonlight, and caught a glimpse of movement in the shadows. Could it be Stewart's boat coming over the creek?

Despair at being caught so close to escape wrenched her. Why had Robin come back to the house? As though he, also, sensed something, Robin looked back over his shoulder toward the water.

Together, they stood like a fixed tableau for what seemed endless moments. Robin's hand remained a vice around her neck. She could not escape. She knew her fate depended on this man she barely knew.

Then, as abruptly as he had seized her in the doorway of the cabin, Robin let her go and stood aside, saying nothing.

She staggered, a little off balance, and hesitated, looking at him. His eyes were unfathomable. He made no further move, though, so she stepped gingerly past him, still expecting the alarm to be raised, but none came. She ran toward the water.

Robin, still as stone, peered through the dark after Mari as she slipped away. Her light form had seemed to float over the ground as it disappeared into the gloom in the direction of the dock. He knew she was off with her sailor visitor, as he also knew the ship *Hazard* would be sailing from Oxford at dawn.

Everyone in and around the port was well aware of the comings and goings of any of the trading vessels. He could have, should have, stopped her. Seizing her at the kitchen door, and realizing her intent, he had felt such rage, he could have broken her neck. The feel of her slim, tender throat under his hand, and the sight of her eyes, wide and dark with fright, like a young animal caught in the hunter's trap, had drained the anger from him, and left his body tight with pain inside.

Staring after her, he knew his rage was at himself more than the girl. In his core, anger and envy churned together. It was strange, he thought.

This slip of a white girl had come here, sailing the wide ocean of her own accord, to land herself in a form of bondage to be used and despised, but had had the determination and spirit to seize an opportunity to escape when it came. Whether she would be successful, he doubted. Neither he nor Sarah, certainly not Peter, had really understood her.

He well knew plenty of poor white folk pledged themselves as bond servants for passage over the sea. They were sold on the auction block alongside slaves and prisoners, but not in chains. The white folk sold in chains were prisoners, sent into exile for their crimes.

Perdita, though, was different. She had followed a lover, it was said, and ended up in captivity of a kind, anyway.

His own plight as slave had not prevented him from having a sneaking, indulgent compassion for her. She had often made him smile with her shows of wit and youthful impulse.

He, too, had had a chance to flee, but had rejected it. One time the captain had been away at sea, Peter had tried to persuade him to break for the north to sign on one of the whaling ships out of Narragansett.

Why hadn't he gone with Peter that time? He knew that white men's trading ships had mixed crews from all parts of the world, and that whaling captains, in particular, had reputations for asking no questions when in need of crew.

He had hesitated though, in conflict. He had thought lovingly of Sarah, who had mothered and protected him when he first came to Plinhimmon, and he had opted for his bond with her, and the relative safety on the estate.

Peter had gone alone, but had not gotten far. He was captured trying to cross the Chester River. He had been well whipped on his return to Plinhimmon.. The man was at this moment lying in a corn-liquor stupor in their shared shack.

Robin knew he would join Peter and drink an equal share himself. It would be easier to claim drunkenness and ignorance when questioned about the runaway girl. He and Peter could, perhaps, have made it together to freedom that time. They had both been young and strong.

He thought again of Sarah. Now, he could not leave her in her old age.

A dull thud interrupted the flow of his thoughts. It was the unmistakable sound of a boat nudging the dock. Robin couldn't resist moving carefully down through the apple trees for a last glimpse of the fleeing girl, and was just in time to make out the silhouette of the craft pushing off from the shore.

There were two men in the boat, he saw in the moonlight, and, although they could not have seen him at all well under the trees, there was a sudden moment of stiffening as though they sensed his presence. The sailors sat frozen and alert, oars held splayed like damsel fly wings above the water. They looked toward his position, straining to see who was observing them.

A quiet murmur came from Mari. "Thank you, thank you."

She turned her face a last time toward Plinhimmon, and a pale hand sketched a salute in Robin's direction. He found himself returning the gesture, unseen, into the night.

As the farmhouse faded into the darkness, Dean and Horrocks pulled strongly across the creek, causing the small boat to rise and dip on the dark water. A light breeze feathered through Mari's hair, enhancing a sensation of freedom.

XIV

From aboard *Hazard*, Mari could hear the murmur of voices as two sailors yarned and supped their watch away.

"Don't worry," Stewart reassured her. "Captain Coxen and most of the crew are ashore for their last night."

"I'll go first," said Horrocks, promptly shinning up the ship's ladder and quickly signaling the others to follow.

"You next," said Stewart unceremoniously shoving Mari toward the steps.

Heart thumping, she climbed, thankful she was in man's garb again. Oil lamps, fore and aft, cast pools of light on the deck, and she could see Horrocks chaffing the on-watch sailors for a drink.

Stewart swiftly led her round the huge capstan and down a companionway to the lower deck.

To her surprise, there were no hammocks. Instead half dozen cots stretched end-to-end down each side of the ship, and each had sliding doors, painted white, to afford both some privacy and security for the sleeping men against the pitch of the ship in rough weather.

Stewart slid open the doors of his berth to show her her initial hiding place. It was the small space beneath his cot.

"It's just until we're underway," he said. "Once we're at sea you can hide in the cargo hold. It's much roomier."

She scrambled into the space. Stewart lowered the planks into position over her, replacing the mattress and bedding on top.

She lay squeezed into the narrow curve. He had stuffed some sacking and a blanket into the hollow to make it more comfortable for her, and, fortunately, she was thin enough to fit comfortably on her side, her back pressed against the hull.

A few slants of dim light given out by the lamps below deck and a drift of fresh air finding its way into the narrow channel eased her.

Twisting her head, she could make out dim, cluttered shapes of sailors' belongings, stowed beyond her head and feet, and saw the ship's ribs that interrupted the long storage space.

"Lie still. It won't be for long."

Stewart's voice came to her quietly from above. Then she heard him clamber back up to the deck as seamen's voices, raised in jollity, came closer, over the water. His shipmates were returning.

She heard some sailors come clattering below, and tensed with apprehension, wondering where Stewart was. It was just two sailors with an inebriated shipmate who they piled into his cot further after. They shoved his bunk door closed and wished him sweet dreams, then laughing, went back on deck.

Mari was left listening to incoherent ramblings for the drunken sailor as he mumbled himself to sleep.

Not a large ship, *Hazard* was a brig of two hundred tons burden with a complement of twelve. She shifted only slightly in the water, lying low and comfortably with her ballast of well-stowed cargo, mainly of tobacco, the familiar aroma filling Mari's hiding place.

Lying in the dark, Mari finally found herself relaxing. She even became drowsy and started to doze, the familiar shipboard sounds and occasional gentle motion of the hull calming and comforting her.

Though there was still the ocean to cross back to England, she felt strangely safe. At last she was gone from Plinhimmon. She reasoned to herself that even were she to be discovered at sea, she could refer the captain to her father for payment of passage.

Stewart Dean, she realized, was the one taking the most risk. She thought of his earnest, intelligent gaze, and his kindly ways, and was truly thankful.

Tension ebbed. For now, nothing more could be done for her safety and wellbeing. She lay drifting in a delicious weariness, and, swaddled in sacking and a rough blanket, gave in to it, rocked to sleep by the boat.

It seemed only moments later that there was noise and confusion as though the ship was being attacked. She swam up from a muddled dream to the sound of many feet milling around the deck.

To her horror, she recognized John Coward's angry voice demanding the right to search the ship. Her mouth went dry with fright, and her heart beat painfully against her ribs.

A whole procession of pushing, shoving men clattered down the companionway, their boots banging loudly on the sole boards.

Mari was terrified, certain discovery was imminent, but, bewilderingly, they passed her by. Then, she realized they were descending into the hold to search the cargo.

Had Robin betrayed her? Why was Captain Coward back to Plinhimmon so soon when he hadn't been due until tomorrow? How could they know she would be on *Hazard*?

There was no time to reason, for the boarding party quickly came back up to the crew's quarters. The rumble of bunk doors being roughly pulled aside grew louder. She squeezed her eyes shut, like a little child hoping if she couldn't see them they wouldn't see her. Coward's voice came again, low and furious.

"The girl has to be on this ship. Strip anything stowed from the bunks. Ames, bring that lamp close here. Back off, Mr. Dean!"

Mari went cold even though she was sweating, expecting any second to be found. There was a thud and rattle on the door hatch concealing her, and she held her breath.

Then, booming over the melee, came another voice, loaded with fury.

"Captain Coward! What's the meaning of this damnable operation? You've invaded my ship like a bunch of scurvy pirates, Sir! You will get ashore now, or find yourself and your party treading river water."

Captain Adam Coxen had returned to *Hazard*, and bellowed like a bull in outrage at finding his ship over-run, and strangers checking his hold without so much as a by-your-leave.

John Coward's response was hard and fast, making his case captain-to-captain, with excuses for his peremptory haste in boarding, uninvited, the other man's vessel.

Fortunately for Mari, Adam Coxen was not to be placated. He was totally incensed at the idea that anyone should think to get away with such a high-handed action, and threatened complaint to the governor and action in the court for Coward's behavior.

There was another explosion of angry words, threats and bluster, before Coward was forced to back down with stiff apologies.

The boarding party retreated, leaving *Hazard*'s crew to a lambasting from their captain for allowing such an invasion.

Mari heard the sailors scuttling about, preparing ship, no doubt subdued and careful not to incur further wrath from Adam Coxen.

Who, she wondered, had allowed Coward and his searchers aboard? It couldn't have been Stewart Dean. Horrocks, who had served on *Integrity* with her, had, perhaps, backed down before his old captain, but he was not in charge anyway while Coxen was away.

Later, there was the sound of sailors coming off watch, and she listened to their comments about the night's events.

"Cap'n's in a blistering mood," one said.

An answer came, "Aye, a good thing for Coward and his crew, not to mention the landlubbers he had with him, that Cap'n was set to catch dawn tide, else he'd have raised hell for 'em ashore. Mayhap will, anyway, when he's next afoot in Oxford town. They'll know to mind their p's and q's. Coxen don't forget a grudge."

Mari lay, quiet as a mouse, eavesdropping on the crew's version of the upset, and heard it had been the first-mate, Ames, who had given over the ship to Coward and his party of interlopers.

"Mate's bin pleadin' he thought John Coward had Coxen's say-so to go through the ship," added another voice.

"He's been tackin' about and whistlin' a fair tune to get back on Cap'n's good side. S'bin a treat, t'see him stalled abluster by Coxen. I'll lay odds the Cap'n will break his back for'im this passage."

Whatever anger Adam Coxen felt, it now had to be subjugated to the needs of his ship. With first light breaking, Coxen needed to make the tide. Orders for getting underway came brusque and clear.

Mari could hear the men going about the business of hauling anchor and setting sail. Then, at last, with unutterable relief, she felt the slow, rhythmic forward motion of the ship.

She imagined the sails belling in the first breeze of the day, as *Hazard* gently curled the bay waters into a wake behind her stout hull and ponderously and smoothly left Oxford and the Tred Haven behind.

* * *

The ship cleared Benoni Point and was crossing the mouth of the Choptank to make the Bay by the time Stewart Dean heard his name called out harshly by Adam Coxen.

Dean exchanged a guarded, tense look with Horrocks, who gave the slightest of shrugs but kept an impassive face, and busied himself

165

with the task of belaying a line. The rest of the crew on deck showed a like concentration, minding their own business.

Dean paused outside Coxen's quarters, and looked back at the receding shoreline, lightening in the early morning. A few sea birds had already taken flight, carving a path down the eastern shore flyway, among them a dozen geese flying in raucous formation beside the boat.

Ames called out the captain's orders, and *Hazard* began a stately turn to clear the river and begin passage down the Bay to the open sea.

Taking a deep breath, Dean knocked on the door, and, on command, immediately entered the cabin.

Adam Coxen was standing at the rear of his quarters, staring back through the casement window. He said nothing for a while, and Dean waited, his mind quickly racing through arguments and explanations for his case and, as quickly, discarding them. He feared the worst.

If found to have smuggled a stowaway aboard he could be flogged, docked pay, and lose his position aboard. He had all but completed a very satisfactory apprenticeship for navigation and seamanship, under the sponsorship of merchant Henry Lowe.

This was his last voyage on *Hazard*, which, when completed, would set him free to pursue his own ship's command. Infinite possibilities lay ahead of him, but despite the risk he was taking, it did not occur to him to regret his impulse to befriend and rescue the girl.

When he had seen her, wretched and miserable, sitting weeping on the banks of the river, his heart was flooded with a powerful emotion, and a kind of wonderful madness had seized him. Though in floods of tears, she had not seemed self-pitying at all, but in despair. One look at her face, and he felt he could have fought any battles for her.

Determining to get her back to England on *Hazard* had seemed, quite simply, the only thing to do as far as both logic and his heart were concerned.

Up until now, he and Coxen had gotten along pretty well together. The veteran merchant-captain was irascible and severe at times, but was a respected commander and seaman, who knew the Atlantic as well as any man sailing. Dean had benefited greatly from working under him.

Coxen suddenly spun around and fixed him with a fierce look. Dean forced himself to stare back and meet the challenge of the piercing gaze.

"Well, Mr. Dean – a pretty fracas in port with our unexpected boarders. I've heard Ames's tale of being hood-winked by John Coward, but, tell me, how many of the party did you invite?"

The sarcasm startled Dean into immediate denial.

"None, Captain."

Crazily, he had the urge to add, "Just one!" but controlled himself.

Coxen's eyes held his, and Stewart felt as though he were staring down the barrels of a pair of primed pistols. The captain then leaned at an angle over his chart table, knuckling the edge with his clenched fist. He was silent for a few moments, apparently waiting for his second mate to speak.

When the younger man said nothing, Coxen fixed him with a wicked, bright look, and came slowly around the table to stand toe-to-toe with his subordinate.

Stewart stood his ground, and awaited judgment.

Coxen breathed in slowly and deeply, swelling his bowed chest with what seemed a barrel full of air. He was a huge man, taller than Stewart Dean by a head, with a wild, resplendent beard, bristling out in every direction, as though imbued with the crackling, angry energy of its owner.

Staring stolidly ahead, Stewart blankly studied the amazing russet jungle spread over Coxen's cravat.

"Mr. Dean."

The captain's voice came low and dangerous.

"Mr. Dean, mark me well – we have sailed fine together, have we not, man?"

Dean nodded dumbly, and the captain nodded back with a vicious smile scything his countenance.

"Aye, and know this - I'll be damned to hell and back again if I'll tolerate St. Peter or the devil hisself to make free with any ship o'mine without my consent, or even a late by-your-leave."

Coxen, still smiling grimly, paused and scrutinized Dean's face.

"John Coward and his crew are lucky indeed that we had to make this tide. I'll give the man his due - high-handed he may be, but he knows the tricks of stowing a cargo safe and tight. So now, as his busy bodies discovered no strays aboard, I'll take it *Hazard* has none.

"So, Mr. Dean, I need not put to the trouble of searching the holds myself, because, o'course, if I do see any such body skulking aboard not earning a rightful passage, why, then, I'll be made a fool of, and I'll be right out of countenance, won't I Mr. Dean?

"And I'm sure that you and your shipmates wouldn't like that, not at all. You surely won't want Captain Adam Coxen distressed. John Coward has yet to pay for his arrogance."

Coxen's eyes bored deep into his second mate's. Dean stood rigid, not daring to bat an eyelid. The captain's voice had trailed off, then he came back with, "You're on permanent night watch, and first in line for double duty this trip, Mr. Dean. Be most mindful of that."

* * *

Mari's stowaway existence could not remain secret, except from Captain Coxen, in the close quarters of *Hazard*. She came to know most of the crew quite well and quickly.

In large part, they accepted her presence with good enough humor, aware of her experience as cabin boy on *Integrity*. Some nights she passed time trying to teach Horrocks to read, which prompted another shipmate to ask her to teach him to write.

On board, she helped with any small tasks when given the opportunity, fraying oakum, mending shirts or canvas, always below deck, ready to make herself scarce should the need arise.

She went on deck only during the night watches with Stewart, and at those times came to understand men's love of the sea. She often went forward and settled herself to gaze at the water folding away from the ship's bow in a glittering curve of foam.

Unlikely as it was, at these times she felt calm and free, even though between whiles she hid away like a thief.

It was best when Stewart was in charge of the watch, with Horrocks at the wheel. In the late hours of the night, Mari would sit in companionable silence with her rescuer, looking at the sky, and he would mark the North Star for her, and point out different constellations. Sometimes, they shared some food, and she developed a taste for warm watered rum, which amused the men.

168

The only bad moment came early in the voyage from first-mate Ames, who threatened to betray her and Stewart to Captain Coxen. He had followed Stewart down into the hold, where she hid amongst the tobacco barrels.

Stewart had used the excuse of finding some spare rope in order to order to take her some food. Sneaking behind him, Ames gave a gleeful bark of laughter and sneered, his face full of peevish satisfaction at having a way to get back at his rival for past insults, real or imagined.

"Well, now – what booty has captain's favorite got stowed for his own use? It'll stick in Coxen's craw when I tell him he's missing out on freight dues."

Stewart, in that instant, grabbed the other man, and pinned him to the bulkhead, threatening him with every harm should he betray the girl. Suddenly, Horrocks and two others of the crew appeared behind the first mate and stood in menacing silence. Ames was surrounded with no escape.

Frustrated, he glared and cursed, and then shouldered past his shipmates, slamming a fist against the bulkhead. The sailors grinned at Dean and hauled themselves after Ames to the upper deck. Stewart stood still breathing hard, a hand on a cask steadying himself against the motion of the ship.

Without thinking, Mari pressed against him, sliding her arms around his waist and laying her head against his neck in relief. His pulse pounded against her cheeks as he reached around her shoulders to imprison her against him. Hemp sacks became a soft enough bed, and, surrounded by the fragrance of tobacco, they coupled with sweet urgency.

* * *

The weeks swung by as *Hazard* worked her way across the Atlantic. The weather remained fair, and steady winds urged them on their course for home over a gentle sea.

Each night Mari would get Stewart to tell her of his life at sea, but he also poured out his dreams. Oxford, he said, was losing its place to other ports like Annapolis and, maybe someday, Baltimore, but he had thought to go further north.

169

He was thinking of signing with one of the prestigious merchant houses sending ships to far places around the world from New York, Salem, or Philadelphia. Albany, he said, was also a possibility.

He had heard that trade was increasing on the great Hudson River. There was already brisk commerce in furs and timbers from the hinterland, concentrated at Albany. Food supplies, such as fish and meat, not to mention a type of flour from local wheat which was considered particularly good, all found ready markets in New York, the colonies further afield, and the West Indies.

He spoke of chafing resentment in the colonies against being held in thrall as to trade and taxes by the mother country. Many folk were fretting under the strictures and demands of crown and government.

"Things will come to a head someday, Perdita, and sometime soon enough. We ought to have much more of a say-so in our own affairs, anyway, quite apart from grumbles and bad feeling about taxes and such. It seems to me we are all making a new country out here, but the powers that be in London don't seem to have sufficient vision to treat the colonies as anything more than a milch cow."

When alone, Mari usually lay in the darkness of the hold, listening to the sound of the ship plowing steadily for England. She often lost track of time when down in the ship's depths, but one day, as she was roused by the bell for the noon watch, there came the call, "Land, ho."

A little later Horrocks came down, stooping under the beams, with some bread and a bowl of stew.

"We've reached the Scillies," he announced, looking excited and invigorated at the thought of soon being back on land.

From Stewart she learned when they had passed the Lizard light. Then, it would be a steady sail, clearing the Isle of Wight, and, soon after, into Portsmouth.

"Getting you ashore shouldn't be a problem," he told her. "Coxen always anchors offshore then goes to the Custom Office to clear things. That will give us our chance."

He knew of a convenient coaching inn, where she could take passage for London.

"Don't worry about money. We'll collect enough to get you home. Not a lot, but certainly enough," he assured her.

Sheer relief and anticipation were suddenly shot through with anxiety at having to fend for herself again, and she realized that Stewart had somehow changed with the prospect of landfall.

After such ease and intimacy on their voyage, they now seemed more awkward and constrained with each other. Stewart seemed tense. Was he, she wondered, looking forward to getting her off the ship and being free of responsibility?

Catching his glance a couple of times, she saw a mournful expression, edged with concern, on his face. She knew that several times on the journey over he had been on the point of pressing her for her identity, and she had been truly tempted to confide in him, but had not.

In the end, this had caused him to withdraw and keep a certain reserve, not even reaching to her for love when the chance arose.

She had hurt him. She had accepted his help, and trusted to his decency and courage to save her, but in the end had withheld complete confidence and trust. In spite of their moments of shared warmth and passion, she must have left him feeling that she was keeping a certain distance.

Overwhelmed by her own needs and the drive to reach back for what she had lost, she dared not acknowledge her feelings too much. She realized she could never thank him and his friends enough, and knew that after this journey their paths were unlikely to cross again.

Knowing this squeezed her heart. Fretting at the idea of simply parting with nothing more done or said between them, she found herself fidgeting with the only item of value she now possessed. This was her mother's gold wedding ring.

At her mother's funeral, Aunt Matty had slipped it from her sister-in-law's finger before she was buried, and had given it to her niece. Her father had either not noticed, or, perhaps, had not cared. Since her mother's death, she had always worn it on a lace around her neck. Many nights, she had gone to sleep, clasping it for comfort.

It was the only gift of enduring gratitude she could offer Stewart.

She wanted to feel that, at least, he had some small token to remember her by, something perhaps to spin a golden thread of memory and friendship between them in times to come.

She lay back in the nest of sacking she had made for herself amongst the tobacco casks. She longed to be on deck, looking to the

171

shores of England, but had to content herself with imagining *Hazard*'s slow progress to port.

Memories tumbled in her head. Her hand found a grimy kerchief of her brother's still crumpled in her britches' pocket. She smiled. Her brother Tom's scruffy old cast-offs had become her uniform for escape, first from London and now from Plinhimmon.

When she thought of it, the urge to run, to escape, had coursed through her blood for a long time. A memory of Tom arguing with his friend, George, came back to her, and she saw herself traipsing happily after them, ever the tomboy, across a spring meadow on Strawberry Farm.

BOOK THREE

MARITAL AMENDS

XV

October 19, 1769 – A chill wind, playing over the chimneys of the Anchor Inn on Portsmouth's harbor front, caused a back draft of wood smoke into the post room. A stout, country wife, seated by the fire, coughed and complained, and slapped a hand ineffectually at the haze as she rummaged in a bundle at her feet.

Mari perversely enjoyed the scent of crackling, unseasoned wood, and looked around at the clutch of passengers waiting with her for the coach to London.

Under the sour gaze of the innkeeper, a potboy trotted to and fro with porter and ale.

The harassed keeper threatened at intervals to cuff the boy, who looked cheeky and calculating, and not at all put out. Hearing the innkeeper's wife scolding them both from the rear court, Mari decided this must be a morning ritual.

Earlier, whilst resting awhile in the inn's attic, Mari had come across a piece of broken looking glass, and had turned this way and that to view herself. Her image had stared back from the fly-blown glass as if not sure of the acquaintance.

Her hair was a spiky, bleached mess under her cap, but, thankfully, her dark tanned complexion from the Maryland summer had faded somewhat from hiding in the ship's hold during daylight hours. Stewart had only dared to let her take the fresh air when he was on night watch, and that, she had relished.

Distractedly, her thoughts flitted to her friends on *Hazard*. The voyage already seemed a dream. Stewart Dean had escorted her to the Anchor Inn, and had been reluctant to leave her.

After all the time they had been together, a deep sweet bond had been forged. Her feelings echoed his, but after a single, hard embrace, they had been almost formal with each other, finally shaking hands in compromise.

As he turned to leave, her feelings were torn and confused, but she persuaded him to accept the gift of her mother's wedding ring as a token of gratitude, realizing belatedly what a poignant memento it could seem.

Stewart Dean would have loved her if she had let him, she knew, but he was also cut out for adventures she was too timid to contemplate. Their paths were not likely to cross again.

She berated herself for a fool and a coward. She had run away to find herself and her love, full of overblown confidence and conceit, only to scurry home depending on Dean and the others to save her.

The men of *Hazard* had scraped together what money they could to afford her lodgings at this inn, and coach passage to London. Her heart warmed again.

Life on board ship was hard, but there was camaraderie, and rough though the sailors were, they had gallantry and generosity. If she had been discovered as stowaway, they could have paid with raw stripes on their backs.

She thought of the times when stars had pricked the dark dome of the sky and the moon had splashed a silver pathway from horizon to ship. The sea passage was good, with *Hazard* making way through smooth, rolling waters.

At night the sea would surge from the bow into a wake full of strange, dancing light. During those moments, Mari fancied she understood the lure of the sailor's life, the utter freedom, flying along with a fair wind curving the sails, and silver fish leaping.

A fresh gust of cold wind rattling the shutters of the inn broke her reverie, and she shivered in spite of the fire in the post room. She scolded herself, again, for failing to keep her thoughts firmly on her situation.

She had no idea how she would persuade her father to welcome her home again. She felt exhausted and empty. The only plan she had was to retrace the path taken through London's streets so many months ago, and she wondered how Joseph Westin would receive his prodigal daughter.

She would sneak around to the back kitchen of her father's house, and beg for Abby's help. The thought of Abby, sitting by her cooking range, supping a late posset before going to bed was cheering. She would hug the cook's comfortable figure, and kiss her soft plump cheeks. She would smell the lavender and baked-bread scent of Abby's apron, and be found again. Mari's spirits lifted.

No more Perdita, the lost one. Mari Westin was back.

* * *

The coach journey from Portsmouth was tedious. Fortunately, the late October weather was clear and dry, but, even so, it took many exhausting hours to reach London. After paying her fare, Mari had little left for refreshment at the coach stations along the road and felt her stomach growl.

Arriving in London at the coaching inn in Aldgate, she proceeded to make her way on foot to Conduit Street. Walking through the busy London thoroughfares was shocking and strange to her.

The sudden change in her situation from that of stowaway on *Hazard*, and her plight at Plinhimmon, was so overpowering that it gave her a sense of unreality and disorientation.

She felt detached and low, stumbling awkwardly along cobble-stoned side streets as though she had not yet found her land legs, trying to remember the way home, instinctively moving west.

She avoided pie-sellers, and hurried past tavern doors with the scent of warm apple cider and roast mutton escaping into the cool autumn air, vying with the less pleasant odors on the city streets.

Passing some law offices, she was hailed, as a street boy, to take a message somewhere for someone, but, head down, ignored the summons and hurried on.

Dusk was falling. Desperately preoccupied with the coming encounter with her father, she allowed her steps to stray toward the center of the highway, and was nearly run down by a coach clattering to its destination. The driver was urging his team at speed on the last short stretch home. A blaring tantivy from the guard's horn, shouts from the streets, and the crack of hooves on cobbles, jolted her to awareness just in time, and she jumped to one side, stumbling and falling against the worn steps of a dingy ale house.

She realized she was on Holborn already, a route much used by the increasing overland coach trade. The road was a maelstrom of activity, even though a few of the shops were closing and boarding up for the evening.

Evening trade overlapped the day's dwindling activities, as chop shops and ale houses, feed stores and milliners, gunsmiths and tailors, all still plied for business.

At least her way was straight forward now. She just had to continue west toward the end of Oxford Street, and there would remain but a few yards to home. It occurred to her, that she was now completing the wide circle of her journey.

She trudged on, finally making a last turn from Swallow Street. Coming in sight of her father's house, her footsteps became slow and leaden.

A great malaise overtook her. She moved slowly down the opposite side of Conduit Street, and stood gazing at the front door of the family townhome. A lamp had already been lit over the portico against the evening gloom, and there was light coming from an upstairs parlor window, where a shadow flitted across the shutters too quickly to identify. Probably Mrs. Pynchon checking the lamps were properly tended, she thought.

Mari found her feet taking her back up the street and through a carriage entrance to the back of the house. There was no way she could summon the nerve to present herself, as she was, at the front entrance. She went, instead, like a peddler, to the back door.

As she stood on the step, the familiarity of it all peeled away the passage of time, and it seemed, momentarily, that it was only yesterday that she had left.

But, as she pulled back the heavy brass lion's head knocker, the realization that she had more than a year's absence to explain almost made her run again.

She shook herself, breathed deeply, and knocked.

There was no immediate response, but she could hear some familiar and reassuring sounds of pots and pans being handled, not the kitchen uproar of a grand supper being prepared, but the recognizably more muted pace of a quiet evening meal for a few.

She was suddenly faint, and, feeling desperate, thumped again at the kitchen door, which was almost simultaneously flung open.

A plump, rosy faced scullery maid, in crisp cap and apron, stood surveying her, barring entrance to the kitchen. Mari did not recognize her.

Poppy, the maid, seeing a thin, scruffy youth having the temerity to come bothering the house at such a time of day, felt free to exercise a superiority and authority she did not have with anyone else.

"We don't want nuthin', and yer not getting' nuthin', so be on yer way and stop beatin' on folks' doors, makin' a nuisance."

Mari stared back at the neatly turned-out maid as though stricken speechless.

This is what she herself had become in America, the lowliest kitchen hand, though this one appeared better fed and clothed, and, however humble her position, would have, no doubt, a proper cot to sleep on at the end of her day.

"Well, go on – are yer daft or what, lad?"

"Who is it, Poppy?" The cook's voice came from behind. "Is it the book-binder's boy with a parcel for Sir Joseph? Fetch Mrs. Pynchon if it is, or ask Henry to come."

"No, it in't, Mrs. Laxby. It's just a cheeky lad, beggin'."

Mari at last found her voice, and stepping forward, pushed firmly past a goggling Poppy.

"No, I'm not," she said as she stepped across the threshold. "I'm Mari."

* * *

The women fussed around her. A concerned and fretted Abby brought a warm posset of egg and Madeira wine with toasted rusks, as though she were an invalid.

When summoned to the kitchen by the distressed cook, the housekeeper's usual, cool demeanor melted, and her face flushed with compassion at the appearance of the master's prodigal daughter. She found the sight of Mari shocking.

To Mrs. Pynchon, it was as if her beloved former mistress, Lady Westin, was staring back at her, eyes large and pleading, gazing out of a face gaunt with fatigue.

She had whisked Mari upstairs straight away to Lady Westin's old boudoir, where Maisie was still clearing up after Tamsin Tallentire's toilette.

The maid seemed dumbstruck to see the daughter of Joseph Westin dressed like a street urchin, entering the room like a sleepwalker in the wake of the bustling housekeeper.

Mrs. Pynchon directed a stream of instructions to Maisie, who tripped to and fro, harassed and excited.

Mari at first sat like a discarded rag doll, leaning against the cushions of a couch once used by her mother when taking her morning chocolate, and, more recently, by Sir Joseph's mistress-in-residence as she fixed new garters over her silk hose.

She slumped as if in a stupor, while Maisie and Mrs. Pynchon hustled and hovered, and prepared a bath for her. The maid offered some laundry soap to the housekeeper.

"No, Maisie, not that. There are some balls of sweet lavender soap down in my storeroom. Poppy knows where.

"Whilst you're there, fill one of the old stocking pieces hanging by the door with oaten bran to soften the bath water – and tell Henry, or Poppy, to bring up some more hot water, and be quick about it. Pass me those towels you have there – hurry now."

Mari had finally allowed them to assist her into the warm, scented water, and the luxury of it relaxed her to the edge of sleep. She lay soaking in the slipper tub, head back and eyes closed, with the sound of the servants' voices spattering around her.

She had hardly bothered to answer any of their questions, except to say she had been journeying all day from Portsmouth after disembarking from a long voyage.

Mrs. Pynchon finally gave up asking, deciding the only course was to get the girl to bed, but didn't allow this until she had lathered Mari's hair and scrubbed her back, as though determined to wash away the contamination of the world.

She deliberately had Maisie pour a large jug of water over Mari's head, both to rinse away soap suds, and perhaps to get some response from her exasperating charge. Roused, spluttering from the dousing, Mari finally showed animation.

She deflected further questions about her absence by asking some of her own. Where were her father, and Tom, Sophie, and Miss Pardoe? Were they away at Ravenhill? Yes, her little sister and the governess were at home on the Essex estate. They had only visited the London house briefly this last spring.

There had been such a furor when Mari's disappearance was discovered, it had been some time before Sir Joseph had allowed his youngest daughter to come to the city again, and, even so, had seemed anxious to get her back to the countryside as soon as possible.

Mrs. Pynchon had not elaborated further, but busied herself toweling Mari's hair, and grimacing at the rough way it had been lopped.

"And brother Tom?" questioned Mari.

"Oh," said Mrs. Pynchon, her face breaking into a smile. "Your brother is away at sea, Miss Mari. The last we heard he was sailing for the Mediterranean, and I think he may be in Gibraltar right now.

"Mistress Tallentire can make you up to date, and she can inform you when to expect your father. He was to return any day now, but there has been some delay, I understand."

Mari felt a certain relief wash over her at this news, and stood as Maisie helped her into a fine, lawn nightgown, beautifully embroidered and flounced with lace. It smelled of flower sachets, and she recognized it as one belonging to her mother, and said so to Mrs. Pynchon.

"We've no clothes of yours here at all. They were all packed off to Ravenhill. I have many of your mother's things packed away though, and I swear they'll fit you well enough, and see you through."

The housekeeper paused, and gently smoothed a fold of the gown.

"For the time being, at any rate."

She turned and glared at the unfortunate Maisie.

"There's no-one here with more of a right to them," she added primly.

Maisie looked somewhat offended, and sniffed, muttering something about Mistress Tallentire not caring for pale colors.

Minutes later, Mari found herself tucked cosily into her own bed in the room she had shared with little Sophie. Mrs. Pynchon left a small lamp burning by the bedside to leave Mari, lying alone at last, to fall into a deep slumber.

Her rest was disturbed only briefly by a strange dream, and once she half awoke and imagined Tamsin Tallentire standing by the bedside, holding a candle that caused soft light to flicker over the copper colored silk of the gown she wore. Her gaze was dark and unreadable.

* * *

The next morning Mari Westin awoke to the soft clink of china, and opened her eyes as the house-keeper gently settled a tray onto the marble surface of the bedside stand. Lying on her side, Mari watched as steam drifted softly from the spout of a silver chocolate pot.

Weak autumn sunlight spilled over rich carpet, as Maisie drew back the window drapes. Mrs. Pynchon moved across the room to check a fire already laid in the grate, and turned again toward the bed as though not sure what to say or how to say it.

She had taken charge of the situation upon Mari's astounding reappearance the evening before, but this morning, looking at the young woman propped against puffed, lace embellished pillows, she was inevitably reminded again of the former Lady Westin, and waited in attendance to learn the daughter's wishes.

Mari was preoccupied, staring over to the window, head slightly to one side as though listening for something amid the street sounds.

Finally, the housekeeper cleared her throat and ventured to ask what Mari would like for breakfast.

The girl stared back at the housekeeper as though looking at a stranger, and before Mrs. Pynchon could repeat her question, she saw Mari's eyes focus on someone behind her. The housekeeper turned to see Tamsin Tallentire standing framed in the doorway.

Sir Joseph Westin's mistress stood there, studying his daughter, one hand resting on the heavy gilt door handle, the other cradling a tisane in a fine porcelain dish. She wore one of her favorite, loose sack robes of peach colored silk, hand-painted with delicate sprigs of flowers.

After a few moments, she came forward and sat herself on the edge of the bed. Mari observed the long line of her throat as she tilted her head back to drink. Then, Tamsin leaned forward and held Mari's gaze with a searching look.

Tallentire's figure looked as opulent as ever, though her face seemed more finely drawn than before. Her hair was its usual unruly, curly, short crop. Her skin was still creamy and flawless, and her eyes danced with life. To Mari, she radiated energy and health.

"We have some talking to do, Mari, and before your dear Papa returns at that."

As she spoke, she turned and waved Mrs. Pynchon and Maisie out of the room.

182

Mari was silent for a moment, staring at her unfinished drink. She finally asked, dreading the answer, "When are you expecting him – today? Tomorrow?"

"No. No," came the assurance.

"Not for a few days yet. He was expected back but has been delayed. He's over in Geneva on some business. He has been away for a month or more."

Tamsin swirled the dregs of the tisane in her cup and set it on the tray by Mari.

"Just as well, Poppet. It gives us time to sort ourselves out, and work out how to get you in your Pa's good graces again."

She flicked a glance at Mari, and, seeing the dubious look on her face at the idea of her father's mistress orchestrating any such thing, Tamsin laughed.

"Oh yes, you have some explaining to do. Stories to tell as well, no doubt. But, first of all, you tell me, and I shall advise what to leave out and what to put in, what to dress with a sauce, and what to serve plain."

Mari laughed in spite of herself, not knowing whether to be offended or relieved at Tamsin's quick assessment.

"Have Aunt Mat and Uncle Frederick been around. I'd like to talk to Aunt Mat."

"You will. You will, but don't fret yourself, Mari. I suspect your Aunt Mathilda and I will not be so far apart in our advice on how to manage you father."

Tamsin sauntered over to the window and stood drumming her fingers on the window ledge.

"In fact, I have sent for you Aunt Mathilda this morning asking her to come as soon as she can. When she arrives, why then, we'll have a council of war."

She appeared amused again. Hands on hips, she turned back to Mari with a brilliant smile.

"I have to say the idea appeals to me. We shall make a good show."

Then, in exasperation, "Mari, Mari! Don't look so down. A mistress, an elder sister, and a daughter can't sort out one Pappa?"

She started for the door, her perfumed gown floating behind her, gold lace slipper skimming the floor.

"Meantime, take you ease and rest where you are. You can have Maisie see to your needs the rest of the day. She won't mind the extra work – she loves to think she's at the center of an intrigue.

"I'll send her up with a better breakfast than this skimpy tray. You are home now, girl. You don't have to exist on hard tack and wormy gruel, or whatever it is that sailors dish up. Cheer yourself up. I have plans for you."

Mari lay back against the pillows, thoughts churning. She could not imagine what the likes of Tamsin Tallentire and Aunt Mathilda could, or would, contrive between them. In spite of her anxiety at the thought of her father, she found herself amused and diverted at the idea of the unlikely twosome of allies.

She set her cup back on the bedside tray, and smiled to herself. Abby's feather light, breakfast puffets and rich, steaming chocolate from her mother's beautiful silver pot were hardly hard tack and gruel!

XVI

The November weather turned crisp and cold.

Mari was amazed at how easily she slipped back into the routine of Conduit Street, though a sense of unreality swept in frequently, especially when her thoughts wandered, as they inevitably did, to Plinhimmon, Stewart, and her sea adventures. She was relieved and thankful that she could enjoy some respite before having to face her father.

She had dreaded the thought of dealing with Tamsin, though, at the same time, had not been sure whether the woman would still be in residence.

Yet, Tamsin had surprised her with gestures of friendship and support. Much as it had galled Mari to accept the presence of a mistress in her father's house, she now had to admit that Tamsin's insouciant attitude to the world of men in general, and her father in particular, cheered and comforted her.

Further, she noted that Mathilda Ashford, whilst deploring her brother's action in keeping a mistress in residence, nevertheless seemed to have had no particular difficulty in establishing a working relationship with Tamsin.

When Aunt Mathilda arrived post-haste from Chelmsford to see Mari, she swept through the front door, waving servants, including Mrs. Pynchon, aside.

She marched upstairs to enter the parlor without ceremony. She stopped abruptly to stand and stare at her niece, who sat by the window. Mari had watched her swift, determined progress from the carriage to the front door with some trepidation. She fully expected an ear-wigging.

As her aunt stood there, silently surveying her, however, Mari saw that Mathilda's usually humorous, intelligent face was distressed, and she rushed over to throw her arms around the older woman and hug her.

"Well, child, well – you're back at last, you're back where you belong, and you've no doubt adventures to tell. Let me look at you."

Mathilda held her niece at arm's length and gazed intently at her.

Echoing Tamsin's reaction, she said, "You must tell me everything – every little thing, and I shall tell you what your father will need to know. We shall have to manage him between us."

Mari sat on the couch next to her aunt.

Where to begin? Hesitating, she looked from one to the other, and Tamsin, pacing the room and sipping a cordial, tilted her head and waved her glass in encouragement. Aunt Mathilda sat intent.

"I...I was looking for Bryce Hunter. He never came. I thought to go to Virginia with him." Her voice sounded forlorn and childish, even to herself.

Mathilda looked over to where Tamsin Tallentire stood. Tamsin simply shrugged and gestured with her glass again.

"You should know," began Mathilda, "before we go any further, the night you went missing young Bryce Hunter died on the Bristol road. There was an accident with the coach, and a highwayman did for him."

Mathilda faltered after this bleak statement, seeing a blank look of shock on Mari's face, then hurried on.

"We only knew of it sometime later from Tom, who visited quite often with the Hunters, as you know."

She paused again. Tears were running down Mari's face but she said nothing.

Mathilda sent a glance of appeal to Tamsin, who quickly said, "Sad as that is Poppet, we have to learn of your adventures. Time later to talk of the Hunter boy."

Mari blinked, staying silent. This news of Bryce came as a bewildering, catastrophic end to her endeavors. What had she hoped for? What had she gained? The whole past year seemed pointless.

Tamsin relented a little, poured another glass of cordial, and pressed it on her.

"Drink up little one, and tell us all. We cannot waste time. Your father is due back soon. You have held up sailing the seas, and serving the colonials. You can survive a sad end to a girl's infatuation."

Mathilda, looking grim and as though about to shake her head, nodded agreement instead and patted her niece's shoulder.

Mari resigned herself to reliving her experience. Scenes from Plinhimmon came so vividly to mind she could almost smell the lazy, warm air of Maryland's summer.

Both the women watched her narrowly when she related the incidents involving the Coward boys and Thorberry, or her exchanges with the sailors aboard ship.

They were both, in their different ways, inclined to disbelieve that Mari had managed to avoid becoming a victim of the more violent and ardent men she had encountered.

Tamsin, especially, was at first cynical and exasperated, and skepticism flickered in her expression as she rose to ring the bell for yet another tray of refreshments.

Eventually, even she was transfixed and rendered silent at the spate of ruthless questions leveled at Mari by Mathilda Ashford.

Studying the girl closely as she answered her aunt, Tamsin was only partly convinced that Mari was being truthful. Raising her eyes to heaven, she bit into an apple, and collapsed back against some cushions on a couch, her sardonic laughter pealing out.

"Heavens above! How could it be? Sailors fit to take holy orders, you'd have us believe. My God! They'd never swallow that draught down the Radcliffe Highway."

Looking sharply at Mari, Aunt Mat frowned. Her answer was tart.

"Enough is enough. It's not the denizens of Radcliffe Highway we have to bother about. Whatever the case, it's her father we'll have to convince, Tamsin. We'll have to smooth his hackles and calm his temper."

Tamsin appeared about to laugh again at this, but kept her amusement in check. She waited, munching on the apple as Mathilda Ashford paced to and fro, slapping at the side of her dress with her fan as she thought.

Mari had retired to the window seat again, and watched the other two women uneasily. Tamsin, at last, shrugged, and wiping her fingers on a napkin, bent over the tea tray.

"You know perfectly well there'll be little choice. Her father will either throw her out of the house, or marry her off the soonest he can. I'll wager he won't even let her anywhere near Ravenhill and little Sophie."

Tamsin had the right of it, Mathilda Ashford had to concede but quickly decided that it would be better if she took her niece back to Chelmsford with her. Mathilda felt she could set the stage more effectively for Mari's acceptance back into Joseph Westin's good graces, and, at the least, have some control over any more family scenes.

It would serve their purpose better, too, were her brother first to encounter Mari back in the calm, simple domestic scene afforded by Chelmsford, rather than to come upon her tripping around London society dressed to the nines in Tallentire's wake.

This was settled upon. Mathilda Ashford would provide the loving family fortress, and Tamsin the concoction of reason sugared by her own charm to prepare Joseph Westin for reconciliation with his daughter.

* * *

Sir Joseph Westin faced his formidable elder sister over the exotic expanse of a Turkish carpet in her private dressing room.

Mathilda sat with every appearance of composure, one hand resting in her lap, the other upon a delicate tea table by the side of her chair. Her only movement was occasionally to trace with a finger the design of inlaid ivory on a bite-and-stir box set upon her tea tray.

Her brother knew he had been manipulated. He slowly paced the edge of the carpet, shot Mathilda a sharp sideways glance, and admitted silently to himself that she had won the first round. He was well aware that she had coached his own mistress to break the news of his daughter's return, and to mollify him before he was allowed to come face-to-face with Mari.

Further, he had had an extra's day's journey from his own house to that of Mathilda in which to calm and rationalize his feelings.

Yes, he conceded the point, it had worked to a degree at least. It had served to oil the troubled waters of his thoughts, but it took little contemplation of his daughter's behavior to bring his emotions back to the boil again.

Fortunately, his earlier insistence upon his daughter's seclusion on his country estate had worked to advantage. His London circles barely knew of her existence, so there had been no particularly difficult enquiries to answer about her return, or, indeed, evasions to make.

He had, at one point, thought of putting it about that he had sent Mari off to a finishing school, or upon extended travels abroad for her education, but it had not proved necessary. Her brief stay in London, prior to her disappearance, had been too short for her to establish any number of friends beyond the family.

As far as more sophisticated society was concerned, she had been merely another young girl, someone's daughter, not present long enough to have made much of an impression.

Westin remembered that he had suspected a possible romantic attachment the girl had had with some merchant's son or other, but, upon his investigation, that had proved a blind alley.

In fact, Westin had quickly assumed his daughter dead. He could not believe that he would have had no news at all of her had she been alive, whatever her circumstances.

Heavy anger moved again in him.

It was all very well for Mathilda to assure him that it was all right, there was no harm done, and that the girl had made out well enough for herself. He could hardly believe that a naïve, closely brought up girl could have traveled to the new world and back, no less, dealing with all sorts of society on the way, including the common rabble, and manage to stay unspoiled in the most basic sense.

He suddenly had had enough of his sister's conditioning and maneuvering,

"Matty, cease and desist, and sup your tea, for heaven's sake. I wish to hear Mari's story from her own lips. Whatever she has to say for herself, I'll be the judge."

Mathilda pursed her lips, but assessing the look on his face, gave in to the inevitable and rang for Mari.

Her brother placed himself, arms akimbo, legs apart, and feet planted squarely facing the dressing room door.

"Don't stand like that, Joseph. You look threatening, and stop scowling so, man. It's your daughter, not some low rogue brought up at the Assizes."

Westin shot a glance of irritation at his sister, and continued to scowl at the door, but silently compromised by clasping his hands

189

behind his back. Mathilda regarded him as he rocked backwards and forwards a little on his heels, and redirected his scowl to the floor.

Even frowning, her brother looked quite handsome, she thought. His fashionable coat was skirted but cut away in front in the newest style, and was of a fine plum colored wool, lined with blue silk. He sported britches in soft silver-gray Italian velvet, buttoned and buckled just below the knee. An immaculate, snowy cravat vied with his gentleman's bag wig and flawless white silk hose in its perfection. Shoes of softly gleaming black Moroccan leather, mounted with plain silver buckles, completed his ensemble.

The picture he presented of the elegant gentleman showed in sharp relief against the sun-washed colors of the oriental carpet he stood upon.

He seemed to be listening intently. Mathilda's expression softened. This last year or so, she noted, her brother had lost a considerable amount of weight, and looked the better for it. She speculated whether it was the result of his entertaining a lively mistress or worry about a lost daughter, but had no way of knowing.

Joseph Westin had always been a cool, reserved man at the best of times. She tensed a little herself as she heard the sounds of approaching footsteps along the hallway.

The footsteps ceased outside the door, and there was silence for a few moments before it was pushed open to reveal Mari standing there.

Mathilda studied her niece with approval. The girl was demurely dressed in a simple watered silk gown of lavender with a square neckline softened by a fichu in a cream-colored lace. Discreet frilled edging adorned the sleeves, and she wore slippers to match her costume. Her appearance was that of a demure young lady of quality, not, Mathilda observed with satisfaction and some relief, that of a young woman in the height of fashion.

The aunt felt confirmed in her judgment of keeping her niece by her in Chelmsford for the confrontation with her father instead of leaving the arrangements to the machinations of Tamsin Tallentire.

"I'll retire if you wish," Mathilda offered.

Her brother's response was immediate.

"No – stay, Matty. I would rather you did."

Westin had not taken his eyes off his daughter, who still stood in the doorway, her wide dark-eyed gaze locked on that of her father

. Mathilda found herself willing the girl to make some show of courtesy and greeting.

"Why was she standing there, so straight and stiff, all pride, no sign of meekness to soften her father?" she thought.

"Come here, Mari."

Joseph Westin finally broke the silence.

Mari hesitated, then complied, dipping a brief, awkward curtsey in front of him, almost as an afterthought.

"Look at me," he demanded.

Mathilda released her breath in a long sigh and bent to study her fan to. Oh Lord, she thought, another staring match, the two of them standing there like book-ends.

Sir Joseph's feelings were in turmoil. He saw before him the living image of his late wife. Quite apart from her physical likeness to her mother,

Mari stared at him with the same blazingly honest eyes. She was apprehensive, but gave the impression of being able to stand her ground.

Westin realized that the question uppermost in his mind was not the one to ask his daughter. He had lived with the thought of her being despoiled and ruined, if not dead, for so long that seeing her standing there at last, he found himself lost and speechless.

His feelings confounded him. He had been set to launch into a tirade against the prodigal, and then to demand her response with her abject apologies. They would be followed, no doubt, by supplications and entreaties for his forgiveness, and acceptance back into his household.

Gazing into her eyes, his words were stilled in his throat, and he felt relief flood through him.

Yes, the girl had much explaining to do, but, reading her face, he was overtaken by the conviction that she was as untouched sexually as she had been on leaving his protection.

She had said nothing yet. This was something he, as a man, felt he simply knew of her in the most detached way.

He continued to regard her closely. Nervousness was there in her demeanor, but pride and defiance showed through. She held herself well, he noted, like her mother before her, even wore a color favored by her mother.

He found himself murmuring absently, "You look well in that dress, Mari, your mother would have approved."

His daughter, looking slightly startled, gazed down at her skirts, smoothing the silk with a nervous gesture.

"Thank you, Papa."

Sir Joseph moved away and paced to the window, staring out into the darkening evening. He continued silent for some time.

Mari looked to her Aunt Mathilda, who sat there with a completely confounded expression on her face.

"Well! Is that all you two have to say to each other? The world jokes of the phlegmatic English, but this is a ridiculous state of affairs."

Westin turned back to his sister.

"Calm down, Matty. I find I need no long rigmarole after all. Mari shall tell me her adventures after I've had a good supper."

He turned to leave the room, pausing by the door, the skirt of his frock coat swinging elegantly.

"Mind, Mari, I have my own plans for you."

He paused and considered her again for a long moment.

"And you need not fear. As you have shown courage, however foolishly, in venturing the way you have over the past year, you will no doubt manage the course I shall set for you with some ease."

On this cryptic note, Joseph Westin left his female relatives to simmer.

Over the next few days, Mari had several long interviews with Sir Joseph on the subject of her adventure.

Aunt Mat contrived to be present, albeit it remaining quietly in the background, settled on a sofa with needlework, or attending quietly to correspondence at her writing table. Her presence had been a reassuring to Mari, especially at the times in her narrative when her father's features had set tight and grim, and his scowl had become fearsome.

Mari had frequently glanced across at her aunt to try and read the expression on the older woman's face, and to gauge whether to expand or diminish her account of her adventures.

She had noticed that Aunt Matty had a way of pursing her lips and raising an eyebrow ever so slightly, when it was best to tone down her story, or to change the subject all together.

One afternoon, after several of these sessions of interrogation, her father dismissed her, informing her that he would be absent for a while. He gave no explanation, but smiled thinly at the expression of relief Mari could not hide.

Whiling away the hours, waiting for her father's return to Chelmsford, Mari had plenty of time to consider her situation. She was filled with frustration again that her life seemed always to be directed by others.

Tamsin and Aunt Matty had been ordering the events of her daily routine in every detail. Now here was her father about to take over, as she supposed, being her father, he certainly should.

Brooding about this, she felt she was still no freer here in England than she had been as a lowly servant on the Plinhimmon estate, but that was self-pity.

She had to admit to herself that here she was free to be indolent and enjoy luxury unknown to anyone at Plinhimmon. She was no more at liberty, however, than she had been as Perdita, to act entirely according to her own will.

Pushing her maudlin feelings aside, she was, even so, uncertain and confused as to her father's plans for her.

Her first interview with him had been so brief, and his manner had appeared abstracted and preoccupied.

On that day he had first arrived, after dinner, he had asked her to give a further account of her experiences, but Mari had the impression that her father was only half listening to her. Could he be so disinterested?

She had expected anger and a storm of words, tirades, and threats. Could he have already formed his own conclusions?

She expressed as much to Aunt Matty, who sighed with exasperation, and set her niece straight.

"Of course, he is thinking ahead, Mari. He is about to find you a suitor, young woman. You must be settled down with someone to take care of you. No more wild adventures. You're no longer a child!"

XVII

A few days later, Aunt Matty came up to Mari's bedchamber, looking a shade tense and thoughtful.

She checked her niece's appearance with unusual care. Mari had just finished dressing to go out visiting with Mathilda, who looked relieved to find her niece was not only neat and presentable, but was looking very well and fresh in a dress of blue and white striped lustring.

"How's your coiffure? No – take off the hat, dear, and come down. Your Papa has arrived with a guest he wishes you to meet."

Mathilda paused and frowned.

"I think your father wishes him to hear something of your story."

Mari stared at her in consternation, and Mathilda, seeing the look on her face, hastened to reassure her.

"No – don't worry, dear, it's Sir Thomas Shirley, a distant cousin of your father and a very good man. A very good man," she repeated, almost to herself.

Mari studied the mixed expressions flickering over her aunt's face, trying to decipher them.

"But why should Papa want me to tell anyone anything, Aunt Mat? I don't understand."

"He's...a....er....um – interested in what you have to say for yourself."

Mathilda paused again, then went on tersely, "I can't say just now. Trust your Papa, but only answer what is asked. For heaven's sake don't rattle on a la Tallentire."

Mathilda had gone ahead to the bedroom door, beckoning Mari to follow.

"At least, for once in a while, your father contrived to arrive at a convenient moment. We could have been comfortable in the parlor, all deshabillé and topsy-turvy. We might have been out and about. As it is, you look perfectly turned out."

Mathilda realized she was chattering on too much as she looked back at a puzzled Mari. Her niece was standing in the middle of the room. A shaft of pale winter sunlight glossed over golden hair and highlighted the sheen of her silk costume.

"Yes, you'll do nicely, Mari."

Mathilda's face was now soft and slightly regretful.

"Come down now, and meet your Papa's guest."

Thomas Shirley sat opposite his host in the Ashfords' drawing room. He appeared to be perfectly at ease as he accepted a glass of Madeira from Sir Joseph, but, in fact, felt a distinct, though well-hidden unease. He wondered why on earth he had agreed to accept Westin's invitation to meet his daughter.

The man's proposal had seemed perfectly feasible a couple of nights before, as they had taken their time digesting a good dinner with accompanying wines and brandy at Boodle's. Westin had run him to earth after first calling at Shirley's London residence, and then trolling the city for a sight of him.

Sir Joseph had made no bones about it. He had been made aware some time before, through mutual connections, that Shirley was in the market for a wife.

Thomas Shirley was due to sail in a few weeks back to his government post in the Caribbean. He was a widower in his fifties, and, following his own family tradition, a veteran diplomat in His Majesty's Service, and a former Army general to boot.

Westin's own father, in fact, had been instrumental, at one point, in procuring the young Thomas Shirley a commission in the Americas.

The men were not close friends, but there were certain old family ties to trade upon and test. Sir Joseph had sat for some hours alone in his study, considering the problems of his willful daughter, and in Thomas Shirley he saw a most satisfactory solution to her plight, if the man could be persuaded to it.

He had been fortunate enough to encounter Shirley at Boodle's as he was about to go into supper alone. He had expressed an urgent need to consult with him, and had been invited to join the man for the evening meal.

Shirley had listened attentively, unperturbed and neutral, as his dinner companion presented his proposal. Sir Thomas's practiced diplomatic demeanor gave no clue to his inner reaction as he listened to Westin. In fact, he didn't know whether to laugh out loud, or recoil, at the man's suggestion that he marry the wayward daughter.

There was a fantastic and rather irresistible irony to it.

Thomas Shirley had no way of knowing whether Joseph Westin realized that the man to whom he was offering his daughter, had been many years previously an ardent suitor to Anna Westin, Joseph's wife. That was, indeed, before Joseph Westin came on the scene to win that lady's hand.

As he had leaned away from the table to savor the lush taste of a particularly good Port, Shirley had reached back in his memory to recall Anna.

She had remained the ideal of unattainable beauty to him, and he had been surprised to acknowledge a dark shadow and ache of sorrow when, many years later, he had heard of her death.

Not that he had spent his life yearning for the unattainable. He had eventually married Selina, a merry younger sister of one of his friends. She had born him three healthy children, two sons and a daughter, and had died two years before of some kind of seizure.

Shirley smiled at her memory. No-one could take her place, but he needed a woman in his life – not for heirs, but as a presence in his home, a comfort and companion in life, and, yes, perhaps, an ally, someone wholly on his side, with his interest foremost - someone he needed to alleviate the isolation of island life in a governor's manse, where stress and frustration alternated with crushing boredom.

He had been feeling bored and dispirited the evening he had been accosted by Joseph Westin. He had deliberately decided to dine alone at his club as respite from the surge of invitations from society matrons touting their daughters for marriage.

He knew he had only himself to blame for letting it be known that he was looking for a wife. He vaguely remembered making some half-joking remark to an acquaintance, that if there were any jolly widows about town who would not have a fit of the vapors at the idea of going overseas, Thomas Shirley was amenable.

What a fool he had been. He had embarrassed himself, and his mortification increased in direct proportion to the number of arch suggestions and ghastly invitations he then received. At least, refreshingly, Westin, sitting opposite him, was direct, no nonsense, man-to-man in his offer.

196

Anna's daughter! In spite of himself, Thomas Shirley was intrigued, and, besides, thought it would be a diversion to get out of London a little while.

He traveled with Westin to Chelmsford.

On the side of advantage, the girl must have gumption, to say the least, certainly not subject to the vapors. On the other hand, she was likely too youthful, reckless and undisciplined for him to take the offer with all seriousness.

Still, he was curious, and had time to fill before his voyage. It could not be worse than sitting in Lady Trench's parlor with her awful ensemble of unwanted females.

So here he was. He swirled the last of the wine in his glass, berated himself for an old fool, and rose to his feet, as a light knock on the drawing room door, signaled the arrival of a liveried footman, who opened it and stood aside for Mari Westin to confront her father and the mysterious guest.

* * *

The young woman stepping gracefully but warily into the Ashfords' drawing room caused Sir Thomas Shirley to be swept back in time. His irritation at himself for consenting to this charade, and resentment at Joseph Westin's machinations, were forgotten.

Anna-Marie's daughter stood before him, the very living image of her mother. Mari was a younger version of the woman he had courted so long ago, and the impact of the resemblance was heightened by the fact that she wore a dress of her mother's. The old-fashioned but nevertheless elegant dress had needed very little alteration to fit the daughter's slightly taller figure.

Both men, for a moment or two, were transfixed, staring silently at her, until Mari herself broke the silence by stepping forward, dipping a curtsey to her father, and murmuring a greeting.

At first, Shirley found himself nonplussed, wits scattered, but quickly pulled himself together enough to step forward for an introduction. He was irritated anew at himself for feeling so stunned at the sight of Mari.

"Like a bumbling, raw recruit of a suitor," he chastised himself.

He bent over the proffered slim hand, which was unadorned and still tinted slightly gold like the rest of her complexion, from the sun on her travels. He raised his head to look into the dark blue of her gaze, and noted, for the first time, the difference from her mother. He perceived a hint of wild independence that Anna-Marie had not shown.

Mari's hand trembled a little, which touched him, and the tremor echoed faintly over the sheen of her silken manteau. She was nervous and on the verge of being intimidated, but not quite, considered the diplomat. She could hold her own, he thought as he held her hand a little longer than necessary and smiled kindly at her, offering a conventional phrase or two.

Shirley suddenly switched a raking glance at her father. Westin, however, avoided his guest's keen regard by affecting to study his daughter fondly, lowering his heavy-lidded eyes to mask a gleam of satisfaction in them.

Shirley was not fooled.

"The bastard knows, and is manipulating me."

He was grimly amused, thinking, "We will play this game my way, Westin, my man."

Shirley turned back to Mari.

"I hear you have had some unusual adventures."

He addressed her as she arranged her skirt on a settle.

"With your father's permission, I should like to hear of them, and ask some questions."

He sounded brisk and business-like, and noted with sly complacency that Sir Joseph seemed startled at his sudden initiative.

"Of course, of course, Sir Thomas...er....what would you like to hear?"

Westin looked straight at the other man, tension suddenly in his demeanor.

Shirley observed him and relaxed back into a chair, deciding to enjoy himself at Westin's expense.

"Well now, there is something I wish to know above all else."

He paused, and took a sip of wine. Mari sat stiff-backed and solemn, gazing unwavering at him. Sir Joseph's eyes narrowed, but his manner remained courteous.

Shirley continued, "Tell me, Miss Westin, though I'm not sure how extensive a young woman's knowledge of the subject would be...."

He waited a moment and surveyed her.

Mari looked back at him, grave and unblinking.

Westin carefully studied a snuff box. Shirley leaned forward earnestly, and continued, "Tell me, does the wonderful Selim continue to take all before him in the colonies. I hear you were in Maryland. Has he trounced the competition at the Annapolis races, do you know? We seem to be exporting some of our best bloodlines to America."

He settled himself back again in his chair, and accepted more wine from a decanter offered by Westin, who smiled sardonically, tipping his own glass in a small salute to Shirley.

Mari was neutral and not in the game. She took Sir Thomas at face value, and proceeded to tell him of her impressions at the Annapolis races. She told her story well. She relaxed.

Sir Thomas was pleasantly attentive and appreciative, prompting her occasionally with remarks about life in general throughout the colonies.

Aunt Mathilda finally joined them, announcing dinner, and went in on her brother's arm, Frederick Ashford being away, and Mari went in on the arm of Sir Thomas.

Once during the meal, Mathilda, with raised eyebrows, discreetly looked a question at her brother, but he had by now allowed Thomas Shirley to keep the reins of the conversation, merely shrugging slightly to communicate equivocation on Shirley's part, at best.

* * *

"So, he's going to think it over, is he?"

Mathilda sniffed her contempt.

"Don't worry, Joseph, if he backs away, and you're so appalled at introducing her on the London scene, Mari can stay here with Freddy and me. I'll find her someone – though society can be a bit dull down here, I must say."

Mathilda tugged at her stays to ease them, and motioned for another brandy.

"And if Chelmsford's environs don't come up with a suitable match, why, I'll take her on one of my trips abroad. Who knows, we'll mebbe catch a count or two."

Perplexed as he was, Joseph had to smile at his sister.

"Damn it, Matty, I'm continually out-maneuvered – first you and Tamsin, and now Thomas Shirley, not to mention that flighty daughter of mine."

He swallowed some of her brandy with grudging appreciation, and was momentarily distracted.

"Dare I ask if this was smuggled, along with the finery of that outfit you're wearing? Don't you think you favor the Kent dealers too often? You know Freddy reckons you'll get caught one of these days."

Mathilda gave an impatient wave of her hand, dismissing the thought.

"It's your own fault. You rushed the man, Tom. He's no fool, after all – and he's not actually given a definite refusal," she added.

Joseph set down his empty glass, and snatched off his wig, tossing it onto the couch beside him. He scratched his close-cropped head vigorously, and sighed, "Well, we will see sister. We'll be off to London in a couple of days. Shirley said he would think it over, and let me know. He is a man of his word."

Sir Joseph lounged back, legs sprawled in front of him, hands clasped behind his head, staring at the ceiling. A crafty smile played on his face.

"He was thrown at the sight of our little beauty, Matty! He couldn't hide it. He stood there, goggling like a moon-struck swain."

Mathilda judged her brother's intentions accurately, and didn't approve.

"You've a reprehensible streak in you, Joseph. And you can be a cold fish, though I say it myself."

Her brother grinned back unrepentant.

"Yes, sister dear, I accept your assessment, but you must admit, Shirley could solve my problem with my daughter in the most favorable way."

Mathilda huffed and rearranged a shawl, but she had no immediate reply, so finished her brandy instead. She could not resist, however, a shot at having the last word.

"In any event, brother Joseph, I shall accompany you to London. I'm determined to keep an eye on things."

She directed another glare of disapproval at her brother, and marched off to bed.

* * *

The Conduit Street house was astir with party preparations, and Tamsin Tallentire was in full flight and voice.

"Percy! Drat you – I'm all in a fog. What do you think you are about - powdering a cake or some gingerbread pudding, man?"

MistressTallentire, attired in a linen dressing jacket to protect her shoulders and costume, was in the powder room being attended by her wig-maker. An apologetic Percy Papplewick stood indeterminately waving a sheep's wool puff of some size above her head.

"How those dames, who have their own tresses done with pomatum and rice powder manage their composure, I can hardly imagine. The doxies must itch and scratch something fierce."

Mr. Papplewick made a moue of protest, but wisely remained silent, and Tamsin waved him aside.

She stood to take off her jacket and hand it to her maid, who looked pleased enough to witness some unfortunate other than herself the victim of her mistress's tongue.

"You do well to smirk, Maisie, my girl – find my patch box, I'll sport a beauty spot tonight."

Tamsin stepped into the corridor and shook out the folds of her dress. As usual, Mari could not help but admire her confident style.

"In matter of fact I'm right," Tamsin added with satisfaction, pausing in her progress.

"Last week I surprised that haughty Madame Peignton, who Ambrose is so fond of, in the water closet. She was poking her frizzed hair with a jeweled toothpick she carries. She had retired behind the screen to relieve herself in more ways than one."

Tallentire smiled at the memory of the proud Madame Peignton's discomfort, and stepped across her dressing room to admire herself in the long glass. Mari trailed behind her.

"Let Percy curl and puff your hair back from your brow, Mari, and wear one of those small flower sprays – on the left side, I think. Percy calls it a French pom-pom. He does them very nicely. Now that we are wearing small panniers of late – I don't think we need to be so elaborate about our heads."

Watching her father's mistress adjust her dress whilst regarding herself in the mirror, Mari fell again into the habit of following Tamsin Tallentire's lead. It was so much easier to go along with both Tamsin and Aunt Matty. They had both, in their ways, acted as a foil and a buffer between herself and her father, and she was grateful for that. She roused from her thoughts of Chelmsford, and turned to watch Tamsin as she put on some chosen jewelry.

"Are many of Papa's acquaintances to be here tonight?"

Mari had submitted to Mr. Papplewick's efforts, but asserted herself enough to refuse powder and the dreaded pomatum. Tamsin was right. They made the head itch. Waiting for her to finish adjusting her costume, Mari regarded her companion again in the mirror. There was no sentiment about Tamsin Tallentire. The woman was entirely practical.

Mari could not imagine her running away to sea on impulse to surprise a lover with romantic daring, to become a cabin boy. More likely, Tallentire would have arrived on board in style to occupy the captain's cabin, and have everyone at her beck and call.

Rueful amusement shaded Mari's face, as she waited for Tamsin to sort through the jewelry box. The scent of powder and Tamsin's perfume was heavy in the air of the dressing room, and diamonds flashed against the creamy column of her throat. Mari suddenly felt stifled and low, and glumly remembered Bryce Hunter.

Prowling through the staid Chelmsford gathering, he had seemed fresh and vigorous, and attractively dangerous to her naïve, girlish mind.

She had been foolish enough to imagine that she had caught his attention and regard enough to venture away with him. Why had he not joined her on *Integrity* instead of losing his life in a muddy ditch?

"Mari – you're day-dreaming. What do you think of this brooch?"

Tamsin's voice cut through her wool-gathering. Mari stared at their reflections in the mirror, almost without seeing for a moment.

"Oh – it's fine, Tamsin," she stammered.

"But I think the small gold bird with the pearls looks better as a hair ornament."

Tamsin leveled a shrewd glance, and, putting down the jewel, turned, taking Mari by the shoulders to study her face. Her regard was sympathetic, and she shook Mari gently, sympathetically.

"It's no use, poppet. He's not here anymore. Surely, you've had enough time to accept that."

Mari was silent, amazed at this perception. Tamsin paused reflectively, and turned again to finger the contents of the jewelry box.

"One way and another, whether your one-time beau meant to or not, he enticed you into danger. You have had some lively experiences this last year, to say the least. Put it all behind you, and....and....take your Papa's plans for you seriously."

Mari understood what Tamsin was saying, but hated to acknowledge the inevitable. She bridled a little, recovering her spirit as her melancholy over Bryce Hunter was replaced by the memory of Stewart Dean's bright, warm gaze studying her face.

"I'm not exactly ancient, Tamsin. Can't Papa wait for a suitor or two to come calling. Even if I were ugly, I'll have some fortune to attract them – and, anyway...."

She deliberately pushed beside Tamsin at the dressing table, and poked through the jewelry.

"Ugly I am not."

Selecting a pin of her mother's, Mari held it against her hair. It didn't look right. She had to admit that Mr. Papplewick's arrangement of small flowers and a feather suited better. Tamsin laughed, and looked merry.

"That's my Mari – come on...find your fan. Let's go down and see who sophisticated society is gossiping about today. Henry announced the immaculate Ambrose Fenster a while ago, and he'll be waiting to chaperone us until your Papa arrives. Thank heavens your Aunt Mathilda and Uncle Frederick have been doing the honors, and greeting the guests."

She proceeded to the stairway, and turned with a wicked smile.

"I don't suppose you fancy Mr. Fenster as a suitor, do you? He is fantastically rich, though, I had a mind to keep him on a string myself in case your Papa tires of my conversation."

Mari found herself giggling as she negotiated the stairs behind Mistress Tamsin. She could no longer be offended by the woman.

Tamsin was outrageous, but Mari had to curtail her giggles. Maisie had tightened her stays too much for levity.

Ambrose Fenster was, indeed, waiting downstairs. They saw him as they entered the drawing room. He looked the very picture of a fop, striking an attitude in the center of the room, studying a glass of sparkling wine. He could have been posing for a portrait.

Tamsin was delighted, and made a bee-line for him, whilst beaming gracious smiles in every direction. Mari resigned herself to be towed in the wake of the mistress.

"My dear, what a fine Macaroni you are – flaunting your new rose-colored peruke. Positively daring – and scented, too! But what have you done to your leg? I know you are much sought after for a dance partner, but it seems you must have practiced a pirouette too many."

Tamsin Tallentire broke off, overcome with gurgles of laughter.

The object of her teasing, Ambrose Fenster, was unnerved enough by his hostess's unfeigned jollity to unbend from a stiff pose of hauteur to glance down, past an exquisite Italian ivory silk waistcoat and matching britches, to examine his lower limbs.

His expression of puzzled concern changed to one of horror. His legs, indeed, looked decidedly odd. The left leg showed itself a full, manly shape, encased in lavender and gray striped silk hose, pulled smooth and tight. The other, however, was certainly misshapen. His lower right calf showed grossly puffed out and lumpy around the ankle, below a spindly thin shank and a knobbly knee.

Mari was diverted, and gazed fascinated, awaiting a reaction. Ambrose yelped with anguish.

"You really are a wretch, Tamsin. You're the one who encouraged me to stuff my stockings and bind my limbs with bombast to impress the ladies!"

Mari was amazed, and continued to stare at Ambrose. His consternation had turned to mortification.

Tamsin was overtaken by mirth again, and quite ruthless, she leaned forward and squeezed his right thigh.

"This ham is well padded, though, and that's a fact."

She spluttered, her ample bosom quivering with suppressed laughter.

"It just looks as though it belongs to someone else, Ambrose."

Mari began to feel sorry for Mr. Fenster, but, then Tamsin chuckled and relented, "You must make use of my boudoir to repair yourself, Ambrose. Call Maisie, if you need her.

"No, no, don't sidle like an awkward boy. Be bold, and move where it's most crowded, dearest, so there'll be little room for company to assess your gait."

So saying, she signaled Henry, and had him escort the embarrassed dandy to the doorway, where guests spilled out from the salon onto the elegantly tiled hall floor.

"Look at him – he's hot and bothered and nothing like as superior as he pretends."

Tamsin paused, looking after her victim with friendly scorn.

"At least he stays in style, though. His blushes match the color of his wig."

This remark brought another outbreak of laughter as she turned to Mari, then a keen gaze from her amazing eyes cut through the amusement.

"What's the matter, Poppet? You're serious again. Do you find us just too frivolous after the stern, God-fearing colonials? Don't find us all too contemptible. There's a fair degree of hard work and maneuvering goes on amidst the nonsense. My friends sometimes have uses your father quite appreciates, you know."

Mari demurred and mumbled a vague reply, feeling, as usual, both uncomfortable and irritated with herself for being so when examined by Mistress Tallentire.

"Look at Wilkes over there," Tamsin continued.

"He'll be tearing strips off some politician's reputation, writing his next inflammatory piece for *The North Briton*, wondering what's for dinner, and conning some grand dame or other whilst eyeing the kitchen maid, all at the same time."

She nodded toward a group of men, who were in animated argument centered around the lanky, untidy figure of John Wilkes.

Mari stared with curiosity. This was the man who had caused street riots in the city the night she had run away from home to find Bryce. He stood now, with a look of mockery and enjoyment on his features as argument erupted around him.

"The people love him, parliament don't," Tamsin added.

"He's for more independence for the colonials – at least, more say in their own affairs – and rights to vote and decide what to tax and what not. He's for abolishing the slave trade, too," she said.

"There are those who would wish him over in the colonies, except he'd cause even more trouble."

Tamsin appeared, for a moment, unusually serious. Then, she shrugged carelessly. "The colonists would wonder what had arrived. He'd shock 'em down to their buskins, no doubt."

The errant Member of Parliament in question suddenly turned and looked over to where they stood as though sensing their observation of him.

Seeing Tamsin Tallentire, he leered merrily at her, all the while standing with arms folded, and an ear bent to the words of a short, portly man, who was addressing him and reaching to pluck at his sleeve.

Tamsin shook with quiet laughter, and gave a quick, dismissive flick of her fan toward Wilkes as she deliberately turned away from him.

Mari was startled and disconcerted to realize that Tamsin and Wilkes were acquainted.

"Don't be so concerned my pet. I've grown to appreciate safe harbor with your Papa. Dallying with Master Wilkes would be high seas adventure, I think, great diversion for the game mistress but highly dangerous."

She linked her arm in Mari's.

"Let us go and get some supper before this crowd eat us out of house and home. I swear you'd think they had never seen a prettily presented jelly before, or tried a rustic confit. They over-stuff themselves and gargle their wine as though there is no tomorrow."

She studied Mari again.

"You, however, look as though it would do you good to plump out a little. Your time in the colonies honed you down too much. Your Aunt Mathilda is here this evening, and I want her to see that I am taking good care of you before your next bout of wits with your good Papa."

This said, she began steering her charge through the throng of guests toward the supper room.

Mari still felt herself in a kind of daze, as though with no will left of her own. She allowed herself to be maneuvered by Tamsin, as she had since turning up at the house a month before.

* * *

Thomas Shirley descended from his carriage. He was late arriving at Conduit Street. He had had mixed feelings about accepting Joseph Westin's invitation. Attending a rout for what Shirley considered the fashionable and frivolous, was not his idea of an enjoyable evening.

He had heard, however, that Westin's mistress attracted a wide range of characters from London's social scene to her soirees, and the Westin house was a useful place to pick up both news and views, gossip and rumors.

The evening should prove an interesting contrast to the night before, he decided, when he had sat through a dreary meeting with officials from the foreign office discussing affairs in the Caribbean.

He admitted also to a curiosity and desire to see Mari Westin again, though he had decided to decline her father's offer of her hand. As Shirley mounted the steps to the portico, the busy hum of a successful party reached him.

A crowd was circulating into and through the hallway between elegant reception rooms. Mathilda and Frederick Ashford stood at the foot of a sweeping staircase, greeting straggling arrivals. They both waved away his apologies for tardiness.

"Heavens, Sir Thomas – we have a positive melee here."

Mathilda waved a hand at the milling guests.

"It's only a wonder we've not had accidents with some of the carriages. You did most sensibly, arriving just now. A short while since and you would have been trapped in a crush."

Sir Thomas enquired after Sir Joseph Westin, and was surprised to find he would be late for his own entertainment. The diplomat decided that the Westins were a slightly odd family, and after exchanging a few pleasantries he bowed to the Ashfords and allowed himself to be directed toward a cluster of card tables at the far end of the long drawing room.

The tables were commandeered by an assortment of social-round veterans, including a duchess with a frowsy wig and grossly over-painted face, who watched the other players like the predator she was.

Sir Thomas eventually skirted the gaming tables, accepted a glass of sparkling wine, and sauntered to stand to one side of the drawing room door to survey the throng.

He was hungry, and decided he would go over to his club for supper alone, rather than jostle around the buffet tables here. He would give Westin a little while longer to turn up, and then make his excuses to leave.

He sampled his wine, which was good, as he listened idly to some heated discussion going on amongst a group of five or six men nearby. He recognized a couple of them. One was the unpredictable John Wilkes, who was in and out of parliament like a dog at the fair, thought Shirley.

It was hard to keep up with where the fellow was at. He saw the mischievous politician suddenly twist his head around and focus a lecherous look at someone behind, and turned to see who the object of this interest was,

Shirley saw Tamsin Tallentire as she laughed and turned away to say something to her companion.

Seeing Mari shocked Sir Thomas anew. Though he was annoyed at his own reaction yet again, he found himself gazing at her with fascination.

She was young, but carried herself well, and seemed, though in a crowd, to stand in a world of her own. She wore a less extravagant style of dress than many women in the room. Her hair was simply done, with a small flower decoration behind one ear. She appeared natural and fresh to him, and he thought she had an air of hesitancy, not timid but as though she had wandered into a world she found puzzling and intriguing, but was no part of.

Sir Thomas was surprised at how strongly this fancy took him. He was convinced, of a sudden, that this young woman, whilst not a naïve maid straight from the nursery, was neither the wild rapscallion fallen into disgrace that one would have supposed from her recent experiences.

He imagined she could in a very few years be a model society hostess, gracing some gentleman's home, but he also thought that she was worthy of a greater challenge. He found himself considering with interest how she might turn out. As she and Westin's mistress moved to the supper tables, Shirley postponed his departure and followed them.

"Sir Thomas! So pleased you have honored us with your presence."

Joseph Westin's voice, just behind him, slowed Shirley in his tracks as he was about to approach Mari and Tamsin. Westin took him by the arm and continued forward to present him to the two women.

"Mistress Tamsin Tallentire, my companion, and, of course, my daughter, Mari."

Shirley was irritated anew. He would have preferred to talk to Mari without Westin present. The daughter obviously found her father over-bearing.

Mistress Tallentire, for all her brash reputation, seemed to discern something of his feelings. She smoothly greeted Joseph and coaxed him away to attend some guests she insisted he had neglected. Westin gave in with calculated grace after giving his daughter a meaningful glare.

Mari knew that Sir Thomas was to voyage shortly to Antigua. She asked polite questions, and was rewarded by interesting replies. Shirley talked to her as a mature woman, not as to a girl.

At one point, when he spoke of trading ships and difficult conditions on board them, she remembered *Hazard* and *Integrity*, and said unthinkingly, "Yes, I know. Oh yes."

Then she blushed and looked confused.

"Yes, of course, you know what life at sea is like first-hand, don't you, Miss Westin? I confess I prefer to travel in more comfortable circumstances when possible."

He smiled gently, and distracted her from the moment by offering to find her some syllabub. He managed to induce her to recount something of her experiences in Maryland, and during the course of this remarked,

"Though your experience was harsh at times, yet you seem to have a certain nostalgia for life in the colonies. You sound a little as though you are speaking of cousins who have been unfair to you and exasperating, yet you feel warmth for them despite yourself. Can I be right?"

Mari pondered this, and, unable to articulate an adequate reply, nodded sheepishly.

"It is odd, I know – I was in such a lowly position, and treated as such, yet I felt sometimes, and in some ways, freer than I am here."

She gazed around the room.

"Amongst this...."

She looked closely at the man standing listening intently to her.

"That sounds foolish, I'm sure, not the wisest thing to say."

Shirley's eyes crinkled with amusement.

"No – go on," he urged.

"I just...I just, er, think..." she faltered to a stop, then started again.

"Some people have to work so hard, so bitterly hard for so little - many of them go out to the colonies simply to find a way of living."

Mari thought of Betsy Murphy as she spoke, and wondered whether her friend at Plinhimmon had found her brother, Liam, or, in fact, had had any chance at all of searching for him.

"Life is so harsh for some, and so easy for others."

She looked over the company again, at the fine satins and velvets of their clothes, and at jewels flashing in the candle light.

"That is life all over, Mari."

He said her name gently and almost absently.

"But, as I'm sure you now know better than most, it is far better to be privileged than not. At least if you hold some position in society, you have a certain choice over your actions and the way you regard others."

He hesitated as if to add more, but before he had the chance, Mari's father bore down on them, eyeing Shirley purposefully across the room as he approached.

Sir Thomas immediately switched his attention to his host, and forestalled any conversational gambit by quickly proffering his thanks and making his farewells to father and daughter.

As he turned to go, he added, "I would, however, like to call on you tomorrow 'fore noon, if I may Sir Joseph. If that would be convenient, of course."

Sir Joseph declared that it would be most convenient, and escorted Sir Thomas to the hall, leaving Mari standing with a dish of untasted syllabub in her hand, a little taken aback by Sir Thomas Shirley's abrupt departure.

Shirley had changed his mind. He had surprised himself, and would not have given prior odds on his final decision. Joseph Westin's blandishments had nothing to do with it. It was the girl herself. Young in many ways, but on the verge of becoming a strong-minded woman.

His initial rejection of the idea of marriage to such a young person had faded. He regarded Mari Westin as an unusual find. She would be pliable, and reasonable, and open to his mentoring and guidance. She would banish boredom and emptiness from his life on the domestic scene. He could watch her grow into her full beauty, and she was beautiful. He could mold her to perfection.

The idea of it was greatly appealing.

XVIII

"There's to be no defying me on this, Mari. You understand? You've been more than willful enough already, and my mind is made up, made up, I tell you."

Joseph Westin was at his sternest.

Sir Thomas Shirley had made a surprise appearance at the Westin town house to present his offer of marriage.

Mari was not summoned to see her suitor. Shirley had declared that he preferred to wait two days for his proposal to be considered, before calling back to hear the decision.

After Shirley left, Westin called his daughter to his study. Delighted and relieved at Shirley's proposal he rubbed his hands together, gloating over the success of his own machinations.

Catching sight of Mari standing silently by the open door, he beamed and waved her magnanimously to sit down.

He began a monologue on how fortunate she was to have the attention and address of such a man as Thomas Shirley.

There was to be no question of refusal. Except she did refuse.

"I can't – I won't."

The words burst out.

"I barely know the man, and he's so much older!"

She was breathing fast and glaring at her father. For a second, Westin was speechless in disbelief at her temerity and glowered back.

"Yes, chit – and wiser. A man of substance and moral rectitude."

He paused, then paced in front of her, coattails swinging as he turned abruptly.

"Shirley is wealthy and well positioned, not some young wastrel, a fortune hunter who would squander your dowry in no time. You need to be settled, and Shirley as an older man is ideal – so fix your mind on it!"

"What sort of life are you wishing on me, Father? I have been errant – but surely I have the right to make such a decision in my own time."

Westin's good humor had evaporated with his benign smile.

"What sort of life?" he rapped out.

"What sort of life? One that will allow you to live in the greatest comfort and under the control of a mature man as you take your position in society.

"That is clearly what you need, and that is what you shall have. And be thankful it is possible in spite of your habit of disobedience and willful silliness."

Mari breathed deeply and answered through tight lips.

"Sir Thomas is a pleasant enough man, but I have no desire to marry at all, let alone to a man his age," she fumed.

"He is almost as old as you are, Father!"

She stood rigidly, with fists clenched at her side, staring her father down, and he recognized the tenacity in her gaze. So like her mother in looks, but decidedly lacking Anna's gentle softness.

Westin held his fire as he stamped around the room, thumping the furniture a few times before delivering an ultimatum, voice flat and uncompromising, face set and unsympathetic.

"Think on it, Mari – carefully. If you would be my daughter with a roof over your head, think hard. Sir Thomas will be back in two days."

He stared at her grimly.

"You had better make the right decision."

He turned and stomped out, leaving Mari to weigh his words. Moments later, she heard the front door crash closed behind him.

Back in her own room, Mari, sitting fuming in solitude, felt the silence of the house around her. The servants must have heard it all. It was as though everyone had scurried for cover. Aunt Matty would turn up soon.

Mari was pretty certain that Sir Joseph would send for his sister to try and persuade, where he had failed to bully. Mathilda was still in London, visiting friends, not too far away.

Mari was washed with anger again. It had been as though years of hurt feelings, held down and crushed into submission, had erupted and blasted out at her father. She knew it was little use, though. She had made no impression, except to fuel his own temper.

She realized that all she was required to do was to agree meekly to everything. That would have been all that mattered. He had no aim or interest but to get her off his hands. He wished only to hear "Yes,

Papa," to sort out the problem, and release him for more important business.

Mrs. Pynchon came to her room eventually to urge her to take some dinner. Mari accepted something on a tray. The housekeeper looked sympathetic and concerned, but said nothing, leaving her alone.

Mari restlessly paced her chamber, unable to come to any conclusion as to what she should do next. She recalled the night, over a year ago, when she had fled from this same room to run through London and take a ship for America, thinking that the man she loved would be on board and waiting for her.

She remembered the boys of the river, Jinty and Tibbs, and wondered if little Perisher was still with them, or even still alive.

She wanted desperately to leave again, but, this time, from despair of being forced into a relationship, not anticipation of a new and loving one with a partner willingly sought for his own sake.

Finally, Mari sat down by the window and was dully watching the street vendors below, when she became aware of someone standing behind her.

It was Tamsin. Mari had not heard her tap on the door, or enter the room. Tamsin stood, arms akimbo, studying Mari.

The mistress was dressed in a dark blue fine wool costume, cut rather more severely than was her usual style. The coat and skirts were fashioned after a riding habit, although Mari knew Tallentire never rode if she could help it.

Without saying anything, Tamsin strode to the armoire and selected a cloak. Mari stared at her, perplexed.

"Cover yourself with this. Don't bother to change, but you might put on something other than those light slippers. We might need to use pattens," Tamsin said peremptorily.

Not even thinking to ask why, Mari asked where they were going. Tamsin was brisk.

"You'll see when we get there, Poppet – I have something to show you – but we must make haste and leave before your father returns. With luck we'll be back before he is, and he'll be none the wiser, and we'll save a great deal of bother and argument."

Mari was amazed and puzzled, but could see the other was determined. She swirled the cloak over her shoulders. It was an all-encompassing, old-fashioned garment, pulled from the back of the

214

cupboard. It was rather like the old dominoes once in style. Mari was dubious about her dress.

"It looks cold outside, Tamsin."

"You'll be warm enough in the coach. We have the loan of your Aunt Mathilda's carriage. It's not so grand as your father's, but more convenient."

Tamsin gave Mari no time to protest, but swept out into the hall and started down the stairs. Mari followed, yet again, in her wake.

The maid, Maisie, was waiting by the door and followed them out. Beales, the coachman, obeyed Tamsin's instructions, and set his team down to Piccadilly and east across London.

As they clattered past The Star tavern on Piccadilly, Tamsin leaned toward the window and gestured, "Look close, Mari, see the well-dressed women, playing the coquette with their beaux. The Star is busy tonight – their backroom will be well patronized."

She smiled a shade too brightly and flared her eyes at Mari, who affected not to understand.

"Now, shall we have a look down the Haymarket, or go along High Holborn? I think we'll view the goings-on in the Haymarket, and then make our way down The Strand. Haymarket has plenty of entertainment, especially for abandoned females, or so they say."

Tamsin had settled back on the cushions, and looked across at Maisie, who was sitting silently with a small, knowing smirk about her mouth.

Mari refused to comment, and stared out at the street market, alive and noisy with its jumble of humanity. There did seem to be a surfeit of women, parading aimlessly up and down. Some were quite prettily dressed. Others looked like simple country maids, and some were tawdry and down-at-heel with weary faces.

"There are some of us well acquainted with life in Haymarket and alleys off The Strand, aren't there Maisie?"

Maisie wiped the smile off her face and tried to look as if butter wouldn't melt in her mouth, as Tamsin spoke again.

"All those literary gentlemen, in and out of the coffee houses and chop shops, getting their pockets lightened one way or another."

Mari still refused to be drawn, and pretended disinterest, although she had already perceived what Tamsin Tallentire was trying to do. She remained silent and resentful.

They reached The Strand, and bowled past fashionable shops, crowded coffee houses, and taverns, with, in between, glimpses down gloomy side streets full of stalls and vendors.

Mari thought of Jinty and Tibbs again, and wondered whether they were busy on the river looking for trade. She tried to remember which lane down to the water had been their escape from the soldiers on the night she ran away to sea.

There seemed to be any number of figures lingering in dark doorways. Drabs, sauntering with dingy skirts swinging, eyed passing men. Quite a few pick-pockets were working the crowds, as folk loitered carelessly to listen to street singers caroling the latest political ballads. They were selling pamphlets from a ha'penny to sixpence, depending on the interest shown.

Mari kept the pretense of insouciance as their coach left The Strand, heading along Fleet Street and over the Fleet ditch. Her heart lurched as they neared St. Pauls, and, finally, she again demanded to know where they were going.

Tamsin smiled, and said, "Wait and see, Mari."

Mari, in irritation, refrained from showing further interest, and contained her curiosity. She was convinced that they were heading toward The Tower, and imagined with a crazy hope that they were aiming for Gould Square and the Hunters' house.

Bouncing along the familiar thoroughfare, her heart lodged in her throat as she thought of arriving at Dan and Alicia Hunter's residence.

Some days earlier, she had thought of trying to get a message to them about Bryce and perhaps to offer condolences, but had abandoned that idea after overhearing Mrs. Pynchon mentioning the Hunters to Tamsin, saying they were away for the winter season and the house was closed.

The coach eventually rattled over Little Tower Hill and down onto a dirty, ill-kept track that led onto Radcliffe Highway.

"Here we are my beauties – old stamping ground. Everything for the sailor, chandlers and taverns aplenty. Do you see anyone we know, Maisie girl?"

Maisie flicked her eyes nervously at Tallentire, then looked quickly at Mari and away again. She turned and mumbled something. Tamsin leaned forward, searching faces as they bounced over the ruts and potholes of the road.

216

The buildings either side were mainly low and meanly built, although Mari recalled Dan Hunter at one time remarking that there had been fine enough houses here. Now there were mainly low boarding houses, cheap lodgings, and taverns for the river trade, with rat runs of narrow alleys behind.

Again, there were street women galore. At one point, Tamsin exclaimed in surprise, and had Beales stop the carriage.

"Maisie – look! That little wench trolling the alleyway there, that looks like little Tilly, don't it?"

Mari peered in the direction she indicated. Maisie started to shrug and turn down her lip in disgust, but then became suddenly still, and leaned forward herself to stare more closely at a slight figure. Checking Tamsin's face, Mari saw that she had an intent, somber look.

"Yes – little Tilly. Never made it from the bottom of the heap. Just look at her."

Mari did. This was obviously the object of Mistress Tallentire's exercise.

The girl in question was standing abjectly at the corner of a lane, by the highway. It was a winter's evening, but she was dressed in poor rags, with no shawl or cloak to protect her from the cold. She was not remotely pretty and looked the worse for wear, with lines of hunger and scars of the pox adding disaster to the dirt on her face. She said something to a burly porter, exiting a nearby tavern, and was brushed aside. She was missing several teeth.

"Well – didn't take her long to sink ter th'bottom, Mistress."

Maisie had found her voice, but her face betrayed no feeling. Tamsin was thoughtful.

"How old do you think that little beauty is?"

Mari shrugged, assuming the question was for her. She found it truly hard to tell. Hunched against the wall, in the gathering gloom of the evening, the waif could have been an old woman – but something about her still said youth, though she didn't seem to stand quite straight. Some affliction was there, apart from poverty.

Tallentire suddenly rapped on the coach door to signal the coachman.

"Take us home, Beales. We've done enough touring the town."

She sat back again, lost in thought.

Mari was puzzled. The outing seemed to have been pointless. Tamsin had not shown her anything she did not already know.

"Tilly Astill."

Tamsin spoke softly, almost to herself.

"Little Tilly Astill – that's her name. Started on the streets by old Mother Clap, at about eight years old, I think. There was something wrong with her, though. Her spine started bending, and young as she was, she turned off some of the customers. Some of your gallants are superstitious, even the sorts who aren't too fastidious. Looks as though she was turned out to fend for herself.

"She must be your age now, Mari, but I wouldn't lay any odds she'll last too long on the Radcliffe Highway on her own, and in that state. What do you say, Maisie – never go back to old haunts?"

Maisie stared out of the carriage dumbly, and nodded without saying anything. Her cloak was pulled tightly around her, and she pushed back into the seat cushions, as if in retreat.

Mari felt rebellious and furious. Who did Tamsin think she was, bringing her to these streets? She pulled her own cloak around her, and shifted into the opposite corner of the carriage, sitting sullenly and silent all the way back to Conduit Street.

* * *

Mari was totally frustrated. Tamsin was obviously very serious in her effort to persuade her to obey her father. She had been berated repeatedly by Westin's mistress on the journey home.

Tamsin was scornful of the months Mari had spent out in the world, shifting for herself. She said that though Mari fancied herself knowledgeable and quite the adventurer, in her arrogance she really had no idea of the danger she now courted. Mari admitted to herself that Tamsin was right, but would not say so.

Tamsin tried sweet reason. After all, Mari could have a fine, exciting life, going overseas with Thomas Shirley. Marriage to such a man conferred immediate status that not many young women her age could expect. Mistress Tallentire even opined that Thomas Shirley was a much more manageable kettle of fish than Joseph Westin.

"But he's as old as my father!" Mari yelled at one point, only to have Tamsin calmly, and infuriatingly, wave her fan dismissively.

"That's to your advantage, Poppet. He'll likely leave you a very rich widow, with society at your feet, and, meantime, before he goes, dote on you like an old fool."

Mari used silence again as her only weapon, and arriving back at the house, made her escape upstairs with no courtesy or apology.

Tamsin was unfazed and marched to her own chambers, trailed by the attentive acolyte, Maisie, but Mari's relief was to be short-lived.

A sharp rap on her bedroom door announced Tallentire's return. She sailed into the room without waiting for a summons, as though all was sweetness and light. She had changed into a loose, becoming night gown of blue moiré silk, and fiddled with sapphire ear pendants as she arranged herself on the window seat. She ordered Maisie to pour them each a glass of cordial.

"Then go and bring me some lavender water for my feet."

Maisie did this so expeditiously she must have had the bowl ready, and Mari had to watch in exasperation as Tallentire lounged back, sipping elderflower cordial and wriggling her toes in the sharply scented water. She sighed with relief, and studied critically a new brocade slipper she held in one hand.

"My, these new slippers make my feet sore."

Mari was nonplussed, hardly able to turn the woman out and send her away with dripping feet. It was absurd. Mistress Tallentire seemed unassailable. Tamsin sighed at the resentful young woman in front of her.

"Don't you understand, Mari? Your father is determined on this marriage, and if you deny him, he is ruthless enough to turn you onto the streets. Then, you really would become acquainted with what it means to fend for yourself.

"And don't think you will be able to go to your Aunt Mathilda. She's a strong woman and can influence her brother in many ways, but in the case of his authority over you as a father, she will not cross him. She is conventional enough for that, my pretty one. Make no mistake."

Mari felt weary and cornered, trapped again. The only glimmer of an idea she could muster, was to pretend to give in. She could say "Yes" to her father and Shirley, and, perhaps gain some period of time to think up a device to aid herself.

She fretted: why couldn't she go to Ravenhill? She could be with Sarah and Miss Pardoe again, stay there quietly for a time, and, perhaps, redeem herself a little. However, she knew the answer to that already.

She had thrashed that through with her father. He meant, as part of her punishment, that she should not be allowed back at Ravenhill to enjoy little Sarah's company. Brother Tom was away, perhaps for years, and could be no ally.

Yet she hated to give in. Maisie, the insolent maid with her sly smirk, and Tamsin Tallentire, her father's mistress of all people, giving her directions as to progress in life. A trollop who had traded and beguiled her way from the back-street slums to a gentleman's mansion!

Looking at her, though, Mari voiced nothing of this. In fact, her fierce resentment was undermined by Tamsin's straight, mocking gaze.

"You never know anyway, Poppet, you just may meet up some young Virginian again," she teased.

"If you did, it would be quite the ton for you to have an affair, and I'm sure any vigorous colonial would be only too happy to oblige."

Having finished her foot bath and monologue, Tamsin shrugged her shoulders as she arranged her robe, and sauntered back to her boudoir, leaving Maisie to clear away the basin and linen, and Mari to ponder on Tamsin's last words as usual. Surprisingly, it was the drab Maisie who brought Mari to the point of decision.

The maid was kneeling and slowly wringing out a towel over the bowl.

"Oh, for heaven's sake, Maisie! Be quick and go. I want to be left alone."

Maisie didn't seem to hear. Just as Mari was about to repeat the reprimand, the maid let the towel drop back into the water and looked up at her. Maisie's face looked drawn and miserable.

"That Tilly, Mistress Mari. That little Tilly. Could've bin me, easily, could've bin me. I was goin' that way, when Tallentire took me in hand."

She stared at Mari with an intense, dark look for a long moment.

The room was quiet, except for the clock ticking and the comforting crackle of the fire in the grate. Maisie broke the silence again.

"You – you'd be gobbled up on London's streets. You'll be gobbled whole, lady. They'd be harder on a Mari Westin than they would on a Tamsin Tallentire. You'll bring out the nastiness of your own kind. Tallentire they take for what she is."

Mari suddenly shivered, though she told herself that Maisie was a simple-minded servant wanting to dramatize for some effect.

* * *

It seemed there was to be no respite.

It was now Mathilda Ashford's turn to persuade her niece of a daughter's duty. The aunt arrived the next morning, waving the servants aside, sailing past them, and entering the upstairs parlor in a bustle of petticoats. She was wearing a severe but becoming outfit in russet colored silk with velvet trimmings on the bodice and sleeves.

Mari had to smile, in spite of herself, as she saw Aunt Matty, who always managed some frivolous touch to her sober outfit. On this occasion, a large curly feather danced over her aunt's hat, at odds with the sober lines of her costume.

Mathilda Ashford plumped down on the couch without ceremony, unpinning the headdress. She sighed, and studied her niece.

"It's time to grow up Mari."

She was silent for a while, and Mari, bereft of argument, made no reply.

"You know, given your situation, you would be better off married to Sir Thomas. Just suppose your father allowed your refusal, and did not abandon you. He will still be determined to have you off his hands the soonest he is able to arrange it, and will pretty much make your life miserable until he has succeeded in that."

Aunt Matty looked down as though contemplating some inner idea.

"Sir Thomas is a decent man, of that I am assured. And I…I think he has an intelligence beyond that of your Papa, even though I say that of my own brother."

She added this hastily, catching Mari's look of surprise.

"You wouldn't merely be safe and well cared for, girl – you would have obligations with a man of his standing, of course, but you'd have a certain direction over your own actions, too."

She looked up at Mari again.

"None of us is totally free to do as we please, Mari. In accepting Thomas Shirley, you would take the best of options facing you, in my opinion."

She kept gazing at her niece worriedly.

"I am not here to push too hard, Mari."

She made an impatient gesture.

"Oh – I don't know what Mistress Tallentire has been saying to persuade you, though I can imagine. I do know your Papa's position. Of that I'm in no doubt. The best I can say, I've a notion you could be as happy with Shirley as I have been with your Uncle Frederick, and I can't say more than that, my dear."

She rose and walked to the bell-pull, and then turned.

"Though, in truth, I could say more than that – Thomas Shirley is more elegant than your uncle, and tidier, too. I've never seen him with porter stains on his cravat."

She tut-tutted to herself, and gave the bell-pull a vigorous tug.

"All this persuading makes me thirsty. What shall we have – tea or Madeira."

Mari sat down next to her, back on the couch, amused again and distracted from the situation.

"You mean," she ventured, "that Thomas Shirley manages to hang on to his wig whilst dancing the minuet, and won't embarrass me by forgetting which is his left or right foot?"

Her aunt chuckled.

"That's better, niece, let's have a touch of humor here. The world's not ending. It's just another door opening for you. You know, too, Mari, you needn't be timorous at the difference in age between you. Whatever their age, men have their weaknesses, too, and, often as not, don't know how to read us. You must learn to manage them, and call their bluff when necessary – not to say take advantage at times."

She added this with a non-committal sideways look.

"Do you take such advantage of Uncle Frederick, aunt?"

Mari couldn't resist, and faked solemnity. Aunt Matty had the grace to look a little abashed.

"Well – yes, but you know only for his own good, of course, he's such a hopeless dear at times."

She managed to finish this statement with an air of comfortable righteousness. The two looked each other in the eyes for a long moment, then smiled at each other, and Mari saw her aunt's love and concern. Who could she trust if not Mathilda Ashford? She did trust her.

"I think Sir Thomas is coming tomorrow forenoon, Aunt Matty. I'll accept his offer, if I can be married at Ravenhill, in the church to be near where Mama lies, and so I can see Little Sophie and Miss Pardoe again."

Her aunt's eyes softened as she gave a firm nod of approval.

"That's without question, Mari, that's without question. It's little enough for that brother of mine to concede."

* * *

Mari watched from the upstairs parlor window as Sir Thomas's chaise drew up to the front of the house. The man himself descended, and stood for a few moments considering the front door, as if undecided whether to approach or not. He eventually strode forward energetically, and Henry, the footman, opened the door to conduct him to Joseph Westin's study.

Mari waited, standing by the fire, to be summoned, and soon there appeared Mrs. Pynchon to escort her downstairs. She was surprised as she reached the hallway to encounter her father leaving his study.

Westin stopped and surveyed his daughter from head to toe, and gave a grunt of approval and a dense stare, as if daring her to say anything.

"Your suitor awaits you, Mari," was all he said, as he strode across the hall to the drawing room.

Mari went into the library-study. It had always been her favorite room, and she was embraced again by the warmth of familiarity.

Thomas Shirley stood by the fireplace, apparently studying the clock on the mantel shelf. She greeted him with a formal curtsey. He took a step forward, and then halted to study her closely.

She noticed he had his hat still tucked under his arm, as if about to leave. He had an air of hurry, and preoccupation about him, emphasized by the fact that he hovered from one foot to the other.

It struck her as a little odd. He seemed as if ready to flee, and she found herself surprised into thinking, "That is the impression I should be giving.

There was no preamble to his address, just a straight forward, "Well then, Mari, will you have me or no?"

Mari saw no reason to indulge in fluttery modesty. Taking a deep breath, she stared back at him, and noticed a trace of hesitancy in his assured, confident expression.

"Yes, I'll have you, Sir Thomas. I accept your kind proposal if you're certain my youth is not such a hindrance to one in your position."

There was an immediate flash of amusement and pleasure in his eyes, which Mari noted were a light gray-green.

"I have to tell you, I have been notified of the necessity of taking ship back to Antigua sooner than I expected. I had thought to remain in England several months more, but that cannot be.

"It means not delaying a wedding too long, and also that you would not have the usual time in which to arrange your trousseau, or other items you might find necessary for such a move."

He looked less assured again, and Mari remembered Aunt Mat's words. She recalled leaving London for the colonies, dressed in Tom's old clothes with a couple of coins in her pocket, and, again, leaving Plinhimmon with even less.

"I am quite ready to go any day – as soon as you please, Sir Thomas. I have clothes aplenty, and I have no need for the trammel of trinkets and boxes galore."

She looked directly at him.

"I enjoy feather beds and brocade curtains, but I don't have need of them."

He was taken by surprise, but couldn't prevent a broad smile breaking out.

"You haven't questioned me about your expectations of our life together – here, or in the colonies, wherever we might chance to be."

Then, without waiting for questions, he proceeded to tell her, and she listened. He was practical and succinct, occasionally looking at her as if to gauge the effect of his words.

He must have been reassured, because he continued describing island life, and outlining his responsibilities. Finally, he wound down, and stood gazing into the fire.

"So, Mari, is your answer still 'Yes?'"

She simply smiled and nodded. He looked pleased, but puzzled.

"You don't seem overly exercised at the idea of such change in your life."

She smiled again.

"Perhaps I'm not such a giddy, excitable young thing as my father and my past led you to believe."

He relaxed again.

"No, no, I don't think you can be."

He slowly reached out his hand to take hers and covered it with both of his. "Shall we end your father's vexation, then, and tell the rest of the world?"

Mari rang for Henry and had him summon her father. When Sir Joseph came back into the study, he took one glance at them standing there together, holding hands, and could not prevent a shaft of triumphant satisfaction on his face, as he made a bow to Sir Thomas, and stepped forward to shake his hand.

Mari felt the warm pressure of Shirley's fingers, as he gave hers a quick, reassuring squeeze and threw her a glance of amusement, as he reached out to shake hands with her father.

"It doesn't matter, Papa, strut all you please – you are not the only winner here," Mari thought.

XIX

Thomas Shirley restlessly paced the length of the balcony, his eyes switching from scanning the sea off Antigua to checking the twisting drive of the Ryder Manor House.

His carriage was not overdue, but he was anxious to be back at English Harbour, and regretted giving in the previous evening to his host's invitation to stay overnight. Peter Romilly was a generous host, but Shirley found socializing for its own sake tedious.

After supper, a long discussion with Romilly over plantation practices and Antiguan affairs generally had been useful and even informative, but the background to their conversation had been a constant flow of shrieks, giggles and demands for attention from the Romilly woman and her coterie of visiting females.

Shirley hadn't blamed his Mari for pleading an indisposition and heading for their chambers early, and, thinking of it, couldn't blame Romilly either for buttonholing him for the evening.

No sign of the carriage.

Below the balcony, a well-laid stone terrace was bounded by a low wall and shade trees from which greensward rolled down toward the dunes and seashore. The sea stretched sapphire blue and appeared motionless except for the edges of soft waves creaming the sand. Apart from a smudge on the horizon of a passing ship, it also appeared empty.

He leaned his elbows on the balcony's edge, brushing against the foliage of some kind of vine which had climbed high enough to send down a cascade of purple flowers to paint the stones below.

The only sounds were a rustling and chirping of some finch-like birds lodged among the tangle of vegetation. The little birds seemed unfazed by humans, and they had amused Mari by occasionally flying into their room to check for any fruit and crumbs that might be on trays or tables.

He had been glad to see his wife relaxed and smiling at the enterprising, cheeky feathered visitors, and to observe her mood lightening again.

Could it be that the sadness that had suffused her since he loss of her baby so many months ago was finally lifting? Momentarily he dared to hope that she would change her mind about going home to England, at least briefly, for a family break.

She was at present dozing on a reclining couch on the terrace in the shade, a book loosely held against her side, the hem of her skirt ruffled slightly by a breeze.

He leaned further over the balustrade to look down at her and thought that he would like to see a painting of the scene.

Physically, the island was what old sailors called a paradise, with its lush green landscape and rainbow range of blossom colors.

His restless eyes were drawn to the huge balls of blazing orange flowers of the Flamboyant trees by the wall, several of which had the bright flame of their color set against the stunning blues of sea and sky.

The terrace wall was pretty well smothered by a scented blanket of creamy blossoms, some kind of honeysuckle perhaps, their profusion imitating the contours of soft folds of snow.

The scene was idyllic, and Shirley smiled again, looking at his wife. It even had the required sleeping beauty, he fancied, then abruptly the fairy tale fantasy showed its dark side.

Sounds of fuss and commotion came from the sunken gardens at the side of the house, and the beautiful scene took on a sinister note as three figures emerged the other side of the terrace wall to sit beneath the Flamboyant trees: Romilly's wife and two visiting friends.

The wife had persuaded her guests to wear a type of hood that Shirley had never seen on any of the other islands. The hood was of calico and covered the head and face. It was sewn simply to a high-point, with round holes the size of a shilling for the eyes. A number of women on Antigua wore the hoods when out in public, and some suggested it was to protect the ladies' complexions.

Shirley didn't see that. As far as he could tell, and Mari agreed, it was more to shield the wearers' faces from observation, though not from shyness or modesty, but rather to enable them to stare rudely and pass commentary that would otherwise be uncountenanced.

The women's figures were nothing if not bizarre, with the nightmarish caricature of the pointed hoods draped over elaborately fashioned European silks.

He recognized which figure was Romilly's wife, Zara, by the habit she had of smothering a giggle, hunching her shoulders and dipping her chin as she clapped a hand to her mouth.

Heads pressed together, the women brought to his mind the three witches at the beginning of Hamlet. Shirley mentally conjured up a cauldron and darkness in place of the bright, surrounding scene.

Looking back at where Mari lay on the couch, he saw that, though still apparently dozing, her head had moved and was tilted toward the sound of giggles and whispering. She had roused from a pleasant sleep to see them marring the landscape.

He watched her suddenly sit up and stare down at the stones of the terrace. Her book was clapped shut, held flat between her hands as if in prayer.

With a shaft of conviction he knew - she's going to leave. She needs to be away from this island. But for how long? Will she come back?

* * *

The ship made its way up the Thames toward the Pool of London. Mari stood on deck for a long period, gazing out at familiar landmarks with a mix of memories crowding her mind.

She recalled sailing down river on Captain Coward's *Integrity* when she ran away to sea in the hope of meeting meet Bryce Hunter more than a decade ago.

An image of the sharp, pale faces of the river boys, Jinty and Tibbs, came back to her with surprising clarity, and she wondered where they were now. Were they still plying the water for passengers, and taking advantage of whatever illicit trade might chance their way? The little one, whose name Mari never knew, Perisher they had called him, he surely would not still be alive.

She imagined a small, wan ghost by the river's edge, at one with the fog and mist, remembering the way in which he had clutched the bread she had given him. He had held the rare warmth of Abby's fresh-baked loaf to his chest and breathed its fragrance with a rapt expression on his pathetic face.

Mari remembered, too, setting sail for the Leeward Isles with Thomas Shirley. That time, she was ushered aboard ship with deference, as the wife of an important officer of the king.

Her mind then jumped to Ravenhill, where their wedding ceremony was held. The affair had, in fact, turned out well, though she had missed the presence and support of her brother Tom, who was away at sea.

Her father had surprised her by laying on a generous banquet, with sports and entertainment for the Ravenhill staff and locals. They had celebrated the union of Westin's daughter and Thomas Shirley with a special enthusiasm as it occasioned a rare and impromptu holiday.

Mathilda Ashford and Mari's father had smiled with approval and complacency throughout.

Tamsin Tallentire had even been persuaded by Joseph Westin to lose her claim on some of Lady Anne's jewelry, and Mari paraded her mother's set of sapphires under Tamsin's watchful eyes.

At one point, Aunt Mat had commented aside to her niece, "A very well-managed affair, Mari. Very well, indeed – like the old days at Ravenhill, when your mother was alive. I think Sir Thomas's relations have been pleasantly surprised too. I've a notion they came a little on sufferance, expecting us to be too rustic and not elegant enough. Well…"

She had smiled to herself with satisfaction, and smoothed a new velvet stomacher encrusted with seed pearls.

"The Westins surprised 'em. Ravenhill takes some beating when it puts on a show."

Mathilda had beamed proudly, and surveyed her childhood home, no doubt sifting through memories of her own. Uncle Fred, standing next to his wife, had winked across at Mari and raised his glass, smiling encouragement.

The hubbub of London's tumultuous dockside broke through Mari's musings and swept memories aside.

Goods were already being loaded onto waiting lighters, and passengers were scrambling to disembark themselves and their baggage, with a mixture of harassment and relief.

Sailors jumped about their business with cheerful alacrity, not forgetting to doff caps or tug forelocks in the hope of an occasional gratuity coming their way from landlubbers utterly grateful to have arrived safely, and desperate to feel terra firma underfoot once more.

Mari waited with her maid, Izzy, for the wherry to take them to the wharf, and, peering over the water, she could just make out a dark, glossy carriage with the bright colors of the Westin coat-of-arms gleaming in cold sunlight. Tom had come to welcome his sister home.

When, finally, the fuss of landing was through, they set off for Conduit Street, and, again, came memories as they passed nearby the Hunters' old house in Gould Square. Mari made no remark, but Tom, studying her face, read her mind.

"The Hunters went back to America long since," he said.

"The Nortons are still there, I believe, and handle some of Dan Hunter's business for him."

He seemed about to say more, but sat back in the coach seat and fiddled with the buttons on his jacket. He appeared preoccupied and tense for a while, but, then, abruptly broke his silence to give his sister the news of their father's death.

Sir Joseph had died at Ravenhill, he said, of some kind of seizure. He would be buried there, next to their mother.

Tom told her they would be stopping at the townhouse to rest overnight, and setting off the next day for the funeral.

He had paused briefly, as if waiting for a reaction from his sister, and then added that Aunt Mathilda and Uncle Frederick would be traveling from their Chelmsford house. Tamsin Tallentire would also be present, Tom said.

Mari, somehow, could think of nothing to say about her father. She was shocked and at a loss for a suitable response.

She found herself inconsequentially thinking instead of the ebullient ways of Westin's mistress. She could hardly imagine Tamsin in mourning dress, and said so distractedly.

Tom smiled, a little puzzled at her apparent calm acceptance of his news. Her face looked solemn with a slight frown.

"Oh, Tamsin's quite the lady now. I think we were all confounded that she stayed the course so long. But, you know, Pa set her up in a place of her own about a year or so ago. She has a rather nice house in Chelsea, a fashionable place, of course. They had an amicable arrangement, and he's allowed for her in his will, so she's well set in life."

He mused to himself for a while.

"She holds quite a salon, I hear. I think all told she was good for Pa, humored him and sweetened him up from his grumpy, sour ways." Tom chuckled.

"She could stand up to him, too."

He turned his attention back to his sister, searching her face with a critical look.

"What about you, Sis? You look very much the fine, beautiful lady, but you've an air of sadness about you – though I honestly can't believe it's because of Pa."

As soon as he said this, Tom looked abashed, but he was right.

Though Mari was deeply sorry that she had not arrived back in England in time to see her father alive, she recognized there was no possibility that she and he could ever have been back on an easy, familiar footing.

After her marriage, Joseph Westin had limited himself to an occasional, formal letter over the years, mostly expressing his expectation that she should continue to fulfill her role as Sir Thomas Shirley's wife with diligence and proper gratitude.

Mari felt no loss of warmth and understanding from his departure. There had been none for her. She felt regret only at what might have been.

Real grief settled like a dark well within her for her lost baby. She thought back to the time she felt his warm little body heavy in her arms, dying of a pestilential ague before he could even walk, and she mentally cursed Antigua.

Mari found it impossible to speak of that, even to Tom, who was probably the person she loved most, and with whom she had always been at ease.

Considering her with a somber but loving eye, Tom acknowledged her strange mood, and accepted excuses of fatigue after the weeks at sea. He assured Mari that she was not expected to have anything to do with the settling of father's affairs. That would fall to him, and Mari was fully content with that.

So, Conduit Street, again. The library was just as she remembered it, comfortable and silent, except for the steady ticking sound of the ormolu clock marking away time that, nevertheless, seemed to stand still in this room. Mari recalled that her father used to wind it himself.

She and Tom breakfasted early, and, waiting for him, she strolled aimlessly to the window, too restless to sit down.

Familiar street sounds punctuated the quiet of the room. She watched a milk maid, sitting on a three-legged stool outside a house a few doors away, milking a pretty, brown cow. The animal was small but showed a good, full udder. Someone's kitchen maid stood waiting for a pail of the milk, looking aloof and superior, not condescending to engage in conversation with the country girl.

Mari sighed, and sat herself down on the window seat, resigned to waiting for her brother. She looked forward to seeing her baby sister, Sophie, still thinking of her as that, though they had not seen each other for years.

Soon, there would be her first view of Ravenhill in all that time, too. According to Tom, things were remarkably the same.

He told her that Miss Pardoe was still employed to care for Sophie, though a governess was certainly no longer required. Miss Pardoe would most likely go with Sophie when she eventually married, which Tom thought likely in the near future. Mrs. Trant, the Ravenhill housekeeper, still reigned as did Mrs. Pynchon at the London house.

Things were not quite the same, of course. Mistress Tallentire was conspicuous because of her absence from the townhouse. Mari appreciated with hindsight how Tamsin had livened things up.

"Yes," Tom remarked.

"She isn't a bad sort, you know. Can hold her own anywhere, and now has some powerful friends to attend her."

Mari smiled at him as they rattled through London's thoroughfares, with the city's noisy pulsing life animating a chill grey backdrop.

She thought, "Of course, of course, Tamsin Tallentire would flourish anywhere."

She acknowledged her old envy and reluctant regard for her father's erstwhile mistress. The woman could still exasperate.

Then she shook herself mentally, and prepared to go and pay last respects to her father. She would see old friends and family, and learn all their doings and scandals. She would enjoy the city, and be refreshed at Ravenhill, gossiping in the parlor with Sophie and the faithful Miss Pardoe.

Imagining their quiet, untroubled lives, she found the prospect of parlor gossip appealing for once, and looked forward to quizzing the pair of them about their plans.

At last, Tom arrived, clattering down the stairs in his usual haste, and, as he entered the library, Mari smiled warmly at him.

"For heaven's sake, Brother, let's be off, or Pa will come back and haunt us for our tardiness!"

Tom looked surprised but relieved, and grinned as he offered her his arm, putting his hand over hers.

"That's my old Mari," he said, and they went out to the carriage. "London air suits you, in spite of yourself, lady."

* * *

Joseph Westin's wake was well attended, unlike the occasion of his wife's funeral.

Mrs. Trant, the housekeeper, under Tom's instructions, had provided a feast of funeral meats for the company, and an equally generous supply of wine soon produced the air of a pleasant social occasion. Not many of the mourners appeared too mournful.

Mari saw doleful, respectful countenances assumed when conventional condolences were offered to any of the family members, but otherwise, as Frederick Ashford remarked, they all seemed to be having a splendid time.

Mistress Tallentire held court with a group of men Mari took to be Tom's friends. She looked as well as ever. When anyone expressed special sympathy, she cast her splendid eyes down and wiped a contrived tear away, but didn't neglect to slant a tragic glance up at the susceptible males, and smile bravely.

She even caught at an attentive man's sleeve with a vulnerable, distracted gesture, causing a skeptical Mari to laugh out loud, attracting a few startled glances from those around her, and an askance look from loyal Miss Pardoe.

Lady Shirley, established matron, found herself succumbing to the gentle authority in the governess's face, and made her own suitably solemn again.

Sophie was the only one of the family who showed signs of real distress at her father's death. Even she, however, looked comforted and somewhat relieved when Tamsin chaffed her out of sadness by suggesting that now she would be under Tom's guardianship, and how much more amiable that would be.

Mari didn't linger with anyone in particular at the gathering, but preferred to wander through the reception rooms lost in her own thoughts and nostalgic memories of Ravenhill.

The general buzz of conversation from the guests broke over her, and she registered fragments of conversation and gossip, ranging from discussion of the latest French fashions to war in the colonies.

She considered, not for the first time, how the revolutionary events causing bloodshed and strife half a world away could have such a different cast here.

People were not indifferent, but there was an interesting range of reaction. There were those, it appeared, who still disbelieved that the colonials would carry on in their efforts for independence, let alone carry the day.

Quite a few of the younger set cheered the colonials on. Uncle Fred himself, a conservative, confessed that he didn't blame the Americans for standing their ground and fighting for their rights as equal citizens.

"The fabric of the relationship has been strained to the point of being torn asunder," Mari heard him declare.

"'Tis a pity senior Pitt is on the scene no longer. My dear Matty, of course, has had a very satisfactory time telling anyone who will listen, that she told them so. And she did. She is a little chagrined, though. She thinks we should have beaten our American cousins to it, and revolted over taxes and overweening government ourselves – years ago."

His voice came to her across the drawing room as he continued to expound his views. Many merchant houses were hanging on, hoping and waiting for the cessation of hostilities. There were those, like the Hunters and Nortons, who had established homes and families, as well as businesses, in both countries.

"Of course, the French jumped to the colonials' aid, and why wouldn't they? The Spanish and the Dutch, too. It's the same old game, after all. The men of business are the only ones with sense. No matter what comes of the times, folks will still need wheat for bread, and tools to work, and clothes for their backs, not to mention American timber for ships to carry it all in," she heard him opine.

Uncle Fred paused in his analysis, a look of almost comical concern on his face as he glanced around for his glass to be refilled. When a footman obliged, he took a satisfying draught of it.

"Yes, indeed. The French jumped on the excuse to cause us grief again, but odds! We're still drinking plenty of their wine, it seems to me."

Mari smiled, as, stalwart Englishman that he was, he drained his French wine to the last drop, and looked at her, as though, in after-thought, he had been rude.

"What do you think, m'Dear?"

As the wife of a governor and diplomat, Mari could hardly voice her own conviction that the American colonials were going to win. She simply shook her head and smiled.

A memory of Stewart Dean's voice returned, telling her of the mounting grievances and ill-feelings against the British government all those years ago, when they sat looking at the night sky on the deck of *Hazard*.

That was long before the Declaration of Independence, and even, later, her husband had confided his serious doubts of the British government's stubborn course and intransigence.

She thought fondly of Stewart Dean, and wondered where he would be now. No doubt, long commander of his own vessel, harassing his enemy's shipping. Mari couldn't think of him as enemy though. The idea seemed ridiculous.

She left off eaves-dropping on Uncle Fred, and wandered over to where Aunt Matty sat. Her aunt sighed and welcomed her by patting the couch.

"Come and join me, Lady Shirley. We haven't had a chance at all of exchanging our news yet."

Aunt Matty looked tired and drawn. Mari felt guilty for failing to acknowledge the older woman's grief.

"We'll share a hot tisane," she said, by way of amends.

"You don't seem too distraught over your father's death, Mari."

Aunt Mat's voice was dry, and she gave a ghost of a smile. Mari didn't reply, but shook her head in a dumb show, taking Mathilda's hand.

They sat for some time in silence, disturbed only by the arrival of the tisane, served by Mrs. Trant herself. Mari sipped at the drink, conscious of her aunt's keen scrutiny.

"So, how has marriage suited the governor's wife?"

Mari delayed answering, trying to summon a response.

"Are you still mourning the loss of your little son, Mari? You know there's hardly a woman, high-born or low, who has not had to come to terms with the death of an infant. They fill the Bills of Mortality from any parish, too much so. 'Heaven's sad crop,' your grandmother called them."

Aunt Matty was both right and wrong. There was still a place in Mari that clutched to itself in grief at the loss of her tiny son, and melancholy had become her constant companion. She tried to imagine her baby as he would have been as a young one, romping around Ravenhill, pestering and teasing his Uncle Tom.

His death had severely affected her marriage.

Thomas Shirley had never been other than a true gentleman. He had been patient and kind, but, inevitably, as she continued to avoid his bed, he had turned elsewhere for female comfort and company.

He hadn't strayed far, but, at least, had steered clear of the wives of island society. Mari's chamber woman, Oleah, had supplied his needs.

Mari had suspected, but had been so wrapped up in herself that she had not acknowledged the fact until, one morning, Oleah was late attending her mistress, and, Mari stepped out to find her.

She practically bumped into her maid coming out Sir Thomas's room. The servant woman was hastily fastening her shift, and froze when she saw her mistress. Oleah's eyes were dark with apprehension.

Instead of outrage, Mari felt relief. She dimly realized, though, the need to wrest some sort of initiative from the situation.

"Did you make sure Sir Thomas took his stomach draught last night, Oleah?"

Mari had spoken to her in a business-like manner.

"Yes, m'Lady." Oleah had been startled and wary.

"I should like breakfast in my room, and we will talk together, Oleah," Mari had said.

The recollection was broken as she suddenly realized Aunt Matty was speaking.

"Is he not still attentive to you, Mari?"

Aunt Mat's voice was gentle but insistent, and Mari found herself chuckling in surprisingly good humor.

"Oh, Aunt Matty, we get along together quite comfortably, but our relationship did not last long in the bedroom stakes."

Mathilda looked shocked and concerned, so, to forestall comments of sympathetic outrage, Mari added. "It's no great matter, Aunt. We are yet good friends and partners."

Aunt Mat still looked a question at her niece, so Mari continued, "A mulatto, Oleah, one of my women, serves him."

Her aunt was dismayed, and squeezed her hand.

"Seriously, Aunt Matty, I have them both in order, and, in fact, of late this last year, Oleah has been far more chamber woman than bedfellow. He has become somewhat frail, and ready for retirement. I think they should allow him to retire."

Aunt Matty managed to look both indignant and nonplussed.

"Really, Mari. What a dispassionate assessment of your husband, and what cold comfort you seem to make of your existence."

She was sitting up straight against the sofa, tisane forgotten.

"No, Aunt Matty, life on the island is pleasant enough, easy and slow for such as I, so much so I feel I have been sleep-walking through it. I'm dutiful, helpful and a decorative wife, and it's very boring. I think I may stay here in London for a while."

Aunt Mathilda was for once speechless. She seemed inclined to chastise Mari, but, at the same time, was in sympathy, finally coming out with, "You are still a young woman, Mari, and you sound world-weary too soon. I'm bewildered, and not a little sad for you – though we all know the bloom on a marriage can soon fade."

Mathilda's expression suited her words, and she went silent for a moment, but then, true to form, cracked out with, "Heaven's sake, girl, it's not as though you're an ugly toad of a female, with no wit about you, and losing a child, sad though that undoubtedly is, is no excuse for letting your whole life slide. You can't simply desert the man, though. He's been good to you, and you owe him loyalty at least. Mayhap a spell in London will kindle a spark in you again. I don't like to see you out of sorts though. There's enough dreariness and turmoil in the world as it is."

True enough, Mari thought, but suddenly and unaccountably, at her father's funeral, she felt the undertow of her old spirit begin to tug at her.

The world was struggling to cope with a new era, and painful experience was the teacher. It was perhaps time for her to venture upon a new era herself.

How that would be accomplished she didn't know, but she would go back to Antigua and her husband, and look to the future.

XX

July 6, 1778 - "Looks like our equal, Mr. Dugdale," said Stewart Dean to his first mate as he assessed the intended prize under full sail ahead, noting its name – *Venture*.

"No, Sir. Our better. She has twelve to our ten," replied Dugdale almost matter-of-factly.

"And she carries carronades, which won't be welcoming."

Dean scanned the guns on the British schooner's deck and registered the high calibre, short barrels that would be so lethal in close combat, and he intended to get close enough to board.

He had never seen these new weapons on a British merchant ship, but was only too aware of their fearsome reputation during close-quarter fighting on Navy men-of-war.

"We have the wind and the speed," he said, noting the prize was sluggish and well-laden, which made her the more beckoning as he thought of her full holds.

"I see no stern-chaser. We'll come in angled on the stern, draw up and give her our best. We must make the first salvo count. The gunners need be fast as we pull alongside, particularly on the bow. We need at least two to their one."

"We've the best, Sir. They'll do it," said Dugdale.

"Sand the decks."

The order was speedily carried out by seamen aware that their own blood might soon be soaked up by the sand they were spreading, but grimly determined that it would not be without cost to the enemy.

"Prepare for boarding," ordered Dean, and in the waist of the ship the bosun organized the pile of grappling irons, pistols and swords for the men to seize once they were close enough for hand-to-hand combat.

As *Falcon*'s deck became a fury of battle preparations, Dean was puzzled to see no similar activity aboard the schooner. She was sailing blithely on, if not unaware of his approach, certainly unresponsive to it.

As the gap narrowed, he could see the British captain conferring with his first mate on the poop deck, but still saw no evidence of any battle orders being given.

Here was a well-armed merchantman that certainly could give as good as she got, and perhaps even better, apparently doing nothing in the face of attack.

From its weathered look and its salt-encrusted sails, Dean took it to be nearing the end of a trans-Atlantic voyage to the islands, probably carrying a variety of supplies and goods that would make it well worth seizing. Probably, he thought, only recently released from the protection of a Navy convoy.

He continued on an angled approach to the schooner's stern, determined to keep his fire to the very last moment. Scanning his seasoned crew, he gave a tight, satisfied smile. They worked well under Dugdale's order.

He had come to rely heavily on Dugdale. The older seaman had a natural air of authority and a canny insight into British ways at sea, gained through years of service in the Navy.

Typical of the British, Dean thought, to lose a darned good sailor through their own high-handedness.

Robert Dugdale had been a young commander of the *Magdalen,* one of the first schooners employed by the Navy against smugglers off the coast of Canada and New England. Whilst in Louisborg, he had agreed to give a local merchant passage to Halifax, and had, thereby, ultimately fallen foul of the authorities.

Giving passage to a local civilian was not a particular problem. Navy ships did this frequently enough. Without Dugdale's permission, however, his passenger had managed to carry aboard a quantity of meat and butter to trade on arrival in Halifax. There, a customs officer had witnessed the man unloading his supplies from the Navy ship, and had informed the port's commanding officer.

Dugdale found himself accused of aiding a smuggler. The court-martial dismissed his protestations of innocence, found him guilty of conniving with the merchant, and ordered him cashiered.

All these years later, Dean sympathized with Dugdale's abiding sense of injustice, but was only too glad to have his services aboard *Falcon,* particularly at moments like this.

"Mr. Dugdale, why do you think they are so quiet?" he asked his first mate.

"Beats me, Sir. They must have something on their minds, or up their sleeves. What trickery can they be up to?"

"Not much without their guns. They are still housed and stoppered," said Dean.

Even as he pondered the puzzling situation, he saw a crewman on the intended prize move to the mast, and, to his amazement, the British vessel's colors were struck.

"I'll be damned," said Dean.

"He's either a coward or a fool. Not a shot fired, and he's done for. Well, let's take no chances."

He ordered Dugdale to keep the guns ready, and the bo'sun to be prepared to board as soon as they were alongside.

The *Falcon* held course steadily and inexorably, covering the heaving expanse of water between the two ships. A dense air of tension before combat remained almost tangible amongst Dean's crew. Their very silence seemed to shout suspicion and disbelief at such an easy conquest.

It made no sense at all, the submission and stricken colors of the well-armed British merchantman.

The final moment came, incredibly, with not a shot fired, nor a word spoken, except for a quiet oath from someone just before the hulls of the two ships crashed together.

The vessels juddered and swung together in a clumsy sea dance, the *Falcon* imposing itself on an unwilling partner. Timbers groaned under the stress. Then grappling irons took hold, and the boats were secured together without resistance.

Dean quickly led his men aboard the schooner, strode smartly across the deck, up the steps to the poop, and confronted the British captain, who immediately threw a smart salute and introduced himself in a grudging, controlled manner by saying with forced politeness, "Blakelock. At your service."

Dean looked at his adversary, the chiseled features of his weather-beaten face, the barreled chest and straight shoulders, the strong legs firmly astride, the hands, after the peremptory salute, now clenched strongly behind his back, the very picture of a man to be reckoned with. Dean's face betrayed his puzzlement as he stared hard at his opponent.

"You, Sir, are extremely lucky," the glowering captain told him unhesitatingly. "Had I not the life of a lady in my charge, I should have given you a drubbing, Sir."

This was said with flat conviction, even though, the man had struck colors without so much as a token resistance.

"I doubt that," Dean replied, equally confident. He turned slowly, and deliberately scanned the deck.

"Even though you have a couple more guns, we were set and ready to seize you."

He turned back to plant a mocking gaze on the man in front of him. The English officer did not miss the underlying contempt of the colonial, and bristled with anger and frustration.

"The only reason I did not take you on, Sir, is that I am carrying the wife of the Governor of Antigua back to her husband," he managed through clenched teeth.

"For her sake alone, I struck, something I would never have thought to do otherwise, as you and your men would have learned to your great cost. I expect you to honor the lady's presence, whatever you choose to do with me."

Dean stared hard at him for a long moment, then gave a brief nod. He believed the man.

"Rest assured - that I shall," he returned.

"You talk a good fight, but your ship is my prize. You and your crew will be taken to America, and held or exchanged, as may please the authorities there. The lady, I give you my word, will be properly treated, and taken home. There will be that honor to your action."

Dean put Dugdale in charge of the schooner with a prize crew, and ordered him to sail the captured ship and the prisoners to Philadelphia, but, first, to transfer the woman passenger, and her bags, to *Falcon*.

As good as his word, he would return her to Antigua - and her husband - under a flag of truce.

* * *

242

Probably Dugdale alone had noticed Dean's distraction when *Venture*'s women passengers stepped aboard *Falcon*. In other circumstances he would have described his captain as a man simply smitten by the sight of a beautiful woman, but there seemed to be something other than that.

Dugdale had mentally shrugged, and made no comment as he had the prize to man with minimal crew, and that was enough to deal with.

After watching *Venture* set a westward course, Stewart Dean settled onto Dugdale's bunk, lost in thought. He tried to tell himself that he could be mistaken, but knew that he wasn't.

It wasn't that Mari Westin had been on his mind all this time. She hadn't. He had thought of her occasionally, with the tender memory and regret for first love, but had moved on as, inevitably, he must, and what did his small passion count for in the surge and upset of a country's revolution?

History had picked him up and swept him along with the rest of his countrymen on an adventure into the future.

Nevertheless, the sight of the woman disengaging herself from the hoist and alighting on *Falcon*'s deck with a touch of a hand on a willing sailor's shoulder, had shaken him.

Images flamed in his head again as the years dropped away. She had her back to him as she thanked the sailor assisting her, and a shaft of sunlight breaking through patchy cloud cover had illumined her dark, gold hair, and played over a supple, long-waisted figure.

He knew it was she, and knowing, turned abruptly to seek the privacy of Dugdale's vacated quarters.

He gave a series of orders with unusual asperity, declining to greet the arrivals immediately. His own quarters were turned over to the governor's wife, and he argued to himself that there she could be confined.

They need have no correspondence, except briefly when he delivered her to her husband.

It was no good, he chastised himself. He had not had the nerve to meet her eyes, though why that was so eluded him. He had not been in the wrong all those years ago.

He called back the sailor entrusted to clear the captain's cabin for the women, and told him to pay his compliments to Lady Shirley, and say that he would be pleased to dine with her later.

He turned his mind back to the manning of his ship. Dugdale, after all, had the more difficult task, with prisoners to ship aboard the prize back to American waters. He issued orders, and *Falcon* obediently set course for Antigua.

XXI

Mari Shirley stood at the small casement in the *Falcon*'s main cabin, staring after the *Venture*, its stern receding as it angled away from them and toward America.

She realized that she was not particularly discomposed, though everyone was treating her as if she were. Her maid and companion, Izzy, was fretting and checking over her mistress's trunk and belongings, wondering how on earth they could be unpacked.

The mistress seemed not to care, and that caused Izzy to fuss more. She felt that being hauled aboard the colonial ship on some kind of sling contraption was just quite enough indignity to suffer in one day for any decent body, though she had managed it very neatly, and had been received with all proper courtesy as she stepped onto the American deck.

Captain Blakelock had assured Lady Shirley with considerable fervor that she should not worry. The American, he told her, had given his word to convey her and her entourage to Antigua aboard *Falcon*, under a flag of truce.

In Izzy's opinion the captain had been more upset than Lady Shirley at the day's turn of events. Blakelock had been deeply distressed at the surrender of his vessel, though he had no real choice when considering the safety of his passengers. In the end Lady Shirley had comforted the captain, reassuring him of his esteem in her eyes and her gratitude at his behavior.

Izzy was both confused by her ladyship's apparent calm, and not a little frightened at the change in their circumstances. She eased her own feelings by muttering some more at the lack of space and comfort on the American ship as compared to the merchant vessel, and prepared to berate any unfortunate seaman who came within scolding distance.

Mari Shirley settled herself down on the cushioned locker which formed a seat beside the aft casement. She continued to stare after the diminishing *Venture*, one arm along the open window, her other hand absently resting upon a pile of clothes, apparently left behind by the American captain's steward.

Izzy had plunked them down as she emptied a locker. Marie casually glanced at the pile of linen, a few shirts neatly squared and folded, and a mariner's jacket. She stroked the jacket absently.

"M'lady?"

Izzy stood looking a question at her.

"I'll take those M'lady. Captain's man at the door – apologized for not clearing captain's effects sooner. The captain himself presents his compliments, and hopes you're as comfortable as maybe."

Izzy sniffed dismissively as she held out her hand for the clothes.

Mari mentally shook herself, realizing with some embarrassment that she had been hugging the pile of linen close to her. She relinquished it quickly to her maid, resisting a startling, insane impulse to bury her face in it. What was the matter with her?

A wave of emotion swept over her, and to hide her face from Izzy she stood and strode across the cabin, only to turn and stare out the casement again at the disappearing *Venture*. It seemed to have a fleeting symbolism of sorts, but her thoughts were too haphazard to recognize exactly what it was.

Izzy didn't miss the dark turmoil in her mistress's eyes, and relaxed herself now that she saw Mari was distressed.

"Don't worry, M'lady. Rest yourself easy. We'll make do quite well."

Suddenly, for Izzy, the *Falcon* was quite a comfortable ship, and, probably, quite a bit faster than the *Venture*. Captain Blakelock obviously knew the American captain would keep his word, and they would be back in Antigua in no time. Izzy's former fretting turned to sympathetic fussing and soothing of her precious charge.

"His man says that Captain Dean suggests you dine with him tonight. They'll be in to set table and such in a while."

Izzy started to hum as she laid out articles of toiletry in a small lavatory at the side of the main cabin. She failed to notice that Mari Shirley had frozen into stillness at the mention of the captain's name.

Mari found herself gripping the back of a chair. The American's name was simply, surely a coincidence. Why, after all this time, was she so obsessed with thoughts of Stewart Dean? He was long gone from her life. A brief, youthful passion that had come to nothing in the end.

She was Lady Shirley, wife of His Majesty's Governor of the Leeward Islands. What was she fantasizing – that a long-lost lover was set to re-enter her life after all these years, and in the middle of the ocean?

Breathing deeply, she decided that Izzy was right: she was upset and shocked, and should contain her thoughts along more sensible lines. She finally paid attention to the busy maid, and gave her careful instructions to lay out her dress for dinner with the captain.

* * *

Mari sat again on the locker settle by the casement, Izzy discreetly observing her. She was surprised that her mistress had taken so much trouble to dress for supper with the American, but, even so, regarded her beauty with complacency.

Lady Shirley's hair was dressed naturally and to good effect. Where she sat, her head and shoulders were dusted with gold by the late sun as *Falcon* slipped south-west down its invisible compass path.

Izzy considered her mistress a picture worth painting, sitting there in a dress of sea green silk shot through with drifts of blue as light reflected from moving water played through the cabin.

Pulling her drifting thoughts to the present, Mari smoothed her dress with a nervous gesture at the sound of a knock on the cabin door.

She stood and moved around the end of the polished cabin table, set simply with plain silver for two people. She noted abstractedly the large, white napkins as she nodded for Izzy to answer the door, and then stood transfixed at the sight of the figure who ducked his head to clear the door frame and stepped slowly through.

"Captain Dean, M'Lady."

"Yes, Izzy. Leave us for now."

Izzy took a breath in as if about to say something, but closed her mouth, bobbed a curtsey, and chose to look miffed instead as she left.

"Captain Dean – Captain Stewart Dean," Mari murmured.

Stewart Dean paused just inside the doorway, as though captured in time. For a long moment, they gazed at each other, saying nothing.

At last, he stepped toward her, and studied her face. She returned the scrutiny, and saw a tall, tanned man with watchful, wary eyes.

His face was that of a stranger, a more grave and weathered face than she remembered, harder and bearing scars from battle. His figure was fit but heavier than she recalled, carrying strength and authority easily and unselfconsciously. Youthful cockiness had worn away, leaving a man to be reckoned with, Mari thought.

Her face, too, was grave, the non-committal face of a diplomat's wife. She paused, then hesitantly held out her hand to him, as though reluctant to touch.

He took the proffered hand and held it, studying her. He noted her hair was dressed attractively but in such a way as to seem too heavy for the slender neck. He found himself imagining it slipping and cascading down. Her elegant form was tricked out in all the finery of her class and position, and he remembered the first sight of her, a servant girl, in that Annapolis tavern.

She appeared now like an image from a master's portrait, incongruous aboard his ship. He had to smile to himself, richly costumed as she was, her complexion was unmarred by artifice and had a golden, light tan about it, unfashionable for a lady. Lady Shirley had obviously not remained in her quarters on the passage home to Antigua.

Stewart realized that he could easily be awash with fresh desire for this woman. Looking at her now, gorgeous enough to grace a royal court, she could never have fitted into his life in the American colonies, let alone be content as the wife of the revolutionary privateer he now was.

He was surprised and perplexed at his emotional turmoil, and sheltered behind a formal show of courtesy.

The awkward situation would be eased at table, and taking a goblet or two of wine together, and, formalities satisfied, they need have little further contact. Still holding her hand, he turned to gesture at the places set for dinner.

He covered his feelings playing host at the supper table. They shared a meal neither really tasted, but, after some awkward moments and helped by the wine, they found themselves talking.

Light was fading and the soft glow from candles took over, playing on the silverware and the silk of Mari's dress. An awkward tension returned, and further attempts at small talk dissipated.

Dean's face was impassive as he twirled wine dregs in a goblet, then, looking stern, he rose to say goodnight. He raised her hand, barely brushing it with his lips, and was startled by a sudden pressure on his fingers as Mari Shirley tightened her own grip, and brought her other hand up to hold his own as if to prevent him releasing her.

She stared down at their linked hands, as if hers were not her own to control, and quickly moved to lace her fingers with his.

They stood silent and immobile. Then slowly, almost dreamily she slid a hand under his sleeve to stroke his wrist, but froze again, appalled at herself. The pulse in his arm bounded warm and reassuring under her fingers, and tightening her hold, she forced herself to meet his gaze.

Stewart saw her eyes were brimming with tears. She had humiliated herself, and was at a loss for anything to say because there was too much tumbling in her head.

What he read in her face, she didn't know, but suddenly something relaxed in his own expression, and he reached for her gently, almost tiredly, like a well-loved friend returning to greet her after a long parting.

She felt herself clasped hard and close, fine silk crushed against rough sea jacket. Tears seeped from her closed eyes and onto his shirt.

She breathed in the salty scent and embraced the firm feel of him, which seemed to permeate her whole being, and the world was well lost for this moment.

Stewart Dean, privateer and revolutionary, master of fine-tuning a sailing ship for battle, solved for himself the mysterious rigging of a fashionable lady's corset.

Silk lacing and fine embroidered stomacher fell to join the folds and spread of sea green silk on the cabin floor as Lady Mari Shirley, gazing at him gravely, unpinned her hair. There was no seduction, simply a joy at claiming this man again.

For both, whatever happened afterwards would be of little account.

* * *

He stirred, suddenly awake, taking in the sounds of the ship. Its motion was full and easy underway, and he relaxed back onto his side in the narrow space of his bed, to take in, again, the sight of Mari, Lady Shirley, lying next to him. Her face was softened by sleep and a slight smile, as from a pleasant dream, brushed her lips.

Silent laughter filled his mind as exaltation shook him. He had just bedded the wife of his enemy.

He had a mild spasm of guilt at the thought of Dugdale, plowing north for the Chesapeake with a skeleton crew and surly English prisoners. He grinned to himself, imagining Dugdale's salty comments at the contrast in their situations.

He gazed at the sleeping woman again, her gold hair spread over the hard, faded pillow of his cot.

He was still dumb-founded. She had disrobed, and discarded her finery like someone throwing away unwanted trammel. Her only nervousness, he realized, had been at the prospect of his refusal of her, not at that of offering herself to him.

Here in the middle of the ocean, in the middle of a war, they had incredibly found each other again.

Stewart frowned at the cabin ceiling, but turned as Mari stirred, to find her observing him. He reached and traced her shoulder, lacing her bright hair around his fingers.

"It's no good, Mari, you know it's no good, my lovely lady."

He hesitated, frowning again, thinking of the way she had wound her arms tightly around him, saying over and over that she had found him at last and couldn't let him go.

He had bedded his enemy's wife, but now he had to give her back to the man on Antigua.

Mari was studying him closely, questions on her face.

"No, Mari – Mari, I'm a privateer, but my Letter of Marque doesn't cover kidnapping wives of high British officials.

"I gave my word to Blakelock, who will soon be restored home. If I don't hand you over to your husband, I'll have the entire British fleet in the Caribbean out after me."

He grimaced, and added after a pause, "They'll be looking for me anyway. I've managed to be a nuisance of late to His Majesty's shipping."

Mari lay and stared up at the dapple of sea light reflected across the cabin.

Of course, this was an interlude snatched from fate. They had been pitched together for a space of time, their lives colliding briefly while nations battled. She remembered resignedly Aunt Matty's advice about returning to Antigua and her husband.

"How long before landfall?" she finally asked.

"A few more days," came the answer.

"Then we shall have those days, Stewart Dean, but when these times are over, if you don't find me again, I swear I shall forego all dignity and come looking for you."

She sat on the edge of his cot by now, looking down on him. She had the look to him of a wild, beautiful figurehead from some romantic ship, belonging to no country or time. He believed her, and held her close.

"Oh, God willing, Mari Shirley, I'll find you. On land or sea, I'll find you."

* * *

Sir Thomas Shirley, focused his telescope on the approaching ship. He saw the flag of truce, and scanned the deck, coming up short against the sight of a woman's figure against the ship's rail.

The colors and outline of her costume and hair stood out against the wood and canvass. He summoned his Navy aide, who came running from the terrace below to be handed the spy-glass.

"What's the ship? What do you make of it?" Shirley demanded.

"American privateer, the *Falcon*." The officer flicked a nervous glance at Antigua's governor.

"That, surely, has to be Lady Shirley on board, Sir Thomas."

They looked at each other, relief and dismay on both faces.

"Blasted Americans. Sailing right in, surveying my harbor, and I can't do a thing about it. M'wife's aboard. They must have taken Blakelock's *Venture*."

Shirley waved the officer away.

"Full courtesies, but keep a close eye on 'em. Let me know when they're in."

The governor moved from the balcony, coughed spasmodically, and eased himself down into his favorite chair.

Mari was back. He felt better. He had expected her to stay in England, but she had proved loyal. They would finish out another year or two on the island. That should see an end to the conflict. He would offer up his position then. That would be time enough.

The islands were beautiful, but they had a way of wearying one.

BOOK FOUR

AMERICAN FULFILMENT

XXII

Nimrod dipped gently at anchor in the Delaware River.

Stewart Dean glanced over the busy wharves of the Philadelphia waterfront as he waited to address the crew of his new privateer.

He was flushed with anticipation. Cadwalader Morris and brothers had served him well. Work on the new ship had commenced with dispatch and gone rapidly under Samuel Morris's keen eye.

A stiff, fresh breeze played over the water, flirting with furled sails. Dean breathed in a lungful of air, taking in the mingled scent of his new vessel, tar and fresh timber, lamp oil and cordage, varnish and canvass. Provisions already were long boarded and tightly stowed.

His sense of exultant optimism matched the bright, clear day. He turned to survey the motley collection of men grouped on the ship's deck.

They looked back at him with expressions varying from the stolid but canny regard of seasoned sailors to the assumed nonchalance of a couple of raw country boys. He knew well enough they were bound together as much by a strong desire for action and reward as any deep-seated patriotism.

He found himself pretty much satisfied with the men taken on. They had been well scanned by his trusted sailing mate Dugdale. He had had to make up numbers with a couple of landlubbers, but they would soon learn the ropes. All in all, he considered they had been fortunate in garnering such an able crew.

Dean gave a cursory outline of the ship's commission and sailing orders, then said, "We sail on the tide."

He relished the sound of his own voice carrying over the deck. He set the crew to their stations. The sailors, neat and easy on their feet, the country boys shuffling and uncertain under the Dugdale's eye.

In a brisk westerly breeze, the freshly painted, fully equipped, and armed *Nimrod* sailed out of the Delaware Bay into the Atlantic, her crisp, new sails powering her along, her windward shrouds stressed taut as violin strings, her broad bow cutting through the waves, heading south along the coast, destined for the Leeward Islands.

The isles were controlled by the British, but fiercely contested by the French out of both long-standing colonial self-interest and opportunistic alliance with America.

Being a crossroads of international trade, they made ideal hunting grounds for privateers on both sides of the war. It seemed, almost, as if every ship in the islands carried its Letter of Marque, giving it the right to fight as well as trade, and Dean was looking forward to joining the fray.

He realized that his new vessel was by no means a mighty warship, but her size couldn't dim his pride in her sleek lines and raked masts that would make her a fast and lethal adversary.

She would outrun all but the fastest of merchantmen, and, with luck, would avoid the better-armed British Navy ships. If he chose his targets well, and his moments of attack carefully, he was confident of many successful encounters.

He was now back in his element, free to roam the seas, looking for opportunities to inflict loss on the enemy and gain profit for himself, his men, the Morrises, and America.

But he knew the Navy ships were everywhere about, ready to pounce on any American vessel setting sail from the east coast, and so he ordered each watch to keep careful look-out, all along the route, for threatening warships as well as beckoning merchantmen.

Dean was resting in his stifling cabin, when he heard the call: "Sails to le'ward."

He leapt from his bunk, grabbed his telescope, and bounded up the half dozen steps onto the deck.

"Two of them," said Dugdale, pointing over the starboard bow to about two o'clock, and Dean aimed his telescope.

"We're in luck," said Dean after scanning the two lumbering merchantmen, and seeing no piercings for cannons or mounted swivel guns.

At first he thought they were both brigs, but then saw one was flying a trysail from a light mast, immediately abaft its main mast, and registered it as a snow.

"Attack stations," he ordered, setting the sails full to catch the prey.

"We'll be upon them in the hour," said Dean to Dugdale. "I doubt they'll put up much of a fight. They seem to be without arms."

He ordered the guns prepared, and the hooks and pistols for boarding brought out of storage, and piled in the waist of the ship. He then turned to getting the last spurt of speed out of *Nimrod*.

The merchantmen, unable to take flight from the fleet Americans or defend themselves, signaled capitulation immediately after the first warning shots.

Dean turned his attention first to the snow, when, suddenly from one of the look-outs, came an urgent shout, "Sails bearing down astern."

He swung round, and through his telescope immediately saw two vessels, mainsails out, their square topsails bulging, and their foresails bent and full, coming on them fast, very fast, clearly set on turning the tables. making the privateers the prey.

In an instant, he realized that they were now the target of two English sloops, big enough and fast enough to outgun and outrun them.

He counted the gun ports along the starboard side of the leading boat - seven. He knew it probably had as many, if not more, swivels. He switched his lens to the other ship. This time he counted ten piercings, and guessed the ship was around 200 tons, twice as heavy as *Nimrod*.

They were in real trouble. Quickly, he weighed the options, which no longer included seizing the wallowing merchantmen and their cargoes.

He might try to outrun the enemy in the hope of eluding them at night, but the moon would be almost full and darkness far from complete, and the pace of his adversaries left him in little doubt of how fatal a gamble that would likely turn out to be.

By his reckoning, they were well south of the island of Barbuda and north-west of the islands of Antigua and St. Christopher. Antigua was a British garrison and hardly beckoned. Their best chance was to race before the prevailing easterly trades for St. Kitts. There, they could find safe haven under the guns of the French.

Once *Nimrod* was at hull speed the advance of the British privateers was less rapid, but still relentless.

Studying them through his glass, Dean saw they fairly slipped through the clear blue waters, throwing up curling white bow waves and leaving a path as smooth as glass behind them. He speculated the ships were sheathed with copper.

Going down the steps to his cabin, he took out his maps, unrolling one of the Caribbean, and holding the curled edges down on his table while he scanned the coastline of St. Kitts, an island shaped like a plump tadpole swimming north west.

He concentrated on the leeward southern coast, which would give more protection. His eyes moved quickly along the shoreline. He studied the small clusters of the inked anchors, which promised good holding ground, off Sandy Point, just to the north west of the fort at Brimstone Hill, and at Basseterre to the south east.

At either anchorage, *Nimrod* would be within sight of French gunners and close enough to the shore so that the English sloops would have to risk full broadsides if they dared to approach.

He decided to head along the coast for the protection of the guns at Basseterre. This was the island's main town and harbor, and he decided it would offer the best protection.

Anxiously scanning the horizon ahead, he looked for the first glimpse of the island that promised them haven. With the British less than a mile away, he finally saw land.

St. Kitts's towering Mount Misery cast a dark, triangular silhouette against the skyline, a crown of white clouds around its peak like a halo. With relief, he realized that they could reach the French-controlled island safely – just.

As they rounded Bluff Point into Basseterre Bay, Dean was surprised to see a forest of masts, perhaps three dozen or more, all merchantmen, some sitting heavily in the water, loaded, others riding higher, their holds empty.

What quickly staggered him was the realization that they were all English.

What was an enemy fleet doing in a French port? Had the English recaptured St. Kitts? Had he sailed not into a safe haven, but a trap? He looked at the coastal forts and, much to his relief, he saw they were all still flying the French tri-color.

He was mystified, but to his further relief spotted two other American privateers at anchor, and soon *Nimrod* settled into the wind, near the compatriot vessels, *Jane* and *Susanna,* as if joining old friends.

No sooner was *Nimrod* at rest, than Dean was astonished to see the enemy rounding Bluff Point into the bay and holding their course, their gunners rolling the cannon out through the ports, priming and loading them.

The lead English vessel headed straight for their anchorage, under the muzzles of the island's guns. Desperately, Dean shouted to his crew, some still aloft tidying the sails, to ready for battle. It was too late.

The larger of the two sloops closed quickly with the becalmed *Nimrod,* and when it was little more than a pistol-shot away, unleashed a full broadside as it glided by. The foremast was hit, and crashed to the deck, flattening two of the American crew and enmeshing two others in a tangle of rigging, narrowly missing Dean.

Another shot passed straight through the bulwark, taking out one of the cannon and its crew with a roar and a flaring cloud of dense smoke. The British sloop then disappeared in the cloud of its own making.

Through the thick haze, Dean saw Dugdale's body stretched over the splintered bulwark, lifeless, even as the second British ship came racing toward the anchorage, ready to deliver another salvo. Dean trained his telescope on the British boats, and saw, for the first time, their names - *Regulator* and *Amazon*. He knew them both of fearsome reputation.

Suddenly, the cannons of the fort opened fire. Dean looked up and was relieved to see the puffs of smoke and the flames as the French joined the battle, but, before he could as much as blink, the blindingly bright flash was followed by a tremendous roar.

The air itself compacted in an instant, whacking him, like a plank of oak, hard across the chest. He was thrown backwards from the stump of the mast, where he had wedged himself next to the wheel for some protection as he shouted commands above the din.

Dazed, he looked at his leg and saw a steady trickle of red oozing down the white, silk hose. He tried to rise, but an agonizing pain shot up his thigh, and he collapsed back down, the blood flowing faster, trickling thinly toward the open scuppers.

He looked to the bow, and saw that *Nimrod* had taken at least two direct shots from the fort. With the British ships turning for another attack, he realized he was caught in cross-fire, and accepted he had little option but strike his colors to save his ship and what remained of her crew.

His gaze on *Nimrod*'s descending flag started to blur. He felt as though he was sinking through the wooden deck, and the ship was sinking into the water, then into the sand, and before the colors were totally lowered he had descended into deep, silent darkness.

Jane and *Susanna,* caught totally off guard and with few crew aboard, were simply overwhelmed without firing so much as a shot. It didn't take the British many minutes to draw alongside, grapple the three American privateers, and seize their crews.

The French in the fort ashore had ceased firing, unable to pin-point friend from foe at the distance. They could only watch helplessly as the prisoners were transferred to one of the British ships, and prize crews put on the captured vessels, which all then headed out to sea, the English captains carefully keeping the almost crippled *Nimrod*, *Jane* and *Susanna,* between their own ships and the French guns.

An agonizing jolt brought Dean to his senses. He opened his eyes to find himself lying beside several of his wounded crew on the deck of what he immediately realized was a British ship. He bit his lip, tasting his own blood as the excruciating pain shot down his leg again. He managed to hold onto consciousness just long enough to hear a disembodied voice from above booming,

"You will be taken to Antigua and held as prisoners of war. Your wounds will be treated as best we can aboard, but we have little to ease your suffering."

Dean passed out again.

XXIII

Francois Claude Amour, Marquis De Bouillé, was sipping an evening glass of Madeira, a drink to which necessity had converted his refined French palate.

He would have preferred his favored Bordeaux, Chateau d'Issan, but he knew it would not survive an ocean crossing without turning to vinegar. Over his time in the Caribbean islands, he had developed a taste for the hardier fortified wine.

He held up the glass and admired the familiar tawny tint, its promise of richness highlighted by rosy rays of the setting sun reaching through the windows.

Sighing with pleasurable anticipation, he leaned back in his ornate, gilded chair, and slowly tilted the glass to his lips, sniffing to catch the aroma that reminded him of his native Auvergne. He was on this evening feeling quite satisfied with his lot.

His capture of the island of St. Kitts from the British four months earlier had been a triumph, albeit a nasty and bloody business at the time. He had been, he felt on reflection and with some complacency, honorable in his dealings with his adversaries, quickly telling the island's civilian leaders that he would spare their lives, houses, and properties, in return for their ready acceptance of his authority - similar to terms he had imposed on the other islands he had captured.

But on St. Kitts, with the sugar cane ripe and ready for harvest in the fields, the marquis decided on a further, unprecedented, step to consolidate local co-operation.

He agreed to allow the merchants and planters to continue trading freely, even with the enemy English, for six months. This would save their harvest and give them time to find new markets.

It would also give the French a ready flow of tax revenue, and, perhaps most importantly, it would send a signal to the British planters on Jamaica, his next target, that life under French control was not to be feared.

True enough, De Bouillé's colleague-in-arms, Admiral De Grasse, had been defeated and captured by the British shortly after the island's conquest. This had been a major setback for French and American interests.

But the word from Paris was that new ships-of-the-line were even now being readied to sail westwards to join the Spanish fleet for a combined attack on the British.

The battle for the islands, he thought, was far from over, but his planned assault on Jamaica, the English Caribbean stronghold, could certainly end it.

And there was this, too - the latest news he had from America was that the English had all but abandoned the land war there after their defeat at Yorktown, and, closer to home, he was quite certain they had given up any hope of re-taking St. Kitts.

New intelligence from London was also heartening. The British people, he had learned, were becoming increasingly disillusioned with their war against America, with parliament actually voting against further hostilities. There were even reports of urgent moves to seek a peace.

Most importantly, on the island of St. Kitts, under the trading concession he had established with the planters, the harvest had now been gathered, the mills had done their work, and ships were being loaded with sugar, rum, molasses and indigo, soon to sail to join a convoy, assembling off Antigua, for England.

He was fully aware that this concession had infuriated the Americans. Members of the Congress in Philadelphia had let it be known to Paris that they saw it as undermining their efforts to cut off all commerce between the islands and England. But, more importantly to him, the trading arrangement had the blessing of his beloved King Louis XVI.

It was to his mind on this pleasant, tropical evening, a moment for a French royalist to relish a quiet glass, but even as he enjoyed another sip, his mood was shattered.

The windows of the drawing room suddenly vibrated to a loud explosion. Then another, and another.

De Bouillé knew instantly that these were not the heavy guns of Fort Londonderry or Brimstone Hill. These were much lighter weapons, and the shots came from Basseterre Bay. It was a sea fight.

Wine forgotten, he ran to the window. To his amazement, he saw three ships flying the American flag at anchor, and sailing past them, its decks already suffused in the dense smoke from its guns, an English sloop. A second English ship was closing.

He blinked, and focused more closely on the scene, which was slowly receding into a thick haze of battle. His outrage clamped him to the spot. The brazen English attacking his American allies right here in his waters? How dare they?

In the secluded luxury of his waterfront residence, the Marquis De Bouillé found himself infuriatingly helpless to take command of the fight.

He could only watch in growing dismay as the English quickly overwhelmed the Americans and made off with their prisoners before his eyes. He was not a man used to accepting such affront under any circumstances.

The glass of Madeira went unfinished, and his demeanor was utterly soured as he paced, struggling to quell his anger.

Even before the British ships and their prizes had disappeared, he swore to himself that he would reverse this business. He would exact a penalty from the English pirates for their insult to France and her allies. But how?

"We have to respond. Can't believe it. In our harbor. Under our noses. What an insult.!" he told Arthur, Comte De Dillon, who had run into the room to join him.

"We have to make them pay a price for the temerity of it. And we have to free the Americans. Your thoughts."

"I don't see many options, Monsieur le Marquis," said De Dillon, flicking a cagey glance at his commanding officer.

He, like De Bouillé, was an aristocrat of military pedigree and used to getting his way, but at this moment was at a loss over what could be done.

"Had we the fleet, we could make them pay a dear price for it, but without Admiral De Grasse, there's no way to stop them reaching Antigua. That's surely where they're headed, and Sir Thomas Shirley is a stubborn man, as we well know," he offered bleakly.

"Clearly, we're in no position for a sea chase. But a price for it, you say?"

De Bouillé was silent for a while, preoccupied with ideas hastily thought up and as quickly discarded.

Then, "Mon Dieu – that's it! And a real price at that!"

De Dillon stared at De Bouillé, who was nodding to himself enthusiastically.

"It will cost them dear by the time I'm done with them."

De Dillon saw a sly, satisfied look on his commander's hot face.

"You have a plan, Monsieur le Marquis? What is it?" he asked.

The marquis smiled, certain he had found an effective riposte: he would ban the St. Kitts' sugar fleet, being loaded in the harbor, from sailing for England.

He would put the Basseterre forts on full alert, and warn the merchants that any ship trying the weigh anchor or slip its cable, would be sunk. He would have to move quickly because the merchantmen were almost ready to sail to join the English sugar convoy assembling off Antigua.

He would summons the community leaders and merchants, and immediately impound their ships. This would deprive the English of a major part of their fleet from the islands, inviting the strongest censure from London, where two dozen ships loaded with sugar, molasses, rum and indigo, would surely be considered far more valuable than three small American privateers.

And the Americans in Philadelphia, it occurred to him with some relish, might actually find themselves benefiting from the trading arrangement they had so vehemently protested to Paris.

If the American prisoners were freed, it would be entirely because of De Bouillé's concession that had so angered their government. That, he thought, would be a nice diplomatic turn of events.

He decided to write immediately to the British governor on Antigua, his old adversary, Sir Thomas Shirley. He would inform that gentleman that if he desired a full convoy to sail east to England, he would have to release the American prisoners.

De Bouillé sat quietly, thinking some more. What else?

Then, the marquis smirked at his own cunning. Yes, a little salt in the wound would be most salutary. The English must also repair and re-supply the damaged American ships if they wanted the sugar.

He had been in correspondence earlier in the year with Sir Thomas Shirley, as he had tried, in vain, to negotiate the surrender of the island's British garrison to forestall the siege and bombardment of the fort on Brimstone Hill.

He now felt he was writing to an old acquaintance. Delicately stroking the surplus ink off his quill into the well of a bronze stand, he drew paper toward him.

In immaculate copperplate, De Bouillé set out his demands. It was a simple quid pro quo which he felt actually favored the English, but he still wondered whether they would accept.

The curt reply he had received from Sir Thomas to his earlier suggestion of Brimstone Hill's surrender still stung.

The English governor had rebuffed him in the brusquest of notes, asserting that the garrison was in good order, his troops in high spirits, and they would fight to the last extremity.

Such defiance had forced De Bouillé to bombard the fort into submission. It took a month, and to his mind the English on that occasion had been too readily victims of their own courage.

Sir Thomas and the senior military commanders he had paroled, allowing them to return to Antigua. The uniformed prisoners he had sent to France for later exchange.

Now, he pondered, would Sir Thomas's stubbornness again prevent him from seeing the advantage of this latest offer?

De Bouillé shrugged as he handed De Dillon the letter of ultimatum to be delivered to Antigua under a flag of truce. Turning back to the desk and his wine, he allowed himself to hope that this time the English would be more sensibly compliant.

* * *

Captain Phillips Cosby was at his wits' end. He sighed with exasperation, stripped off his jacket, and mopped his face with an outsized kerchief, quickly tossed to one side. His mind chafed at his problems.

Putting together a sugar convoy to England of more than a hundred ships from the Caribbean islands was proving almost impossible.

He had wanted to sail in May, now it was June. First one island, then the next, requested delay, and, all were demanding escort frigates to ensure their ships' safe passage to the rendezvous at Antigua.

He puffed his cheeks, blowing his breath out explosively. Didn't they realize that, apart from his own ship, *Robust*, he had only one other frigate at his disposal, *Convert*, and she was in bad shape?

It was to be Cosby's last convoy before retiring to the family home, Stradbally Hall, in Ireland, which he had inherited from his uncle some years ago.

He was a sailor at heart, and had been in no hurry to take up the life of the country gentleman, but now, with the war against America winding down, it seemed timely enough to strike his colors, though he knew he would miss the sea

He should, he reflected, already have been in Ireland, had not *Robust* all but foundered during a winter storm.

She had been so badly damaged in a December crossing from New York to England that he had to break off from the convoy he was escorting, and seek repairs in Antigua.

At the time, he was leading a fleet of 130 ships, with *Robust* carrying Lord Cornwallis and other British officers home to account for their defeat by General Washington at Yorktown.

The violent winter storm forced him to order the ships to lay-to, but the gale was so strong that most of the fleet separated, and his own main yard was snapped clean in two, making him labor in the heavy seas.

When *Robust*'s newly-laid copper sheathing failed and the ship started to take on water, he transferred Lord Cornwallis and retinue to another ship, and made for safe haven in Antigua

That recent experience had left him acutely aware that another disastrous crossing would not sit well with their Lordships in the Admiralty, and he was determined to make the coming passage both safe and profitable.

There was, though, an added and unexpected complication, which needed to be handled delicately. He was taking home the widow of Antigua's governor. Sir Thomas Shirley had died suddenly from a tropical fever.

Cosby had come to regard Lady Mari Shirley as a warm friend over his months on Antigua, and, in the absence of the governor's deputy and the Navy Yard's commissioner, it had fallen to him, as the senior officer on the island, to escort her to her husband's funeral.

A couple of days later, she had asked if she could sail home to England aboard *Robust*. Without hesitation, he had offered her his cabin, and now had to reshuffle the quarters.

This addition to his problems produced mixed feelings of sympathy and reluctance which together created a certain awkwardness in him.

He didn't approve of female passengers, even one of the standing of Mari Shirley, on any Navy ship. He had, though, sincere regard for her. She had seemed to him a somewhat sad, gallant figure.

He knew that she had carried out her social duties on the island as the governor's wife while somehow contriving to hold herself a little apart from Antiguan society.

The consensus among the islanders, he thought, was that she felt herself some sort of superior being. Cosby differed.

The Mari Shirley he perceived was unhappy and ill at ease, sometimes unnerved perhaps, at many of the excesses of the island's small, closed and privileged society.

The sound of hurrying footsteps and exclamations cut short his ruminations. Shrugging thoughts of Mari Shirley and her problems aside, he prepared to finish the day's business.

He looked up as Captain Henry Harvey, commander of the *Convert*, entered the room to announce the imminent arrival of two English privateers bringing three American prizes into harbor.

"Seems they were cut out from St. Kitts," Harvey announced, grinning. "What shall we do with them?"

Cosby slapped his desk with annoyance at the new problem, standing up to curtly reel out the usual drill.

"Search 'em for deserters, and press any you find for the convoy. We'll need every hand we can get. Impound the prizes for The Crown's share, and detain the enemy crews. I'll deal with it all later."

"Yes, sir. Immediately."

"Who's bringing them in?" he asked.

"*Regulator* and *Amazon*."

"Those two again. They're worse than bloody pirates."

"Good at what they do, though." Harvey said this grudgingly.

He shared the Navy's respect for the seamanship and courage of many privateers, but judged the ruthless opportunism and insatiable greed of this particular pair with jealous self-righteousness.

Usually, Cosby would have been happy enough to take possession of captured American vessels, which could be converted to warships or stripped of much-needed spares for the Navy, not to mention the value of their cargoes, to be split between the privateers and The Crown. But on this day, he had no need of the additional bother.

XXIV

"Fold it more carefully, Izzy, be more mindful of creasing the skirts. That's a favorite, you know," Lady Shirley chided, as she watched her maid fold an abundant, complicated petticoat into a traveling trunk.

Izzy said nothing, but frowned and pursed her lips.

"The Polonaise style's very difficult to fold well, M'lady, 'specially when the folds is stitched afore."

Izzy tugged and tucked in an effort to smooth the pleats of the dress. Mari stood over her, eyeing the costume. She leaned forward to stroke the dress's fine surface of painted pale yellow, Chinese silk.

"It's a pretty fashion," she murmured.

"But going out of style at last, I think – if not already passé back home."

She sighed.

"Perhaps I should leave it here, or give it away."

Izzy managed to look scandalized.

"You said it was a favorite," she pointed out sharply.

"Yes, yes – but I'm in widow's weeds now."

Mari Shirley paused, and regarded the dark blue of the costume she was wearing.

"Or what passes for them, at any rate. I'll hardly have use of such pretty finery for a while – in or out of mode."

She strolled over to the balcony doors of her chamber, which opened to a view of the harbor at some distance. She felt she had wasted too much time, sorting and supervising the packing of both her own and her late husband's wardrobe.

That morning she had spent with Sir Thomas's man, who had placed his master's collection of suits, britches and assorted linens in cedar-lined trunks to be shipped back to the family home in England.

Mari had been overcome with a mixture of sadness and relief, as she looked over the servant's efforts.

Particular items had brought back memories of different occasions. A sudden fit of nostalgia and regret had caused her to hesitate over a particular coat of blue-green corded silk jacket. It had been a favorite of Thomas's.

It was a simple cut-away coat in the manner of a riding coat, with large buttons on simple cuffs. No elaborate embroidery, but the cut had suited her husband's still-trim figure well, and the color had enhanced that of his eyes. It had a fine, elegant style, "like the man himself," she had thought, tears stinging her eyes.

Thomas Shirley had striven to keep his marriage bargain with her, and she knew she had been the first to default on it. The man servant had looked a question at her.

"No, pack that one away too. All his things must go back to his family in England."

The servant had then given her a curious glance, and Mari instantly realized that she had spoken as if she were a housekeeper, detached and no relation to the Shirley family, let alone the governor's widow.

Her husband had become a victim of an ague a few weeks earlier. He had never regained robust health after returning from the island of St. Kitts, where he had surrendered the British garrison to the French earlier in the year.

It had been a bitter time for him, though his French counterpart had been honorable and generous in his treatment of what remained of the British force after the long siege and dreadful losses at Brimstone Hill.

Sir Thomas's poor health had been undermined further by low spirits and what seemed to be a bone-deep fatigue. A recurring bout with the ague had scoured his weakened system, and he had succumbed finally after typically, and with heart-rending doggedness, handing over the affairs of the island to his deputy. He had left unsentimental instruction that he should be buried on Antigua, on the point overlooking the harbor.

Mari had found this a heavy irony. She was convinced that her husband's final illness had been caused by the fetid, unhealthy atmosphere in and around the Navy dockyard at English Harbor.

It was a place Shirley had cause to visit frequently, and he had, as often, fretted at the filth and stench of the ordure accumulated in the waters there, as well as the steamy, insect-ridden swamp nearby.

He had dictated his last farewells and wishes in letters to his family. When he had died there had been little for her to do, except carry out his instructions and prepare to leave herself for England.

There were those who criticized her for her cold temperament, and for not sending the governor's body back to his homeland for burial in a family plot, but Mari did as Thomas wished, and did not dignify outside criticism with any explanation.

She had not in the past, in any event, put herself out particularly to please island society. Sir Thomas's impeccable diplomacy had made up, for the most part, for this lack in his wife.

Her husband's death had shocked her, but in the aftermath, relief had trumped grief. She was at last free to leave the island.

In memory, she would forever couple the fetid swamps and polluted bay with the dark mood and mentality of plantation life, holding the vision of the rest of the lush sunlit island in stark contrast. She had lived her years on Antigua, apart and isolated, waiting and longing for something else.

Now, her thoughts were firmly on her departure with the next convoy, which was due to sail, under Captain Phillips Cosby.

Already a sizeable fleet was assembled off the harbor of St. John's. The departure, she understood, depended on the arrival of the ships from Barbados, St. Lucia, St. Kitts and Nevis, and, once all were together, they would sail for England, under the protection of the Navy.

She couldn't wait for the moment. She stared, unseeing, into the distance, lost in her own thoughts.

The sea stretched blue as sapphire to the horizon, and suddenly her gaze focused sharply on a small flotilla making its way to harbor. Two of the ships were badly damaged.

Obviously, the stricken vessels must be prizes, their crews prisoners-of-war. Captured vessels were regularly brought into the harbor to be converted by the Navy into fighting ships, or readied for transfer to England, where the Admiralty would decide what to do with them.

She had seen such arrivals many times before, but, this time, the little flotilla struck her as particularly forlorn. Clearly the captured vessels were in a sorry state. She found herself intrigued.

She knew that Sir Thomas, in his day, would have dropped whatever he was doing to be at the dock by the time the small fleet arrived. But, she wondered, could she, should she, so assert herself? It was, after all, none of her business.

She pushed the idea away, and recommenced pacing her room, absently getting in Izzy's way, causing her maid to throw glances of irritation as she maneuvered around her restless mistress.

Mari tried to distract herself from the action down in the harbor by sifting through her ideas of how she would live in England.

She tried to imagine herself living as the dowager Lady Shirley at her husband's estate, and failed. She had fortune enough of her own, apart from any marriage settlement, and could well afford to set up and maintain a private establishment.

She had not, in any case, had any real acquaintance with members of her husband's family since she had wed him, and she would have, of course, her sister, Sophie, and brother, Tom, for support and comfort.

Her pensive mood was interrupted by a knock on the door, and a servant announced the arrival of Captain Cosby, who presented himself with a slight click of the heels and a perfunctory bow.

She was both pleased and curious. She liked the Navy officer, who had assumed command on her husband's death and in the absence of Sir Thomas's deputy.

She found him deferential, but personable and easy to talk to. She appreciated the sympathy and support he had offered her, assuring her of safe passage home on the convoy under his command.

To her mind, he was acting as befitted an officer and a gentleman, and had become a trusted ally, though she did not regard him as an intimate friend.

"Ma'am, excuse me," he said, entering the room.

"How go your preparations? Better than mine, I hope."

"I'm all but finished," she replied. "But what do you mean, Captain Cosby? Is there a problem with the convoy?"

"Several, Ma'am. The islands keep wanting delays, and now there's been an incident in St. Kitts which does not bode well."

Cosby crossed to the balcony to stare at the vessels easing to anchorage. Mari joined him to look out once more.

"What's happened?" she asked. "Is that to do with those ships just in? Who are they?"

"Indeed, it is, and it's a problem I could do without."

Cosby's facial expression might have been comical if not so genuinely worried.

"A privateering action, Ma'am. Three captured American vessels from St. Kitts, and they may delay our sailing."

Mari gave him a sharp, puzzled look.

"Why should it do that?" she asked.

Cosby paced the balcony, preoccupied with the newcomers, and had some difficulty minding his courtesies. He was not accustomed to confiding Navy matters to any man not concerned, let alone a woman, governor's wife or no. Mari Shirley, however, was gazing at him in a sympathetic but determined way. She questioned him again.

"Why should their arrival delay our convoy, Captain Cosby?"

Phillips Cosby shrugged, and employed a handkerchief to scrub the back of his neck.

"Fact is m'Lady, we have had an unusual accord with the French on St. Kitts, which is why they are allowing the planters' ships to join our convoy. This could upset it all."

Mari was still not sure of Cosby's reasoning.

"They seemed in bad way - the ships brought in."

"There was a short, fierce fight. The Americans must have thought they could find safe haven with the French on St. Kitts. No such luck for them though, with *Regulator* and *Amazon* in their wakes."

Cosby paused in his pacing, exasperation showing again.

"Those two are as ruthless a pair of privateers as ever sailed the seas."

Captain Cosby sounded a shade self-righteous and prim in his condemnation of his fellow countrymen, and Mari couldn't help but raise an eyebrow, and suppress a smile at such an outburst.

She and he, both, well knew that the Admiralty had an eagle eye for any share of spoils from privateers.

Cosby went on, "One of the American captains, a Captain Dean, is wounded in the leg, and several sailors have much worse injuries. We'll do what we can for them, but some may be beyond help."

Cosby made as if to leave, but was arrested by a gesture from Lady Shirley. He waited, a quizzical expression on his face.

272

She stared back at him, her own face unreadable.

"Dean," a common enough name, had conjured up memories – the hold of a ship and the dense aroma of tobacco leaves; warm bodies locked in embrace on a bed of rough sacking; an ardent young man and his hurt pride; then, stolen love on the high seas again in the middle of the war, and a vow to find each other with an intent that had faded with time.

Surely chance was too frail for their paths to cross again after all the years. There was a sharp knot of excitement, causing her breathing to tighten and pulse to quicken. It was undeniable.

She was compelled to find out. She considered Phillips Cosby, trying to judge his temper and inclination.

"I wonder, Captain, whether I could see the prisoners?" she said, her voice amazingly even.

"What do you think? I shouldn't wish to impose myself, but I should be interested to see what we have."

Seeing doubt in his face, she offered, "Perhaps I could even be of some help, always assuming you think it proper."

Cosby hesitated, then acquiesced reluctantly.

"Ma'am, it is up to you. The wounded captain has a shot in the leg, but the other captains are in fine fettle. Both may be a lot less comfortable if they're shipped off to England shortly as prisoners-of-war."

Mari made an effort to mask interest. A hope was burgeoning at the back of her mind, crazily it seemed if she examined the idea. She tried to sound casual.

"Do you know the names yet of the American ships?"

"No, Ma'am. I know very little of the incident as yet. All I know is that one of the captains is in a bad way, having lost much blood."

"I can see them, then?" said Mari. "I won't interfere, but I would be most interested to set eyes on them."

Cosby bowed, puzzled but giving assurances he would arrange the meeting, and escort her at her convenience.

* * *

The Transport Officer put forward his hand to assist the Governor's widow from her carriage.

273

He was still not convinced at all of the propriety of allowing her ladyship access to the prisoners, but had yielded to her powers of persuasion. He helped her step neatly onto the stone causeway leading to the crumbling portico of the old fort where the Americans were being held.

The place looked ruinous, as though permeated and decayed by the heavy air. He wrinkled his nose reflexively at a drift of sour odor as they approached. It was no place for a fine lady, but Mari Shirley seemed not to notice.

Cosby saw that she seemed to have decided that mourning dress was satisfied by limiting herself to shades of blue and violet. This day Mari Shirley had chosen an overdress of lavender lustring, sporting a deep frill, striped in shades of lavender and gray. She looked formal, but very feminine. Slim, brocaded slippers, unsuited to dusty streets, matched her costume, and she carried a parasol.

As she passed under the portico, Cosby felt, again, how out of place she was. The pristine colors and immaculate form of her skirts showed in startling contrast to the grim, mildewed stones.

At least he had prepared the guard, whose small ante-room had been freshly swept and sanded, and the man had thought to provide a chair for his elite visitor.

Inside, as they adjusted sight from the bright exterior sunshine to the dimness of the room, the jailer smirked and bowed clumsily, unsure whether first to salute the Transport Officer, or offer Lady Shirley a chair.

Captain Cosby wasted no time on explanations, or courtesies. Wishing to curtail the visit, he prevailed upon the man to provide a list of the American crew in custody, and show it to Lady Shirley.

He then watched her face closely, as she looked over the list, and saw a stillness settle over her. Without knowing why, he perceived a change in her. He sensed tension and excitement, though she sat quietly. She turned to him.

"Captain Cosby, I should like to interview Captain Dean of the *Nimrod*, if you please."

Cosby stared back at her uncomfortably.

"I'm still not sure that this is quite proper, Ma'am. Our prisoners should not be on show. Forgive me."

Lady Shirley looked taken aback, but quickly recovered.

274

"Oh, Captain!"

She hesitated, apparently studying her shoe, but then looked up with a slight smile. Her eyes were huge and dark.

"I'm not here from idle curiosity, Captain Cosby."

He waited for her to explain.

"You actually have here, a man who - enemy or no - I have reason to hold in high regard. He has rendered me, and Sir Thomas, too, great service in the past. He is on a side deemed enemy these days, but, yet, I am still in debt to him."

She tried to read the Transport Officer's face for signs of sympathy or lack of it, and added, "It is most important that I assure myself of his wellbeing and comfort, and I will vouch for the cost of anything necessary to that end."

Cosby, by now, was intrigued, and unable to resist allowing her to play the scene through. He had heard old rumors of the governor's wife having some connection with an American privateer, who had gallantly restored her to her husband after her ship to Antigua had been taken as war prize.

He nodded to the guard to fetch Captain Dean, and waited with Mari in silence. She stood still, listening, but as they heard footsteps returning down the passageway, she retreated to lean against the guard's table, as though bracing herself for a shock.

The door was opened, and the American prisoner limped in, leaning heavily on crutches.

Assessing him, Cosby saw a man handsome and robust, though weak from loss of blood, his pallor contrasting with the dark powder burn on his cheek, battle-scarred and weary. His clothing was stained dark and torn, and his open jacket hung loosely as he bent on his crutches. His bandaged left leg he held gingerly off the floor.

The man was clearly shocked at the sight of Mari Shirley, and looked almost mesmerized, but said nothing.

Cosby switched his scrutiny to Lady Shirley, and, once more, he noted a change in her.

She was leaning against the table, and from the tilt of her head and lowered eyelids, it was as though a languor had overtaken her.

Phillips Cosby thought, "Vanquished – she looks vanquished, ready to be taken."

Flicking his gaze back to the prisoner, he saw the American's eyes, dark and unfathomable, locked on the woman's.

It seemed to Cosby that Dean's form had become more tense and heavy as if some powerful force of will had overtaken his injured body.

Cosby experienced a frisson, and uncomfortably felt himself a voyeur at a lovers' meeting. The dingy, nondescript room seemed full of charged emotion pulsing between the two of them.

Lady Shirley was the first to break the tension, pushing away from the desk and moving to look closely into the prisoner's face. She suddenly surprised herself and the men by saying enigmatically, "A third time pays for all, Captain Dean."

She disregarded the startled expressions on the faces of the two men. What had she meant? A wave of mixed anger and resentment overtook her.

These men sailed the seas, fought and strove to bend others to their will, leaving whole nations and the world in upset. She was tired of men dictating terms. A stubborn sense of contrariness swept over her. She was tired of living her life as others would have it.

Time fell away, and the wild possibility of freedom beckoned again. She changed her demeanor to that of the coquette.

"Well, Captain Dean. What a to-do for you. How *Amazon* and *Regulator* have inconvenienced you, besting you at your own game."

The men could only display polite bafflement. She glanced round to Cosby.

"And, Captain Cosby, you know, is severely inconvenienced, too, in his affairs, not least, perhaps, by me."

She smiled brilliantly at Cosby.

Both men exchanged wary glances, enemies on the same side for the moment, not sure where this was leading.

Looking at them, an irrational burst of amusement sped through her. She regarded Dean, propped on crutches, longing for her with his eyes, yet denying her a greeting. Then, there was Phillips Cosby, a strong man, tough and honorable, bent on carrying out his naval duties. His weather-beaten face was perplexed and cautious.

Mari couldn't guarantee herself where this would lead, though growing sure that from now on she would forge her own path. The shade of a plan formed in her head, a fantastic possibility. She had a goal.

Stewart Dean and Phillips Cosby, both, might prove difficult to manage, she reflected. There was the on-going war, and stiff-necked authorities to consider, but, in spite of all this, Mari felt a burst of exhilaration.

There was always war and stiff-necked authority of some kind or other, but ordinary folk still managed to live their lives, obeying the rules, bending them, or ignoring them. Mari Shirley was determined to prevail.

Dean had not moved his gaze. It was unreadable, and caused her a flutter of dismay and a small misgiving that she was wrong.

Mari started guiltily at not mentioning his wounds. Her face now flushed with concern. She stared at her former lover in consternation.

She now became brisk and practical, curtailing the awkward reunion by ordering clean bedding and medicine for Stewart Dean and the other wounded Americans.

She wished to have Dean at the Governor's house, but Cosby rejected the idea, saying it was more than his position was worth. She even pleaded a case for his release, inviting further rejection.

Cosby appreciated the fact of her previous relationship, but was shocked at her vehement intercession on Dean's behalf. He reminded her,

"They are prisoners-of-war, Ma'am, and, unless we can exchange them for some of our own men, we should take them to England with us. If the French held some of our troops, we could arrange a prisoner exchange, but they don't. It's hard to see what else I can do but ship them to England."

He sympathized with his petitioner.

"They will likely be exchanged quickly once we're there. That must be some consolation for you, Ma'am."

Mari decided to demur gracefully and retire, her first sortie unsuccessful. Cosby promised her that he would try to find a solution, but the same day a packet boat brought word that the fleet from Barbados was finally on its way, driving the plight of the prisoners from his mind as completing preparations for the convoy's sailing again became again his main concern.

* * *

Days later, as he checked the convoy's provisioning list, Cosby was informed that a French ship, flying a flag of truce, was entering the harbor.

He got up from his desk, buttoned his jacket, and strode briskly down to the quayside, where he watched a pinnacle, lowered from a French frigate, move steadily toward the quay.

The crew shipped their oars, grabbed the mooring rings, and held the craft alongside while their officer leaped ashore and bounded up the stone steps, seemingly mindless of the slippery moss that covered them. Cosby threw a brisk salute.

Arthur, Comte De Dillon, returned the recognition, introduced himself, and handed Cosby a letter.

"The Marquis De Bouillé sends his regards," said De Dillon, giving the slightest of bows.

Cosby took the letter, and saw it was addressed to Sir Thomas Shirley

"Unfortunately, Sir Thomas is recently deceased, and his deputy is away for a period," Cosby told the Frenchman. "I will deal with the matter myself. Come and refresh yourself, while you wait a reply?"

"You will find the business is urgent. I will attend, Sir."

With the governor dead and his deputy away from the island, Cosby, as the senior Navy officer, would have to handle it.

He walked back to his office, slapping the letter lightly against his thigh as he wondered what its message was. Once there, he quickly took out an ivory paper knife and neatly slit open the envelope.

His French was good enough to allow him to understand clearly just what De Bouillé was proposing. His eyes followed the words as his mind translated them: the incursion by the English privateers into French waters was "*piratical*," and unless the American prisoners and their ships were released immediately, the St. Kitts merchantmen would be blocked from joining the convoy for England.

At first exasperation and temper rose at this latest threat of delay, but it soon occurred to him that the French demand was not so unreasonable, and, in fact, could turn out to be entirely advantageous.

He could well understand De Bouillé's anger at the action of the English privateers. He would be furious, he acknowledged to himself,

278

if French corsairs ever had the temerity to defy Antigua's defenses and invade St. John's Bay or English Harbor.

In this frame of mind, De Bouillé's use of *"action de pirate"* struck Cosby as not unjust. He reasoned that the Admiralty would hardly object if he acceded to the French demand: the exchange of three small American privateers for three dozen sugar-laden merchantmen would seem not only sensible but compelling in these particular circumstances.

Here, he realized, was a way to serve his own interests while also answering Mari Shirley's plea for the release of the particular man in her life.

It had been almost two weeks since the Americans were captured, and most of them, including the wounded captain, were recovering well under the careful scrutiny of the governor's lady and the island's doctor.

Their damaged boats were tied up in a corner of the harbor. Cosby reckoned it would take three or four days to make them seaworthy enough to return to St. Kitts, where they could be fully re-equipped by the English planters there.

He took out his pen, and wrote quickly, accepting the French terms. As he handed his response to De Dillon, he said, "Tell the marquis his demands are understandable, his anger, too. The action by our privateers…"

Cosby shrugged, "that, after all, is the nature of their game. The American ships will be readied as quickly as possible. They and their crews should be returned within the week. I'll send an escort with them under a flag of truce. Tell the marquis that I expect the St. Kitts fleet to sail promptly to join the convoy in St. John's Roads. This business can be cleared up without further delay."

The French officer took the envelope from Cosby, saluted, and left.

* * *

Phillips Cosby stood at the window of the governor's office, waiting upon Lady Shirley and surveying the horizon, where a forest of masts was gathering. He felt easier than he had for many weeks.

279

The problems with the convoy had all been solved at last, and he could grant the golden-haired widow her wish.

The interview went well. She dazzled him with her smiles of gratitude, and delayed him from his duties to take some refreshment with her. When he was comfortably sat down with a glass of cool wine, she stunned him with further news.

"My own plans are altered, after all, Captain Cosby."

She stood up, pacing before him, but now turned squarely to face him and deliver a broadside of her own.

"I have determined to go to America with Captain Dean."

The naval officer sat transfixed, staring back at her in disbelief, then grasping that she was sincere. Expostulations and questions buzzed in his head, but died on his lips. Instinctively, he knew not to patronize her or treat her as any but an equal. That much, he had learned from her comportment and actions over recent days.

She had effectively taken charge over the prisoners' treatment and welfare, receiving a daily report from the island's doctor. The jailer had trotted after her like a lap dog on her daily visits to the fort.

She had initially spent much time with Dean, and had helped to nurse him back to health. Impressed by her regular visits to the fort, Cosby had finally relented and allowed Dean to visit the governor's manse. Even so, he had not been prepared for this bald announcement from her.

"But m'Lady."

Cosby leaned forward.

"You are Sir Thomas Shirley's widow. How can you contemplate such a thing? How can the Americans condone such an idea?"

He almost found himself arguing as though on the part of the Americans - that she would be an unwanted responsibility, even a severe hindrance to them.

Looking into her face, he realized such remarks would appear lame and even ridiculous. Her decamping to the enemy would be a scandal. He couldn't allow it, but he felt he hardly had authority over Lady Shirley. She had placed him in a predicament, and he was not exactly sure where authority lay.

He silently cursed the earlier, repeated delays of the trade convoy. Had it left on time, Lady Shirley would have been long gone from the island, and his life much simpler.

Cosby marched across the room, poured himself a generous portion of wine without asking, and gulped it down.

"Lady Shirley, you have to know that you are putting me in an untenable position. I can hardly hand you over to the enemy. I'd lose my commission."

He sank down on a sofa, empty glass in one hand, decanter in the other, his eyes rolling in anguish at the thought of his fate so near to retirement. Mari Shirley burst out laughing. She realized his distress and sympathized, but was resolved.

"Captain Cosby – wait awhile."

She took the decanter from his hand, and refilled his empty glass.

"First of all, you and I both know full well that this conflict with our colonies has all but played its course. The government at home and people in general have long wished for an end to it all. What we are finishing out here, on our little island in the middle of nowhere, is of scant lasting consequence.

"The real game is finished. We will settle with the Americans, and have the usual intermittent bouts of spleen or cosy collaborations with the French. Territories will be taken or exchanged, like pieces on a chessboard, and life will go on until the next upset.

"I am the late governor's widow – yes. But truly, of what consequence to anyone am I now? I have no intention of settling back on Sir Thomas's own family estate, with people who are strangers in all but name. My own family, yes, I shall visit some time, when all this is over."

She encouraged him to finish his wine and have more by waving the decanter at him.

"I plan to go to America as Mari Westin, in any event. Even as a governor's widow, going amongst the enemy, I have no real value. I know nothing of import, and I never moved in elevated circles back home in England. No-one is going to remark my absence."

Phillips Cosby was not so sure of this, but had to concede her remarks about the war were true. These affairs, so huge and alarming, and even world-wide in their effect, always boiled down in the end to some sort of compromise.

Deals were done over territory and trade, and the dead and ruined were reduced to numbers in dry reports, hardly regretted, let alone mourned, except as contributing to success or failure in the eyes of the living powers. Relaxed by a sufficiency of wine, he fumbled to a conclusion.

"I would be remiss in my duty, m'Lady, if I did not urge you to reconsider such an action. But, if you are determined on this course, the least favor you can afford me is to leave Antigua on the escort frigate, which I have ordered to accompany the privateers back to St. Kitts.

"The convoy sails for England on June twelve, and the escort will rendezvous with us at sea after delivering the Americans. Should you have inclination to change your decision, you may remain on the escort until she rejoins the convoy. Should you persist with your plans to….ah…"

He hesitated to say "defect, " and continued, "to…ah…reach America, it is certain the Marquis de Bouillé would entertain you courteously and well until the Americans are ready to leave. Needless to say, it would be as well, in any case, for island society to bid you bon voyage on a Navy ship."

He paused, and examined his suggestion for flaws. It was something of a fudge, he knew, but, damn it, if the woman was determined to jump ship, let the French take the blame!

A warm smile lit Mari's face. Men were men. Captain Cosby was not such an adversary as she had feared. Her glance became positively flirtatious.

"I will behave impeccably for you, Captain, and shall give the islanders a most appropriate and nostalgic farewell banquet. I shall remain in your debt."

XXV

To Mari, the royal Virginian capes of Henry and Charles at the mouth of the Chesapeake Bay brought back bitter-sweet memories of herself at fifteen.

That first passage through them had landed her in servitude. Now, here she was, standing close to Stewart at Nimrod's rail. She gazed toward the sandy beaches either side, knowing that ahead lay the challenges of a new, unsettled society.

She looked at Stewart, who was relaxed and happy as he held her in the shelter of his arms.

"Home waters, my love," he smiled at her.

She returned his smile. This was how she had imagined it would be all those years ago.

Dizzy and silly though she had been then, she had now found her love. How could she have known that it would take so many years and ocean crossings, and a war that was barely over, before she should find what she had always wanted.

On arrival in Virginia, they planned to stay briefly with Walter and Elizabeth Dean, Stewart's uncle and aunt, in Richmond. They would have to regularize Mari's presence with the governor, but, given her status and their intention to marry, Stewart anticipated no great difficulty.

Local society was another matter, as attitudes to the British were mixed and unpredictable.

"With the governor's permission and family support we'll manage very well," said Stewart.

"And I can't think of any society matron who would care to take on Aunt Liz."

He grinned at the prospect.

"We'll get over to the plantation as soon as we can. Father spends most of his time there, and he'll be delighted to welcome you and enjoy your company. You'll be safe and comfortable, whilst I get *Nimrod* up to Philadelphia.

"Virginia should take it as a great compliment anyway," said Stewart, striking a pose as he declaimed, "Lady Shirley has thrown her cap to the winds again for Virginia's sake."

Then, seeing the self-doubt in her face, he looked at her with tender mischief.

"Or at least for mine – and I'm their favorite privateer. So, they'll soon love you as I do."

Mari immediately took to Richmond, with its open aspect by the river. Many of the houses, stacked up the slope of the hill, faced the water as though enjoying the view. It was a home-coming for Stewart, and she savored his pleasure with him.

With surprisingly little delay or formality, Mari had an interview with Governor Harrison. He was at first intrigued and disbelieving, then riotously amused at the idea of a British governor's wife decamping to the Americans. She was charming and beautiful to boot.

"A feather in your hat, Captain," he remarked, then added, shaking with laughter, "and a prize and a half. You are most welcome home."

* * *

The man climbing the hill toward Henrico Parish Church reminded Mari of Uncle Fred Ashford so much she had to smile. He had the same ambling gait, swaying a strong portly frame from side to side. Even his feet were like Uncle Frederick's, large, splayed out and planted with a firm tread.

The man was engrossed in a book he held in one hand. His other hand held a stout stick, more an Irish knobkerrie than a gentleman's cane, that he touched on the ground marking a leisurely progress.

As he drew near, she recognized the amiable face of Rector Miles Seldon, who would be officiating at her wedding in a few days' time. She raised a hand to wave to him, but absorbed in his reading, he failed to see her and passed by.

From her perch at the upper parlor window of the Deans' house on Grace Street, she could look down over the vista of the James River and the lush surrounding countryside.

Richmond was spread before her, its houses scattered over folds of green hillside down to the water's edge. The rush and play of the falls upstream could be heard as a murmuring backdrop to the sounds of the town, and she watched the river's current nudge and swing ships at anchor off Shockoe's Landing.

Thinking of Uncle Fred and Aunt Mattie brought a pulse of nostalgia and regret that neither they nor her brother, Tom, and sister, Sophie, could be here to join the wedding celebrations.

"They could have sailed almost to my front door, if it weren't for this wretched war," she thought, then pushed the fancy aside.

The war was not officially over, though it was known that preliminary articles of the peace treaty between England and the colonies had been signed in Paris the previous November. In deference to French allies Governor Harrison had announced there would be no official celebrations until England and France had also come to a final settlement.

Since arriving back in Richmond, Mari's impressions of Virginians had been mixed to say the least.

Amongst the people fierce patriotic fervor was tempered by an ambivalence toward the British, and she herself had, in fact, benefited from this by obtaining dispensation from the governor to remain on Virginian soil as an obvious non-combatant.

However gracious the dispensation, this description of Mari had caused Stewart's aunt, Elizabeth, to sniff in disgust. She was, yet again, confirmed in her view that the male sex were skilled at combining hypocrisy with idiocy.

Elizabeth Dean and her daughter, Anne, had enthusiastically taken over responsibility for the wedding preparations, leaving Mari with little to do but sit and twiddle her thumbs.

She and Stewart were to be wed when he returned from Philadelphia, and she wished heartily that she had gone with him instead of staying behind, feeling as though life had stalled like a ship in the doldrums.

She had succumbed, though, to the hospitality and concern of the Dean clan. For safety and comfort, they had urged her not to travel too far afield until she was established as Stewart's wife.

Her presence in Virginia was, after all, equivocal, in spite of the governor's favor. She accepted their advice, perversely irritated at herself for doing so and in a fever of anxiety for Stewart's return.

Mari's quiet reflection in the parlor was suddenly interrupted.

"I declare this child is full of dumplings. He's growing bonnier by the day."

Mari looked up as Elizabeth Dean pushed busily into the room to plump her grandson, Benjamin, promptly down onto the carpet to be distracted by his toys.

Stewart's aunt settled her tall, angular figure onto the couch and leaned back thankfully on the cushions. She was flushed from the effort of carrying her two-year-old grandson up the stairs and managing her skirts at the same time, but had been determined to show the imp and his mother that she could still manage it.

With her long legs, thin frame, and sharp features, she put Mari in mind of some kind of water bird, a heron perhaps. The older woman was elegant enough at rest, but a flurry of sharp angles in movement, somehow combining efficiency with awkwardness.

Mari smiled at the sight of her now. Elizabeth was lolling, inelegantly back, knees apart as she set her lopsided cap straight, trying to tame untidy wisps of graying hair as she did so. She caught the smile and responded with a wry grimace of her own.

"I can confess I'd forgotten what a pother and to-do children can be – even be they our darlings."

She leaned forward over her skirt, pushed a whirligig toy nearer to Benjamin, and chuckled.

"Anne thinks I'm a trifle overbearing with Benjy, and says that I annoy his nursemaid, but they needn't worry, I shan't interfere too much."

Elizabeth paused, puffed her cheeks and chuckled again, "Maybe just once in a while."

She switched her attention suddenly from Benjamin to regard Mari closely, and essayed a question.

"How are you bearing up m'dear?"

Mari allowed the question to hang in the air, wanting to avoid answering too little or saying too much. She made a small, dismissive gesture and tried to smile, knowing that the older woman's sharp eyes and understanding didn't miss much.

"You were all aglow when you had just arrived with Stewart, Mari, but I fear our new world has disappointed you."

Still getting no response, Elizabeth forged ahead.

"It must be admitted we have a very unsettled state of affairs here between patriots, returning loyalists, and those who don't care as long as they can profit one way or another."

Elizabeth had regained her usual brisk, confident style.

"You must feel some confusion, and maybe doubt, Mari, but you've done the right thing, a brave thing. You'll do fine in your new life, and will be well in Philadelphia, I'm sure."

She paused, patting her knees as if to reassure herself of something on a list.

"You shouldn't worry about ill-feeling here anyway, though there remains considerable animosity against the British, of course. You have made a particular stand in your choice of husband."

As though suddenly aware of the sound of her own voice, Elizabeth looked vexed, then repentant and anxious.

"I'm sorry my dear, my Walter is right. I have a tendency to hector sometimes."

Mari found herself laughing at Elizabeth's unaccustomed uncertainty. She rose to join her soon-to-be-aunt on the couch, and sat down to give her shoulder a squeeze.

"Aunt Liz. I'm not regretting my action. It's just that I'm appalled at myself sometimes. It's as though there's still a fifteen-year-old inside, naïve and arrogant, who plunges ahead on impulse only waking to the enormity of a situation when the die is cast."

Mari looked so rueful that Elizabeth laughed in her turn.

"You've a deal to adjust to, that's for sure, Mari."

She held Mari's gaze.

"But I've a mind in your case that a change in your social circumstances is not so much the problem."

Elizabeth set her head on one side, studying her house guest.

"You have still an air of restlessness about you. You're still reaching for freedom. I think that's why you couldn't resist coming back."

Mari protested.

"I've always loved Stewart."

"Yes – yes," interposed Elizabeth.

"But you sense and love the possibilities of this land."

She paused. Mari was slightly exasperated.

"I'm not so naïve, Aunt Liz, that I think all is gold and wonderful. But yes..."

She stood and crossed to the window again, opening the casement to a breeze rustling in from the water.

"Yes – I feel I breathe easily here," she said simply.

Elizabeth gave a satisfied nod, and watched as Mari turned again to pull a willing Benjamin onto her lap. She fiddled and straightened the collar of his smock.

"It's just that I seem to have a natural bent for saying the wrong thing in company here. You'd hardly think I've been a diplomat's wife."

A flicker of merriment skittered over Elizabeth's face. She turned a warm gaze on Mari.

"We're still coping with the idea of our own freedom and how we'll manage it, and there's plenty of disagreement about that, not to mention the jockeying for position of who has the say-so."

Elizabeth was silent again, then looked at Mari mischievously.

"You still have beauty and charm, Mari. Sweeten your lectures with those.

"Men are ever ready to be charmed after all, though come to think of it, I have to say that I myself have neither the looks nor temperament to practice those arts. I rely mostly on intimidation, though Walter sees through me most of the time."

Mari was completely distracted again and gave in to amusement at the idea of Elizabeth Dean as a coquette, practicing winsome ways with the men. She imagined any male receiving such attention from the lady would be flummoxed if not outright terrified. That was certain.

"In any event, my dear, sensible folk get over these little upsets - it's all water under the bridge diluting the sentiment." she stopped, considering her words.

"Lord, I sound as prim and prosy as my late mother-in-law."

"But not as fond of the elderberry wine, I trust, aunt."

The mocking voice came from a grinning Stewart as he strode unannounced into the room, his eyes searching for Mari.

He appeared travel-stained, but elated at being home. Elizabeth laughed with surprise and delight as her nephew hugged her and Benjamin together. She pretended to scold.

"You're back at last, and not before time, sloping in here like a villain, hoping to catch us unawares no doubt."

She cast a bright look at Mari, and back at Stewart and became heavily tactful.

"Much as I should like to stay and bandy words with you, nephew, I must be off with my charge to annoy Anne. I shall wait dinner to hear of the goings-on in Philadelphia."

She proffered her cheek for a kiss and added with mischief, "I've just been advising Mari to run away to sea again until Virginia remembers its manners – and by the by, young man, I prefer my brandy to elderberry wine."

Stewart responded by bowing her out of the room with a courtly flourish, and she made a merry exit with Benjamin.

Stewart turned and smiled happily across the room. Mari's gaze had hardly left him since he arrived, and he noted anxiety as well as amusement in her face.

He stepped over to pull her close, squeezing her hard and lifting her off her feet.

"We're going to Philadelphia, my love."

His enthusiasm was irrepressible.

"Uncle Walter wants us to set up there. The idea is to have a foot up in Philadelphia. After all, Congress is there – we'll be at the hub of decision-making – politics, trade and finance."

Mari saw his face suddenly dreamy as, locked in thought, he rocked her to and fro stroking her hair. She had to suppress a smile.

He didn't look like a man of the city. He had been a mariner too long, she supposed. He looked vital and healthy, skin burnished bronze by sun over open sea. His face was weathered and keen, definitely the look of a sailor, she decided – slightly unkempt even in newly-tailored clothes with fancy buttons and silver buckles. He could never be taken for a city dandy or sober financier.

His mood was contagious as he talked of where they would live in Philadelphia. There was always another horizon, it was true she thought. She tried to imagine him confined to a fusty office, though, and failed.

"Won't you miss the sea?"

He laughed and swung her round.

"No, beloved, I shan't because I'm not giving it up. I have plans."

At her look of surprise, he went on, "Yes – I have some interesting ideas on future trade with China, no less.

"So, the ocean beckons. And, as far as office business is concerned, Anne's husband is setting up with us. He knows the city scene like the back of his hand, and he's a lawyer to boot with a financier father. Fancy - dizzy, little Anne settling on such a man for a husband. Who'd have thought it?

He shook his head, smiling at the thought of his cousin.

"Perhaps she livens him up, and he calms her down."

He turned his attention back to Mari, and kept her close.

"I know it's been unsettling for you coming to Virginia, but though things are still at sixes and sevens it will get better. The Paris treaty will be ratified and the country is already forging ahead. There are splendid times to come, Mari. What can we not do?"

Mari laid a cheek against his chest, feeling the warmth through his cambric shirt, and hearing the thud of his heart. A chuckle shook her, and he raised her chin with his hand, looking a question.

"What is so entertaining of a sudden?"

"Oh, the idea of going to Philadelphia pleases me. It will be very interesting, and, indeed, what can we not do?"

Her smile was brilliant, as, tilting her head, she added, "I might just take Aunt Liz's advice and run away to sea again."

She caught an intense look from him.

"Yes, Aunt Liz may have been chaffing, but she has a point. I could go to China with you and choose myself some beautiful porcelain, and, of course, some silk for Anne for staying behind in Philadelphia to tend to the home fires."

Stewart looked askance for a heartbeat, then burst out laughing.

"You might at that, my lady. You might at that – and no cabin-boy drudgery this time."

He stood musing, studying her face again.

"I have to confess the idea of adventuring with you on the high seas again appeals, though there's always danger," he reminded her.

She looked at him, pleased at his consideration of her suggestion. Elizabeth had no doubt been joking, but Mari suddenly realized that despite the teasing, she herself was not.

People might declare that it was not the normal, proper thing for a woman to do. A wife should stay at home out of harm's way and tend to the domestic hearth, but the recent times – were they normal? Society was changing, new vistas were opening and expanding, and who avoided danger anyway? Danger was everywhere, in any quarter.

She remembered the wasted years apart, and quickly wrapped both arms around him, pressing against his body, trying to contain the bubble of excitement and anticipation in her breast. Jerking her head back to take advantage of the moment, she fixed her eyes on him.

"I will go to sea with you, then."

He stared back, shaking with inner laughter, and raised a hand to trace the curve of a breast pressed against his shirt.

"Yes, dear heart, we'll sail toward the sunrise and search for treasures."

"I'll hold you fast to that, Captain Dean," came the answer.

* * *

"Mari, Mari! Widow Gault's here to see about your wedding gown. Shall I send her upstairs, or will you come on down?"

Anne's girlish voice floated up the staircase, breaking the mood, and Mari laughed as Stewart waved his hand in mock horror, signaling his intention to escape.

"No – I'm coming down."

Leaving him in the sanctuary of the parlor she stepped out to meet the widowed seamstress recommended by Aunt Elizabeth to trim any gown in the finest way.

"She's by far the best in Richmond. She doesn't do needle work for just anyone – doesn't have to – so treat her prettily. I like to keep in her good books.

"She's such a boon when Benjamin needs new clothes," Elizabeth had said emphatically, explaining that the woman had brought her business to Richmond from Williamsburg when it was decided to change the capital.

Remembering Elizabeth's admonition, Mari put on a welcoming smile which changed to a gasp of disbelief as she stopped halfway down the stairs. The years fell away as she looked at the figure of the woman standing patient and erect in the hallway.

"Betsy? Betsy Murphy, is it really you?"

The two women gazed at each other amazed.

291

Betsy, slightly flummoxed, saw the elegant figure of a society matron descending the stairs toward her. She recognized straight away a one-time gawky, young friend who had been desperate for love and adventure, and spirited enough to search for it. Mari saw an old trusted confidante she had never thought to see again.

Betsy, as she stood there, seemed not to have changed much. Her dress was plain, much as Mari remembered, as if she had helped iron the snowy white collar only yesterday.

Stepping closer, she was about to embrace her old friend, when Betsy suddenly dipped an awkward curtsey, as though in afterthought.

Mari took hold of Betsy's shoulders and studied her face. Time had left its stamp of hardship and stress, but grave and indomitable character was still there. Betsy's calm gray eyes crinkled with pleasure and amusement at the former lady rapscallion, as she had often thought her.

There was nothing for it, but to retire and exchange news.

Mari was riveted to hear that a year after she herself had fled back to England with Stewart, John Coward had sold Betsy on to Thorberry.

Mari grimaced at the memory of this man, but Betsy reassured her that though life with him had been relentlessly hard, she had counted herself well-placed to care for her brother, Liam.

Thorberry, it seemed, had been sensible enough to recognize worth in a servant when he found it, and over time had come to value Betsy so much that he had proposed marriage.

She had refused, but continued to work for him for Liam's sake, her own character and experience arming her sufficiently to keep Thorberry at bay and even outwit him.

After the declaration of independence, he had fled the country for England leaving the plantation to the care of a factor. Before going, however, he had even been moved to be generous with the money and goods owing to her from her debenture, but had given nothing for Liam.

They had then moved to Williamsburg, Liam to find work as a pot-boy at an inn, and she to set up as seamstress and laundress.

Later, when the powers that be moved to Richmond, she followed, and, for once, Liam had been the occasion of his sister's good fortune. He had gained work at Gault's Tavern, and thereby Betsy had met

Simon Gault and eventually married him. Betsy smiled at the telling of this.

Mari's own story had not surprised Betsy at all. That the young run-away should have been married off to an older man for protection, discipline and convenience to her father seemed inevitable to her.

That Mari, once widowed, had opted to run for freedom to the newly-independent America was all in character for the girl she once knew.

The afternoon mellowed toward dusk before they were through. The rest of the household had left them mostly to themselves. The matter of the wedding dress was finally discussed, and they settled on minor embellishments to the gown with little ado.

Before parting, Mari extracted a promise from Betsy to attend the ceremony.

"You will be my only family from the old country," she said sentimentally.

Betsy was touched and amused, and slipped back into an old reassuring role, squeezing Mari's hand.

"I'll be there – I'll be there."

She turned back at the street doorway as she was leaving, and Mari was astonished to see her stifling a giggle.

"We've both waited a long enough time for this after all – haven't we Perdita? I couldn't possibly miss it. Could you?"

* * *

Mari's wedding dress was a simple one of fine lawn with a blue silk sash and deep soft frills falling from the neckline. Betsy Murphy had been pleased to make it over from a hardly worn summer dress.

"The blue of the sash matches your eyes, Mistress Mari," Betsy said.

Mari's hair was dressed with a simple spray of flowers, and she carried a small prayer book borrowed from Anne. A blue velvet book marker echoed the shade of the sash, as did the band around the bride's neck, supporting a gold locket containing a fine miniature of Mari's mother.

Elizabeth, at first, thought the dress too young and informal for some-one of Mari's age and station, but changed her mind as she watched the bride come lightly down the stairs and swing, laughing into Stewart's embrace.

"I have to say I had looked forward to a more formal occasion, with some display," she admitted to her husband.

"Mari does look so lovely, but in following her we'll look as if we're off to a picnic."

Elizabeth paused before adding, "An elegant picnic, though, I suppose."

Mari and Stewart walked up Grace Street to Henrico Parish Church. Elizabeth declared it a gem of a day, but, no, she wouldn't walk but would share the chaise with Anne and Benjy.

Mari knew that Elizabeth considered her contrary in refusing the carriage on her wedding day, but she insisted to Stewart, "I am not being willful or making a to-do.

"I just want to walk to church on your arm in the sunshine – no display, just ourselves and close ones. We'll make our vows and be wed, and walk out with the rector's blessing to the good wishes of friends and neighbors."

XXVI

March 28, 1783 - Rector Miles Seldon sat in his vestry in a reverie. His little church had a worn but comfortable air. Light filtering through the tall, plain windows put a sheen on the high-backed, well-used pews.

The place could do with some sprucing up, he knew. There were still scars and pock-marks on the walls from two years previous when Benedict Arnold and his British troops had been briefly quartered here.

It seemed like yesterday to the rector. They had ransacked Richmond, doing the usual quota of looting and burning. They ate, slept and laughed, swore and groaned in his church until they were sucked out of it by the prevailing currents of war.

Seldon thought that Henrico Parish Church had given them better ease and shelter than most places. He realized that, perverse though it might be, he had not really begrudged the enemy soldiers that comfort. This church had witnessed great events.

The couple to be married today would be wed only a few feet away from where Patrick Henry had galvanized the delegates to the second Virginia convention, held in the church eight years earlier.

Miles Seldon had been chaplain to that convention. George Washington, from Fairfax, and Thomas Jefferson, from Albemarle, were among the 120 delegates.

The convention debated the idea of establishing a well-trained Virginia militia, prepared to defend the state against further oppression by George III.

Seldon remembered the shouting and jostling as arguments and opinions flew back and forth across the aisle. Some delegates had been outright fearful of declaring opposition to the king and breaking with Britain. Some had been impassioned and emotional, others implacable and not to be swayed.

Patrick Henry had crystallized sentiment in a dramatic final challenge, flung out to echo from the walls of the church, "Give me liberty – or give me death!"

The spark of his passion crackled through the room, and delegates swayed by him roared approval. The convention had adopted Henry's amendment in a tight vote, and Seldon recalled that some of the faces had looked blank with shock as if the knowledge had just hit them that that is what it might truly come to – liberty or death.

Miles Seldon had stared at Washington, whose expression was stern and serious, but detached and calm as though contemplating a distant horizon.

Thomas Jefferson had made a good fist of suppressing his excitement, but Seldon had seen the gleaming eyes and tight smile. Patrick Henry had been all afire, his foxy, handsome features the focus of attention.

"He's done it – We're away!" Seldon had thought, praying for wisdom for the delegates with a pounding heart.

Seldon broke from his thoughts to take a quick look through the vestry door. The pews were almost full. There was scuffling and a shaking out of skirts as folk made room for newcomers and resettled themselves.

He had the impression that a good many of those assembled would be strangers to the Deans but were there out of curiosity, and, maybe, simply to enjoy the occasion in a holiday spirit.

And why not? They had all been through violent, unstable times, and the stresses and dangers of war were stark in their minds. His people deserved some respite time to celebrate and recoup energy for what he was sure would be trying times ahead.

Seldon knew that the Treaty of Paris had been signed though not yet ratified, and George III himself had already declared America to be free at the opening of Parliament the previous December.

He also knew that Governor Harrison had deliberately delayed official celebration until America's French allies had sorted out their own differences with Britain. That, with more European shenanigans, had taken longer. Finally though, it was done, and tomorrow Virginia would celebrate.

People from all points of the compass had been flocking into Richmond for days, both for a session of the assembly and the festivities, to include illuminations. So crowded were the streets, that folk were exercised constantly dodging horses and wagons. Inns and taverns were full to popping, as was his church right now, the rector noted with satisfaction.

There was gentle murmur of conversation, then a flutter of heightened interest at a stir of activity outside.

The wedding party had arrived, and was making its way up the red brick path to the church door. Seldon went to greet them, and preceded them into the church.

Standing waiting for the inevitable resettling and discreet coughing to quieten, the rector studied the pair in front of him with pleasure.

The bride's appearance seemed to sing of summer, gold hair gleaming in the church's soft light, her gown floating around her.

The groom looked weathered and worn, as well he might having fought for his country's freedom, but stood robust and happy beside his betrothed.

The notion took Seldon that this was a good start to the town's festivities - an English lady and an American gentleman making happy union. He hoped and prayed it presaged the future.

Mari glanced around and saw respectful, smiling faces anticipating the ceremony.

Stewart looked as elegant as she had ever seen him, in dark plum colored coat and britches, with, for once, a finely tied cravat. He smelled strongly of bay rum, and she wrinkled her nose at him when he glanced sideways at her. He grinned sheepishly, knowing that Elizabeth had doused his face too liberally with the stuff to staunch a nick made whilst shaving.

The rector's homely, intelligent face beamed at them. He smoothed his hand over the worn Book of Common Prayer and began, "Dearly beloved......"

The familiar words floated over the now-quiet company, and, finally, on the pastor's prompting, Stewart fumbled in a narrow pocket, and reaching over slipped the ring onto Mari's finger.

It was a perfect fit.

The ring was not new but worn and smooth. She recognized it, and stared up at him startled. His eyes sparkled with laughter at her surprise.

"It was always meant for you," he murmured with a pretense of solemnity.

It was her mother's own wedding ring that Mari had given him all those years ago in gratitude and as a memento.

A pulse of bitter sweet memory flashed across her mind.

Miles Seldon cleared his throat to end their distraction, and nodded brusquely at Stewart to continue.

"With this ring, I thee wed, Mari….."

* * *

The next evening, Richmond was aglow with candles in the gardens and windows of almost every house and building. The peace celebrations were in full swing.

People everywhere were carrying cressets, the flickering light from the paper torches turning their faces into so many mysterious but happy gargoyles.

Laughter jumped through the crowds thronging the streets. Canon fire cracked out a salute to victory, causing horses to skitter and children to cry, and fireworks exploded all around.

The Deans arrived at the governor's ball, with Elizabeth declaring it a rout, a complete rout.

Inside was a melee worse than that outside in the streets, with the variety of costumes and finery confounding any notion of what was fashionable and what was not.

They had by-passed the laden supper tables, having over-indulged in a late dinner at home. It was time to dance to distraction, and Anne in particular was determined not to miss the lottery drawing for who would have the honor of opening the ball as the governor's partner.

She and Elizabeth, both, had been vastly amused by reports of offense taken by Governor Harrison's ladies at the idea of a lottery for the right to take such precedence. Anne wanted to see how cranky they would look should none of their names be drawn.

Mari held onto Stewart's arm, happy to follow in the wake of Aunt Liz and Uncle Walter as they ploughed through the crowd to find seats.

She was excited by the buzz. It was a carnival of all sorts. People were jubilant, triumphant, euphoric over the arrival of an exciting, new future.

Luck was with the Deans. They found a good position, that is one from which Elizabeth could observe the goings on and assess the dancing.

There was a lull while the fiddlers tuned up, and the governor dipped his hand into a bowl that held the names of Richmond's fair citizens. The governor's ladies stood behind him, the younger smirking and pretending to examine their fans.

Anne frowned, "Just look at them. They are preparing to fake surprise when Governor Harrison reads one of their names from the draw."

She found herself somewhat shocked, yet still had the grace to look shame-faced. when the governor chose, paused, chuckled, and then read out the name of his partner for the first dance.

It was a local shoemaker's daughter.

There were a few gasps, and a wave of laughter as proud parents edged her forward, flushing with pleasure, to curtsey to the governor.

Anne fully enjoyed watching expressions of disbelief and consternation wipe smug smiles off the faces of the Harrison ladies. They protested to each other, tossing curls and pouting.

The governor ignored them, graciously offering his arm to the chosen girl to lead the dance with him. He collected a round of applause from the company, and seeing the stunned delight on the young girl's face was pleased he had insisted on an honest lottery.

"Bravo for Governor Harrison," Elizabeth exclaimed.

"Though I'll give odds he'll be dancing to the tune of his womenfolk for this!"

Mari marked the attitude of the governor's friends and relatives at the break in precedence. The men seemed to take it in stride, but the ladies were obviously scandalized and in a huff.

"Old habits die hard," she thought, trying to imagine a scene like this in Antigua or London, with Thomas Shirley, or her father, presiding.

The idea of either of them cavorting with a tradesman's daughter, unthinkable as such a thing was, caught her fancy and made her giggle. At the same time, she felt the burden of her former life slough off her shoulders.

Stewart squeezed her hand, firmly pulling her behind him toward the music. The milling crowd was thoroughly motley with judges, lawyers and military, politicians and planters in a happy, riotous mix with the town's traders, craftsmen, laborers and their kinfolk. There were elegantly coiffed ladies in silk, and others comical in their effort to dress up to the occasion.

Embroidered slippers scuffed the floorboards next to dusty, cracked leather boots, and as more revelers surged forward, behind the governor and the shoemaker's daughter, Mari and Stewart were swept onto the dance floor to join the celebration of new beginnings.

END

Acknowledgments

In researching this book, we used the resources of the Talbot County Library, Easton and Oxford, MD; Howard County Library, Columbia, MD.; the Maryland State Archives, Annapolis; the Maryland Historical Society, Baltimore; the Maryland Diocesan Archives, Baltimore; the Chesapeake Bay Maritime Museum Library, St. Michael's, MD; the U.S. Library of Congress, Washington, DC; New York State Library, Albany; The Mariners' Museum, Newport News, VA; the Naval Historical Center, Washington, DC; the Public Record Offices, London; London's Docklands and Guildhall Libraries; the National Maritime Museum and the Caird Library, Greenwich, England; the Northern Ireland Public Records Office, Belfast; and the internet, particularly www.google.com, and www.accessible.com.

We are particularly indebted to: Catharine M. Sedgwick, whose short story, "Modern Chivalry," introduced us to the core elements of this romantic adventure; Lucinda L. Damon-Bach, President and founder of the Sedgwick Society, for sharing her copy of Sedgwick's book; Pete Lesher, chief curator of the Chesapeake Bay Maritime Museum, for introducing us to the Jane Foster Tucker Collection, with its insights into the early history of Oxford, and the booklet "Perdita" that Foster produced for Oxford Museum; Ellen Moyer, Mayor of Annapolis and curator of the 2001 exhibition "It All Began Here," for sharing her knowledge of colonial horse-racing in the town; Edmund Nelson and Byrne Waterman, of the Maryland Historical Society's Library, for unearthing the shipping records of Captain John Coward's *Integrity* and Captain Adam Coxen's *Hazard*; Bob Aspinall, Librarian of London Dockland Library, for his insights into the operation of the Legal Quays on the River Thames in the mid-18th century; Charles Brondine, of the Early History Branch of the Naval Historical Center, Washington, DC, for his advice on privateers; Cathy Williamson

Public Services Librarian at the Mariners' Museum, Newport News, VA., for her attentive help in plumbing the museum's rich resources; Monique Gordy, curator of the Maryland Room of Talbot County Free Library, Easton, MD., for her unfailingly gracious response to our numerous enquiries about life in 18th century Maryland; Peter Day, our indefatigable researcher in London; Antoine Deram, in Paris, who researched the French conquest of St. Kitt's; our friend and colleague Muriel Dobbin, in Washington DC, for her enthusiasm and encouragement for the project.

Authors

Gilbert Lewthwaite is a retired national and foreign correspondent of The Baltimore Sun (1971-2001) and The Daily Mail, London (1960-1971). He has won numerous awards, including a Pulitzer Prize nomination in 1997 for a series of articles on slavery in Sudan.

Valerie Lewthwaite is an English registered nurse, who brings to the table her professional understanding of human strengths and frailties, and her international experience of raising three sons in four language zones.

They have lived and worked in London, Moscow, Rome, Washington, Paris, and Johannesburg. They currently make their home in Maryland.